OF TRUTH
AND BEASTS

By Barb and J. C. Hendee

The Noble Dead Saga—Series One

Dhampir

Thief of Lives

Sister of the Dead

Traitor to the Blood

Rebel Fay

Child of a Dead God

The Noble Dead Saga—Series Two

In Shade and Shadow

Through Stone and Sea

Of Truth and Beasts

Also by Barb Hendee

The Vampire Memories Series

Blood Memories

Hunting Memories

Memories of Envy

OF TRUTH AND BEASTS

A Novel of the Noble Dead

BARB & J. C. HENDEE

A ROC BOOK

ROC
Published by New American Library, a division of
Penguin Group (USA) Inc., 375 Hudson Street,
New York, New York 10014, USA
Penguin Group (Canada), 90 Eglinton Avenue East, Suite 700, Toronto,
Ontario M4P 2Y3, Canada (a division of Pearson Penguin Canada Inc.)
Penguin Books Ltd., 80 Strand, London WC2R 0RL, England
Penguin Ireland, 25 St. Stephen's Green, Dublin 2,
Ireland (a division of Penguin Books Ltd.)
Penguin Group (Australia), 250 Camberwell Road, Camberwell, Victoria 3124,
Australia (a division of Pearson Australia Group Pty. Ltd.)
Penguin Books India Pvt. Ltd., 11 Community Centre, Panchsheel Park,
New Delhi - 10 017, India
Penguin Group (NZ), 67 Apollo Drive, Rosedale, North Shore 0632,
New Zealand (a division of Pearson New Zealand Ltd.)
Penguin Books (South Africa) (Pty.) Ltd., 24 Sturdee Avenue,
Rosebank, Johannesburg 2196, South Africa
Penguin Books Ltd., Registered Offices:
80 Strand, London WC2R 0RL, England

First published by Roc, an imprint of New American Library,
a division of Penguin Group (USA) Inc.

First Printing, January 2011

10 9 8 7 6 5 4 3 2 1

ROC REGISTERED TRADEMARK—MARCA REGISTRADA

LIBRARY OF CONGRESS CATALOGING-IN-PUBLICATION DATA:
Hendee, Barb.
Of truth and beasts: a novel of the noble dead/Barb & J. C. Hendee.
p. cm.
ISBN 978-0-451-46375-3
1. Vampires—Fiction. 2. Quests (Expeditions)—Fiction. I. Hendee, J. C. II. Title.
PS3608.E525O4 2011
813'.6—dc22   2010030890

Set in Adobe Garamond
Designed by Alissa Amell

Printed in the United States of America

OF TRUTH
AND BEASTS

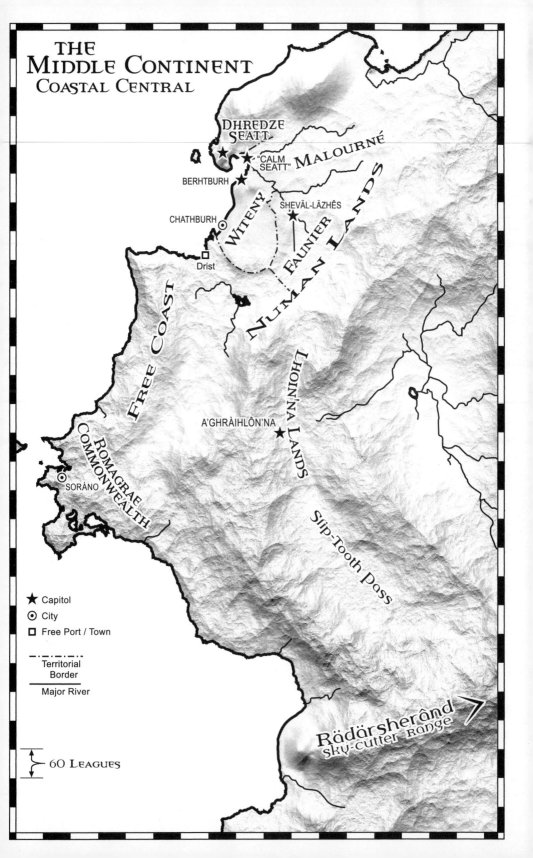

PROLOGUE

. . . never close your eyes again . . . not ever . . . not until they all die. . . .

Byûnduní—Deep-Root—halted in the dark of a chamber so tall and empty that he heard the frightened clench of his own massive hands. And why should there be light or sound in the temple of his people? The hall of the Bäynæ, the dwarven Eternals, was now a place filled only with false hopes. The people's greatest ancestral spirits had abandoned them.

Suddenly, he heard the pounding behind him, though it seemed to hammer within his skull, until it took shape in a thunderous gale of breathy, tangled voices.

. . . they will kill you, if they can. . . . They will; you know this . . .

He wanted to scream in rage at the chorus of overlapping whispers in his head. They had torn at him for so long, he could not tell if those words of warning were his or theirs. He could not remember when he had last closed his eyes, though he felt as if he were asleep. Not in a dream, but in an endless nightmare where silence had been slain.

In the depths of Bäalâle Seatt, there was but one long ever-night of fear and madness.

The pounding would not stop, and he could almost feel it upon his broad back. He turned about and stared in panic at the great doors of the chamber of the Eternals.

Each was the height of four dwarves. Each had been hewn whole from the trunk of a great oak and was as thick as his forearms were long. Yet he could hear those who crowded outside the doors, pounding . . . so many of them it began to sound like a rain of stones upon the wood. They were pounding to get in, though their voices could not breach the barrier like the hammering of their fists.

"What are you doing?"

Deep-Root spun at the threatening whisper and reached to his belt. All he saw at first were the great silhouettes in the dark. They reached to the hall's impossible heights. Three lined the wall of the door, and three more stood at the far side. All these statues of his people's Eternals were silent, their stone faces lost to sight.

A flickering light caught his eye.

An approaching flame wobbled toward him. Behind it was the reddened glow of a craggy old face, perhaps worn down and shriveled like the corpse of a human. The closer it came, the more he made out its features—and the two black, olive-pit irises of one of his own people.

Broad featured and gray bearded, the elder's eyes widened in wariness, exposing bloodshot whites around his irises. The torch glimmered upon the steel-shorn tips of the black scale armor of Master Kin-of-Far.

"You would let them in!" the old stonewalker accused.

"No . . . not anymore," Deep-Root denied.

"Liar!" the other hissed, and his free hand dropped to the black-lacquered hilt of one of his daggers.

In reflex, Deep-Root reached for a blade sheathed at his own waist.

"Where have you been?" Master Kin-of-Far asked, cocking his head. "To your prattling brother? Is that how it started?"

The elder stonewalker watched Deep-Root with one eye, while the other tried to see whether the doors had been opened as he crept forward.

"All of them turned against us once the siege began," he continued. "What deceits did you spit into the people's ears . . . through your brother?"

And the whispers rose like a torrent in Deep-Root's head.

. . . no one left to trust . . . never turn your back . . . they are coming for you. . . .

Deep-Root released his dagger's hilt and slapped his hand to his head.

But one voice, so much louder than the others, cracked through his mind.

Listen only to me—cling only to me.

The other voices began to grow again, making it too hard to think.

"No . . ." he whispered, and then gripped his head with both hands as he shouted, *"Leave me be!"*

"Leave you be?" asked the elder, feigning puzzlement. "Why would I? You—you did this to us, traitor. You and your brother . . . made them come for us!"

"No . . . my brother has no part in this."

"More lies!" shouted the elder, jerking his blade from its sheath.

Do what is necessary and come to me.

Deep-Root closed his hands tighter upon his head.

The elder dropped his torch and charged, raising the dagger as he shouted, "Keep your treachery, Byûnduní!"

Do not listen. Come to me.

And again the other voices raised such a cacophony that he tried to cling to the one clear voice. He tried to crush the others from his head.

Byûnduní—Deep-Root—snatched out one dagger at the sight of his caste elder coming for him.

This tainted place had to end. There would be sleep and silence once Bäalâle fell and was forgotten.

CHAPTER 1

Wynn Hygeorht paced the floor of her room inside Calm Seatt's branch of the Guild of Sagecraft. Shade, a large wolflike dog with charcoal black fur, lay on the small bed, watching her through crystal blue eyes.

Wynn was in trouble, and she knew it.

Only one night before, Wynn and Shade, and her other companion, Chane Andraso, had returned from Dhredze Seatt, the mountain stronghold of the dwarves. In that place, Wynn had disobeyed every order and every warning from her superiors. The repercussions were staggering. By now, word of her return had surely spread through the guild to its highest ranks. It was only a matter of time before she would be summoned before the Premin Council.

"Where's Chane?" she whispered absently, still pacing.

Whatever happened tonight, he'd want to know. He'd taken guest quarters across the keep's inner courtyard, but it was well past dusk, and he was late.

She nearly jumped when the knock at her door finally came. Pushing strands of wispy brown hair away from her face, she hurried to open it.

"Where have you . . . ?"

It wasn't Chane outside the door.

There stood a slender young man only a few fingers taller than Wynn. He was dressed in the gray robe of a cathologer, just like her. His shoulders were slumped forward, as if in a perpetual cringe.

"Nikolas?" Wynn said, then quickly dismissed her confusion and smiled. He was one of the few friends she had left inside the guild.

He didn't smile back. In fact, he wouldn't even look her in the eyes.

"You . . . you've been summoned," he whispered, swallowing hard halfway through. "Premin Sykion says you're to come straightaway to the council's chamber. And you're supposed to leave the . . ." He glanced once toward Shade. "You're to leave the dog here."

Wynn just stared at him. But she'd known this was coming. Hadn't she? She straightened, smoothing down her own gray robe.

"Give me a moment," she said. "Go tell the council that I'll come directly."

He hesitated nervously, then nodded. "I'll walk slowly. Buy you a little time."

Wynn gave him a sadder smile. "Thank you."

She watched him disappear down the passage, but she closed the door only partway. She took a breath before turning about, for the next part wouldn't be easy.

"Shade, stay here," she said firmly. "You cannot come."

Wynn used as few words as possible, as Shade's understanding of language wasn't fluent yet.

With a low rumble, Shade flattened her ears and launched off the bed.

Wynn was ready. She spun through the half-open door and jerked it shut. The door shuddered as Shade slammed into the other side with her full bulk. Then the howling began.

"Stop that!" Wynn called through the closed door.

With no time for Shade's drama over being left behind, she gathered up her robe's skirt and hurried down the passage to the end stairs, and then out into the night air of the courtyard.

She made her way across to the old stables and storage building, long ago converted to workshops, laboratories, and, of course, the guest quarters. Slipping through one outer door, she headed upstairs to a door she knew well. These were the same quarters once used by her old ally, Domin Ghassan il'Sänke of the guild's Suman branch, far to the south. She knocked lightly.

"Chane, are you there?"

No one answered, and anxiety swelled inside her. Where could he be? She had to at least let him know she'd been summoned.

She knocked again, more sharply.

"Chane?"

A scuffle rose beyond the door, followed by the sound of rumpling paper and a sudden screech of wooden chair legs on a stone floor. This time, the door opened, but the room beyond was dark. Wynn looked up at Chane Andraso towering over her, his face pale as always.

"What in the world were you . . . ?" She stopped midquestion.

Chane's clothes were wrinkled, and his red-brown hair was disheveled. He blinked several times as if she'd just roused him from dormancy. And . . .

"Umm, you have a piece of parchment stuck to your face."

His eyes cleared slightly, and he reached up. Instead of grabbing the torn scrap, he swatted at it with his hand, and it fell past Wynn into the passage.

"Did I wake you?" she asked in confusion.

Chane always woke the instant the sun fully set. Light from the passage's small cold lamp seeped into the guest quarters' outer study. The chair behind the old desk was pushed at an awkward angle against the wall. A pile of books and papers was lying haphazardly all over the desk, and some had even fallen to the floor.

"I must have read too late . . . near this morning," he rasped in his maimed voice.

Wynn raised one eyebrow. Chane had fallen dormant at the desk, not aware that dawn was coming? She shook her head, for they had larger problems.

"I've been summoned."

Realization spread over his handsome features as he came to full awareness.

"I am coming," he returned instantly, stepping backward to grab the room key off the desk.

Then he hesitated, glancing down at himself. He still wore his boots from the night before, along with his rumpled breeches. He quickly began tucking in his loose white shirt.

Wynn didn't care how he was dressed. It didn't matter.

"Only me," she said. "I was even ordered to leave Shade in my room."

Chane froze. He knew Shade almost never left Wynn's side. The dog rarely tolerated that. He returned to tucking in his shirt.

"I am as responsible as you," he insisted, "for all that happened. You are not facing them alone."

As he came to the door, Wynn looked up, meeting his eyes in silence. She felt ashamed by her relief at the thought of his standing beside her to face the council. But that wasn't the way this would work.

"I don't think they'll let you—"

"I am coming," he repeated, and stepped out, closing the door.

He headed down the passageway toward the stairs before she could argue further. Without intending to, she sighed—in relief, resignation, or at the weight of her burdens. Perhaps all three.

Wynn still felt cowardly in her relief at Chane's presence as they climbed the stairs to the second floor of the guild's main hall. With all that had happened in the Stonewalkers' underworld, deep below Dhredze Seatt, she could imagine the Premin Council like some Old World mock court. Its verdict would be predetermined before any trial began.

But it wasn't a trial. This was a guild matter, and what she'd done would never be revealed publicly. She would have no statute of law to protect her against any unofficial conviction.

She glanced up at Chane beside her, his expression grim with determination. Perhaps his presence might keep the council in check, for there were internal affairs they might not raise before an outsider. But she doubted it.

When they stepped onto the upper floor, two sages waited outside the council's chamber down the broad passage. Chane never slowed, and Wynn tried not to falter, but the closer they came to the council chamber, the odder it all looked.

A middle-aged woman in cerulean, from the Order of Sentiology, and a younger man in a metaologer's midnight blue stood in silence on either side of the great oak double doors. Wynn didn't immediately recognize either one, although, with their differing orders, they made a strange combination. She'd never seen attendants outside this chamber before.

Both watched her as she approached, which made her nervous. Then they both reached out at the same time and opened the doors without a word.

Inside, standing about, waiting, was the entire Premin Council. And Domin High-Tower, the only dwarven sage and head of Wynn's order, was present, as well.

Folklore of the Farlands, Chane's world, spoke of dwarves as diminutive beings of dark crags and earthen burrows. High-Tower, like all of his people, was an intimidating hulk compared to such superstitions. Though shorter than humans, most dwarves looked Wynn straight in the eyes. What they lacked in height, they doubled in breadth.

Stout and wide as he was, he showed no hint of fat under his gray robe. Coarse reddish hair laced with gray hung past his shoulders, blending with his thick beard, which was braided at its end. His broad, rough features made his black-pupiled eyes seem like iron pellets embedded in pale, flesh-colored granite.

He glowered at her from where he stood beyond the council's table. Suddenly, his glower turned to an incensed glare, quite disturbing from any hulkish dwarf. He rounded the table and tall-back chairs, coming straight toward the opened doorway, his long red hair bouncing with each stride.

"Does your impudence know no limits?" he rumbled, halting within arm's reach.

For an instant, Wynn had thought Chane was the domin's target, but High-Tower's anger was fixed on her.

"This is a guild matter," he growled. "It is no business of any outsider!"

Wynn glanced up at Chane—who stared down at the broad domin.

"You need to leave," she said quietly. "Wait for me in my room."

"No," Chane rasped.

Wynn stiffened. Most times, she no longer noticed his maimed voice. But there was warning in that one word. Chane passively looked at everyone inside the chamber, and this only heightened Wynn's tension.

Chane's resolve might have given her relief at first, but now it was making things worse.

"You will leave," someone else said flatly.

Wynn followed the sharp shift of Chane's eyes.

Premin Frideswida Hawes of Metaology stepped straight toward them in a smooth gait that didn't even sway her long, midnight blue robe. Within the shadow of her cowl, her hazel eyes watched them both. She stopped six paces off and focused fully on Chane. In place of High-Tower's anger, she appeared mildly disdainful.

Chane didn't move—and Wynn began to panic. What could anyone here possibly do to force him?

"High-Tower," Hawes said.

The dwarven domin lunged and grabbed Wynn's arm, jerking her into the chamber.

Chane took one step. "Release her!"

A sharp utterance cracked the air between the wide chamber's walls.

Wynn twisted her head to see.

Hawes's eyes narrowed as she stamped the floor and lashed out with an open palm.

The echo of High-Tower's steps seemed to vibrate in the floor, and Chane wobbled, as if about to topple, his eyes widening.

The floor beneath his feet suddenly lurched. Its stones rolled like a wave rising on a tidal beach. He fell backward through the open doors and toward the passage's far wall. Hawes swept forward to stand before the opening, her back to Wynn.

"Why are you doing this?" Wynn asked, and jerked forward, but she couldn't break High-Tower's grip.

The two attendant sages grabbed the door handles, pulling the great oak doors closed. Hawes raised one hand before the narrowing gap.

"Wynn!" Chane rasped, trying to scramble to his feet.

"Wait for me in my room!" she called.

The doors slammed shut, and he was gone from her sight.

Hawes swept her hand down with another sharp utterance.

Wynn went limp in High-Tower's grip as the doors' aged oak began flowing together along the passing of Hawes's hand. The gap blended downward along the seam. In an instant, the twin doors became one solid barrier, the wood's grain now looking as if it were cut from one piece.

Premin Hawes laid her fingertips on the wood, cocking her head as if listening.

Wynn stared numbly at the barrier as High-Tower released her. Even Chane would be hard-pressed to break his way through from the other side. More than once she'd heard Domin Ghassan il'Sänke's innuendos about this branch's metaologers compared to his own. During his visit from the Suman Empire's guild branch, he'd made plain how little he thought of even Premin Hawes's skill as a thaumaturge.

Il'Sänke had been very wrong.

Everyone within the room remained silent for the longest time.

Premin Hawes finally turned and nodded to the others. She glided toward the long table's right end, and the rest of the council turned to follow. But her gaze fell upon Wynn as she passed. There was no malice or anger there, merely a cold and calculating study.

Council members began taking their seats, and Wynn turned to face what awaited her . . . alone.

Hawes settled silently in one of the smoothly crafted, high-back chairs at the right end of a long, stout table that stretched across the room's rear. All the chairs were now filled with the five robed members of the Premin Council.

Premin Adlam, in the light brown of Naturology, sat at the table's left end. Next, on High Premin Sykion's left, sat portly Premin Renäld of Sentiology in cerulean. Sykion, as head of the council, sat at the table's center, dressed in the gray of Cathology—Wynn's own order. On her right, Premin Jacque of Conamology had his elbows on the table. His fingers were laced together, and he rested his high forehead against them, hiding his face.

And Hawes at the far right end still studied Wynn, almost without blinking. Her hazel irises now seemed the color of the walls' gray stones.

Wynn stood straight, meeting that gaze, but then she couldn't help glancing at the sixth person present.

As with the last time she'd been called here, Domin High-Tower, her immediate superior in Cathology, returned to standing beyond the table. He wouldn't even look at her and stared out one of the narrow rear windows. He'd once been a beloved teacher, but was now her fiercest, most open opponent, trying to hobble her efforts at nearly every turn.

"Journeyor Hygeorht," Premin Sykion began slowly, "I hardly know where to begin."

Wynn shifted her gaze.

"Lady" Tärtgyth Sykion, once a minor noble of the nearby nation of Faunier, was an aged but tall and straight willow of a woman. A long silver braid snaked out of the side of her cowl and down the front of her gray robe. Beneath her usual motherly and temperate veneer, she was as untrustworthy as the rest. Tonight, there was no nurturing care in her expression.

Strangely, that took away all of Wynn's shame and fear.

She wasn't about to give them the slightest chance for a long recitation of her offenses. She wouldn't subject herself to more subterfuge hidden beneath righteous indignation, no matter her guilt.

"I request to go south," she said immediately, "to the Lhoin'na, and our guild's elven branch."

Sykion sat upright, like a willow suddenly revitalized in resistance to an autumn gale. Her eyes barely betrayed shock, but not so for Premin Jacque. He lifted his head from his laced fingers, his broad mouth gaping for an instant.

"You are not here to request anything!" he said. "You are here to answer for your actions."

Wynn clenched her jaw.

Sykion lightly cleared her throat and straightened a stack of papers. The topmost appeared to be a letter of some kind, but Wynn couldn't make out its contents from where she stood. Then she spotted the sea green tie ribbon lying beside the stack. She grew sick inside, thinking of a royal wax seal that must have bound the ribbon enclosing that letter.

"Journeyor Hygeorht," Sykion began again, "it has come to our attention that a number of journals secured with the texts are missing."

Wynn was ready for this, the first and least of her "crimes."

Six moons past, she'd returned from abroad, bearing a treasure like none before it—a collection of ancient texts from the time of the Forgotten History, presumably penned by forgotten Noble Dead. These texts hinted at an ancient enemy who'd nearly destroyed the world a thousand years ago . . . in a war that many now believed was an overblown myth or had never even taken place.

Wynn knew better.

To her shock, upon returning home, she'd lost this treasure. Out of fear of the contents, her superiors had seized the texts—along with her own journals. They'd locked everything away, to be translated in secret. Wynn had uncovered hints that the original texts were hidden somewhere in the underworld of Dhredze Seatt. Against all orders, she'd found them again, but was only able to take back her journals.

"The journals are not missing, but back where they belong," Wynn answered. "I wrote them."

Perhaps they'd expected her to be contrite. Why else would they make her stand alone before them like some miscreant schoolgirl about to be expelled?

"You don't deny that you took these journals?" Adlam asked, perhaps a little uncertain.

"They're mine," Wynn answered.

"You will return them immediately," Sykion said.

"No."

"Journeyor Hygeorht—"

"By law, the texts are mine, as well," Wynn interrupted. "I found them. I brought them back. If you make any attempt to regain my journals, I'll engage the court's High Advocate . . . with my own case to have *all* the texts returned to me."

She spoke without wavering, but her stomach knotted.

Making threats gave her no pleasure, but she'd learned a thing or two about what was right and what was necessary. This place had been her home since the day someone found her abandoned in a box at its outer portcullis. She had no wish to be expelled from the only life she knew. On the other hand, the premins wanted her gone—and yet still under their control. They couldn't have that without her continued connection to the guild.

But as Wynn's last words escaped, any pretense of formality vanished from the chamber.

High-Tower turned her way. He was not a premin, and so not part of the council. He didn't speak, but his breath came strong and hard.

Premin Renäld glared at Wynn and whispered, "And what of the loss of Prince Freädherich?"

He may as well have shouted.

This was the worst of it—her true crime. This was the reason she'd been commanded before the council. Next to the loss of Prince Freädherich, stealing back her journals was a child's prank.

Wynn slid one foot back a half step before catching herself. She'd known this was coming, but the quick shift in their assault had caught her off guard just the same.

A gleam of righteous ire—but also horror over the consequences—sparked in Renäld's eyes.

"*If* the worst comes . . . you have cut our hopes in half!" he spat at her.

Wynn knew it all more than he did. During her ordeal in the Stonewalkers' underworld, she'd uncovered a dark secret unrelated to her purpose.

A prince of Malourné, thought drowned years ago, was alive and locked away in the Stonewalkers' underworld—to protect him from himself. His wife, Duchess Reine Faunier-Âreskynna, princess of Malourné by marriage, had been caring for him in secret. The family line of the Âreskynna had an ancient blood connection to the Dunidæ—Dwarvish for the "Deep Ones." A fabled people of the sea, only the Stonewalkers and the royal family knew of them.

Freädherich had been slowly succumbing to sea-lorn sickness, carried in his blood from a forgotten ancestor married in an alliance to one of the Dunidæ. Wynn had unwittingly drawn a black wraith named Sau'ilahk into the underworld, and the threat of the wraith's presence had accelerated the prince's illness and its transformation.

Prince Freädherich had fled, escaping to the open ocean with the Dunidæ, who always sought him out at the highest tides. Because of Wynn's actions, Malourné had lost not only a prince, but the prime emissary to the Deep Ones, and an ancient alliance along with him.

Duchess Reine had lost her husband for the second and final time.

Wynn's certainty of her choices wasn't enough to hold down her guilt. She tried not to let it show but smoothed her robe a bit too obviously. The council was watching for weakness, anything to use against her, and they had more than enough.

"If this hadn't been kept secret for so long," Premin Renäld went on, "you wouldn't be standing before us. You would be facing the High Advocate yourself, on trial for—"

"As far as the public is concerned," Wynn cut in, "the prince died years ago."

It was a shabby, cruel response, but there was nothing else she could say. What happened couldn't be undone. She had no intention of justifying herself to those whose fears overrode necessary action, who denied obvious conclusions for all of these events.

The Ancient Enemy was returning. Another war was coming. There was no *if*; only *when*. And Wynn had to continue in her determination to stop it.

"So, you deny any part in the prince's loss?" Premin Jacque demanded.

"I deny its relevance . . . in the present," Wynn answered. "It has no bearing on my request to travel south to the Lhoin'na's guild branch."

This was her goal. In the brief time she'd regained access to the ancient texts, searching for clues of the Ancient Enemy's return, Wynn had found hints of where to look for the mystery's next piece.

Bäalâle Seatt: a great dwarven settlement, lost in the mythical war at the end of the Forgotten History.

Her best guess placed it somewhere south, nearer the great desert and mountains separating the north from the southern Suman Empire. The Lhoin'na—elven—branch of the guild was not far from that range of mountains. Each guild branch had gathered lost fragments of the far past in their own regions. The archived library of the Lhoin'na sages might be the better place to find clues to the location of that lost seatt. She now staked everything on the hope that her own guild branch wanted to rid itself of her presence.

Wynn stood in a long silence, watching her superiors. During some moment she hadn't noticed, Hawes had pulled down her cowl. The premin of metaologers was the only one who hadn't spoken as of yet.

Premin Frideswida Hawes appeared to be late middle-aged, but her short, cropped hair was as fully grayed as dull silver. With smooth, narrow features above a pointed chin, her expression rarely betrayed mood or thought.

Hawes's silence, versus the others, seemed out of place.

Wynn viewed metaologers as logical, willful, used to the subtleties and hazards of balancing belief and knowledge. She wondered if blunt honesty would now be a useful tactic.

"I wish to go south. You wish me gone," Wynn said, looking at Hawes, but then she turned to Sykion. "Simply give me approval. A quick word serves *all* our needs."

Shocked expressions rose on both Sykion's and Adlam's faces, but no one spoke for the span of three breaths.

"The council will discuss your *request* . . . later, in private," Sykion said. "For now, as you clearly won't face your transgressions, you are dismissed." Then she leaned forward. "You are confined to the guild grounds."

Wynn tried not to stiffen, but failed. "You cannot order me to—"

"Journeyor Hygeorht, you will remain on grounds!" the high premin commanded. "Or I will have your status revoked. I may face the consequences of that, but it would be a price worth paying."

Wynn was too stunned for her growing anger to escape.

"Understand this *clearly*," Sykion went on. "No guild protection, no funding, no status whatsoever as a sage. Threaten us again with action to regain the texts, and I will have you charged with the theft of the journals, which were in the dwarves' possession at the time. We shall see whose case the High Advocate takes . . . and whose word stands unblemished before the people's court!"

Her aged features were strained with a fury that Wynn had never seen there before. But open hostility was preferable to politely veiled aggression.

They were in a deadlock. No matter Sykion's warnings, she was desperate to keep a hold on Wynn. And no matter what Wynn threatened, she couldn't afford to be cast out, or she would have no right to enter the archives of Lhoin'na sages.

"Do you understand?" Sykion asked.

Wynn nodded curtly.

"Then you are dismissed . . . for now."

Wynn turned slowly and found herself staring at the impenetrable barrier of solid wood. By the time she glanced back, Hawes's hand finished an upward sweep, thin fingers curling lazily inward at the last. When Wynn turned back, only normal, old oak doors stood before her.

They began to open under the push of the outer attendants.

Looking out hesitantly, Wynn was relieved not to see Chane outside. He must have followed her request and gone back to her room. Trembling slightly, Wynn left the now silent council chamber, trying not to break into a jog until she was out of sight of the attendants.

A short while later, Chane paced Wynn's small dormitory room, listening to her recount what had happened with the Premin Council. Seething, and still startled by how easily he had been locked out of the proceedings, he listened carefully to all that had transpired.

"They gave no answer to your request?" he asked.

"Only that I'm confined to guild grounds."

She sat on the bed, one limp hand on Shade's back. Chane studied them both.

Wynn looked less troubled than he expected. Her wispy brown hair hung around her pretty, olive-toned face. He suppressed an urge to push a few strands behind her ear.

Shade still appeared put out at having been left behind. Reading a canine face was not always easy, but she had almost taken on an air of petulance. Though she was an elven breed of dog called a majay-hì, anyone who did not know this saw only an oversized, long-legged, near-black wolf.

Wynn ran her hand down Shade's neck.

"I think they'll let me go in the end," Wynn said. "Once they believe they have the means to get me out of their way *and* keep me on a leash."

Chane stopped pacing. "How soon do you think we can leave?"

"I can't even guess, but we'll make use of our time while we wait."

He stood there a little longer, debating his next words. An uncomfortable concern had nagged him since returning from Dhredze Seatt. Wynn had more than enough burdens, but with another journey ahead, he could no longer put this off.

"Then we should discuss safeguards," he said carefully. "Once we leave civilization—"

"I know," she broke in tiredly. "I'll be away from so many other mortals, and we'll be traveling through isolated places where the Fay might try to seek me out."

At that, Shade raised her head, rumbling softly into Wynn's face.

This was going to be harder than Chane thought. Before Wynn or Shade could start in about the Fay, Chane cut them off.

"Whenever possible on the road, I need to keep my ring off."

Chane wore a brass ring that he called his ring of nothing, which had been created by his old undead companion Welstiel Massing—who was now truly dead. The ring protected Chane against anyone sensing his nature as an undead. But it also dulled his own heightened senses, including his awareness of the living and the undead.

Wynn blinked at his reference to the ring. It had nothing to do with the Fay hunting her because she was the only mortal who could hear them, spy upon them whenever and wherever they manifested near enough. And then realization of what he truly meant finally spread across her oval face.

"Oh, Chane," she said. "Sau'ilahk is gone. I burned him to nothing down in the sea tunnel."

"You burned him once before in the streets of Calm Seatt," he countered. "And yet—"

"This time was different," Wynn insisted. "I destroyed him, and that's the fact."

Perhaps . . . but this was the point of contention. It was not a fact, as there was no proof of it.

In the underworld of the dwarves, Wynn had used her only weapon against the undead—her sun crystal staff—to vanquish the wraith. It was true that this time she had had powerful help. Cinder-Shard, the craggy-faced master of the dwarven Stonewalkers, those who guarded the remains and spirits of the dwarven honored dead, had somehow been able to seize Sau'ilahk's incorporeal form with his massive bare hands. And that sardonic elf called Chuillyon, dressed in white robes like a false sage, had held the wraith at bay with little more than serene, smiling whispers.

Those two, along with the other Stonewalkers, had hindered and bound Sau'ilahk. They had given Wynn time to burn the wraith with her staff, its crystal emitting light akin to the sun.

She was convinced the wraith was gone.

Chane was not.

"Compared to the wraith, I am a common vampire," he countered.

He could hear himself shifting from his normal, voiceless hiss to something more raspy, grating, and heated. He tried to sound calmer, more rational. "Yet you watched as Magiere severed my head from my body."

This was also how his voice had been permanently maimed.

Wynn fell silent, glancing away.

"Yet here I am," he finished quietly.

He hated feeling forced to bring this up. Watching him die his second death had been more than difficult for her. He still had no understanding of how he had later managed to come back. All he remembered was waking up soaked in blood and covered in freshly killed bodies in a shallow-earth hollow. He was whole again—and Welstiel had been looking down at him, as if waiting.

"I traveled with Magiere, Leesil, and Chap for a long time," Wynn finally answered. "They—we—destroyed vampires who did *not* come back." She gestured toward her desk, at the stacks of journals piled there. "I've recorded it all, regardless that my superiors have no interest in the truth."

Chane glanced at the journals. Another notion resurfaced, one that he had mulled over in recent nights. He had never even seen those journals until Wynn managed to steal them back.

But she had written everything in them about her travels with Leesil and Magiere, about her experiences with the undead and the an'Cróan, the elves of the Farlands. If he could read them, he might better understand her . . . comprehend her true drives, goals, hopes, and fears. Even if she had not recorded events literally, he knew her well enough to read between the lines of her script.

His one task was to protect Wynn, including from herself. This gave him purpose, and to do so, he needed to understand everything she had been through.

"May I read them?" he asked, nodding at the stack.

Wynn turned pale.

"I wrote them in the Begaine syllabary," she blurted out. "You won't be able to."

"I read a little of your guild symbols." He stepped closer. "And you can help me. Studying your works will teach me to follow the script."

Wynn started to say something more but it never came out.

Chane did not understand her reluctance. He had already strained her patience by pushing his point about Sau'ilahk, but now that he had made the request, he would not stop.

"The information in those journals could help me—us—in the journey to come."

This reasoning was sound. If they were to travel to another guild branch in search of more answers, how else would he know what to look for? She viewed him as part of her purpose now. He should be allowed to know everything.

Wynn was still silent.

Chane understood her well enough. Everything she had brought to the guild had been taken from her. Now that she had regained some of her prized possessions, perhaps she was reluctant to relinquish them again, even to him.

"As you said," he went on, "we must pass time constructively until the council decides. I will need to purchase the supplies for our trip if you are confined. Otherwise, I must better understand what has brought you this far."

And still she hesitated.

"Were they not written to recount your experiences, share your knowledge?"

Wynn looked up at him.

"Of course, yes." She stood up, stepping to her little desk table. "I recopied this one while on the ship from the Farlands. This recounts my journey to Droevinka with Magiere, Leesil, and Chap. You can start here."

Her sudden acquiescence was a relief, but something in her eyes troubled Chane. Even as she held up that first journal, her small fingers were white from clutching it too tightly.

What was she hiding?

CHAPTER 2

Seven nights later, Wynn knelt on the floor of her small room, feeding Shade bits of dried fish. All was quiet except for the dog's clacking teeth and smacking jowls. She glanced at the door again, wondering why Chane still hadn't arrived, and then looked around at her simple room: the bed, desk, small table, and one narrow window with a view of the keep's inner courtyard.

Once she'd felt safe here, in what was now her prison. The council had maintained a deafening silence, and she had begun to wonder if they'd ever decide her fate. She and Chane had pressed ahead, anyway, itemizing supplies for him to acquire and making preparations for a journey. He stopped by her room each night before heading into the city to either tell her what he'd acquired or to see if anything new had been put on the list—or to return a journal and pick up another.

Wynn clenched all over every time he did the latter.

It wasn't that she minded him reading her journals. They were a scholar's records, after all. But a fair portion of their content dealt with the undead, with hunting and eliminating them. Chane often grew sullen or even bitter whenever she mentioned her old companions, Magiere, Leesil, and Chap. She could only imagine his state while reading so much about them.

Wynn's relationship to those three was . . . complex.

Magiere was a fierce, dark-haired rogue and the only dhampir Wynn had ever even heard of. Leesil was half-elven, raised in his youth to be an assassin enslaved to a warlord, a life he had escaped. Chap was a majay-hì like no other, a true Fay who'd chosen to be born into a pup of the Fay-and-wolf descendants of the elven lands.

In Wynn's time in the Farlands of the eastern continent, she'd journeyed with these three in search of an artifact once wielded by the Ancient Enemy of many names. Their journey's last leg ended in the far south of the region, in the high, desolate range of the Pock Peaks. There they'd finally uncovered the artifact—the orb—as well as those old texts that had given Wynn nothing but misery since returning home. She and her companions carried away what they could, and upon their return to the new little guild branch in Bela, Wynn had been given the task of bearing those texts safely back to Calm Seatt.

Magiere, Leesil, and Chap had sailed with her, bringing the orb. Their journey encompassed the better part of a year. They stayed together until the city of Calm Seatt loomed into sight and then parted ways. Wynn's companions—mostly Chap—had decided the orb was too dangerous to bring to the sages. So they'd left to find a place of hiding for it against those who might seek it out.

Wynn still missed them. Magiere, Leesil, and Chap had become more than friends to her. They were like blood . . . like family. She was lonely for them, and Chane knew it.

He'd wanted so badly to read her journals, and she understood his reasons, but each time he returned one and took another, he grew more silent, tense, and matter-of-fact. Even worse, he feigned ignorance if she asked why. His darkening mood might have nothing to do with the journals, but she doubted it.

And to make matters worse, he kept returning to the topic of Sau'ilahk.

Sau'ilahk was gone—Wynn knew this. She'd seen the end, and Chane hadn't. She'd described every detail to him that she could, though she couldn't explain the influence of Chuillyon or the Stonewalkers upon the wraith any more than he could.

But he hadn't *seen* it happen.

Chane was many things to Wynn. He'd appeared at some of the worst times in her life, when it seemed no one else could protect her. He'd thrown himself in front of her and done whatever he deemed necessary to make certain nothing got past him. But he was a vampire, one of the higher forms of the undead, known in some cultures as the Noble Dead. By any account, as a predator of the living, he went too far at times in defending her.

Much as Wynn trusted him as an ally, how could she dare feel anything more than that? Still, she wished she understood him better. Was he worried about their journey or about their limited chance of blind success? Or was it what else they'd pieced together in their time in Dhredze Seatt? Between more passages she'd translated from the ancient texts and a scroll in Chane's possession, they'd uncovered a deeper burden.

Magiere, Leesil, and Chap had not carried off the only orb.

The Enemy had created five for some unknown purpose, one for each of the Elements of Existence. The one Wynn's friends possessed was likely that of Water, and they were somewhere to the north of this continent, trying to secure it in secret.

At the great war's end, the Enemy had given thirteen vampires known as the Children the task of scattering the five orbs into hiding. A thousand years later, it seemed the orbs still existed . . . somewhere . . . the last tokens of a war so few believed had ever happened at all. The Enemy now had minions—old and new—on the move, seeking the orbs again.

Wynn suspected one orb might still be in Bäalâle Seatt. If so, she had to find it before any other servants like the wraith reached it first.

Shade finished the last of the fish and whined for more.

"You'll not become a glutton like your father," Wynn said, stroking the dog's head. "Time for your language lessons."

Shade scooted backward on her rump, flattening her ears with a low snarl.

"Shade . . . no more arguing."

Wynn's head suddenly filled with a chaos of her own memories. In each image, she was touching Shade and communicating by sharing mental pictures. But the rushing cascade made her head pound.

"No . . . no memory-speak," she said. "You will learn words, even if I have to pin your ears back to hear them."

Like her father, Chap, and other majay-hì, Shade communicated through memories with her own kind via touch rather than any form of speech. Wynn called this memory-speak. Shade's father was unique, for he could speak words into Wynn's head. Both father and daughter could also raise another being's own memories so long as they had line of sight. But, unlike Chap, Shade couldn't speak words in Wynn's head.

In place of this, Shade could send her own memories to Wynn when they touched. She could also share memories she'd picked up from others. To Wynn's knowledge, no other majay-hì and human could do this.

"Shade, come here," she said.

Shade curled her jowls, and the pink tip of her tongue flicked out and up over her nose—just like Chap used to do.

Wynn exhaled.

"I barely tolerated that from your father. Don't think I'll give you half as much. Come here!"

Recently, Shade had made a slip. Wynn had uncovered that her young majay-hì guardian indeed understood spoken words—to a point. Shade couldn't speak, but she could listen, and she'd been doing so without anyone knowing it. She was going to listen now, and learn.

Shade abruptly launched straight from a squat.

Wynn lurched back in surprise, but the dog only hopped to the bed, turning a full circle before settling. Shade curled up, facing away, toward the stone wall.

Wynn scrambled to her feet. "Don't be obstinate."

Shade resented being forced to communicate like "jabbering" humans, but Wynn was determined to expand the dog's vocabulary. The grueling process of memory-speak might be all right for fluent majay-hì accustomed to nothing else, but it wasn't efficient enough for Wynn.

Wrestling an animal bigger than a wolf would've made a sensible person hesitate, and yet . . . it didn't stop Wynn from grabbing Shade's tail.

Shade whipped her head around with a snarl.

Wynn didn't let go. "You wouldn't dare."

Then Shade's ears stood straight up. She looked across the room, rumbling low as her ears flattened again, and she scrambled up to all fours.

Wynn released Shade's tail and turned around, looking to the door.

"Chane?" she called. "Is that you? Come in."

The door didn't open, and Shade's rumble turned to an open growl of warning.

Before Wynn looked to the dog, the wall to the door's left appeared to shift. She backed up until her calves bumped the bed.

Gray wall stones bulged inward, as if something pushed through them.

Wynn rushed for the corner beyond the door and grabbed the staff. She ripped the leather sheath off its top, exposing the long sun crystal, and thrust it out toward the rippling wall stones.

Something like a cloak's hood overshadowing a face surfaced out of the wall. Thudding footfalls landed upon floor stones, and a cloaked and stout hulk stood within the room, easily twice as wide as Wynn, but no taller. An overbroad hand swiped back the hood, and a stocky dwarf glowered at her, eye-to-eye.

Wynn's initial fright turned to anger. "What are you doing here?"

Ore-Locks cast one glance toward Shade, who was still growling. Beardless, something uncommon for male dwarves, his red hair flowed to the shoulders of an iron-colored wool cloak. He looked young, perhaps thirty by human standards, so likely sixty or more for a dwarf. Wynn knew better still.

Ore-Locks was older than that due to his life among the Hassäg'kreigi—the "Stonewalkers" of Dhredze Seatt.

"Why do you still delay departure?" he asked, ignoring her question.

She clenched her teeth. He'd left his own sect, determined to join her in search of Bäalâle Seatt, but she didn't trust him. He was an even darker complication beyond dealing with the council.

From what she'd gleaned of Bäalâle Seatt, its fall—its destruction—had been the work of a traitor. That one's name had been forgotten long ago, and only a cryptic title in ancient Dwarvish remained: Thallûhearag, the "Lord of Slaughter." Only Ore-Locks seemed to know his true name.

Byûnduní—Deep-Root—had been a stonewalker of Bäalâle Seatt, just as Ore-Locks was in Dhredze Seatt. But the connection went deeper than that, for Ore-Locks claimed it was this spirit of his ancestor that had called him to sacred service as a stonewalker, a guardian and caretaker of the dwarves' honored dead.

Ore-Locks worshipped this genocidal traitor, claiming that Deep-Root—that Thallûhearag—was not a Fallen One, those who stood for the opposite of all that the dwarves' Eternals represented.

Chane claimed, by his truth sense, that Ore-Locks truly believed Deep-Root was no traitor. But there was no proof in mere believing. Knowingly or not, it all made Ore-Locks a potential tool of the Enemy through the spirit of a mass murderer. Perhaps he already was.

Wynn wanted no part of him.

Then she noticed his attire.

He no longer wore a stonewalker's black-scaled armor. He still bore their twin battle daggers on his belt, along with the new, broad dwarven sword in its sheath. But the long iron staff in his large hand was the first bad sign. He was dressed plainly in brown breeches and a natural canvas shirt, and through the split of his cloak, Wynn saw the burnt orange, wool tabard.

Stunned, she stared at his vestment. "What are you wearing?"

"I am in disguise," he answered quietly.

That was something else about Ore-Locks; he didn't behave like a typical dwarf. Most of his people were slow to anger and quick to laugh. They wore their emotions on their broad faces, their feelings expressed proudly with booming voices.

Ore-Locks's voice was too often low and quiet, his dark eyes devoid of his people's heartfelt emotions. She could never be certain what lay behind his words. And while she wasn't religious, his choice of disguise, that tabard and staff, were blasphemous.

Ore-Locks had "disguised" himself as a holy shirvêsh of Bedzâ'kenge—"Feather-Tongue"—the dwarves' saintly Eternal of history, tradition, and wisdom. That was as far removed from the deceits of Thallûhearag as possible.

"Take that off," she told him.

"The shirvêsh of Feather-Tongue are well received in most northern lands. I do not wish to be noticed along the journey."

"I said . . . take it off."

Anyone who worshipped a servant of the Enemy had no business masquerading as a shirvêsh, a religious servant, of Feather-Tongue.

"When do we leave?" he asked.

"I never agreed to let you come."

"That was settled in fair barter with your companion."

Wynn glanced away.

Chane had broken his sword trying to get them past a massive iron door because of her obsession with finding the Stonewalkers. When they'd returned to the guild, Ore-Locks had appeared. He'd brought Chane a new sword made of the finest dwarven steel, which Chane never could have afforded.

Chane distrusted Ore-Locks only half as much as Wynn did, and he needed a new sword. At the offer of one of such craftsmanship, he hadn't said a word to refuse it.

"When do we leave?" Ore-Locks repeated.

"I don't know. I'm waiting for funding and . . . other matters to settle."

She wasn't about to tell him anything more than necessary.

Ore-Locks turned away. "I am at the Harvest Inn, west of the Grayland's Empire district. Send a message when you are ready." He paused with his back to her. "You would do well not to leave without me."

Shade's rumble turned to a snarl. Though Ore-Locks's quiet tone hadn't changed, those last words had sounded like a threat. Or perhaps Shade had snatched a memory that rose in the dwarf's conscious thoughts. Either way, Wynn kept silent as Ore-Locks strode toward—through—the wall.

She sank on the bed's edge, feeling stretched thin on all sides, and snarled her fingers into Shade's scruff. Shade shoved her head against Wynn's neck, but soft fur and a warm, wet tongue weren't comfort enough as Wynn glanced at the door.

Where was Chane?

Upon rising at dusk, Chane dressed quickly, pausing briefly at the mirror over the short dresser. He tried to smooth his raggedly cropped, red-brown hair. Several objects, the results of his nightly errands, rested upon the dresser. As of yet, he had not told Wynn about these extra acquisitions.

The sword that Ore-Locks had brought him now had a plain leather sheath. A fresh cloak of deep green wool, with a full hood, was folded atop the dresser's end. Upon it lay a matching scarf, a pair of new, fitted leather gloves, and two small leather triangles with attached lacing for their final purpose.

He still had two more items to attain, and tonight, he was already late in seeking one.

Rushing through the small study and into the outer passage, Chane locked the door to his guest quarters and hurried to the end stairs. When he reached the building's ground level, he did not head for the courtyard. Instead, he ducked into one ground-floor chamber laden with workbenches, books, and glass contraptions and other tools. Rounding to the back, he headed down another flight of stairs.

Emerging in the building's first level of underchambers, he stepped into a narrow stone corridor lit by two sage-crafted cold lamps set in wall-mounted metal vessels. Alchemically mixed fluids provided mild heat to keep them lit. By their steady light, he counted three wide iron doors on both sides of the passage. These were the lower laboratories of the guild.

In two previous visits over eight nights, he had never seen what lay behind any but one. He had tried opening others to peek in and satisfy his curiosity. Not one budged, though there were no locks or bars on their outsides. He headed for the last on the right, but tonight it was shut tight, like the others.

Chane let out a sigh, an old habit left over from living days. He knocked, listening for an answer, but none came. He tried the heavy iron handle, anyway, expecting the door would not open. To his surprise, it slipped inward as he twisted the handle. He hesitated and glanced along the other heavy doors.

This was wrong. Still, perhaps *she* was within and had not heard him. He pushed the door wide.

"*Géorn-metade*," he called in Numanese.

No one answered his formal greeting.

A short, three-step access hallway emptied into the left side of a small back chamber. He had come here twice before, just past dusk, both times in haste before going to Wynn's room. He never told her where he had been.

Chane entered, quietly closing the door. All he could see from the hallway were shelves pegged in the chamber's left wall. They were filled with books, bound sheaves, and some slender, upright cylinders of wood, brass, and unglazed ceramic. As he stepped out of the passage, the room filled his view.

Stout, narrow tables and squat casements were stuffed with more texts, as well as odd little contraptions of metal, crystal and glass, and wood and leather. A rickety old armchair of tattered blue fabric barely fit into the back right corner beyond the orderly mess upon the age-darkened desk of many little drawers. Atop the desk's corner sat the dimming cold lamp, brighter than he had first thought.

Someone had been here recently to rub its crystal to brilliance.

Chane scanned stacks of parchment and three bowls of powdered substances. An array of brass articulated arms anchored to the desk's other corner each held framed magnifying lenses. They were mounted so that one or more could be twisted into or out of alignment with the others.

Chane stood in the private study of Frideswida Hawes, premin of the Order of Metaology. And he was tempted to dig through everything in sight.

He understood a little of thaumaturgy, the physical ideology of magic, as opposed to the spiritual perspective of his own conjury. Still, something here might shed a spark of light on his own research. He leaned over the desk, touching nothing as he examined the stacks of parchment and paper. Most appeared mundane, concerning daily guild operations and Hawes's own order. Considering the top one's immature topic, one stack seemed to be papers written by initiates.

Chane returned to the left wall's pegged shelves.

Spines and labels on texts and containers were all marked in the Begaine syllabary. Even after nights of stumbling through Wynn's journals, he still struggled to understand the sages' mutable writing system. He reached for a ceramic cylinder with a wooden cap to verify that it was a scroll case.

"So . . . disrespect is not your only flaw."

Chane spun at the voice behind him and came face-to-face with a mature, slight woman in a midnight blue robe.

"Do we now add thievery to the list?" she asked.

Chane studied the narrow face of Premin Hawes. With her cowl down, cropped, ash gray hair bristled across her head, though any lines of age were faint in her even, small features. Severe-looking, she was not unattractive.

"My apologies," he began. "I was . . . only . . ."

Chane glanced down the short passage to the chamber door.

Hawes could not have passed by without bumping into him, so how had she entered unnoticed? He flashed back to their first meeting.

When Wynn had been called before the Premin Council and he had been ejected, Hawes had stood inside the chamber doors. As the doors shut tight, the seam between them began to vanish. In a mere instant, the doors became one solid barrier. The image of Hawes with one hand raised, as she glared at him through the closing doors, had remained fixed in his mind. Her revealed abilities that evening were why he had ultimately sought her out in private.

"Well?" she said.

Chane remained calm, facing this deceptively academic-looking woman.

"Is it finished?" he asked.

She scrutinized him a moment longer and then turned toward her desk. Opening its top left drawer, she lifted out a narrow pouch of brown felt stacked atop two torn half sheets of paper and one of Chane's own books. Much as he hungered to know what she made of the latter three items he had shown her, the first was the most important.

Premin Hawes loosened the pouch's drawstring and slid its contents into her hand.

"This pair is smaller," she said, "as you requested."

She held out a pair of glasses much like those Wynn wore when igniting the sun crystal.

"They are the same?" he asked.

"Yes, simple enough to duplicate . . . though these have structural improvements."

Smaller compared to Wynn's, their round, smooth lenses were framed in pewter. Unlike the straighter, thick arms of the original pair, these had tin wire arms with curved ends to better hook around a person's ears.

Hawes had likely engaged her apprentices to make them—considering what little Chane discerned of her. Wynn had mentioned that Domin il'Sänke had scant respect for this branch's metaologers compared to his own. Ghassan il'Sänke had not known with whom he was dealing.

The premin, like a mage of worth, did not put her skills on display unless necessary. Only petty dabblers made a show. From what Chane had seen at the council chamber, she was far beyond some academic practitioner.

"They were created from your specifications," Hawes continued, "though they will not fit you."

Chane said nothing. These glasses were meant for Wynn, to replace the ones she had. As to the first pair . . .

He stepped around Hawes to her desk. Fingering aside the two half sheets of paper, he picked up the book he had left with her.

Chane had scavenged and saved as many books, journals, and sheaves as he could from a remote keep of Stravinan healer monks, ones that Welstiel had turned into feral vampires. This text, thinnest among them all, had held Chane's attention from the start, though he could not truly say why. An accordion-style volume of grayed leather cover plates, it had one thick parchment folded back and forth four times between the plates. Its title read *The Seven Leaves of . . .*

That final word in old Stravinan was too obscured by age and wear.

"Did you make anything of this, based on my attempted translation into Numanese?" he asked.

Hawes barely glanced at the book. She slowly pivoted the other way and retrieved the first half sheet of his notes—his translation. There were now more notes written in her own hand.

"Of ingredients mentioned, some are rare. They are mostly herbs and substances considered beneficial to healing . . . but not all."

Her explanation made sense, considering where he had acquired this text. To some relief, he realized what the last word of the book's title must be.

The Seven Leaves of . . . Life.

But not all seven substances in the translated list implied leaves. Two he could not make out at all, proving difficult to copy them rote into Belaskian letters of similar sound. He glanced at Hawes's notes, looking for those two.

"What is . . . a *muhkgean* branch?" he asked.

"A mushroom grown by the dwarves," she answered. "Its cap spreads in branched protrusions that splay and flatten at the ends."

"Like leaves?" he asked.

She shrugged. "Yes, that might come to mind in looking at one. But I know of no medicinal purpose for them."

This left another puzzle for Chane. To his knowledge, there were no dwarves in his part of the world. So how would those healer monks have known of this mushroom, let alone what it was called by dwarves?

"What of this . . . an-os . . . a-nas-ji . . ."

Chane still struggled with the last of the seven terms. It was not Belaskian, old or contemporary Stravinan, or any language he knew. When Hawes said nothing, he looked up.

She was scrutinizing him again, as if deciphering him like some ancient tome.

"What is this text to you?" she demanded.

"A curiosity. I would think any bit of recovered knowledge would interest a sage as much, if not more. Are these ingredients for something? Is it a type of healing salve, like I have seen Wynn sometimes carry?"

"Not a salve . . . a draught, a liquid concoction, at a guess."

She paused long, never even blinking, and Chane grew unnerved. Before he spoke, she cut him off.

"I'm uncertain of the full process, since it isn't described in detail. By your translations, the text contains only cryptic references, perhaps key points or reminders of some more explicit procedure. It does not appear to be thaumaturgical—or, rather, alchemical—in nature, so perhaps a mundane process."

Chane sagged a bit. Even for these grains of knowledge gained, he had hoped for something more conclusive. His own body was almost indestructible, but Wynn's was not. He would use anything that might keep her whole and sound. Yet if Hawes could not decipher the process hinted at, what chance would he have to do so? He was no thaumaturge, let alone highly skilled as a conjurer. He worked mostly by ritual, sometimes spell, and rarely ever artificing, even in its most common subpractice of alchemy.

"What is this seventh item?" he asked again.

Open suspicion surfaced in Hawes's expression.

"*Anasgiah* . . . is perhaps Old or even Ancient Elvish," she said, correcting his failed pronunciation. "I found no translation for it, though I've heard something similar. *Anamgiah*, the 'life shield,' is a wildflower in the lands of the Lhoin'na."

Chane wanted more, but clearly Hawes's patience thinned with each answer. Instead of pressing her on this, he picked up the second sheet of his scribbled marks before her patience ran out. This one he had shown her with hesitation; it concerned a starkly different topic.

"And this list," he said. "Do you know any of these ingredients?"

Hawes whispered in warning, "What kind of . . . *man* . . . carries works of healing, only to stack them with something of deadly harm?"

Malice flickered so openly across her stern features that Chane tensed.

"It is a poison, as a whole?" he asked. "Or is only one component so?"

He already knew some ingredients for Welstiel's violet concoction were benign. Others baffled him, particularly the flower he knew as *Dyvjàka Svonchek*— "boar's bell" in Belaskian. Hawes might be as puzzled as she was suspicious.

"Do you know the flower?" he urged. "Perhaps by a name other than those I translated?"

In one quick step, Hawes closed on him.

"Who are you?" she demanded. "And make no mistake: I have no fear of you!"

Her claim was obvious, though Chane could only guess how skilled she might be beyond what he had seen. After their encounter at the council chamber, it made him wonder again why she had assisted him at all.

"You do not agree with the way the guild has treated Wynn," he said, hoping to throw her off balance.

"Agreement is irrelevant," she returned instantly. "The guild's purpose comes first. Answer my question."

To Chane, there were few who mattered among the common herds of human cattle. Fewer still who would be a loss at their death. Wynn was foremost among these.

Hawes was obviously well beyond the unworthy masses, and beyond many here within the guild's walls. Had he stumbled upon a hidden, if adversarial, ally that Wynn had not recognized?

"I am the one who keeps Wynn safe," he answered.

Hawes lifted only her eyes, not her head, glaring up at him, as if his superior height were nothing but an annoyance.

"It has been called Léchelâppa," she said.

Chane frowned. It sounded Numanese, but he could not translate it in his head.

"Corpse-Skirt," she added in different terms. "It was used by some in the past as a common way to draw out and kill vermin . . . foolishly, considering livestock were attracted to it. I know of no one who carries it or sells it . . . or would be allowed to do so."

So it *was* known in this part of the world.

Chane was grateful for the information, but one thing disturbed him. Hawes openly discussed an illegal substance, but she never asked what this second deadly concoction was for. This left him wary.

He slowly reached out and took the list of components from *The Seven Leaves of Life* out of her hand. Clutching the book and his note sheets, he held up the glasses, peering once through their clear lenses.

"My thanks," he said. "I am late in meeting Wynn."

If his sudden desire to leave startled the premin, she did not show it. She cocked her head to the side, still eyeing him, and simply nodded.

Without another word, Chane strode out and down the passage. Late as he was, his own quarters were close, so he took both flights of stairs two at a time. Fumbling briefly with the key to unlock his guest quarters, he went directly to the desk, hiding the glasses and his other burdens in a lower drawer. As Chane turned to leave, his gaze fell upon Wynn's stacked journals, and he winced.

The mere sight of them hurt for what he had found—or rather not found—in their pages.

At first, he had allowed Wynn to work with him, helping him interpret so many symbols he could not follow. The further he traveled within her stories of the Farlands, the more he wanted to study and absorb her writings by himself. He later took to struggling alone in his own room with copious notes made in her company.

Doing so without her assistance was daunting, but he began to grasp the syllabary's premise of compressing and simplifying multiple letters into symbols of fewer and fewer continuous strokes. These were combined with special marks to account for pronunciations and special sounds in any language. It was all elegant, concise, adaptable, and so much could be condensed within a single page.

Fascinated as he was by each of the experiences he wrested from the symbols, something odd began to trouble him. Soon he stopped paying attention to actual events, paged backward, and focused on her accounts of the Noble Dead, most specifically the vampires.

She wrote of Toret—Chane's own maker—once called Rat-Boy, and of Sapphire, Toret's doxy. There were many passages concerning Welstiel Massing, Magiere's half-brother, and Li'kän, that ancient undead now trapped beneath the castle in the Pock Peaks' frozen heights. Wynn wrote of the feral monks Welstiel had created to fight his battles as they had raced for that castle. She even recounted meeting a vampire boy named Tomas in a decaying fortress outside of Apudâlsat in Magiere's homeland.

Chane paged faster, but some of Wynn's encounters with the undead that he knew of were missing.

At times, he had been an intricate part of her life—of her stories. But she had omitted how he had protected her from an undead sorcerer named Vordana, simply noting that Vordana escaped to be later destroyed by Leesil. She omitted how he had saved her from two mindless undead sailors in those same swamps and marshes. The account of Magiere severing his head was missing entirely.

As for the orb's discovery, guarded by the deceptively frail Li'kän, Chane found only a mention of "another undead" in Welstiel's company. And, that in the end, one of Welstiel's "servants" had betrayed him. That one was never described, let alone named.

It had been Chane himself. There were so many holes in the tales, and he felt as if he were falling through all of them at once into nothing.

Chane Andraso was not mentioned once in the journals of Wynn Hygeorht.

Standing in the guest quarters' silence, he could not bear to pick them up again. As if touching them would make the truth all the more real. Wynn had written these journals as if he never existed. All record of him had been blotted away from later becoming a reminder to anyone, especially to her. Chane did not need to ask why.

He was a *thing* not suitable for her world.

That realization—that intentional omission of him—cut him worse than Magiere's falchion severing his head. Yet he could not leave Wynn.

His place was at her side for as long as she would allow him. He swallowed the pain and locked it away, but he still could not touch those journals again.

Chane left the guest quarters, heading out across the courtyard to the old barracks that served as a dormitory, trying not to let himself think. As he reached the dormitory's second floor and Wynn's door, a part of him did not want to see her. But he always went to her just past dusk. He stood there for a while before he could finally knock.

"I am here," he rasped.

Chane heard Wynn's quick footsteps within the room trotting closer to let him in.

CHAPTER 3

The following afternoon, Wynn sat in a deep alcove of the archives with Shade on the floor beside her. She was searching for anything to help locate Bäalâle Seatt, but her efforts gained her little.

She'd found an older map of the western Numan lands, all the way to the Rädärsherând, the "Sky-Cutter" mountain range blocking the southern desert and Suman Empire beyond. Paging through a sheaf of obscure dwarven ballads, she found one that mentioned something called the *gi'uyllæ*. It didn't pertain to what she was after, but stuck in her head just the same.

The dialect was so old that the meaning was only a guess—something like "all-eater(s)" or "all-consumer(s)." At first, it seemed some ancient reference to goblins, but the verse hinted at massive size.

Wynn tried to keep sharply focused, but her thoughts kept wandering.

Last night, Chane had acted more strangely than ever when he'd finally arrived. He'd paced about, barely speaking to her. When she'd asked him again what was wrong, he wouldn't answer. She'd tried talking to him, but pushing him harder seemed to make things worse. And for the first time, he hadn't mentioned the wraith—Sau'ilahk—even once. After only a few moments, he'd left early on more errands.

So what had he been worried about?

Wynn felt quite alone in the world except for Shade and Chane, but he was making her nervous about the journey ahead.

Shade's ears suddenly perked. She raised her head to peer at the alcove's archway.

"What is it?" Wynn asked, looking up. Then she heard shuffling footsteps.

"Young Hygeorht?" a reedy voice called.

"Here," she called back.

Light grew upon the shelves outside the archway, and Master Tärpodious shuffled into view in his sagging, old gray robe. As someone who rarely ventured into the light of day, Tärpodious's wrinkled skin looked almost pallid. With a glimmering cold lamp in his boney hand, the effect was even starker, like an apparition gliding through a dark, abandoned library. He blinked at her, his milky eyes enlarged by his oversized spectacles.

"Ah, there you are," he said.

Wynn stood up. "Is something wrong?"

"No, no, just an initiate down with a message. High-Tower wants to see you in his study."

A hollow formed in Wynn's stomach. Had the council finally made its decision? She glanced at the stacks of books and sheaves on the small table.

"I'll see to those," Tärpodious said, voice crackling like rumpled paper. "Don't keep High-Tower waiting. . . . He might swallow his own tongue."

Wynn half smiled at his jest and gathered up her journal, quill, and cold lamp.

"Did the initiate say anything else?" she asked.

"No, just to go straightaway." Tärpodious began pushing sheets back into a sheaf. "Off with you."

She nodded and headed out with Shade. The prospect of a private meeting with High-Tower wasn't attractive, but perhaps the stalemate with the council had finally ended—one way or another.

Crossing the old archivist's entry chamber, Wynn reached the stairs before Shade and hiked her robe's hem as she hurried upward. The stairs actually ended at the base of the northern tower, where High-Tower's study was two levels up the next spiraling staircase. She stopped at the landing before his door, all the more anxious over what he would say. Her entire future could be decided within moments.

Shade whined.

"I know," Wynn said, and, unable to hesitate any longer, she knocked.

"Come," someone called in a deep voice.

Wynn opened the door. She'd expected to find him at his desk, but he stood before one of the narrow window slits in the nearer stone wall. His massive bulk blocked most of late afternoon's light. She'd learned basic Dwarvish under his tutelage, and he had been fond of her . . . once. Now, the only emotion left between them was a constant exchange of suspicion, if not open animosity.

"You asked for me?" she said, stepping inside. Shade followed, and Wynn closed the door.

Without a glance in her direction, High-Tower headed to his desk and picked up what looked like two wax-sealed, folded parchments.

"The council is sending you south," he said, his voice more gravelly than usual. "You'll deliver two messages along the way."

Wynn's small mouth parted, but she was too stunned to speak, and High-Tower went on.

"One is for Domin Yand of the small annex at Chathburh . . . the other is for High Premin T'ovar of the Lhoin'na branch—*immediately* upon your arrival there."

"Messages?" she repeated.

The council hadn't simply granted her request; they were giving her two tasks.

"I've booked passage for you," he went on, "and the majay-hì and your . . . companion. A Numan merchant vessel is bound for Chathburh. From there, you'll travel inland, south to the northern tip of the Lhoin'na lands. Stay inside their forests all the way to a'Ghràihlôn'na, their southern capital."

"Inland . . . from Chathburh?" Wynn asked.

Regional maps were fresh in her mind. If she disembarked at Chathburh, she'd be forced to cross most of Witeny and the Tillan Ridge at its southern border. The overland trip alone would take several moons, barring complications from oncoming winter and delays in the sea voyage.

The council wanted to be rid of her all right, and for as long as possible. But the delay to her destination was unacceptable.

"It's faster to continue by sea," she said. "I can make port farther south at Drist and bypass the Tillan Ridge."

High-Tower's complexion reddened like a slowly heated fire iron.

"A cesspit like Drist is no place for a sage!" he sputtered. "The last thing we need is you getting your throat cut in broad daylight or ending up on some slaver's vessel. Your request was approved, even funded . . . and you still question duty and common sense?"

Wynn hesitated. She couldn't lose what little ground she'd gained.

"Are you refusing the council's orders?" he demanded.

"Of course not. I was just suggesting a quicker route between both destinations."

High-Tower calmed slightly. "Traveling through Witeny is safer."

You mean longer, Wynn thought, but said, "Yes, certainly."

Stepping forward, she took the letters from him.

"And the funding for food and lodging?" she asked. "And possibly horses in Chathburh . . . if I'm to cross half of Witeny."

High-Tower grunted, opened a desk drawer, and pulled out a small pouch.

"This should suffice, if you are frugal." Then he dug in his robe's outer pocket and handed over a folded slip of millet paper. "A voucher for your return passage from Chathburh. Any Numan vessel will honor the guild seal, possibly even some Suman, but stay off vessels coming out of the free ports . . . like Drist!"

She took the voucher and the pouch. By its weight, the council hadn't given her much for anything but basic needs. Certainly it wouldn't be enough for further sea passage, but it didn't matter. In truth, this was more than she'd dared hope: guild approval and some financial assistance. Once she was out of their sight, there were other options to consider.

"I'll deliver both messages," she said, and turned away without thanking him.

"Wynn . . . ?"

She slowed to glance back, and he looked uncomfortable, as if he had something to ask that was difficult to get out. She offered him no help and stood waiting.

"Have you," he started, and then paused. "Ore-Locks has not been seen since you left Dhredze Seatt. Do you know of his whereabouts?"

Another strange state of events in an odd maze of connections—Ore-Locks was Domin High-Tower's brother. But why in the world would he think she knew anything of Ore-Locks?

"No," she lied.

Her response had nothing to do with loyalty. She didn't want anything to do with Ore-Locks, but she wasn't about to give High-Tower any more information than she had to.

He kept studying her, perhaps uncertain if he believed her or not, then scowled and looked away.

"Then go. I am sick to death of your deceptions."

This was the last thing he should've ever said to her.

"My deceptions?" she returned. "While I was trying to keep sages from dying in the streets, you swore to show me all the translations and the codex. But it was Master Cinder-Shard who gave me access to the texts—*all of them*—while I was with the Stonewalkers."

"You mean you gave him no choice, considering what followed you there! You used that to get what you wanted in the first place!"

His face resembled a dull beet, likely at the thought that she'd once more gotten around him and the guild.

"I saw the second codex," she said, her voice rising. "The one *you* wrote and kept from me, along with any texts or translations not listed in the first one! Or did you and Premin Sykion keep it from others, as well? Don't you lecture me about deception."

He uttered no further counter, for what could he have said? He had lied to her. They'd all deceived her, holding back anything they could.

"And what of your tall companion?" High-Tower asked.

The shift threw Wynn off. "What about him?"

Chane had kept to himself here. No one could say he'd been any kind of inconvenience.

High-Tower rounded the desk an instant after Shade began growling in warning. He slowed, though he didn't glance once at Shade.

"Your friend left a little something behind when you were all thrown out of the seatt," he said. "A shirvêsh at the temple was cleaning his room. What use would he have for a large urn full of blood?"

Wynn went still. She'd arranged for the goat's blood so Chane could feed. The fact that she'd forgotten about the urn—and it had been found—should've been the first thing to fear. But it wasn't.

"Full?" she repeated without thinking.

High-Tower's eyes narrowed.

It was too late to cover her slip, though he wouldn't understand her exact meaning.

"Yes, *full*," he repeated.

High-Tower was the enemy here, not Chane.

"It was probably for some dish from his homeland," she lied, shrugging. "I saw his people make blood puddings and sausages, just the same as yours. We were in a seatt, after all."

She tried hard to be outwardly disdainful as she turned for the door and gripped its handle. After a slow breath, she glanced back. "When does our ship leave?"

"Tomorrow. At dusk."

They weren't giving her much time, but sooner was better, especially now.

Opening the door, Wynn stepped out, and she jumped at a flash of brown in the corner of her sight.

Regina Melliny's bony form stood just behind the opened door. Shade pushed past, bumping Wynn against the doorframe, and Regina instantly backed away.

"What are *you* doing here?" Wynn asked.

Regina was an apprentice in the Order of Naturology, and she'd recently made Wynn's life miserable. No doubt the nickname of "Witless" Wynn had been Regina's doing.

"As if that's any of *your* business," Regina answered haughtily, but with a nervous twitch of her eyes toward Shade.

"But it is mine, apprentice," High-Tower growled, his voice close behind Wynn.

Regina's gaze shifted as the venom drained from her expression.

"I was just . . . I was up above," she faltered, "taking my study time on the tower roof, sir."

"In late autumn?" High-Tower asked. "Not wise or healthy . . . *Miss* Melliny."

That he hadn't called her "apprentice" this time didn't escape Wynn's notice—or Regina's. It was clearly a warning. Regina spun and scurried down the tower's stairwell.

"Off with you, as well," High-Tower said, his voice now somewhere farther across the study.

Wynn shut the door without looking back. She had no time for Regina's spiteful antics. But High-Tower's mention of the urn—the full urn—still confused her. She started down the stairs with Shade, but by the time they reached the bottom, she'd begun worrying more about money.

There wouldn't be enough for anything other than what the council had planned for her, and she didn't possess anything worth selling. Did Chane? Even so, they had little time to go off bartering his possessions. So how could she get more coin or something worth selling later?

An awful notion occurred to Wynn. It was almost sacrilegious, but it was all she could think of for the best profit anywhere, at any time.

She and Shade passed quickly through the main floor and out into the courtyard. The sun hadn't yet dipped, and she looked toward the northwest building, the one with Chane's guest quarters.

And below that were the guild's laboratories.

"Come on, Shade," Wynn said. "One more stop before supper."

Chuillyon's white robe swished about his felt boots as he strolled through an open archway and into the royal castle's manicured garden copse.

The second and final loss of Prince Freädherich Âreskynna still weighed heavily upon him, as well as the renewed grief of the prince's wife, Duchess Reine. There had been little he could do to console her or himself.

With his cowl down, a chill shift of air blew his faded and streaked golden brown locks across his narrow mouth. Prominent creases lined the corners of his large amber eyes set around a narrow nose a bit long, even for an elf.

Late autumn, when fiery colors began to fade and fall, was to him the saddest time of each year, making his mood much worse. He did not like it. Even the wispy white of snow and glistening icicles were better than this. He strolled on through hedges and past one rose bush still bearing dead buds that would never birth light blue petals before winter came. The royal family always preferred blues and aquamarines.

The garden was empty, with no sign of the one he had come here to meet in private.

Nearly four centuries past, before Calm Seatt could truly be called a city, the first of the Âreskynna, rulers of Malourné, had resided in a much smaller castle. In a few more generations, they had embarked on plans for a new and greater residence. The royal family moved in, and the first castle became the barracks for the nation's armed forces. Two centuries more, and Queen Âlfwine II—the "Elf Friend"—desired something new yet again. Scholars thought she had preferred a more lavish residence, suitable for a monarch. Others claimed that like her descendants, she hungered for a view of the bay.

To Chuillyon, the latter was obviously correct. Any in the bloodline of the Âreskynna—Kin of the Ocean Waves—had always shown strange affinities for the open sea.

Âlfwine II oversaw designs of this very castle. The nation's armed forces, including the newly established city guard contingent, moved to the vacated second one. The first castle, by far the oldest and smallest, was given over to the Guild of Sagecraft. Or, rather, to its founding Numan branch.

It had been long years, decades that Chuillyon served discreetly as counselor to the Âreskynna. He spent so much time here as to have rooms of his own. But he preferred this garden, even in the sadness of late autumn . . . and what had come to pass in Dhredze Seatt.

He strolled among elaborate obelisk trellises of thinning ivy and between sculpted evergreens and half-denuded oaks and maple trees.

"Psssst! Here, sir!"

Chuillyon slowed at that too-loud whisper, took a deep breath, and assumed his most serene demeanor. This was not a meeting he relished, but it was necessary all the same. He turned slowly, facing a large myrtle shrub clipped into the form of a conch shell. A flash of brown slipped around it, and a bony girl in a brown robe stepped into view.

Regina Melliny bowed briefly, too much eagerness in her small human eyes.

"I have heard that your Premin Council held a short private meeting today," he said. "Was there anything of import?"

She looked him over, trying to be proper, but the more she tried to hide her glee, the more obvious it became. She knew nothing of his true position or the reach of his influence—only that he served the royal family. And the Âreskynna held sway and favor with the guild.

"Wynn Hygeorht leaves tomorrow night," she said.

"Leaves?" he returned, and then waved her to silence before she confirmed it.

He had hoped Wynn might stay put, at least long enough that preparations could be made.

Chuillyon suppressed disdain at Regina's lust for his favor. He had spotted her one day while visiting the guild with Duchess Reine. By her frustrated and spiteful demeanor, he had instantly spotted a pair of willing eyes within the guild's Numan branch. Arranging a quiet chat with her had been effortless.

"Continue," he said.

Regina stepped forward, nervously smoothing the front of her brown robe.

"The council approved her request. As always, they give her anything she wants."

Chuillyon made an effort to remain passive. This petty young woman would never attain journeyor status on her own merits.

"Where is she going?" he asked softly.

"South, to Chathburh, and then inland across Witeny . . . to your guild branch."

"To the Lhoin'na?"

"That's what she wants. She's been begging for it since she got back from Dhredze Seatt. As I said, they give her whatever she wants . . . or she pesters them until they do."

"Why does she wish to visit the guild's elven branch?"

Regina shrugged. "Who knows? She may act deranged, but no doubt she's up to something. She thinks she's better than anyone because she tripped over a pile of old books halfway across the world."

The girl's endless spite again wore on Chuillyon. "She gave no clear reason for this journey?"

Regina shook her head. "But she's to take a message to Domin Yand at the Chathburh annex . . . and then one to your branch and High Premin To . . tov . . ."

"Yes, I understand," Chuillyon cut in before the girl butchered the name or his people's language.

His mischievous nature sank like a log under troubled water.

Wynn was not whimsical. She always had reason for whatever she did, and was methodical, even if reckless. But why had the Numan sages' council given her the pretense of messenger duty?

"This is what you wanted, yes?" Regina asked. "I tell you what she's up to, what I can . . . and you speak to Premin Adlam for me? I'm ready for a journeyor's duties. I have been for more than a year! Please make him see this."

Her desperation haunted Chuillyon, much as it made her useful. Looking into her hungry eyes, he saw no readiness. Doing as she asked would be no true favor. It would only send her to a harder fall.

"Of course. Soon," he assured. "You have been most helpful, apprentice."

Regina took a deep breath of relief and triumph. "Good. I mean, thank you . . . sir," and she backed away.

"And to you, apprentice."

Before he turned away, her high brow furrowed. "Sir . . . I know Premin Adlam and some others treat you as a sage, but I don't know of any others who wear white robes. I don't even know how to refer to you properly . . . by our ranks."

"It is complicated," he answered softly, "and I have an urgent task to attend. If you would not mind, perhaps another time?"

That "other time" would never come for her.

He did not watch her leave. Instead, he walked on through the remainder of the obelisk trellises nearly barren but for brittle vines. Wynn Hygeorht had requested to go to his own guild branch. But why? She sought portents of the returning enemy and the prospect of another great war. In that, she knew almost as much as her superiors. It was quite surprising how far she had foraged, regardless of all obstacles. Even he was impressed.

But too many secrets—that should be left buried—had long been hidden in the forests of the Lhoin'na. Some he could not let Wynn Hygeorht root out, but others . . .

Such a precocious little human, aside from her growing skills as a sage, and even just thinking of her actually made Chuillyon smile. He could not help it.

There was a time, perhaps fifty years ago, when he would've found even greater delight in her exploits and antics. Perhaps he might have joined her, just for the surprises along the way.

Oh yes, he would have joined her, but these were not those days. He needed to remain apart and alone—in preparation for what was to come. That thought took away his smile.

Chuillyon pressed on, entering a small, manicured clearing with but one barren tree at its center. From anywhere else in the garden, it was always hidden from sight. It was not shaped like a typical tall and straight ash. From its thick trunk, stout branches curved and wound and divided up into the night. Even that might not be noticed at first.

Leafless and barkless—yet alive—a soft, golden glow emanated from its fine-grained, tawny wood to dimly light the clearing. It glistened, from its wide-reaching roots creating lumps in the earth to its thick and pale yellow trunk and limbs.

"Not so soon, I beg," he whispered, as if to that tree—or perhaps something greater that it represented. "A little more time . . . it is not so much to ask."

Chuillyon stepped into the reach of the tree's glow. A little of his sadness washed away, but not enough.

Wynn stood hesitantly outside the iron door of Premin Hawes's study.

Before coming here, she'd stopped by her own room and put her things away. In recent times, she'd justified some astonishing betrayals for the sake of a higher purpose. But what she was about to do felt extreme, even to her. Taking a deep breath, she knocked.

"Yes?" a voice called from inside.

"It's Journeyor Hygeorht," she answered. "May I come in?"

No one responded, but barely a pause passed before the door opened.

Premin Hawes looked out, her normally flat, cold expression betraying a hint of surprise. She glanced briefly at Shade.

"I assumed you would be preparing for your trip," she said.

"Yes, that's why I needed to see you. I have a confession to make."

"A confession? I'm neither the premin nor a domin of your order. Why me?"

"Because . . ." Wynn forced her voice into a contrite, distressed tone. "Because I lost my cold lamp crystal at Dhredze Seatt."

A frown hardened Premin Hawes's hazel eyes.

For a sage, this was an egregious oversight. Only those who reached journeyor status were given a crystal of their own as a mark of rank, achievement, and a presumed life devoted to the guild—to sagecraft itself.

"I couldn't bring myself to tell anyone," Wynn rushed on. "So much had happened. My belongings were confiscated several times. I'm not even certain when or how it went missing."

The premin's frown deepened.

"Please don't lecture me," Wynn begged. "I feel terrible as it is, but I'm heading south tomorrow." She paused, as if grief stricken. "I need a replacement . . . to prove my status at the Lhoin'na branch."

Hawes seemed about to speak but didn't. The disapproval on her narrow face shifted to something more guarded and passive.

"Haven't you been down in the archives?" she asked. "How were you studying without your crystal?"

Wynn swallowed hard. "Master Tärpodious took pity on me. He loaned me one reserved for apprentices approved to work in the catacombs."

It was plausible, and hopefully Hawes wouldn't check—at least not before Wynn was long gone.

Premin Hawes stepped forward so steadily that Wynn backpedaled out of the way. Shade was forced to retreat, and hit her rump against the passage's other side.

"Come with me," Hawes said.

She glided down to the middle iron door on the northward side. Just as Wynn caught up, the premin touched the tips of her narrow fingers against the door right where there should've been a lock. She closed them like a pincer.

The door's iron bulged between her fingers and thumb.

A palm-sized disk formed out of the iron between the premin's fingertips.

Wynn knew—everyone here knew—that the iron doors of the laboratories had been fashioned decades ago to be as impenetrable as possible. But in all her life, she'd never seen how they opened.

Hawes rotated her hand with a whisper, though the disk didn't turn. Her delicate fingertips slid smoothly along the disk's edge, and then she flattened her palm against it. The disk sank, vanishing flush into the iron.

With one quick twist of the handle, Premin Hawes pushed the door open.

"Wait here," she commanded.

Wynn was still staring as the premin disappeared inside, closing the door to the barest crack. Again she wondered at Hawes's skills compared to Domin il'Sänke's dismissive comments. She didn't have long for those thoughts.

Narrow fingers curled out around the door's open edge.

Premin Hawes pulled it partly inward and stood blocking Wynn's sight of the inner room. From behind her back, she held out one perfectly formed cold lamp crystal.

Wynn's breath of relief was genuine as she took it. "Thank you . . . thank you so much!"

With a respectful nod, she turned off down the passage. Shade scurried ahead in a clatter of claws on stone, quite eager to leave.

"Wynn."

That one word made her flinch to a stumbling stop and turn.

Premin Hawes came down the passage in that glide that barely moved her robe. When she halted an arm's length away, her hazel eyes never blinking, a tense moment followed that Wynn would never forget.

The premin held up another cold lamp crystal, as pure as the last.

Wynn stared dumbly at it, unable to move, until the premin snatched Wynn's hand holding the first crystal. Shade only let out a half snarl before swallowing audibly. The premin opened Wynn's hand with her own thumb and placed the second crystal beside the first in Wynn's palm.

Wynn studied the pair, her thoughts utterly blank. When she finally looked up, Premin Hawes had turned away down the passage.

"In case your misfortunes continue," the premin said evenly, "and you . . . *lose* the first one."

Frideswida Hawes turned into her study. The last iron door on the right shut with a clang that echoed down the passageway.

Wynn stood frozen. Had the premin of metaology known what she was up to? If so, how did she know?

Chane, lying on the bed in his guest quarters, opened his eyes to darkness. He sat up, fingering the brass ring still on his finger from last night's foray into the city.

Climbing out of bed, he walked out of the bedchamber and into the study. Dusk's tinted residue of light filtered through the canvas curtains beyond the desk, filling the room with enough for his night sight. As he glanced down toward the desk, the first thing he saw was one of Wynn's journals. He looked away.

He had slept in his breeches and shirt. Both were now quite wrinkled, and he started back for the bedroom to change before meeting Wynn. His attention lit upon a recently added item among his scattered belongings on the desk.

The paper-wrapped package's twine binding was already severed. He had checked the contents last night upon finding it left outside his guest quarters' door. This was the final item of his secret needs before the journey could begin, and the sages had not supplied it. He had arranged to have it made in the city.

He grabbed the package, paper crinkling in his grip, and headed into the bedroom. Setting it atop the piled cloak, scarf, and gloves, he slowly opened the paper to stare once again at its content.

Thick but pliant, the shaped leather had laces on either side, with two openings set high and parallel. Chane lifted it to his face, aligning the holes with his eyes as he looked into the mirror. It was exactly as he had specified, spreading back to his ears, halfway across his scalp, and under his chin to his throat. But even he could not deny what it looked like. . . .

An executioner's mask.

Chane quickly lowered and rewrapped it in the paper, hiding it away in a dresser drawer. He now possessed everything he required, though he had yet to reveal his purpose to Wynn. He would have to let that wait until there was no time left for her to escape him. The night before they planned to leave would be best.

After pulling on a fresh shirt and his boots, he ran his fingers through his hair, though his hand was shaking when it came down. He left the room, locked the door, pocketed the key, and quickstepped all the way to the inner courtyard. Trying to wipe his thoughts clean, he was distracted as he approached the southeast dormitory.

Young voices rose on the entry door's other side, but he did not truly hear them.

"You don't know that, Kyne!" said one.

"It's just a wolf," said another. "A big one . . . but just a wolf."

"No, it isn't!" shouted a third, a girl. "It's a majay-hì!"

Chane was in no mood for nonsense. He reached for the latch, but the door suddenly swung open. The iron handle cracked against his fingers, and he lurched aside as the door struck his elbow and shoulder.

Three small forms in tan robes boiled out of the opened door.

"There's no such thing," grumbled one pudgy boy.

"I looked it up in the library!" a girl about eleven or twelve shouted back.

"Oh, pish!" grumbled a second, gangly, red-haired boy.

"Just because you two can't read Begaine doesn't mean it isn't there," the girl insisted.

And the pudgy one wrinkled his face in a pout.

"What do you think you are doing?" Chane snapped.

At his sharp, nearly voiceless rasp, all three initiates sucked in a breath. The girl's eyes widened until the whites showed all around, and she stared up—and up—at Chane.

"Oh . . . I'm . . ." she stammered. "I'm . . . I'm so sorry, sir."

Her little nose and ivory cheeks were smattered with faint freckles. Two equal braids held back her dark blond hair. She looked nothing like Wynn; acted nothing like a sage. None of them did.

Chane felt the beast stir within him.

He could not see a possible hope that such whelps would ever understand what it meant to be a sage. He hung there, glaring down at them, until they began inching together, clustered yet unable to take their frightened eyes off him. How had these *things*, these calves of the human cattle, ever been allowed inside this place?

Chane jerked the door wide, sending the trio scurrying out of his way and running for the keep's main doors. He was still shuddering as he headed up the stairs for Wynn's room.

Even within the guild, there were those who did not matter, who did not belong.

Wynn sat at her desk, making a list of things to gather and tasks to complete before embarking tomorrow night. Shade lounged on the bed, her crystal blue eyes half open, but the dog seemed to be watching intently.

A knock sounded at the door.

"I am here," Chane rasped from outside.

Wynn paused. He sounded sharp, almost loud, even for his limited voice.

"It's open," she answered.

Chane stepped in and shut the door. As was his habit, he wore a white shirt, black breeches, and high boots—simple attire, like that of the young nobleman he'd once been. She studied his face, looking to see if he appeared hungry or weak. He just looked disturbed.

If he hadn't consumed the blood in the urn, what had he fed on while they were at the seatt? What had he been feeding on since? She wasn't sure how to broach the subject.

"We're leaving tomorrow night," she said. "We have passage on a ship to Chathburh."

Chane straightened. "Tomorrow?"

Wynn touched the two sealed letters behind the pouch of coins.

"They gave me a supposed mission to deliver these. More likely they want me gone straight off and for as long as possible, where they think I'll do no harm. I'll need any of my journals you still have, and the rest of the supplies you've been buying, so we can go through this final checklist."

She held up her list, but he barely glanced at it.

"It is too soon," he whispered. "I am not ready."

Wynn turned in her chair to fully face him. "I thought you'd be relieved. This is what we've been waiting for."

"Yes, but . . ."

He paced the length of her room, a mere four steps. When he stopped, he stared at her staff in the corner beyond the door. Its sun crystal was fully sheathed, but that was the part his eyes locked upon.

"Get your cloak, your glasses, and the staff," he commanded. "Come with me. . . . But Shade stays here."

Shade lifted her head from the bed's blankets and growled.

In all the time Wynn had known Chane, he'd never ordered her to do anything, at least not like this. He looked openly angry now, as if expecting her to argue.

"What is the matter with you?" she asked.

"Just do it!"

Wynn crossed her arms and didn't even get up. Chane looked away, anxious, almost defeated.

"Please," he whispered. "Leave Shade here."

Something in Chane's pleading voice pulled at Wynn. Maybe if she did as he asked, he'd finally tell her what was wrong. With a sigh, she pulled her cloak off the chair and got up.

The glasses were always in her robe's pocket these days, and she stepped around Chane to retrieve her staff. An instant of relief flooding his pale face was alarming.

She glanced toward Shade. "Stay."

Shade jumped off the bed, snarling.

"Stay," Wynn said more firmly, pulling the door open.

Shade rushed in and slammed headfirst into door. It closed with a loud bang as the dog backed up. Her snarls turned into a rolling growl.

A short wrestling match followed in which Wynn held the dog back while Chane stepped out. Wynn quickly slipped out after jerking her robe's skirt out of Shade's teeth, and Chane pulled the door closed. Shade immediately began howling, barking, and snarling.

"Stop," Wynn called through the door. "Or you'll have a crowd of apprentices come running. We'll be back soon."

Wynn motioned Chane onward, hoping Shade would quiet down once they were gone—although she had no idea where they were going.

Chane was silent all the way to the courtyard. He headed straight across for the northwest building that contained his quarters. Confused, Wynn followed, but he stopped her at the door. When he looked down at her, she almost backed up.

His irises had turned clear and colorless, as they did when his undead nature fully manifested itself.

"Wait here," he said. "I will return shortly."

Chane's voice was as cold as his irises, and he slipped inside.

His erratic mood shifts sometimes left Wynn unsettled, but she waited, shivering a few times in the chill night air. True to his word, Chane reemerged shortly, wearing a forest green cloak with the hood up. She'd never seen it before. A matching scarf was wrapped multiple times about his neck, leaving only his hood-shadowed face exposed. He wore new, fitted calfskin gloves, suggesting they'd been custom made.

Chane didn't need protection from the cold.

"What's all this for?" Wynn asked.

He didn't answer. Then she noticed a scrunched bulk of leather in his right hand. Two laces dangled from his curled fingers along with the strings of a brown felt pouch.

"This way," he said, and headed for the gatehouse tunnel. As he turned, the side of his cloak wafted open.

The hilt of his new sword protruded above his hip, its mottled dwarven blade now couched in a new sheath. He never walked the guild grounds while armed, as it was considered poor manners.

"Chane . . . ?" Wynn called, but he strode away, and she had to trot to keep up.

When he exited the tunnel, he didn't go on to the bailey gate, but turned left into the inner bailey. They'd nearly reached the barren trees and garden below the southern tower when Wynn got fed up.

"Chane, what is going on?"

He turned to face her. Without answering, he jerked the leather sheath off her staff with his free hand, exposing the sun crystal's long prisms.

Wynn stepped back in alarm, catching the crystal's sheath as he tossed it at her.

"Give me your glasses," he said, fiddling with the pouch he carried.

"First you tell me what we're—" She stopped.

Chane held up another pair of glasses like her own. These were smaller, with delicate arms curved at the ends.

"Made for you," he said. "Put them on, and give me your old ones."

Confused but curious, Wynn pulled out the glasses made by Domin il'Sänke and handed them over. The lenses were clear, designed to go dark only when struck with harsh light. They allowed her to see when the sun crystal ignited.

Chane took them, shoving the new ones into her hand.

Wynn hooked their thin arms around her ears. They fit snugly and did not shift like the old ones.

"Better," she commented, adjusting them on her small nose. "What made you think to have them made?"

But Chane was off again.

Wynn glanced at her staff's crystal in puzzlement and had to hurry. She'd barely caught up as he rounded the southern tower and stopped. He looked up once, and Wynn did so, as well. All the windows in the tower were dark.

He pointed toward the barren corner garden. "Stand there."

"Chane, what is this about?"

With his back to her, he stopped a few paces down the keep's left side and lowered his head. Whatever that leather object was in his hand, he appeared to be tucking it inside his hood. When he raised his head again, he didn't turn to her. He just stood there with his hands limp at his sides.

"Ignite the crystal," he said, his rasp sounding strangely muffled.

"What?" Wynn gasped, and then she had a notion of what he was up to.

From the gloves and scarf to the cloak, he'd planned this. What was he trying to prove?

"You don't know if that's enough protection," she said. "And you're too close."

"Ignite it!"

"No."

Chane held to his resolve. Reason had not been enough, as she would not listen. She had to see one thing, beyond a doubt.

"I'm not playing this game," she said.

Chane heard her footfalls in the autumn leaves as she began walking away, and he reached for his sword's hilt.

"This is not a game."

In one motion, he ripped the blade from the sheath and turned with a level slash. The tip of mottled steel passed a hand's length before Wynn's throat as she lurched back. Her eyes widened in sudden fright, but Chane did not stop. As the beast rose within him, he lunged in, reversing his slash without a pause.

"Chane!" Wynn cried out.

He brought the blade tip back along the side of her head, so close that she could hear its passing in the air. Brittle aspen branches snapped as Wynn twisted away along the autumn trees. She lost her footing and toppled into the bailey wall.

Chane faltered for an instant, but he could leave her with only one choice, and he cocked the blade for a direct thrust.

"*Mênajil il'Nûr'u mên'Hkâ'ät!*" Wynn shouted.

The world flashed blinding white in Chane's eyes.

*   *   *

Wynn sucked in cold air that burned her lungs, as the lenses turned black against the glare.

This wasn't some reckless test of Chane's to withstand the crystal's light. He'd been the one to demand Shade stay behind. Why had he turned on her after all the times he'd fought to keep her from harm?

The glasses' lenses quickly adjusted, and Wynn shed no tears from the intense light. She gripped the staff with both hands as she saw Chane. At first he was little more than a black silhouette beyond the burning crystal.

He just stood there with his sword's tip dangled against the hardened earth.

"Chane?" she whispered, and the sight of him grew more distinct.

Inside the cloak's hood she saw the glint of round glasses with black lenses, the ones she'd exchanged with him. But she didn't see his pale features around them.

She saw only pure black, like when she'd stared into the cowl of Sau'ilahk's black robe. There was no Chane, just a featureless darkness broken only by those round, pewter rims that focused on her.

Why had he attacked her? And why did he now just stand there?

"Look at me!" he rasped. "Do you understand what this means?"

Wynn didn't answer, for she didn't understand. She finally shook her head, holding on to the staff so tightly that her hands began to ache.

Chane lunged at her.

Wynn tried to swing the crystal into his missing face. He grabbed the staff above her hands and turned it aside. She tried to pull it free, but her effort was futile, and she knew it.

He didn't take the staff from her. He just stood there, gripping it, his missing face much closer now.

A leather mask completely covered his features.

The look of it made Wynn cringe. Then she felt something else. The staff was shuddering in her hands. She glanced only once, fearful of changing her focus too long.

Chane's arm was shuddering, the tremor spreading into her staff. She spotted the quiver of his hood's edge. He was beginning to shake all over.

"Look at me," he said. "If I can stand in the sun crystal's light . . . if I can resist it with so little preparation . . . how could you *know* Sau'ilahk is gone?"

All her terror and anger at his seeming betrayal twisted in her throat.

"The wraith . . . cannot . . . not . . . that easily," Chane whispered, and the shudders were now in his voice. "You only *believe* . . . wish it so."

Wynn felt something fracture inside of her. Her worst swallowed fear, the one she'd pushed down so hard, leaked from that crack. She shoved at Chane.

"No!"

Chane stumbled back as he released Wynn's staff, though her little force would have done nothing to him. He lowered his head, turning from the searing light . . . and from the agony on her face.

All of his skin prickled and stung, like the memory of a blistering sunburn in the youth of his lost life. It sank deeper and deeper with each moment, eating away his strength, but he was not burning . . . yet.

If he had to, he could now withstand the crystal's light for a while. But he could not bear to look into her eyes. He heard her breaths come in shudders, perhaps sobs, but she still said nothing more.

If he had to burn for her to make her face the truth, then he would.

Chane let the sword fall and thud upon the cold ground. When he saw Wynn's feet shift and stumble, he reached across and jerked the glove off his left hand. Without looking up, he thrust it blindly out at her.

"Look! It did not even burn me."

But it did so now. He bit down against the pain. The air around him became laced with the stench of searing flesh. Wynn's breaths ended in a sudden inhale, and all light winked out instantly.

Everything went pitch-black.

Chane drew back his hand, curling it against his chest. He tried to remain steady as he fumbled to pull off the glasses and mask with his good hand.

"That wraith . . . a spirit . . . is centuries older than me," he said, panting. "More powerful than I could ever become. You *believed* you had burned it to nothing . . . in the streets of Calm Seatt the first time. How can you *know* you succeeded . . . the second time?"

Even his night eyes took a moment to adjust to the sudden return of darkness. And he dared to look at her. What he saw was worse than the torment of his hand.

Wynn stood clutching her own glasses, the staff pulled so close to her face that Chane made out only one wide eye over a tearstained cheek. Her breaths came too fast as she shook her head ever so slightly.

"You weren't there in the tunnel," she said, sobbing. "You didn't see what happened. I destroyed it!"

"You have no proof! You are about to set sail and head into the wilds, yet you cling to a false belief you only wish was the truth."

Wynn broke right before Chane's eyes. Half buckling, nearly dropping, only the staff held her up. Her eyes clenched and tears flowed fast, dripping down her chin.

"You bastard," she whispered.

Chane wanted to run, to hide from her sight.

Anger and fear twisted inside Wynn as those words had leaked out.

In the last few years, she'd traveled with a mix of companions, from a dhampir and half-blood rogue to a Fay spirit in the body of a majay-hì, and elven assassins as either allies or enemies. They had all possessed innate talents, which gave each a chance against the Noble Dead.

She was just a small, mortal human possessed of only one weapon: the staff and its sun crystal she'd begged from Domin il'Sänke. Now Chane made even that sound like nothing—like she was powerless.

Didn't they have enough to fear without him making it worse? Couldn't there be just one small victory for her in the face of all that might come?

She would never forget the sight of him in that mask and those glasses, swinging a blade at her throat. Not ever. She wanted to hurt him.

"And aren't you hungry yet, for all this effort?" she asked. "Do you need another urn of blood to help heal your hand? No, wait. You didn't even need the first one. . . . Did you?"

Chane straightened, his eyes widening this time. Any pain faded from his features—his pale, undead face.

"Don't lie to me," she rushed on. "The shirvêsh at the temple found it still full in the room you had there."

"The urn would not help me," he said so quietly she almost didn't hear him. "Blood is only a conduit for the life . . . that must come from a living entity . . . for my need."

Perhaps this was truth. Perhaps it wasn't just an excuse. Still clutching his seared hand, he twisted his head so far to the side she could no longer see his face at all. The sight brought her no sense of victory. She had hurt him, and some part of her now wished she could take the words back.

"I could not bring myself to tell you," he whispered, "that your efforts would not help."

"What . . . what have you been feeding on?"

Chane hesitated far too long. By the time he answered, she wasn't sure she believed him.

"Your notion of livestock was not wrong, but the animal must be alive."

He wouldn't meet her eyes, and the discomfort inside Wynn began growing again.

"You and Shade are all I have left," she said, sidestepping around him to go back toward the gatehouse tunnel. "But if you ever . . . *ever* feed on another sentient being, I will leave you behind. You will never enter my presence again. Do you understand? Never."

Chane still hung his head and said nothing.

Wynn turned and strode off along the inner bailey. By the time she reached the gatehouse tunnel, she was running. She didn't stop until she'd shut the door to her room, collapsed against it, and slid to the floor. There were so few certain pieces left in her fragile world. Two had just shattered.

She could no longer deny that the wraith might still exist.

She could no longer trust Chane.

Wynn finally noticed that Shade now stood right before her. Shade looked to the door.

Her ears flattened as her rumble grew, and her jowls pulled back, exposing her teeth. No doubt Shade picked up everything from Wynn's memories of moments ago.

Wynn sobbed once and threw her arms around Shade's neck, burying her face in the dog's thick charcoal fur. The only one Wynn could count on now was an obstinate, adolescent majay-hì.

On the rocky shore, south of Calm Seatt and high above the foaming waves of the bay, the night air shimmered. The outline of a tall shape slowly began taking form.

A dark figure garbed in a flowing robe and cloak shifted and swayed. Then it twitched and jerked, as if writhing in pain. No face was visible within the pitch-black pit of its sagging cowl. One arm rose, and its sleeve slipped down, exposing a forearm, hand, and fingers wrapped in black cloth strips.

Sau'ilahk came into consciousness amid the agony of Beloved's anger. And only then could he scream. Heard from afar, the sound would have been a sudden shriek of wind.

As he became aware of himself, startled that he had not ended in Beloved's embrace, he realized he had returned to the world of the living. Turning, he searched to see where he was. Calm Seatt spread before him with a multitude of night lamps illuminating the city. He did not know whether to feel rage or gratitude.

The last he remembered was being trapped by the Stonewalkers as Wynn burned him to nothing. And yet he had returned to the edge of Beloved's dream. In the punishment for his failure, his disobedience, he wished he had perished instead.

But Beloved would not let him die.

Now fear and suspicion clouded his every guess.

Sau'ilahk had believed that he could control his own fate—that he could tease and twist the hints to his salvation from his god. A thousand or more years past, at end of the great war, Beloved's thirteen "Children" had divided into five groups. Each group had been given one of the Anchors of Creation—the orbs, so called by the ignorant few who had now learned of them—and the Children had dispersed to the ends of the world, taking the orbs into hiding.

Sau'ilahk, highest of Beloved's Reverent Ones, its priests, knew only this much, and not where those five journeys had ended.

But as reward for his own service, he had asked for eternal life, for his beauty to never end. Beloved consented, and then cheated Sau'ilahk with a twist on that promise's words. Sau'ilahk's body decayed, but his spirit remained. He received his eternal life, but not eternal youth.

All Sau'ilahk wanted was the Anchor of Spirit. Through it, he could have flesh and beauty again. Yet his search had proven fruitless through the centuries, until one pitiful little sage uncovered words penned in ancient texts by three of the Children. Wynn Hygeorht was his one hope to force Beloved to fulfill what had been promised. Through her, he would learn the long-lost paths of the Children and the resting place of the orbs.

He had believed that *he* was manipulating Beloved into assisting him, but Beloved had raged over his recent failure, his destruction, in the underworld of Dhredze Seatt . . . and Beloved had punished him.

And yet now, here he was just outside of Calm Seatt, Wynn's home.

Follow the sage . . . to your desire. Serve, and she will lead you.

Sau'ilahk whimpered, a sound like breeze-ripped grass. He cowered down, feeling dormancy threatening to take him at the sound of his god's demand. Then his mind began to clear of terror.

Perhaps the texts were not the true answer? Perhaps Wynn Hygeorht's interpretation of them was the key? Was Beloved using him again, or did they share the same goal?

Sau'ilahk did not know. But if Beloved knew his desire for the orb, the Anchor of Spirit, then why else would his god return him to the world?

He floated on the cliffs south of the city, watching its lights. There was fear, doubt, suspicion, and one more emotion fought against these, almost as strong as the desire for flesh.

Revenge against the sage.

She had been the cause of his suffering, or at least of his continued failure. Once flesh was within Sau'ilahk's reach, once he satisfied his god, he would show Wynn Hygeorht a glimpse of the torment Beloved had given him.

CHAPTER 4

The following night, Wynn waited on the docks, watching a wide, three-masted frigate anchored in the bay. Shade continued to glower at Chane, who stood a few paces behind them. The dog's jowls quivered, revealing her teeth.

Nothing about this night had been easy.

When Wynn had left her room that evening, Chane had been waiting for her in the keep's courtyard. Before she could do anything, Shade charged him, snarling, with hackles raised. She terrified two passing apprentices as she backed Chane against the northern building.

Wynn had tried over and over through memory-speak to explain what Chane had done and why. Either Shade didn't understand or didn't care; she knew only that Chane had attacked Wynn.

Shade became even more enraged when Wynn made it clear that Chane was still coming with them. She had woven back and forth in the courtyard as if looking for a way to get at him. All Chane did was raise empty hands and wait. Wynn had to drop her belongings and grab for Shade. From that moment on, amid the rush to port, Wynn and Chane stayed focused on the task at hand. Neither of them spoke of what had happened the night before in the inner bailey.

Tonight, Chane was dressed the same, minus glasses and mask. The only noticeable difference was his old sword strapped on his other hip. He'd mentioned taking it to a blacksmith and having the broken end ground to a point, so it would be usable again. The old sheath's end was cut short for the blade and crudely closed with leather lacing.

Wynn wondered why he'd brought it at all, as the sword he'd gained from Ore-Locks was far superior. But she didn't ask. Chane had both of his packs—or, rather, his own and the one he'd taken from Welstiel—hooked over his shoulders. More than ever, Wynn didn't like that insidious vampire's toys being in Chane's possession, with the possible exception of the brass ring.

Wynn wore her old elven tunic and pants beneath a knee-length gray travel robe and a heavy winter cloak. She carried her staff, its long crystal sheathed, and her own pack stuffed with scholarly needs. She'd also belted on Magiere's old battle dagger. The last of their baggage was a medium-sized chest that sat at Chane's feet, loaded with supplies, clothing, and Wynn's journals.

They were as ready as they would ever be.

Chane pointed outward. "The skiff is coming."

But Wynn looked back toward Calm Seatt's great waterfront.

She saw no sign of Ore-Locks, though she'd sent him a message that morning as to the time and place of their departure. Only a few moments after, she'd second-guessed herself, but if he was determined to follow, there was little she could do to stop him, anyway. Still, if Ore-Locks missed the boarding, it wouldn't be her fault.

"How many cabins do we have?" Chane asked.

Wynn welcomed the question, as the silence was getting thick. Anything mundane put off talk of what had happened between them.

"Two," she answered. "I told Ore-Locks to make his own arrangements."

She and Shade would need a cabin to themselves. Chane valued his privacy for obvious reasons. Ore-Locks could fend for himself.

"Perhaps he'll change his mind," she said.

"I do not think so."

Chane was probably right. Ore-Locks's estranged sister, a master smith fallen on hard times, had made Chane's new sword. Wynn couldn't guess what it had cost Ore-Locks financially and personally, and she wondered how he'd acquired it to barter for his inclusion in this journey.

The skiff had almost reached them. Wynn made out the beard stubble of one sailor kneeling in the prow. When the boat neared the dock's ladder, the slim man climbed up to meet them and glanced down at the chest.

"Anything else?" he asked.

"Just our packs," Wynn answered. "We'll keep those."

She'd done well in using only one chest, considering they had no notion if they'd find horses, let alone a cart, when they hit final landfall.

"In, Shade," she said, pointing to the skiff.

Shade circled behind Wynn, still watching Chane closely.

Wynn regretted not trying harder last night to suppress her memories from Shade, but she'd been too overwhelmed. Hopefully, Shade would come to her senses and remember how Chane had always protected Wynn in the past. They needed him on this journey.

"Shade, go," she said.

The dog circled back, growling as she approached the dock's edge. At the sight of her, one of the sailors at the oars looked up. His eyes widened at the massive wolf above, and his hand dropped to a knife in his belt.

"Leave off!" commanded the stubble-faced one.

High-Tower must have explained about Shade when he'd booked their passage.

Shade dropped off the dock's edge. She landed in the skiff below, and it rocked sharply. Both oarsmen grabbed pier lashings to steady the vessel. As their foreman heaved the chest, the sound of heavy footfalls vibrated in the planks beneath Wynn's feet.

She didn't need to look.

Ore-Locks came down the dock, stopping at Wynn's side with his long, red hair glinting under the lanterns. An overburdened sack was slung over his broad shoulder. He still dressed like a shirvêsh of Feather-Tongue, iron staff and all.

Wynn bit her tongue as he proffered a slip of paper to the bearded sailor.

It seemed he could pay his own way. How a stonewalker acquired money was a puzzle, but Wynn now had no legitimate excuse to leave him behind. Then she felt an unwanted spark of petty glee.

Ore-Locks looked down at the skiff and grimaced slightly. Most dwarves disliked sea travel intensely. Not that they couldn't learn to swim, but rather that it didn't matter—because they sank.

The sailor carrying the chest eyed Ore-Locks anxiously. He glanced at the voucher and then down at the skiff. A dwarf's weight alone might make it sit very low in the water.

Chane ignored them both and lowered his packs, doing likewise with Wynn's, and waited while she climbed down. Once she was safely aboard the skiff, he followed, but Ore-Locks still stood above.

"Are you coming?" Wynn asked, settling in the skiff's rear with Chane.

The bearded sailor frowned. "Please, sir, sit close to the center, near the oars."

Ore-Locks's expression tightened ever so slightly. When he began scaling down, two ladder rungs creaked slightly. He hesitated again before placing one heavy-booted foot into the skiff.

"Careful," Wynn warned.

He looked at her. "Do you fear sinking?"

"Goodness, no," she answered. "I can swim . . . or at least float."

Ore-Locks stepped down with his full weight.

Wynn's petty glee at his discomfort vanished as the skiff rocked so hard that she grabbed one side.

Ore-Locks moved with surprising speed, shifting quickly to crouch toward the center. The small vessel steadied, and with a sigh of relief, the bearded sailor climbed into the prow, using the chest for a seat.

Wynn was finally embarking on a long journey to both find and secure a powerful tool of the Ancient Enemy—and she had few skills or weapons of her own. Her only companions were the secret worshipper of a dwarven traitor, a vampire obsessed with her, and an adolescent majay-hì.

As the sailors locked their oars into the cradles and began to row for the frigate, Wynn sat silent in a moment of self-pity. But she couldn't turn back now.

Sau'ilahk materialized on a barren spot down the rocky shore from Calm Se-att's port and watched as the tiny skiff pulled up to the large frigate. Much to his surprise, the last passenger in Wynn's skiff had the bulk of a dwarf and red hair. Sau'ilahk was puzzled.

He searched his memories of all dwarves Wynn had ever met while in

Dhredze Seatt. He recalled only one with such hair. Ore-Locks, a stonewalker, was no longer dressed like his sect. Had he abandoned his way of life in the underworld? Even so, what was he doing with Wynn?

Sau'ilahk waited until activity aboard the vessel picked up as the men prepared to set sail. He was patient as the moon climbed higher. The ship eventually sailed outward, leaving Beranklifer Bay and turning south down the coast. For now, that was all he needed to know.

Sau'ilahk sank into dormancy for an instant. Focusing on the southernmost point along the shore, he "blinked" to that place to wait and watch again.

Chane stood near the ship's bow, with sea spray glistening upon his face. The last half-moon of the voyage had passed quickly, one night blending into the next.

Wynn had given the captain an excuse they had used before: that Chane suffered from a skin condition and could not be exposed to sunlight for any reason. As with most people, the captain's need to accommodate a paying customer took precedence. By now, none of the sailors even noticed Chane's presence on the deck at night. Leaning against the rail, he closed his eyes for a moment, feeling the night wind blowing damply over his skin.

"Can you see the lights?"

Chane opened his eyes at Wynn's approaching voice. She pressed up against the rail an arm's reach away.

"Chathburh," she said, pointing outward. "We've arrived."

Shade came trotting up beside Wynn and reared, hooking her front paws on the rail.

"Where will we lodge?" Chane asked.

"The guild annex has guest rooms. I've heard the library is small but unique. You might like it."

His chest tightened. He had almost felt as if Wynn were *safe* on this ship. Their sea voyage was about to end, and they would be back in the real world. The search for impossible clues would continue, opposed by even those who might have the power to assist them.

Wynn would throw herself into danger again. His place was to protect her, to keep her alive. They couldn't just sail on like this forever.

And he had been growing hungrier over the past three nights.

Chane had disembarked once—by himself—during a stop at Witenburh and tried feeding on a goat. That revolting experience had provided some life for his need. Since then, he had mulled over other options without further fracturing Wynn's confidence.

The lights of Chathburh grew brighter, closer, in the distance.

A sailor hurried past, and Chane called out, "How long to port?"

"Soon," the sailor answered. "We'll dock by second bell . . . late evening."

Chane knew that with this stop, Wynn's search for Bäalâle Seatt would truly begin. Of course, he did not wish her to find it.

He had seen both the guardian and the safeguards placed upon the orb that Magiere had found. He did not want Wynn getting near anything so dangerous, not if he could stop it. But his place was at her side for as long as she would have him. A journey, any journey, ensured his usefulness. For now, that was enough.

Chane gazed toward the city, bracing himself for whatever might come.

"This . . . is a guild annex?" Chane asked in surprise.

He watched as Wynn trotted toward what looked like an aging four-story inn. Its unusual height was its one remarkable feature.

"I've never seen it before," she answered. "But it was once a lavish inn for wealthy patrons. When the owner passed away, there was no heir and no one bought it. It became city property, left in disrepair for many years, until the guild finally purchased it for almost nothing."

Wynn scanned the front of many windows, appearing well satisfied.

All Chane saw was a nondescript building that had been too hastily stained without the boards being properly stripped and cleaned.

"The front parlor should be part of its library," Wynn added. "I've heard it's well designed to serve our needs." She stepped up onto the porch landing and knocked at the front door. "Hello?"

Though well into the evening, it still was not late. The second bell for quarter night had not rung until they were off the piers. Chane assumed someone would still be awake, and he was not wrong.

The door opened, and a short, middle-aged woman in a teal robe looked out. Taking in Wynn's gray, short robe, she smiled pleasantly. Chane wondered if Wynn might be better treated where no one truly knew her.

"Journeyor Hygeorht of Calm Seatt," Wynn introduced herself, "with a message for Domin Yand. Do you have rooms to spare?"

"Of course," the woman answered, waving them all inside. "I'm Domin Tamira. The annex is never but half full. You can take your pick of rooms on the top floor. Have you had supper?"

Wynn and the domin continued chattering away as Chane stepped in, though Shade pushed past, hurrying after Wynn. Ore-Locks came last. They all passed through the wide foyer and into a comfortable sitting room filled with old, overpatched armchairs and small couches, along with bookcases stuffed with volumes, some as old and worn-looking as the building itself.

Chane backed around Ore-Locks to the parlor's entrance. "Wynn?"

The domin's thin eyebrows rose at his maimed voice, and Wynn paused in her chatting.

"Yes?"

"I will go out . . . for a few missing supplies and return in a while."

She tensed slightly before nodding. "Yes. Find me when you're done."

Chane set down the travel chest and pulled off his own pack, leaving it by the door with his old sword. He kept Welstiel's pack over his shoulder.

"What could we need at this point?" Ore-Locks asked, watching him closely.

The ship's crew had seen to their meals on the voyage. They had not delved into their supplies.

Chane ignored him and left.

Sau'ilahk materialized in a cutway beside a fishmonger's stall down the street from the old building. He had kept his distance along the way, so that neither Chane nor Shade would sense him. As Wynn knocked, a domin of Conamology had answered.

Sau'ilahk knew of guild annexes, though he'd never bothered with one in his centuries. What could Wynn possibly seek in this out-of-the-way place?

He had not risked getting close to the ship to hear anything she might say, and tonight was his first safe opportunity. His only method was through a servitor—a minor but complex elemental with enough awareness to be his eyes and ears. He cleared his thoughts, preparing to exert energy into conjury.

The annex's front door opened again, and Sau'ilahk paused.

Chane stepped out alone and strode off inland along an adjoining street.

In brief moments in Dhredze Seatt, Sau'ilahk had clearly sensed Chane as an undead. Other times, as now, he seemed more like a solid apparition— seemingly *not there* to Sau'ilahk's senses, and yet somehow *there* to see, hear, or even touch.

Sau'ilahk hung in indecision, wondering whom to spy on: Wynn or Chane? He finally blinked to the corner, spotting Chane moving on with a steady gait.

Chane picked up his pace when he breached the city's inland edge. Trotting into the surrounding farmlands, he let his senses widen fully. Even with the brass ring on, somewhere ahead he smelled life, alone and isolated. Perhaps it was his hunger that overrode the ring's dulling of his senses.

He kept on, losing track of time, and wishing to be farther away before attempting what he had planned. Traipsing through a copse of near-leafless maples, he peered out over a fallow field to a small, thatched barn. Smoke drifted lazily from the clay chimney of a nearby cottage. He silently closed on the barn, pausing, listening for anyone nearby before entering.

It was a poor little place, with only three cows stabled inside. The nearest one had a black face and tan body. Kneeling on the hay-strewn floor, he dropped Welstiel's old pack and dug inside it to pull out an ornate walnut box.

Chane opened the box to study three hand-length iron rods with center loops, a teacup-sized brass bowl with strange etchings, and a white ceramic bottle with an obsidian stopper. All rested in burgundy padding. He slipped back in memory to the first time he had seen Welstiel use the cup.

They had been starving in the rocky, jagged wilderness of the Crown Range north of his homeland when they came upon an elderly wandering couple huddled by a campfire. Chane had wanted to lunge, but Welstiel stopped him with a warning.

"There are ways to make the life we consume last longer."

True, and Chane now reenacted exactly what he had seen Welstiel do.

He took out the rods, intertwined them into a tripod, and set his dagger on the ground beside it. Placing the brass cup upon the stand, he lifted the white bottle. Its contents—thrice purified water—were precious. Pulling the stopper, he half filled the cup, remembering Welstiel's cold, clinical explanation.

"Bloodletting is a wasteful way to feed. Too much life is lost and never consumed by our kind. It is not blood that matters, but the leak of life caused by its loss."

Chane glanced at the black-faced cow. To his best knowledge, Welstiel had never tried this on an animal.

The very idea of the cup was revolting, not to mention the humiliation of feeding on livestock. But he needed life to continue protecting Wynn. He could not risk feeding on a human, or she might hear rumors of someone missing or found dead and in a pallid state.

Chane approached the cow. The animal raised her head and blinked liquid eyes at him with no fear. Grasping her rope halter, he led her out of the stall and moved her to one side into a clear place to fall. He pressed slowly and steadily with his foot into the back of her front knee. As she began to kneel, he tipped her over, pinning down her head. She bellowed once in panic, struggling to get up, and then relaxed.

He took up the dagger and made a small cut on her shoulder. Once the blade's tip had gathered leaking blood, he carefully tilted the steel over the cup.

A single drop struck its pure water.

Blood thinned and diffused beneath dying ripples as Chane began to chant. He concentrated hard on activating the cup's innate influence. When finished, he waited and watched the cup's water for any change.

Nothing happened.

His incantation was based on researching Welstiel's journals and the tiny engravings on the cup's inner surface. Something was wrong. As with any mage, their workings were individual, and seldom could one successfully use the workings of another.

The cow let out a low sound. Suddenly her ribs began to protrude, as if she were turning gaunt.

Chane released his grip and scooted back.

The cow's eyelids sank as her eyes collapsed inward. Jawbones began to jut beneath withering skin. It was not long before the animal became a dried, shrunken husk as vapors rose briefly over her corpse. As Chane heard the cow's heart stop, he turned his gaze to the cup.

The fluid was so dark red, it appeared almost black, and it now brimmed near the cup's lip.

Chane did not know whether to feel elated or revolted. He knew what awaited him in drinking the conjured liquid. The first time, Welstiel had warned him with only two words.

"Brace yourself."

Chane shuddered once before he downed the cup's entire contents. When he lowered the brass vessel, it was completely clean, as if it had held nothing at all. For a moment, he tasted only dregs of ground metal and strong salt. Then he gagged and collapsed on the straw-strewn dirt.

His body began to burn from within.

Too much life taken in pure form burst inside him and rushed through his dead flesh, welling into his head. Curled up, he waited with his jaws and eyes clenched until the worst passed and the convulsions finally eased.

Had he used a mortal human in this fashion, he could have gone a half-moon without feeding again. He did not know how long the life energy of a cow would last.

Sitting up, Chane stared at the shriveled husk until his false fever subsided, and then he carefully packed away his equipment. Strong and sated, in control of his senses, he prepared to drag the carcass into the distant stand of trees. It would be a few days before it was found. He and Wynn would be gone by then, and any talk of its condition would never be connected to him.

He paused once upon opening the barn door and glanced toward the quiet cottage. Then he dragged the husk across the fallow field.

Sau'ilahk lingered well beyond a copse of barren maples, watching in fascination as Chane dragged a desiccated carcass toward the trees. What had Wynn's guardian been doing in that barn? Then he felt the tingle of a living presence and heard dead grass crackle in another direction. He froze in place, a still, black shadow barely more than a deeper darkness amid the night.

Something else moved along the copse's left. Only a dark hulk at first, it circled around the outside of a leafless tree into sight.

Ore-Locks stood hidden at the copse's backside, watching Chane, as well.

Sau'ilahk was certain the dwarf had not been there an instant before; he would have sensed a life in this empty place. So where had the dwarf come from so suddenly? His attention shifted as Chane walked out the copse's far side, becoming more obscured by the small stand of trees.

His pale face had a hint of color. Had he been feeding on the cow? No, that could not be. The animal was shriveled to the bones. Bloodletting would not have had this effect.

The puzzle of Wynn's companion only grew.

Once again, slight movement pulled Sau'ilahk's attention.

Ore-Locks watched Chane leave and then turned about, placing one great hand on a tree as if bracing himself. Unlike Sau'ilahk's fascination, the dwarf was scowling. Perhaps the errant stonewalker did not know Chane's true nature. Had Ore-Locks seen anything that happened inside the barn?

The dwarf straightened, arms slack at his sides beneath his cloak, and appeared to sink—drop—straight down.

Sau'ilahk quickly drifted to the side of the corpse. Few things surprised him after a thousand years of wandering in the nights. He found heavy footprints where the dwarf had stood, but none coming in or out. Ore-Locks had appeared from nowhere and vanished the same way. This matched what Sau'ilahk had seen in the dwarven underworld.

Stonewalkers had leaped out of the walls at him. Now it appeared Ore-Locks and his caste could pass through earth as well as solid rock.

Two more things became clear as Sau'ilahk circled back to watch Chane striding the inland road toward Chathburh. First, mystery though Chane might be, he required life energy like any other undead, and second, he had taken effort to slip off and do this in secret.

Mulling this over, Sau'ilahk blinked out of sight.

After a late supper, Wynn delivered her sealed message to Domin Yand, head of the annex. A jolly elderly man in the Order of Naturology, he had eaten a few too many honey cakes in his life. He was quite puzzled but in no hurry to open the message so late in the evening. Ore-Locks had finished his own supper quickly, not bothering even to sit, and then vanished to find a room. He never reappeared.

From what Wynn observed in the Stonewalkers' underworld, she guessed he'd spent much time in dim light, in the Chamber of the Fallen. Sailing under the open sky, constantly surrounded by other people, must feel quite foreign to him. Perhaps he longed to be alone.

She didn't miss his company, and lingered downstairs in the annex's library. At least until Shade required her nightly trip outside before bed.

When they finally headed up the central staircase, all the way to the top floor, Wynn found Domin Tamira true to her word. Most of the rooms were empty, and those available had their doors fully open. Wynn picked a large room with a window overlooking the front street. She could just make out the lights of the port between the high rooftops. The faded, four-poster bed was draped with a soft, thick quilt, and old velvet curtains graced the windows. Shade immediately turned a full circle before settling on a washed-out braided rug at the bed's foot, and then she gazed watchfully at the closed door.

Wynn pulled out one of her three cold lamp crystals. Once it was glowing, she shut the curtains, stripped off her boots, and sank to the floor before the scrollwork dresser.

"Come," she said. "Time for more words."

Shade simply wrinkled her nose and remained watching the door.

"Come on," Wynn repeated, holding out her hand.

Shade rumbled and began to squirm. She fidgeted all the way around, until she faced fully away from Wynn.

"You have to learn, Shade. It'll make things easier."

So far, lessons had focused on simple terms for common objects and actions, as well as basic commands. The last were certainly demeaning, considering the intelligence of the majay-hì.

"Shade," Wynn said, clearing her mind, so as not to give any clues by memory, "show me . . . High-Tower."

She reached out and touched Shade's haunch, hoping the dog understood enough to call up or send an image of the stout dwarven domin.

Nothing came. Wynn tried to think of other ways to describe High-Tower, from his gray-shot red hair and braid-tipped beard to his—

Suddenly, the domin's image rose in her head. A brief moment of elation came, followed by disappointment.

"No cheating!" she said, taking her hand away. "You must get it from the words, not my memories."

Shade had to use words as cues and understand which one of Wynn's memories to call up to answer back when they weren't touching.

"Show me . . . my room."

Clearing her head, Wynn waited, but again nothing came. She slumped where she knelt. A simpler exercise might be better, something that didn't have to do with Shade calling back a previously seen memory of Wynn's. Perhaps something could be used to check Shade's growing vocabulary.

"Shade, look at . . . the window."

The dog just lay there like a pouting adolescent. How Wynn wished Shade could simply speak words in thought like her father.

Suddenly, Shade's ear twitched, and a vivid memory rose in Wynn's mind.

She was sitting on the hearth's ledge in the Sea Lion tavern on the night of Magiere and Leesil's wedding feast. Chap lay beside her, silent and pensive. They both knew his kin, the Fay, were now aware of Wynn's ability to know of them, hear them. He was deeply concerned about her safety.

"What am I to do without you?" she'd whispered to him.

Remembering that moment from more than a year past made tears well in Wynn's eyes. No mortal should've been able to hear Chap's communion with his kin, and as a result, they wanted Wynn dead. They'd tried to kill her once, because the taint inside her allowed her to hear them, just as she heard Chap in her head. If it hadn't been for him, turning on them . . .

Once you arrive, stay where many are around you, Chap had warned that night on the hearth. *They will shy from approaching where they might be noticed.*

"You know something dark is coming," she'd replied. "Is it your kin . . . from what you sensed in the orb's cavern? Are they behind all of this?"

No . . . something more, beyond them. And I have made other . . . arrangements, which I hope will come through for your well-being.

Wynn hadn't known then what that meant. But she did now. Through his mate, Lily, Chap had sent Shade. He'd sacrificed a daughter he'd never met to try to guard Wynn in his absence.

Wynn wiped away fresh tears, uncertain why Shade had called up this memory. Perhaps it was a reminder from Shade that she was the intended guardian and Wynn the ward, and not the other way around. And soon enough, they would be leaving the tenuous safety of civilization.

"Shade, pay attention," Wynn said, lightly poking the dog's rump.

As her fingertip sank through charcoal-colored fur, another memory erupted in her head.

Wynn was looking at herself, as if she were two separate people.

The other her looked too tall, as if Wynn was lower to the floor. The other Wynn glared down, pointing a finger at . . . Wynn. She said something that came out like a series of sounds parroted without an understanding of the words.

Obviously, this was one of Shade's own memories passed between them as Wynn's finger touched the dog. All memories that Shade passed this way had problems when it came to spoken words—which tended to come out muted and dulled. This time, when the memory passed, it instantly repeated, and Wynn caught the words scolded at her . . . by herself.

"Shade . . . no!"

She jerked her finger back, so startled that she wobbled on her knees. The obstinate meaning behind the reflected memory was clear. Shade was telling Wynn no, quite plainly.

"Oh, you little . . . Don't you tell me . . . !"

Wynn fell into mute shock as the greater meaning in the memory dawned on her. She had a sudden bizarre notion, so simple that at first she couldn't believe it was possible.

"Get up," she said, pushing on Shade's rump.

Shade got up all right, and spun around with a snarl, but Wynn grabbed the dog's face with both hands.

She tried to recall any *word* that Shade had heard often and that meant something important to both of them. She was just as careful not to let any true memory come to mind. She needed not just a person, place, or thing, but a concept connected to moments—to memories—with a like *meaning*.

"Wraith," she whispered.

Shade's hackles rose and her jowls pulled back. A cascade of moments involving Sau'ilahk, a mixture of both their memories, flickered through Wynn's mind. It ended with Wynn's own perspective of thrusting the ignited sun crystal into the wraith's hood.

That was one word that Shade had heard many times—and understood. Likely, she understood far more words than she let on. This time, Wynn didn't scold Shade for using memory-speak. Instead, she lifted one hand, touched her right temple with one finger, and then pointed more directly at herself.

"No Shade memory. Yes Wynn memory. Show . . . Wynn hear . . . *wraith.*"

Wynn lifted her other hand from Shade's face and sat back, not touching the dog, so that Shade could not send her own memories—but only call up Wynn's. The dog stepped forward, reaching out with her nose.

"No," Wynn said. "No memory-speak. Wynn memory."

Shade's eyes narrowed an instant before the assault came.

Every moment in Wynn's life when she had spoken of the wraith to anyone went racing through her head—too fast! It felt like the world was swirling around and around amid a living nightmare of black-cowled, black-robed, faceless figures. Nausea in Wynn's stomach lurched up into her throat, and one fleeting, remembered voice sounded inside her head.

—*wraith . . . cannot be gone*—

Wynn flinched, breathing hard. "Stop."

Of course it would be that moment, so ugly and fresh, when Chane had come at her in the inner bailey wearing that horrible mask. But the sounds were nearly clear. Wynn held on to that memory herself, hoping Shade still caught it.

"No see . . ." she said, and then touched her own ears. "Hear yes. Memory of words . . . of *wraith!*"

Shade's jowls trembled.

An echo rose in Wynn's mind. Fragmented sounds came out of her own memories of Chane's toneless voice, saying . . .

—*wraith . . . not . . . gone*—

Wynn grabbed Shade's face. "Yes . . . yes, Shade!"

It was a broken set of words, and this would never be like talking with Chap. Shade could use only words found in memories that the dog understood, and unless they were touching, it could be only words Shade had ever heard in Wynn's own memories. But this was still more than Wynn had ever hoped possible.

She'd found Shade a voice, stolen and broken as it was.

Another moment rose in Wynn's mind.

Chane had come to her room that night to cryptically demand that she follow him out and leave Shade behind. The view in the memory was twisted, two views of the same moment overlaid from two perspectives—Wynn's own mixed with Shade's as the dog had lain upon the bed.

—*Come . . . Shade stays here*—

Wynn stared at Shade, wondering what this recalled memory meant. Then broken words, still in Chane's voice, shuffled in order and came again.

—*Wynn . . . stays here*—

Wynn was so elated that she didn't even think about what it meant. Shade was doing more than repeating memory words. She was using them to express herself for her own meaning.

Wynn hugged the dog, murmuring, "Oh, thank goodness!"

Then Shade let out a low rumble, and a flash of different moments rose to Wynn's awareness. They were hazy, muted, and more garbled than any other past memory that Shade had shared. Wynn had experienced this before, the first time Shade had shared memories passed on by other majay-hì—by Chap to Lily, and then to their daughter.

Wynn saw through Chap's eyes on the night the Fay had tried to kill her.

Lily's pack of majay-hì scrambled over a massive, downed birch tree as its unearthed roots came alive. Those wooden tentacles lashed at them. Through Chap's perspective, Wynn saw herself jerked out from beneath the downed tree's branches by a root. She tumbled across the earth, her tunic torn at the shoulder, and lay there, barely conscious.

Wynn instantly let go of Shade, shrinking away. Those same broken words in Chane's voice came at her again.

—*Wynn . . . stays here*—

It had happened on a terrible night in the Eleven Territories when the Fay had been communing with Chap and realized Wynn had overheard them. A tainted mortal had been spying on them, and they'd tried to kill her.

Shade began to growl at Wynn. More fragmented words came, this time echoed in Chap's strange mental voice from the night at the Sea Lion hearth, after Magiere and Leesil's wedding.

—*stay where many*—

Shade lunged, shoving Wynn back with her front paws.

Wynn toppled and her back flattened against the dresser. A hodgepodge of differently voiced words came out of her memories.

—stay . . . Wynn . . . here . . . no . . . forest—

Shade was trying to command her with what few words she understood. Even in finding a flawed voice, it was unsettling how quickly the dog caught on.

Shade had always had her own purpose, one that Wynn too often forgot. Shade was worried about Wynn traveling where there were too few mortals for the Fay to fear being noticed.

"Oh, Shade . . . I can't stay," Wynn stammered.

Words from her memories came instantly back.

—Fay . . . kill . . . Wynn—

Wynn threw her arms around Shade's neck, hearing and feeling the dog's distressed rumble. How could she reassure Shade when she couldn't even do so for herself?

"We aren't heading inland yet," she whispered, though Shade might not understand all of the words. "I haven't told Chane, but we were going farther down—"

A knock at the bedroom door stopped her, and then Chane called from outside, "Wynn?"

Such bad timing made her wish he'd stayed away a bit longer. She sat up, one hand stroking Shade's neck as she placed a finger over her lips before she answered.

"Yes, come in."

The door opened, and Chane stepped inside. The look of him startled her.

His face, though still pale, now had a hint of color. He looked . . . at ease, yet more alert than earlier that evening. As if guessing her first question, he said, "A bovine, well outside of the city."

After the full urn of blood left behind at the temple, Wynn took nothing for granted.

"That will work for you, taking just some life from an animal?" she asked.

He hesitated, and then answered flatly, "Yes."

A strange grimace, a kind of revulsion, twisted his features for an instant. She'd never seen that before where his *need* was concerned. She felt a little guilty for doubting him, but not for long.

"You should pick out a room," she said.

"I will, but with winter coming, we should begin the inland trek as soon as possible. How long do we stay here?"

This time, Wynn was the one who hesitated.

"A night or two, at most," she began, "but we're not traveling inland just yet. Tomorrow, I'll book us passage on another ship. We're bound for Drist, a free port to the south."

"Another sea voyage? Is this other port a better place from which to embark?"

"The farther south we travel by sea, the shorter our journey to a'Ghràihlôn'na."

"Can we afford this?" he asked.

She should've told him all this sooner, but waiting meant less chance of an argument.

"I'll have to spend a fair bit of our funding," she admitted, "which means at some point, we'll need to fend for ourselves. But don't fight me on this. It's the only way. The council wants us to take moons to reach the Lhoin'na, and the same or more coming back."

"I will not fight you," he said. "Why do you think I would?"

Wynn didn't answer, but for some reason, his expression had changed. He seemed almost relieved. Did he look forward to more sea travel?

"Have you told Ore-Locks?" he asked.

"He can wait until it's already settled. I'll go out in the morning and see what I can arrange."

"Take him with you. I would come myself, but—"

"Ore-Locks? No . . . Shade is protection enough, and Chathburh is a perfectly safe—"

"There is no such thing as a safe port, in any city," Chane cut in. "They are favored by the baser factions of all societies. You are less likely to be bothered with Ore-Locks along . . . instead of just an animal."

Shade growled at him.

"At least to a stranger's eyes," he added, for he knew how aware Shade was.

Wynn tightened her mouth—only because he was right. For better or worse, Ore-Locks had to at least be treated as part of their group. Then she blinked as something appeared to shift near the ceiling.

It had seemed as if some breeze had found its way through the old ceiling boards, puffing out a bit of dust. But when she peered upward above Chane's head, she saw nothing.

Chane looked up, as well. "What?"

Wynn squinted and shook her head. She just needed sleep after the strain, and she had a slight headache from struggling with Shade's lessons.

Outside in a cutway beside the fishmonger's shop, Sau'ilahk heard the soft swish of air as his servitor returned. He could conjure small constructs of the Elements to serve his needs, and this one of Air captured sounds within its presence. He waited as the round mass of warped air drifted near.

Repeat, Sau'ilahk ordered.

Like a warp upon a desert horizon, it began to reverberate with the sound of voices. Only one recorded utterance was important to him.

. . . Tomorrow, I'll book us passage on another ship. We're bound for Drist. . . .

. . . the farther south we can travel by sea, the shorter our journey to a'Ghràihlôn'na . . .

This filled Sau'ilahk with renewed hope. Wynn was headed to the Lhoin'na sages in their capital city, "Blessed of the Woods." Had she uncovered something of worth in the ancient texts that he could no longer reach? She traveled with her council's approval, though likely they just wished to be rid of her for as long as possible.

Yet Wynn Hygeorht would again veer off any course planned for her.

Useful as this might be, for now all that Sau'ilahk could do was track whatever ship she took. Another sea voyage would again limit him from drawing near, but following her would be less troublesome. He could freely forage for himself, knowing where to easily pick up her trail.

Banish!

The servitor vanished, and mundane air popped as it rushed in to fill the space.

The energy to create it had cost Sau'ilahk. He drifted down the alley, slight hunger gnawing at him as he searched for sustenance in the night of a sleeping city.

CHAPTER 5

Two nights later, Chane stood with the others on a small schooner's deck, watching the lights of Chathburh. Though they had boarded, the captain would not set sail until dawn.

Wynn had been eager to leave the annex. On the morning after delivering her message, the sages of Chathburh had begun to politely avoid her.

Chane did not need to guess why.

Likely the message that Wynn had delivered contained some warning from the council concerning her. Though she would never admit it, the changed attitude of the Chathburh sages bothered her. Chane sympathized in his own way, as he himself would always be an outsider where the guild was concerned.

Only Ore-Locks seemed unhappy about further sea travel. However, out of the corner of his eye Chane noticed more than once that the dwarf was watching him carefully. He pretended not to notice.

"Quarters are cramped, but the price was less than I expected," Wynn said, and she glanced at Ore-Locks without her usual slight frown. "Especially after you haggled with the captain."

Ore-Locks merely shrugged and leaned on the rail. "I made a fair barter. He asked too much for what he had to offer."

Ore-Locks was soft-spoken for a dwarf, but Chane had seen the dwarven customs of barter in Dhredze Seatt. Should he have cared, he might have pitied the ship's captain, though the notion also made him feel inadequate. He could not walk in daylight and had not been there to aid Wynn.

At least while her goals held some hidden value to Ore-Locks, the wayward stonewalker would be one more safeguard for Wynn. The more, the better, as Chane contemplated the future.

They would need to join a caravan to travel safely inland, which meant following someone else's rules and schedules. He might be trapped inside a wagon all day while dormant—prone and helpless. The very idea left him anxious.

"We should get settled," Wynn said, waving him toward the aftcastle.

He nodded and hefted their chest to follow.

"A deckhand loaned me some cards," Wynn added. "Do you know faro, or maybe two kings?"

Chane raised one eyebrow. "Do you?"

"A little . . . Leesil taught me."

Chane went silent at that.

Sau'ilahk materialized beneath the docks of Chathburh, half-submerged in undulating, dark water. His wafting black robe and cloak were unaffected by the water's motion. He watched Wynn's chosen ship anchored in the harbor, its sails still furled. She was headed first to the free port of Drist and then on to the Lhoin'na homeland.

He would not need to follow directly, as there were few ports between Chathburh and Drist. Perhaps he could head south and await her arrival, but first he wished to restore all his life energy lost in conjuring servitors. And taking a few extra lives would bolster him further.

The thought of Drist pleased him. It was a place where the rule of law depended upon the power to enforce it or to ignore it. He could feed there to his heart's content, as no one would give much notice to another corpse in an alley. There were so many who died or vanished in the free ports without a clue as to why.

He winked into dormancy, preparing to awaken on the outskirts of Drist, a place he knew well enough for that. In that brief instant on the edge of eternal dreams, an oppressive presence clawed at him.

Sau'ilahk . . .

He could not help but answer. *Yes, my Beloved.*

Do you follow the sage?
Yes, your . . . servant obeys.

Shortly before dawn, Chane sat on the bunk in his cabin, which was hardly bigger than a walk-in closet. He had passed the night playing cards with Wynn under Shade's watchful gaze. Not that he cared about the game or Shade's scrutiny, and he did not mind indulging Wynn in a harmless pastime. But fear of his own limitations never left his thoughts.

Chane stared at Welstiel's pack on the floor beside his bunk. With a slight shudder, he finally reached inside it. He drew out a leather-bound box, longer and narrower than the walnut one that held the brass cup. Opening it, he looked upon six glass vials with silver screw-top stoppers, couched in velvet padding. All but one was empty, and that one was filled with murky fluid like watery violet ink.

Chane took it out and rolled it between his fingers. A thin, fishy-sweet odor lingered around it as he watched the fluid swirl. He had recognized that scent the very first time he had seen this box.

The fluid's primary component were the petals of a special flower, yellow at the tips and deepening to violet nearer the pistils. *Dyvjàka Svonchek*—"boar's bell" in Belaskian—was named for the belief that only wild boars and heartier beasts could eat it. It had other old names with meanings like "flooding dusk," "nightmare's breath," and "blackbane." Premin Hawes had called it corpse-skirt in Numanese. In other words, poisonous—toxic, and even mind altering if smelled too deeply by the living.

Welstiel had found another purpose for it, one that Chane suspected but had not put to the test.

In their time together in the healers' monastery, it seemed Welstiel had not fallen dormant during the days. Only later had Chane uncovered clues to some concoction that Welstiel had been making in the monks' medicinal chamber. Its smell, which revealed one thing that was in it, and its unnatural implications had kept Chane from trying it on himself. All he truly knew was that he had once seen a vial half full, implying the possible dosage.

Now he was desperate. He needed to know if it would serve him, and thereby help him in protecting Wynn. If so, he would need more of it—much more, if this journey could not be cut short. There would be no foreseeable safer time.

Chane unscrewed the stopper. He steeled himself, pouring half the vial as far as he could into his throat.

After a breakfast of biscuits and dried fish, Wynn didn't feel like sleeping just yet. She walked the decks with Shade in the cold air, but the rising sun promised a bright day. She'd grown accustomed to her upside-down world, sleeping part of the day and staying awake part of the night with Chane. She often headed off to bed midmorning, under the curious eyes of Ore-Locks, and then woke in late afternoon, doing the same between midnight and dawn.

She'd given the captain their old excuse about Chane's skin, the same that Ore-Locks had heard. She told the captain that due to this condition, Chane had his own food, as well. While this captain had been less concerned than the last one, he grunted acknowledgment. At least no one expected Chane to appear for meals or daylight hours.

Sailors were busy all around, preparing to set sail, but none seemed to mind Wynn's presence. She settled on a deck chest beside Shade, one hand on the dog's back and the other on the rail wall.

"Rail," she said, patting it for Shade's attention.

Shade curled one jowl in annoyance at another vocabulary lesson.

—*sleep*—

The word rose in Wynn's mind without warning, in the sound of her own voice.

"You're tired?" she asked.

—*Wynn . . . sleep*—

"Yes, I probably should."

She got up and headed for the aftcastle and down the narrow stairs just below it. But her tiny quarters could hardly be called a cabin. There was barely room to walk in beside the fold-down bunk supported by chains on one wall. And the mattress was hard enough to please a dwarf, though she was suspicious of sharing it with possible insect life.

As she passed Chane's cabin door, she heard a loud thump, and she stopped. The thump came again, followed by a groan. Chane should've been long dormant by now, and Wynn reached for the door latch. It wouldn't open—wouldn't even turn.

Their cabin doors didn't have locks, yet somehow his was barred shut. She tried harder and couldn't budge it.

"Chane, are you all right?"

There was only silence but for the sound of the wind and waves above deck that carried down the passage.

"Chane?" When no answer came, she tried the door again. "Open up."

Heavy footsteps thudded in the passage behind her, and she glanced back.

Ore-Locks had stepped halfway out of his cabin, turning sideways to squeeze through the overly narrow doorway. He wore only breeches and a black shirt, and his long, red hair hung loose.

"What is going on in there?" he asked.

So far, Ore-Locks had held his tongue regarding Chane's eccentricities. His doubt concerning Wynn's story was plain, but he hadn't openly questioned it. The three of them maintained a sort of unspoken state of limbo on the matter. No matter what Ore-Locks might speculate about Chane, he could never be told the truth.

In Dhredze Seatt, the Stonewalkers had shown their hatred for anything undead, and, admittedly, Wynn understood and agreed. But where Chane was concerned, she couldn't take any chances.

"Nothing," she replied. "He's a heavy sleeper. Perhaps he just rolled out of the bunk."

Ore-Locks rumbled almost like Shade, and then frowned and glanced into his own cabin. Likely he slept on the floor. A dwarf would never fit on one of the bunks, even if it didn't break under that much weight. Then he looked back at her hand upon the latch—both hands, actually—and stepped closer.

"I can open it," he said, his tone suggesting a genuine assistance.

Shade growled at him in warning. Wynn turned quickly, taking a step and cutting him off.

"It's all right."

Ore-Locks looked into her face, eye to eye. His expression shifted to a rare flash of frustration.

"What does he eat?" he asked suddenly, leaning slightly to gaze around her toward Chane's door. "He has not joined us for a single meal, nor do I believe he has touched our meager stores."

"Why were you looking in our stores?"

Her response gave him pause. Dwarves were a communal people.

"We take this journey together," he answered.

"No, I take this journey. You're here only by my unwilling consent."

She'd been looking for a chance to make it clear who made the decisions here. She also wanted to know what real reason he had to demand following her.

What did he really want at Bäalâle Seatt?

He'd never tell her outright, but she hoped he might slip up and let some hint leak out. So she didn't antagonize him further.

"Chane will be fine," she said. "I'll check again later."

Most dwarves were open and forthright. Ore-Locks had proven himself otherwise. He crossed his arms, his gaze intently shifting back to her, but no hint of emotion showed on his broad features. With a slow breath, he returned to his cabin.

Wynn stood guard a few moments longer and then put her ear to the door.

"Chane?" she said softly, but not a sound came from the locked cabin.

Chane crouched on his bunk, his arms wrapped around his pulled-up knees, and he tried not to claw off his own skin. He could not stop shaking.

The beast chained inside him, that feral nature Welstiel had once warned him of, screamed a last time. It collapsed, still and silent, as if retreating into some inner dormancy.

But not Chane—no such relief came to him.

Wynn's soft footfalls rose in the outer passage.

He scrambled, falling off the bed as he fumbled with shaking hands to shove the chest against the door. Full fright took hold immediately. The chest was not enough. Wynn might still push the door open and see him . . . awake in the daytime. He clenched the door's inner handle—and it bent in his grip.

He felt Wynn weakly attempt to turn the latch from the outside.

"Chane . . . are you all right?" she called softly.

Chane quietly gripped the bent handle with both hands.

He could not hold in the soft whimper, imagining the terror of having to look into her eyes. He realized too late that he was panting, though he did not need to breathe. He tried hard to stop himself, listening to her voice, and then to Ore-Locks's as Shade growled.

It was all too loud, as if they stood within his cabin, shouting over the wind he heard outside the ship. The notion horrified him, as if Wynn had come upon him while feeding or looked into his face after a kill . . . and saw his euphoria.

In Dhredze Seatt's underside, she had twice forced him into wakefulness during the day. They had been deep inside the mountain, shielded from the rising sun. Even so, he had suffered, hazy and disoriented and unaware of half of what he did.

This was not the same—he was fully *awake*.

Every nerve tingled with an ache. Every muscle vibrated from within. The cabin's porthole was covered with nothing but burlap. The sun burned just outside, radiating a dim glow behind that fabric.

Only a curtain and the ship's thin wall veiled him from daylight.

He had never been so aware of the sun.

It was there, just within reach of him, waiting to burn him. He could not even hide from it, because no matter how he tried, he could not fall dormant.

"Chane?" Wynn whispered through the door.

A part of him wanted to shove the chest aside, open the door, pull her in, cling to her until nightfall. But he could not let her see him like this, see him so weak.

He hung on to the door latch until he heard her walk hesitantly away. Then he crawled to the bunk, its mattress tearing under his fingernails as he climbed up, and curled into the corner at its head. Clutching his knees again, he watched the porthole, its one layer of burlap all that lay between him and the sun.

And no matter how Chane tried, he could not fall dormant.

What had he done to himself?

CHAPTER 6

Thirteen days later, Wynn stood at the starboard rail as the sun nearly touched the ocean's distant horizon. A sailor suddenly stepped in beside her and pointed to the other side, down the coast.

"Drist ahead, miss. You can't see the port yet, but there are ships harbored out from it."

Wynn stepped to the port side, and he followed, trying to stay away from Shade.

"Yes, I see them," she said. "How long?"

"Shortly after the day's final bell, so you might as well pack up." He paused, looking at her. "Watch out for yourself, miss. It's a pitiless place. Most of us don't even get off there . . . except for exchanging cargo."

She only nodded her thanks at his warning, and then brushed Shade's ear with a fingertip.

"Come on, girl. We're going below."

The journey from Chathburh had been unpleasant at best. Ore-Locks had stayed in his cabin much of the time—not that Wynn minded his absence. Maybe it was the typical dwarven dislike of the sea. But his self-imposed isolation made the tension even thicker when he came out for meals. They both ate in silence. He often stared straight ahead, his dark eyes focused on nothing, as if he spent much of his time living in a world no one else could see.

And worse, she spent the first six days wondering if Chane suffered from some form of seasickness. He hadn't come out for two nights. When he did, he looked awful—pale even for him.

He was anxious, twitchy, and distracted, often sharp and short in his replies. He showed no interest in cards or any other pastime. She once bluntly asked him what was wrong. To her surprise, he told her to leave him alone. As he turned to go, he'd had difficulty opening her cabin door. His hand shook visibly.

Over the following nights, he slowly returned to his old self. Wynn never thought she'd be relieved to have him return to the brooding, cold state he'd adopted in his days at the guild. But last night, they'd played two kings nearly till dawn. All seemed back to normal, so to speak.

No, she wasn't sorry to see this particular voyage end, and she would certainly be choosier about their accommodations next time—if she could afford better. Heading belowdecks, she knocked at Ore-Locks's door.

"We're almost to port," she called. "Get packed. We'll disembark as soon as Chane wakes."

Time passed quickly while Wynn readied for what came next. Unable to squelch her curiosity about the notorious free port of Drist, she thought of High-Tower's fuming shock, if and when he learned she'd ignored his warning. Then someone rapped softly upon the cabin door.

"Wynn?" Chane rasped.

She peeked through the porthole and saw that dusk had come, but the dimming light outside wasn't completely gone. Somehow he'd come early again. Before this trip, he never roused on his own until full darkness.

"Yes, come in."

He stuck his head in.

"Grab the chest," Wynn said. "We've made port."

Not long after night's first bell, Chane fidgeted anxiously on deck. The harbor was so crowded that the crew had to wait their turn to even dock the ship.

"Ah, dead deities in seven hells," Wynn muttered under her breath.

Chane frowned at her language, but he could not argue with the sentiment. And he still felt *wrong* inside. Whatever side effects he suffered from Welstiel's concoction had faded to lingering, nagging nervousness. At least now that the fluid had been tested, he knew its purpose.

It would keep him from falling dormant.

A fervor of deck activity pulled him from his thoughts. The crew's demeanor had changed drastically. Half the men strapped on cutlasses, while others began hauling cargo on deck before any signal that the ship could dock. One sailor climbed to the crow's nest with a large crossbow and a case of quarrels strapped to his back.

Chane grew more uncertain about Wynn's chosen destination.

By the light of massive pole braziers, six long piers jutted from the port far out into the water. A vessel filled nearly every available space, except for the largest ships, which anchored offshore.

Looking over the piers, Chane could not help his rising trepidation.

Too many people, uncomfortable numbers, filled the port even at nightfall. Dockworkers and sailors clambered everywhere, hauling cargo to and from ships, handling mooring and rigging, and shouting over the general din. A medium-sized schooner pulled away from the nearest dock and finally drifted past, out beyond their ship's prow.

"Weigh anchor! Gentle to port!" their captain shouted.

Their smaller vessel drifted inward and soon settled in an open slot. Chane, along with his companions, stayed clear as sailors threw mooring lines to dockhands below. Once the ramp was lowered, four armed sailors sprang forward. Two ran down to stand post at the ramp's bottom, while the other pair took stations at the top, watching all activity below.

Chane looked about and saw similar safeguards on other vessels. He had never seen sailors behave in such a fashion in Calm Seatt or the king's city of Bela in his country. Perhaps High-Tower's warning to Wynn had been legitimate. What kind of business did their ship's captain have in this place?

"I do not like this," he whispered.

The city loomed before them, couched between dark, high hills cresting above the shore to the north and south. Buildings of mixed sizes and shapes, dingy and worn by coastal weather, were so closely mashed together that only a few vertical roads showed between them. Warehouses lined the shore, and the air was tainted with myriad scents, from fish to oiled wood, salt brine to people and livestock. The stench of burning wood, coal, and oil from the immense braziers tainted all other smells.

"Look at all of them," Wynn whispered, but she was not looking into the city.

A wild array of people hurried about the docks and milled around the large bay doors of warehouses. Every color and form of attire that Chane could imagine was scattered among them.

Caramel-skinned Sumans in colorful garb led goats harnessed in a line. A group of even darker-skinned people he had never seen, with tightly curled black hair, were dressed in one-piece shifts of cloth, or pantaloons and waist wraps of strong colors with ink black patterns. They tried to navigate a cart of cloth bolts, perhaps silk, around a cluster of garishly armored men. Another band in hides and furs leaped off a thick-hulled vessel with many oars raised upright around its one square sail. This group shoved their way down the dock with shields and broadswords in hand, as if waiting for someone to challenge them. They had to be Northlanders, a people Wynn had mentioned a few times.

The number of Numans was almost overwhelming. Some dressed like vagabonds, while others wore finery beneath voluminous wool cloaks.

"Go ahead," the captain barked.

Startled to awareness, Chane turned.

The captain waved them forward. "The ramp's secure. . . . Off with you all."

Chane had his new sword strapped on, but he picked up his old one that had been left leaning against the chest. Couched in its cropped sheath, he strapped it over his other hip. Ore-Locks appeared no more pleased than Chane at the sea of people below. The dwarf wore his broadsword, and his grip tightened on his iron staff. Shade let out a quiet rumble. The dog hated crowds in general, and this crowd hardly qualified as general. Only Wynn seemed undaunted, with a tense eagerness on her face.

"I will lead," Ore-Locks said.

With his own bulky bag lashed to his back, he hefted the chest onto his shoulder, keeping one hand free for his staff. Chane waved Wynn and Shade onward, and brought up the rear as they descended the ramp. Ore-Locks's bulk proved useful in clearing the way up the dock.

Once they approached the shore, Chane spotted a floating walkway along the rock wall beneath the piers. Between every other pier post were switchback ramps and stairs leading upward from the lower floating platforms for small boats.

"*Vanâkst Bäynæ*," Ore-Locks growled.

Chane looked up to find the dwarf had stopped and was scraping his boot on the shorefront's cobble. There was a line of dung left by the passing of the Sumans' goats. Passersby gave it no notice.

"This place is a giant gutter," Ore-Locks said quietly, shoving on through the crowd.

With little choice, they made their way through the throngs. Chane kept close behind Wynn, ready to jerk her back in an instant.

"Ore-Locks is not wrong," he said. "This place appears to be little more than a haven for pirates and smugglers."

"That's because it is," Wynn replied without looking back. "Keep moving."

Chane slowed. She had known this and still gone to secret lengths to bring them here?

"Wynn!" he rasped. "How could you—?"

"Look over there," she interrupted, pointing. "That might be a row of inns."

"Inns?" he repeated.

"There is no guild annex here. We'll have to fend for ourselves."

They entered the city's edge beyond the waterfront, and Chane grew more irritated by the moment. Wynn had willingly walked them into a lawless port, and now nosed about for an inn like some traveler on holiday?

"You cannot stay here," he said. "This place is not safe."

She turned to face him. "I'm in the company of a majay-hì, an armed dwarf, and . . . and you. I could hardly be safer."

Ore-Locks waited on them, his expression flat. Shade ceased growling and pressed up against Wynn's leg and hip. Chane was speechless, aghast at Wynn's nonchalance.

"We can't just stand here arguing," she told him.

He clenched his jaw, finding his voice. "Fine . . . where is this row of inns?"

"That way," she answered with a flick of her hand.

The gesture almost made Chane heave her over his shoulder to toss her back on the ship.

Again Ore-Locks led, and Chane brought up the rear, watching anyone who came too close. But the farther they went, the more the crowds thinned.

In a block and a half down a poorly cobbled street, they soon passed only hard-looking, worn women in faded, low-cut gowns, sailors swilling from clay bottles, and a mix of what might have been merchants, both prosperous and shabby. Everyone kept to his or her business or pleasure, as if expecting others to do the same.

Chane passed a small shop of rough-cut planks. A simple sign above the door had one word written in four different languages: the first said "Apothecary" in Numanese. He slowed as notions rose in his thoughts.

"What?" Wynn asked. She had stopped a few paces ahead.

"Nothing," he answered, but he noted the shop's location.

Ore-Locks occasionally drifted to either side of the street, examining eateries, taverns, or inns along the way. Chane could tell nothing from the fronts of these bland, almost neutral establishments. He guessed at the gambling, coin bending, and other illicit endeavors that went on behind their closed doors.

He would not have Wynn sleeping in any such place.

But as naive as she could be at times, she was no fool. As he watched, her brow wrinkled every time Ore-Locks cast a quizzical glance her way before some establishment. When she shook her head, they moved on.

"What about that one?" she said suddenly.

Chane followed her gaze.

At the street's end stood a large, well-situated, three-story building nearly half a block wide. Constructed of thick planking with not too badly cracked sky blue paint, its white shutters were stained by city smoke and filth. The building sported a sweeping, ground-level veranda with two armed guards standing by the front columns.

As Chane followed Wynn, he was uncertain whether the iron grates over the windows were a good sign. The guards were relaxed but watchful as Ore-Locks stepped between them to the front door. Guards could also be a good or bad indication. A white sign above the door held one gilded word in only Numanese: DELILAH'S.

Wynn hurried up to the nearest guard, a stout man, cleanly shaven though rough featured. As Ore-Locks peered through the open front door, both guards eyed Wynn. The closest nodded respectfully.

"Commander Molnun, at your service," he said. "Welcome."

"Does this establishment offer rooms?" she asked.

"The finest in Drist."

"And secure?" Chane asked.

The "commander" looked Chane up and down with only his eyes, never moving his head.

"Yes, sir . . . the best to be had."

Chane looked the man over in turn. His outer leather tunic did not hide hints of a chain shirt beneath it, likely with quilt padding under that. Though properly closed, the tunic was a loose fit; the commander valued mobility over show. His sword hung low rather than being cinched against his belt like some preening noble wanting to look dashing would wear it. This one had to be ex-military.

If the establishment hired standing mercenaries, it would not be cheap.

Wynn seemed to realize this, too, and cast Chane a troubled glance.

"I will pay," Ore-Locks cut in, perhaps guessing the problem. "We should stay here."

Chane warmed with discomfort but did not argue. He should have procured more money by now. The commander nodded to Ore-Locks.

"Be certain you carry a lodger's voucher whenever you plan to leave and still return."

Chane nodded and reluctantly ushered Wynn in.

As Wynn followed Ore-Locks through the weatherworn, hand-carved front door, she tried to stifle her growing annoyance with Chane. Much as she was accustomed to his overprotective nature, tonight he was dangerously close to overbearing. He'd known from the start that this journey would hold surprises. True, Drist was worse than even she'd expected, but they were here. They—he—had better make the best of it. But once inside, she stopped thinking about Chane at all.

A huge oval rug of deep brown with a circular pattern of white flowers and light green, leafy vines was spread under her feet. The foyer walls were stained a rich shade of cream, with amber curtains on the windows from the high ceiling to the polished wood floor. From somewhere unseen, the soft, resonant tones of a skillfully played wooden flute filled the air, which was scented lightly with sandalwood.

"Oh . . . no," she said softly.

Unlike the old guild hotel in Chathburh, the interior here was in its prime. This was going to cost more than she'd first feared.

She half turned left to see a solid walnut counter with gold inlay. The young man behind it was well dressed in a white linen shirt and black satin vestment. His face was oval, and his skin was as olive toned as hers. His hair and eyes were both light brown, like hers.

Chane stared at him.

"May I help you?" the young man asked politely, and his gaze dropped briefly to Shade. "I am Mechaela. What do you seek this evening?"

The question seemed odd. What would weary travelers seek besides lodging?

Two men, dressed similarly to this host, walked past Wynn and into a wide parlor on the right. Neither was armed, and Wynn took a few steps, peering after them.

Low couches of plush padding filled that room. Small tables held crystal vases loaded with fresh flowers, though where such came from in late autumn, she couldn't guess. Seascape oil paintings of unimaginable clarity graced the walls.

She spotted an archway at the far side that led into another room of similar decor. Three men sat playing cards at a polished obsidian table. Their finery might have marked them as nobility, if this had been any city but Drist. A willowy girl appeared from out of sight and poured wine for the gentlemen. Her gown of overlaid gauze was a bit revealing.

To the far left of the nearer room was a tall set of closed doors. Closer still was a curving staircase that stretched upward. What kind of place was this?

"Three rooms," Ore-Locks said.

Wynn turned back to find him at the counter with the young host. He was already untying a lanyard strung with punched dwarven coins, or slugs.

"Two rooms," Chane corrected, and looked down at her. "You are not staying here alone. I will sleep on the floor."

Wynn bit the inside of her lip, not wishing to make a scene.

Mechaela raised an eyebrow, but said nothing, though he did glance at Chane's and Ore-Locks's sheathed blades. He reached out with one finger to tap the long iron staff leaning against the counter.

"Of course, you'll need to relinquish your weapons. You can retrieve and return them upon coming and going."

Chane blinked. "No."

Ore-Locks appeared equally surprised.

Shade rumbled, perhaps sensing the sudden tension.

"Chane!" Wynn whispered. Would he ever stop being so difficult?

"No," he repeated.

"Is there a problem, gentlemen?" said a smooth voice from behind them.

Wynn spun around.

A slender woman stepped out of the parlor. Delicately built, she was far taller than Wynn. Her teal silk gown, embroidered with curling vines of white blossoms, was so smoothly fitted that it moved with her, revealing her subtle curves. Shining black hair hung in long, faint waves that sparkled in the foyer's lamplight, though her bangs were held back with a band of polished silver.

She had skin the shade of soft ivory, perhaps a bit warmer, and eyes so deep blue, they mesmerized Wynn at first. Her lashes were long, and her eyelids were powdered to match her gown.

She was . . . unreal. Even Ore-Locks appeared stunned at the sight of her.

"Is there some confusion?" she asked.

Her tone didn't imply a true question, but her voice was almost a breathy echo of the flute's resonance. This was a woman who could stop almost any man in his tracks at twenty paces—maybe fifty.

Unfortunately, Chane was not one of those men.

"I will not relinquish my swords," he said.

"I am Delilah, owner of this establishment," she answered, and her gaze passed over Ore-Locks with polite interest.

Wynn felt Chane's hand settle on her shoulder.

"I do apologize," Delilah went on, "but all patrons, regardless of what they come for, must leave their weapons before entering. Do not be concerned. Your safety—your needs—are secured and assured by my staff."

Wynn glanced nervously about. Their needs? Shouldn't that be obvious?

"How," Chane challenged, "when your interior guards do not carry weapons?"

"Mechaela requires no weapon," Delilah answered.

Her eyes traced a smooth path from one newcomer to the next, perhaps assessing who truly made the decisions, and a smile spread across her small mouth.

"And what *needs* bring you to us . . . sage?"

Wynn was a bit stunned. She wore only her short robe over her elven travel clothes, yet this woman knew what she was, and that she was supposedly in charge. Wynn glanced through the parlor arch at the lounging furniture, and into the room beyond that, and at the other woman in the revealing gauze dress. . . .

Chane sucked in an audible breath and exhaled. *"Domvolyné!"*

Before his meaning sank in, Wynn felt his fingers clench her cloak's shoulder and tunic. He jerked her backward toward the front door.

"We are leaving," he said.

"Oh . . . oh . . ." she stammered, flushing red in the face.

A *domvolyné* was a house of leisure in Chane's country. Wynn had just walked them all into a high-line brothel in the middle of a pit called Drist.

"What is wrong now?" Ore-Locks asked, and stared blankly at Chane.

There were no brothels among the dwarves.

"Oh, please, please," Delilah called, suppressing a brief laugh with delicate fingers. "Forgive me. I meant no offense—only a playful jest. We can accommodate you. . . . We care well for all our patrons, by their own needs."

Behind the counter, even Mechaela was hard-pressed not to smile.

Wynn grabbed the doorframe before Chane could haul her into the street.

"Chane, stop it. It could be the same—probably worse—everywhere here."

"Yes, there is worse," Delilah added, no longer amused. "Mechaela, they will need the quieter and more peaceful of our accommodations."

He nodded. "I will place them properly in the east side of the second floor."

"But," Delilah added, "you must leave your weapons."

Wynn looked to Ore-Locks, hating to turn to him for support. He sighed and handed over his iron staff before beginning to unbuckle his sword. A startled Mechaela fumbled a bit under the weight of the staff. Wynn looked back and up to Chane, his expression curled in a silent snarl.

"Chane?"

With a seething, unintelligible rasp, he released her and headed for the counter. He unlashed the shorter, ground-down sword, then did the same with the new dwarven blade.

"This is everything?" Mechaela asked politely, eyeing the sheathed end of Wynn's staff.

She pulled off the sheath, displaying its long crystal, and Delilah nodded approval. After a brief hesitation, Wynn pulled Magiere's old battle dagger out from behind her back, as well. Delilah watched in interest as Ore-Locks began tugging steel and copper slugs off his lanyard.

Much to Wynn's relief, neither Mechaela nor Delilah balked at payment in dwarven slugs, and Wynn tried to count her own mixed blessings. At least she'd reached Drist and found safe, if questionable, accommodations.

Now if she could just get Chane to calm down.

Entering the lavish rooms, Chane thought that, aside from the fact that it was no place for Wynn, the whole interior smelled wrong. The room itself stank of too much perfume. On their way up, they had passed three young women and an effeminate young man of exceptional beauty, who were obviously not patrons. But they met no one else as Mechaela led them northward down a long corridor of sumptuous carpets on the second floor.

Ore-Locks's room was across the hall, but he followed them inside their own room, looking about. He set the chest down, shut the door, and then dropped his bulky sack. It clattered strangely. Then he walked to the bed covered in quilted raw silk of varied violet hues, pressing his hand down until it sank through the puffy bedding to the soft mattress.

"Like sleeping in a sinkhole," he said.

Chane wanted to go out by himself, but he was uncertain how to broach the subject. How long did Wynn intend to stay in Drist before heading inland?

"What now?" he asked. "Winter is so close that we will find few caravans on the move. I should try to procure a wagon."

Wynn glanced away nervously.

"Wynn?" he asked.

After a slow breath, she answered, "We're not headed inland . . . just yet."

Ore-Locks's complexion flushed, and he beat Chane to the obvious. "What?"

Wynn rolled a shoulder, fidgeting in sudden discomfort. She swung her pack onto the bed and began digging through it, finally pulling out a journal Chane had not seen before. She paged through it and flattened it open.

"Look at this. I copied a map I found in the archives."

Why did she keep everything from him until the last moment?

"We're here," she said, pointing to one inked dot on the coastline. "If we take another ship south, all the way to the port of Soráno in the Romagrae Commonwealth, we'll—"

"Another ship?" Ore-Locks cut in. "I have no quarrel with a good walk."

"And I want to reach the Lhoin'na as quickly as possible," she countered. "Soráno is nearer to our destination. This is the fastest way."

Ore-Locks sighed but otherwise remained silent.

"Instead of going inland, south by southwest," Wynn continued, "and all the way through Lhoin'na lands, we'll come in below and take the shorter route directly east. By the time we reach their forest, we'll be on top of a'Ghràihlôn'na, the one great elven city, and their branch of the guild. For a slightly longer sea voyage, we'll cut our journey time in half, and keep us in . . . civilized areas a bit longer."

Chane glanced at Shade, who was watching him, but he shook his head, incredulous.

"Then why did we stop here at all?" he asked. "We have no business in Drist."

"To throw the guild off my trail."

Chane did not understand. Wynn looked up at him, a bitter anger in her eyes that he had not seen there until recent times.

"High-Tower laid out my route," she answered, "not only to waste my time, but to track me. Think about it. Our funding was barely adequate, and I was commissioned to make two stops, both at guild locations. Whatever was in that letter to the Chathburh annex, someone might have checked if I booked passage anywhere else. By landing here, all they can report is that I went to Drist."

She tilted her head. "If . . . when High-Tower hears of it, he'll think my trail ends here, only to be picked up once I reach the Lhoin'na, but I'll be there long before he expects. And there's no one here to report that I booked passage farther south."

Chane crossed his arms. Every day there was something more about Wynn and her guild that became tarnished in his view. Besides her, the guild was the only thing in this world he had ever believed held value.

"As you said," Chane countered, "we were not given enough money for another voyage."

"I'll take care of it."

Chane lost all patience with more surprises. "Wynn, how are—?"

"It's taken care of."

"What have you done?"

She bit her lower lip but did not answer. Instead, she reached into her pack. When she withdrew her hand, she opened it, exposing a cold lamp crystal.

Chane was still baffled. He had seen her crystal many times and even used it once or twice himself. Then she put her other hand into her short robe's pocket and pulled out two more.

"These are spares," she said quietly.

Chane began growing suspicious. Only journeyors and above were given a crystal as a mark of status and accomplishment. Such were nearly sacred among sages. So how had Wynn acquired a second, let alone a third?

Before Chane said a word, again Ore-Locks beat him to it.

"Did you steal those?"

For once, his expression was completely unguarded. Ore-Locks knew the implications as well as Chane.

"No!" Wynn answered.

"Wynn?" Chane warned.

"Premin Hawes gave them to me . . . when I told her that I'd lost mine."

So she had lied to get them.

"No one is hurt by this," Wynn said. "I knew we'd need more money and wouldn't get it."

What she intended was now clear.

"Even just one of these will bring more than we need," she went on heatedly, almost daring either of them to argue. "We simply trade it to someone who has no wish to reveal where or how it was gained."

Chane remained silent. He had seen Wynn give in to questionable— sometimes dark—rationales to justify her endeavors, not that the effects mattered to him. He had done worse for far less and more self-serving motivations. But he had never thought her capable of lying to her own for this kind of purpose, or to barter away something so honored. The act was so . . . premeditated.

Ore-Locks was quiet as well, but any ethical considerations on his part seemed to vanish.

"One of those is worth a good deal more than a sea voyage," he said.

Wynn looked at him. For a brief moment, she spoke to him as a companion.

"So much the better, if it buys silence, as well, from whoever takes it in exchange for the fastest passage."

The dwarf studied her for the span of two breaths, and then held out his thick hand.

"I can exchange one for what it is worth."

Wynn hesitated.

"Can you barter better than a dwarf?" he challenged.

Chane knew Ore-Locks was right, though it did not make Wynn's plan more palatable. Wynn slowly dropped a crystal in Ore-Locks's large hand.

Still, Chane said nothing, and that made Wynn glance sidelong at him.

"I didn't have a choice," she said, as if needing to defend her actions. "There was nothing else small enough to carry but worth enough in trade or sale."

Chane looked away. He should have found a way to gain more coin. She should not have been cornered into doing this.

"Everyone should eat and retire," he said, changing the subject. He had his own agenda for the night, and he wanted Wynn locked safely away. "But a meal could be expensive here."

"We will have enough," Ore-Locks said, "once I trade this to cover it."

He rolled the crystal in his large hand, watching the motion trigger the tiniest glow within its prisms.

As casually as he could, Chane said, "All right. While Ore-Locks settles into his room, I will go down and order food."

The dwarf looked at him for a long moment, finally nodded, and stepped out. As soon as he was gone, Chane turned to Wynn.

"I need to go out."

She shifted uncomfortably. "I know."

Sau'ilahk hovered in an alley across from the large inn. His quarry appeared to have settled for the night. He pondered conjuring another servitor of Air to slip inside and function as his ears. But the place appeared too active. Indoors, within lit, contained areas—possibly with low ceilings—his creation might be spotted before it located Wynn.

Chane suddenly stepped out the front door.

Sau'ilahk lost his train of thought. Chane was no match for Sau'ilahk's conjury, but this enigmatic undead had exhibited some arcane skill. It would be prudent to know exactly what he was up to, as Sau'ilahk had never been fond of surprises.

He blinked to the next corner, watching Chane stride back toward port.

Chane did not like deceiving Wynn. She assumed that he needed to feed, and he had chosen not to correct her. Between the brass cup's draught and the still-lingering influence of Welstiel's violet concoction, he did not feel hungry. By now, he should. But not even a twinge of hunger had come since Chathburh. Chane had other needs this night, new ones only beginning to nag at him.

He had not been prepared for what Welstiel's concoction would do to him. Even in knowing, the thought of consuming it again left him frightened. Suffering through those days in his cabin had been horrible. But soon enough, Wynn would leave civilization.

There might come a time when he would need to remain conscious, whether it was day or night. He had only one more dose of the violet concoction. And worse, he had not told Wynn that he had taken their pouch of guild-funded coins from their travel chest. But tonight he needed the money.

With his cloak's hood pulled forward, he ignored passersby. He made his way back to the shops inward from the port, to find the shabby multilingual sign above a door: APOTHECARY.

Late as it was, he reached for the latch but stopped short, staring at Welstiel's ring on his third finger. It hid his nature from unnatural detection but also dulled his awareness more and more the longer he wore it. He could still sense some deceptions when spoken, but that ability and his senses were more acute without the ring.

Chane slipped off the ring and tucked it into the coin pouch.

The night world instantly took on a bizarre shimmer, like the air in summer heat. It passed, and the night grew bright in his eyes. He heard a rat in a nearby alley fussing with some piece of discarded paper, and the soft lap of water on the floating walkways below the piers another block away.

Grasping the door handle, Chane pressed down—and it opened. Upon entering, he was instantly assaulted by musty air wrapped in too many scents to separate them.

Small lanterns sat on faded tables or hung from low rafters, illuminating walls lined with close-spaced shelves laden with hundreds of glass, clay, wood, and tin vessels of all sizes. The counter to the right supported a long box tilted so customers could see into it. In its little divided cubicles were powders and flake substances beneath cheap, poorly cast glass lids.

"I'm just closing up," a scratchy voice said.

Chane started slightly and turned.

An old woman stood in an archway to a back room filled with small tables and strange apparatus. Wild, steel gray hair hung in straggles over her face, which had one missing eye. She didn't wear a patch, but had inserted a polished orb of jet or obsidian with a red dot in place of an iris. Two large moles decorated the left side of her nose, and her hooded robe might have once been red. She leaned on a gnarled cane.

"I need several components," he said. "One in particular."

She looked him up and down. "Why would the likes of you come here for such a . . . component, as you call it?"

Her mockery of the term suggested she knew he was after something more important—more expensive and perhaps questionable—than was on display in the shop. It was also to probe to see if he was willing and able to pay for it.

"Because it is . . . very rare," he answered.

CHAPTER 7

After Chane left, Wynn took advantage of the privacy and the rare luxury of the inn. She stripped down to her shift, then lifted the pearl-glazed pitcher and basin and fresh towels off the dresser and settled down on the floor. Before she'd even finished pouring water in the basin, Shade stuck her face in the bowl and started lapping. Wynn let her drink, for the water wasn't soapy yet. The dog was probably hungry, as well.

"We'll have supper soon," she said.

She took her time washing. She'd barely finished and pulled on her short robe when a soft, triple knock came. Shade's nose rose in the air, along with her ears, as she sniffed repeatedly, and Wynn didn't need to guess as she opened the door.

A slender woman in a lavender gown stood outside, holding a huge tray with three covered plates.

"Your dinner, miss."

"Thank you . . ." Wynn trailed off.

Should she pay the girl now? How much would this cost? The girl was watching her and offered a demure smile.

"Mechaela will settle accounts upon your departure."

"Thank you," Wynn said, taking the tray, which was heavier than it looked. After a brief nod, the girl vanished down hall.

Wynn shut the door with her hip and hauled the tray to a small table. When she lifted one plate cover, she found a grilled salmon fillet, steamed green beans, and roasted potatoes—and the same under the other two covers. After so much time on a ship, the food probably smelled more exquisite than it truly was. But where had the staff found fresh green beans at this time of year?

Obviously, Chane had ordered a plate for Shade, who already fidgeted at Wynn's side. Wynn set one plate down and had barely taken her hand back before Shade was halfway done. She shook her head at the sight and sighed, but the third plate gave her pause. It couldn't be for Chane.

Reluctantly, she picked up the plate, opened the door, and knocked on the one across the hall. "Ore-Locks, supper."

He opened the door almost immediately, but he looked past her, into her room.

"Where is Chane?" he asked.

"Out," she said, offering the plate.

He didn't take it. "How long?"

"He's just getting supplies," she said.

"Again . . . at this time of night?"

Why would it matter to Ore-Locks where Chane went or what he did? The dwarf looked at her, the barest crease forming on his brow and between his eyes.

"Is not his purpose to protect you?" he asked. "Leaving you at a guild annex was one thing. Not the same as . . . *here*, and without even telling me."

Wynn blinked. Ore-Locks was angry that Chane had left her unguarded?

"I will stay with you until he returns," he said, taking a step.

"No—I'm fine," she said, shoving the plate out into his chest. "Shade is with me . . . and I'm just across the hall."

Ore-Locks's jaw muscles bulged. "You will stay inside your room?"

"Yes," she answered, uncertainly, wondering if he had some genuine concern for her.

"Bäalâle Seatt is our purpose," he added. "At present, you are the one best suited to find it."

Uncertainty vanished as Wynn stiffened. *This* was the Ore-Locks she knew.

He would never let her come to harm as long as his only path was to follow her. Another realization hit her: this was the same reason he hadn't pressed her regarding Chane's strange habits. From the first moment Ore-Locks had met

Chane in the Chamber of the Fallen in the Stonewalkers' underworld, Chane had proven himself more than adequate at protecting Wynn. That made him useful, and the dwarf would turn a blind eye as long as Chane remained so.

Ore-Locks didn't care about anything but his own end goal—whatever that was.

Wynn pushed the plate into his chest again and let go of it. She spun around as he huffed and staggered, likely fumbling to grab the plate.

She walked directly into her own room and closed the door.

Sau'ilahk felt an undead presence suddenly manifest in his awareness.

Chane had paused before an apothecary's shop, his right hand moving to his left. Then he slipped something into a small pouch.

Sau'ilahk quickly blinked into the deep night shadows under an awning half a block farther on. He had felt this same sudden change before in the underworld of Dhredze Seatt. Although Chane somehow hid his nature, there were moments when he seemed to *unmask* himself, and, once revealed, he appeared to be no more than any mundane vampire.

Sau'ilahk watched as Chane entered the apothecary's shop, and he desperately wanted to know what was happening in there. But if he could sense Chane's true nature, he might be sensed in turn if he drew too near.

Sau'ilahk needed a spy.

He focused inward, expending excessive energy in his rush. In his mind's eye, he shaped a glowing circle for Spirit in the air, the size of a splayed hand. Within this, he formed the square of Air, stroked glowing sigils in the spaces between the nested shapes, and then fixated upon the grand seal as if seeing it hanging before him. Part of his will bled away in a wave of exhaustion.

A silent breeze rushed through Sau'ilahk, though it rustled neither his cloak nor his robe. He ignored this side effect and called the air into the seal. The pattern's empty center undulated like the heated air above a smokeless fire. That barely visible distortion held its place—a servitor of Air with a hint of consciousness.

Sau'ilahk imprinted it with purpose.

Into the space with a lifeless presence within . . .

Record all sound until it leaves that place. . . .

Return and reiterate what you record.

Sau'ilahk released the great seal from his mind's eye. The servitor shot away, slipping through the top crack of the shop's door.

The repulsive apothecary eyed Chane carefully.

"Jasmine and heartsease for a love potion?" she asked. "To win your lady from a rival?"

"No."

He stepped closer through the haze of airborne dust illuminated by lantern light. One did not simply walk into an apothecary's shop and ask for poison. Or did one in a place like Drist?

Chane pulled a pack from his shoulder and dug out a slip of paper. "I need everything on this list, especially that last item."

She took the torn half sheet in her bony fingers with their long, yellowed nails. For the most part, there was nothing on it that could not be found in a typical apothecary's shop. Nothing truly unusual, from glass vessels, a small oil burner, wood alcohol, and varied components he had guessed at.

He watched her, waiting for her to spot the Numan reference at the end to the deadly flower he knew as boar's bell.

She read it as if it were nothing, but her eye—her one real eye—flickered before she looked up.

"I'm sorry. I can't help you."

Chane did not feel any warning within.

No rumble from the beast sounded inside him. No tightening prickle ran over his skin. But he had not cleared his head to listen for deception in her words. Still, it was not necessary in order to know that she would lie. Even here, a poisonous substance would not be sold openly to a stranger.

Chane drew out the pouch that High-Tower had given to Wynn and jostled it once, making it clink.

"Yes, you can," he whispered. "You will sell it to me . . . or I will find it here myself."

This time, her eye did not flicker, though she did not appear intimidated by his close presence and height. Still leaning on her walking rod, she raised her other hand, shaking the paper slip and her head at the same time.

"No need for poor manners," she chided.

Without warning, she snapped her hand with the paper out.

White powder exploded from her ragged sleeve into Chane's face, filling his eyes and nostrils. With startling nimbleness, she rushed backward, watching him expectantly.

Chane wiped a hand down his face, clearing his eyes. He briefly wondered whether the powder was lethal or merely something to incapacitate the unwary. For the first time since he'd entered, the wretched woman appeared uncertain as he took another step.

"Bring me everything on this list."

She studied him closely, perhaps waiting to see whether the powder took some latent effect. When it did not, she slowly smiled, a gruesome expression. She obviously suffered no moral dilemma over what he'd requested.

It would be so much easier to just kill her.

But word of a dead or missing apothecary, her shop ransacked, would spread by morning when the other businesses opened nearby. There was no telling how long before Ore-Locks found them passage south. Wynn might remember one shop with a simple sign that Chane had paused at on their way through the city. She would remember the particular night that he had been out on his own.

The old crone leaned her cane against the wall, now amply nimble without it as she made her way around the shop, assembling his needs upon the front counter. It was a larger burden than Chane had estimated.

"Do not touch corpse-skirt with your bare hands," she warned without real concern in her voice.

"And the grain alcohol . . . for purifying equipment?" he asked.

She glanced at him from the corner of her one good eye and reached under the counter to pull out a brown glass bottle.

"Perhaps instead you wish to remove a rival or two?" she said. "Clear the way to your heart's desire, the one you covet?"

Her ironic needling bothered him. The one he coveted was so much farther beyond his reach than something that simple. His rival, if any, was only himself—what he was. That was something Chane could never clear away between himself and Wynn. Without reply, he counted out coins, stacking them on the counter.

When he finished, the old woman smiled again and shook her head.

Chane counted out more until he'd gone through nearly half the coins in the pouch.

It would have been so much simpler—more satisfying—to just kill this decrepit wretch.

Sau'ilahk watched Chane step out of the shop. The vampire paused to shift his pack to a more settled position, and then he took something shiny from his pouch and extended a finger.

Chane slipped on a brass ring.

Sau'ilahk almost lurched out of the awning's dark shadows as Chane's undead *presence* vanished from his awareness. In a thousand years, he had rarely been surprised like this. Was it as simple as a ring?

For all that he had discerned of Chane's skills, he had never seen this undead display an aptitude for artificing. Chane had not displayed talent enough to make such a device. Why would a vampire need such a thing, when the living would never know what it was until too late?

But Sau'ilahk could see its use. For those brief instances, when he manifested himself fully, that ring could hide him, as well . . . from Chane and the dog.

A shift of air broke his obsessed thoughts. The servitor returned and immediately began reiterating all sounds it had recorded inside the shop.

Sau'ilahk listened, though there was little of use that he heard—except perhaps for one term. The servitor vanished with a puff of a breeze, its task fulfilled, but Sau'ilahk continued to ponder.

What could Chane possibly want with corpse-skirt?

He suddenly knew.

Chane sought a remedy to stave off dormancy.

Sau'ilahk had seen such a work only once, long ago in his time among Beloved's Children. How had Chane uncovered this rare secret? Where had he learned it? Who could have possibly known in order to teach him?

Three times when Sau'ilahk had gone to Beloved beneath the mountain during daylight, one or more of the Children had been present, fully awake! Why was never clear, but it had nagged him so much that he had gone to the

Eaters of Silence. He'd threatened that trio of mad servants to his god until they revealed the truth. One of them had assisted in the making of a concoction containing . . . What had it been called then? Something from Chane's own region? Ah yes, *Dyvjàka Svonchek*—boar's bell.

Perhaps Chane was nothing more than a common vampire, a mere dabbler in conjury with a growing bag of minor tricks. But did this make him more dangerous or more dependent on what could be taken away from him?

Sau'ilahk hung in the dark, uncertain.

Chane headed away from the waterfront district, realizing one more task was necessary before returning to Wynn. The apothecary had asked for more than he expected. Half the money from the guild was gone, and he had to replace it.

At a loud voice, Chane slowed and glanced left.

A sailor tumbled out of a tavern door, as if shoved, and stumbled into the middle of the side street.

"Curse you, Ramón!" the man shouted, slurring the words. "You cheat! You cheated me . . . and I won't forget it!"

A shorter, more sober man stepped in the doorframe, his features shadowed amid the light spilling out behind him from inside the establishment. A raucous mix of voices from inside could be heard as well.

"I never cheat, Dusin," the second man answered. "I don't have to. You're too drunk to play the tiles as well as others . . . let alone against me."

Chane kept a steady, slow pace as he crossed the intersection. He casually turned in against a building to peer back around the corner.

The drunken sailor, Dusin, charged and took a wild swing at the object of his rage. Ramón easily sidestepped, letting the door close, and hooked his assailant's ankle with his foot. Dusin teetered, slamming face-first into the doorframe, and immediately flopped onto the building's landing.

"Sleep it off," Ramón called over his shoulder as he walked away. "Try me later . . . when you've got enough coin."

Dusin rolled on the landing, holding his face and moaning.

Chane caught the thin scent of blood in the side street's shifting air. It was so good, that smell, but he had no interest in the loser—only the winner.

Ramón strolled up the way toward the intersection.

Chane flattened against the wall around the corner, watching him pass. He stayed there, waiting as Ramón headed straight onward. Once Ramón was beyond the intersection, Chane hurried to the far corner and looked around the edge.

He was not watching the man but trying to see beyond, to the closest alley or cutway. He was also overburdened, as he had not cared to leave his packs and possessions back at the hotel. Quietly, he set both packs against the wall of the corner shop and ducked around, eyeing his target's back.

Ramón had his head down as he walked, and Chane heard the click of metal. In this of all places, the haughty winner of some game of chance counted his meager fortune alone in the night. Chane crept along the building fronts, nearer and nearer.

His quarry was only six paces from a narrow access between the buildings on the far side when Chane rushed into the street.

Ramón turned, still walking, at the sound of Chane's boots.

Chane lashed out before the man's eyes had focused upon him. His fist struck his target's cheekbone, changing the man's turn into a spin. Chane heard the chink of a coin pouch striking the cobblestones, and that sound cost him an instant of hesitation.

His quarry flopped down hard onto the street.

Chane grabbed the body by one arm and dragged it into the narrow cutway. Ramón lay against the alley's sidewall—unconscious but breathing—as Chane glanced back.

The pouch lay in the middle of the street.

He crept to the cutway's end, looking both ways along the street. It was empty, and apparently even Dusin had crawled off. Chane rushed out, snatched the pouch, and retreated into hiding.

The pouch was full of copper and silver, but only half the coins were from Malourné. Wynn would notice if he used foreign coins for the balance. There was no option but to put the Malourné coins into Wynn's pouch. He dropped the rest back into the new pouch and tucked it into his belt.

Ramón still lay unconscious, a pulse pounding in his throat. The earlier scent of blood was still thick in Chane's head.

This man was not like that old woman in the shop. How many were found dead in the streets of a place like Drist? No one would miss this man or connect his death to Chane, not even Wynn. All he need do was raggedly, recklessly slash the man's throat once he was finished.

Chane pressed his hands against the alley wall above the man, hanging his head to stare down at the slumped form. He could *smell* life waiting for the taking.

Two bells rang in the night, and a third followed after a brief pause.

Chane lurched back to the alley's far side, regaining himself. It was later than he realized, and Wynn would be waiting and wondering where he was.

"You have more luck," he hissed at the slumped form, "much more than you will ever know."

He ducked into the open street at a run, grabbing his packs along the way. When he reached the lavish brothel masquerading as an inn, he did not even acknowledge the guards or the attendant as he relinquished his weapons. Taking two steps at a time, he brushed past several young women along the staircase.

Opening the door to the room he shared with Wynn, he looked inside.

She was curled upon the bed, sound asleep. Shade lay at the bed's foot, not even raising her head, though her half opened eyes never blinked as their crystal blue irises watched Chane.

Two empty plates lay on the floor beside a porcelain washbasin and pitcher. Wynn must have eaten, tried to wait up for him, and fallen asleep. She was dressed only in her cotton shift and wrapped in her short robe. Such tiny feet she had . . . and slender ankles at the end of sleek, olive-toned calves.

Chane stepped to the bedside and pulled the dangling side of the silk quilt up over Wynn. Shade was still watching, but she did not growl. He and she were both determined to protect Wynn.

They had that much in common, if nothing else.

Chane awoke upon the floor past dusk to the sound of Wynn already digging through their chest and repacking their belongings. Shade sat beside her, alternately watching him but watching Wynn even more, and only occasionally she sniffed at something wrapped in cheap paper.

"Are we leaving?" he asked.

Wynn jumped slightly and spun around to look at him.

"Yes. Ore-Locks went out this morning," she answered. "I think he wants us out of this port as much as you do. He sold the crystal and found passage to Soráno on a larger cargo ship. The captain was eager for a little profit now that his holds are emptied."

Wynn frowned anxiously, looking into the chest. "Chane, do you have our coin pouch? I can't find it."

He sat up quickly, for he had forgotten to put it back.

"Yes, I brought it in case I needed it when ordering your dinner last night."

Wynn sighed in relief. "Oh, good. I thought I'd lost it. You keep it for now. I have some of the money Ore-Locks got in barter." Then she paused, as if something else was wrong. "He was angry when you went out and left me alone."

Wynn patted Shade's head, looking away in a pensive moment.

"What else?" Chane asked.

Again she hesitated. "I think he's getting close to demanding some answers. I wish . . . I wish he wasn't with us. I don't trust him."

That much had been obvious from the beginning. Chane could not help a stab of guilt that she had been dealing with Ore-Locks on his behalf—especially considering the last part of his outing. But he would do anything to protect Wynn, at any cost.

"When do we board?" he asked.

She glanced at him, as if surprised by the change of subject. "As soon as we're packed."

CHAPTER 8

For Chane, this third sea voyage was a torment of trial and error. He disembarked at a few ports along the way, heading off alone just past nightfall, to collect small bottles from various shops.

Several times he sought out livestock, looking for collections of cattle or goats so that one missing animal would not raise immediate notice. He drank only once from the dark, life-giving substance gathered via Welstiel's feeding cup. Overflushed with life, he began using the cup to fill his collection of bottles. These he stored in the bottom of his pack for times ahead when there might be less opportunity to hunt alone.

Soon, however, he came to a decision, one he could not put off. He began excusing himself from Wynn's company on the ship to work alone in his cabin. He did not reappear for several nights. His first attempt at recreating Welstiel's concoction was a painful failure.

He spent three delusional days and nights between dormancy and coherence, where fear of the sun escalated. Either he had not used enough corpse-skirt—boar's bell—or he had incorrectly estimated other ingredients. When the concoction's effect wore off quicker than expected, he increased the amount of corpse-skirt by half.

The result was so much worse.

He squirmed in convulsions on his bunk, the sounds of waves pounding upon the ship's hull nearly deafening him. During the days, he could not stop the sense of burning, as if sunlight crawled and wormed through the hull to seek him out.

Wynn repeatedly knocked every night, calling to him through the blocked door.

But on the fifth night of so much horror, even the beast within him fell silent as if dead and gone, and he knew he was closer to the correct formula. When he came out late on the sixth evening, still not having gone dormant, Wynn was on him in an instant.

"What are you doing in there? Why are you locking yourself in your cabin?"

Her tone was demanding, but her eyes were filled with worry.

"I need privacy," he said, clasping his hands behind his back so she would not see them shake. "Soon we will be among crowds again. I take my solitude while I can."

She looked sad and frustrated at his obvious lie, but she did not press him further. There was no way to tell her, not for the way she always viewed Welstiel's pack of toys. That was always the way she would see it, or anything to do with him. And what would she think of Chane trying to recreate anything of Welstiel's, the one who had plagued her and her companions across half a continent?

Three nights later, Chane tried again, though the last dose had not fully worn off. Worst of all, he was running out of thrice-purified water.

During the journey's earliest part, he had caught clean rain in a bowl held out of a porthole. This was boiled in a glass vessel sterilized with wood alcohol, and he had to hold both glass and burner steady against the ship's rolling. Steam rose into a ceramic, elbow-shaped pipe, cooling and dripping into another sterilized container. The process was repeated twice more with the same water. Less than a fourth of the rain remained in a thrice-purified form.

It had not rained again since before he had prepared the last dose.

Chane had only enough water for one more attempt, with no possibility to continue trial and error once they reached Soráno. When he finished the third batch before dawn, its color, consistency, purity, and opacity perfectly matched the remaining half vial that Welstiel had made.

Side effects seemed inescapable, though Chane was learning to bear the amplified terror, that paranoia of the sun just outside the covered porthole. But as he held up a vial's capful, far less than the dosage he had first thought necessary, he hesitated with the draught a fingernail's breadth from his lips.

How had Welstiel ever borne this . . . drug of the dead . . . without one sign of discomfort?

Chane watched the violet liquid in the cap betray his trembling hand. He threw the fluid into the back of his throat, washing it down with a gulp of water from the ship's casks. As he stared at the three remaining vials made from this batch, he hoped he would not have to discard them like the last two.

He did not—but final success brought him no relief.

When the sun rose outside the ship, Chane was curled in the corner at the bunk's head, shuddering in a wide-awake hell for the third time. On the fourth night, rather than the fifth, he managed to leave his cabin to find Wynn, though she was no less worried.

Time lost meaning as waves rushed past, one after another. One night past dusk, Chane stood on the deck, wind at his back as he heard Wynn's light steps.

"Soráno is close," she said. "We'll make dock before another bell."

He looked down to find her gazing toward the passing coastline, though her living eyes would never make it out in the dark. Wisps of brown hair danced across her olive-toned cheek below her eyes.

They were going back into the world again.

Wynn didn't know what they would find in the port city of Soráno. She'd read a good deal on the Sumans, farther south, and knew something of the Lhoin'na to the east. But as she walked beside Shade through the streets, she couldn't help noticing something startling about these people. That realization came only a breath before Chane's shocked rasp.

"They all look like you."

He wasn't wrong.

Wynn had never been in this part of the world, never been farther south than Witeny. While growing up, she'd seen people in Calm Seatt with her complexion, hair, build—but very few.

Fine boned, though round cheeked, the people of Romagrae Commonwealth weren't as tall as the Numans of Malourné, Faunier or Witeny, nor as dark-skinned as Sumans. Nearly everyone walking past wore strange pantaloons and cotton vestment wraps of white and soft colors. But they all had olive-toned skin with light brown hair and eyes, just like her.

Wynn was still a little daunted when she noticed Chane staring at every passerby. His open fascination began making her uncomfortable.

Soráno's streets were clean, most of them cobbled in sandy-tan stones. Smaller, open-air markets appeared more common than in Numan cities, or at least Calm Seatt. She spotted three in sight along one wide main street. Everyone appeared to be either some kind of merchant or farmer with crops that grew well beyond the seasons up north. The number of items available was overwhelming.

Arrays of olives, dried dates, fish, and herb-laced cooking oils were abundant. Occasionally some scent reminded Wynn of what Domin il'Sänke or his quarters smelled like during his visit—spicy and exotic. She slowed briefly as they passed stacked bolts of fabrics with wild, earthy patterns common in the Suman nations farther south.

Suppertime was long past, so most vendors were closing up for the night. Chane was still staring at the inhabitants as he walked beside Wynn. It was getting annoying.

"So, this is where you are from," he said. "These are your people."

"Don't be ridiculous," Wynn answered. "I'm a citizen of Malourné and a sage of Calm Seatt. That is my home, my people."

"But . . . how did you come to live there?"

Whenever asked, Wynn referred to herself as an orphan, stating that her parents had passed over. In truth, she knew no such thing, but they were certainly dead to her. Chane had never before asked for more than that.

"Domin Tilswith found me in a wooden box at the front gates," she said finally. "There was no note and only a large purse of coins hidden beneath the blanket, enough to meet an infant's needs for quite a while."

Chane stopped walking. "But this must be the land from where you came."

Wynn didn't believe in ancestral memories or cultural links by blood. People were shaped by their experiences and environment—and by themselves. Any half-wit knew this. The vendors and patrons of the market street were just another crowd of strangers encountered along the way.

Chane kept studying her.

"What?" she asked.

He shook his head quickly and looked away, watching the people. They all went about their lives beneath the strange street lanterns of colored glass, which bulged evenly like perfectly made pumpkins of pale yellows, oranges, cyans, and violets.

"And now?" he asked. "Do we find an inn or procure a wagon to leave immediately?"

Shade rumbled softly and closed on Wynn with a sharp huff.

"What's wrong, girl?" Wynn asked.

She was about to reach down and touch Shade's head when the dog darted off straight through a market stall's remains.

"Shade! Come back," Wynn called, and ran after the dog.

She heard Chane shout something from behind her, but she ignored him. She was too busy trying to keep Shade's whipping tail in sight as it bobbed and weaved through the thinning crowd and the remains of closing stalls.

"Shade, this is no time for games! Come back here . . . now!"

Shade slowed briefly, tauntingly, at a corner. Wynn almost caught up, but then Shade bolted off again, vanishing from sight.

"What is the matter with that beast?" Ore-Locks called, his voice farther behind than Chane's.

Wynn ran on. Stalls and shops gave way to larger buildings and quieter streets. Nearly out of breath, she stumbled into an open area. The shore was in plain sight, and she guessed she might be south of the docks on the city's outskirts.

There was Shade, sitting by the side of a dirt road.

Wynn caught up, panting too hard to scold Shade anymore. She grabbed the dog's scruff, more to brace herself than anything else, and bent over with long, heaving breaths.

"Don't . . . do . . . that," she said, gasping. "What is wrong with you?"

Chane joined them, though he wasn't panting. Ore-Locks took a little longer, huffing and puffing on his thick, shorter legs, iron staff in one hand and their chest heaved up on his shoulder.

"Get that animal a leash," he coughed.

Shade wrinkled her jowls and whipped her tongue over her nose at him. But Chane was looking ahead, beyond all of them.

"Can you not smell it?" he said. "Shade did from farther off."

Wynn straightened up, following his gaze.

Back from the shore, wagons of all shapes and sizes were stationed about large timber buildings with corner posts the size of the nearby palm trees. At least six campfires glowed in the dark, illuminating those milling about. Men and women loaded boxes or tended to horses tied off at rails. One elder woman led a team of mules into a nearby stable half as big as the other structures.

Wynn felt soft pressure against her leg, and looked down as Shade pressed closer.

—no . . . Chane . . . wagon . . . stay . . . Wynn . . . people—

Shade's broken words, spoken in Wynn's own remembered voice, made the dog's intentions quite clear.

"A caravan station," Wynn whispered.

Shade huffed once.

Chane glanced down at Shade. He had already decided they should travel inland on their own. With Ore-Locks and Shade, they could camp by day and journey by night, just as he and Wynn had done on their way to Dhredze Seatt.

Wynn stroked Shade's head, thoughtfully watching the caravan camp, and Chane knew she had changed their plans again. Or this time, Shade had.

"Let's see if any are headed inland and barter for passage," Wynn suggested.

"I will do so," Ore-Locks said, about to stride off.

"Wait," Chane cut in, stepping closer to Wynn. "We should just purchase a small wagon and go on our own. We can set our own pace."

She looked up at him, some realization dawning. Clearly she understood what he had not said. There were complications in traveling with others, with no place for him to have secure privacy during the day.

"Are you sure?" she asked. "The caravan might be—"

Shade snarled loudly and clacked her jaws at Chane.

"Stop that," Wynn scolded, and grabbed Shade's muzzle.

Chane watched the two of them lock gazes in sudden stillness. Ore-Locks watched closely as well, though he did not ask what was happening. Suddenly, Wynn flinched.

"What?" Chane asked, wanting to pull her away from Shade.

"She . . . she thinks," Wynn began. "She insists her way is safer."

"No," Chane said, his attention shifting between her and Shade. "We are better off on our own. I can protect us."

Shade snarled so loudly that Chane looked about, fearful the noise might gain unwanted attention. Wynn seemed troubled at being caught between them. With a slight shake of her head, she closed her eyes, still holding the dog. When she opened them again, she glanced uncomfortably at Ore-Locks before she stood up.

"Shade's not going to agree to that," Wynn said to Chane.

"Shade?" Ore-Locks repeated. "Since when is the animal making our decisions?"

Wynn looked only at Chane. "She's worried about the Fay, that if I'm too isolated in the wilderness . . . they will try to kill me again."

"Fay?" Ore-Locks asked. "Kill you? What are you talking about?"

No one answered him.

Chane closed his eyes briefly. Shade was right, and it should have occurred to him before the dog forced the issue. It unsettled him just how much Shade seemed aware of and how far she might go for her own agenda concerning Wynn. But the dog had made her point, and Wynn had clearly agreed. They needed to travel in greater numbers.

Ore-Locks stood waiting for an explanation.

Chane stepped forward, waving the dwarf along. "Come. We will speak more later. For now, it is time to barter."

Following behind, Wynn was still shaken by Shade's vehemence. The dog had once again shown her the same frightening images of the Fay trying to lash her to death with the roots of a downed tree. And Wynn had felt a more personal fear, a determination from Shade that she had not felt before.

Once Shade set her mind on something, shaking it from her jaws could be as difficult as with her father, Chap. In spite of Shade's harsh methods for making her point, Wynn couldn't disagree.

They soon reached the nearest team of mules being disconnected from a weathered wagon twice their height. There were some faded hints of its once garish paint. All around, people loaded or unloaded, hauling bundles in or out of the great timber buildings with shake roofs high above. Some tended animals, while others prepared communal meals over open fires. Low voices filled the air.

While a few bore the same coloring as the people of the city, others were paler or duskier. There were two Sumans, perhaps from desert tribes, though no Numans among the caravans, and certainly no dwarves. It appeared that race or culture did not matter here. Most wore thick leather clothing, tough enough for their long journeys, and either floppy hemp and reed hats or head wraps of rough cloth.

A young woman in leather breeches and a patchwork vestment of earthy colors crouched at a nearby fire. She tended a large iron kettle, boiling some eggs, and she was about to drop in tea leaves as well, making a meal and drink all at once.

"May I speak with a team leader?" Wynn asked, hoping someone here understood Numanese.

The girl rose, her black coiled braids not even shifting. She pointed at a large man in a suede coat crouched before a wagon's wheel, which he inspected with great attention.

"A'drinô," she said. "Chieftain A'drinô handles all trade for our clan."

"Thank you," Wynn replied, heading off, though Ore-Locks was already on the move.

She hoped the dwarf would follow her lead before trying to strike any deal. She untied her cloak to expose her gray sage's short robe.

"Master A'drinô?" she asked.

He turned from the wagon wheel and stood up, hands on his hips, as if the interruption was unwelcome. Then he saw her companions and grew puzzled. He was as tall as Chane and clean-shaven, with a long, red-gold braid down his back, tied in place with a fraying golden ribbon.

Wynn offered him a polite nod. "I am Journeyor Hygeorht of the Calm Seatt branch of the Guild of Sagecraft."

"Calm Seatt?" he repeated, his accent marked with elongated vowels. "You're a long way from home."

"Yes. I'm delivering an official communication to the premin of the Lhoin'na guild branch. Are any caravans headed that way?"

"What do you offer for passage?" he asked bluntly.

"Service as guards," Ore-Locks cut in, gesturing to himself, Chane, and even Shade.

He already sounded too assertive—which was the way of dwarven barter. But Wynn hoped he wouldn't get any worse.

"We have guards," A'drinô returned, but he did eye Ore-Locks and then Chane for a moment.

"Not like us," Ore-Locks said flatly. "Not even close."

His manner had the wrong effect. Wynn could almost see the chieftain's expression closing up. Ore-Locks was normally quite effective at bartering. A'drinô clearly thought the only gain here was for the dwarf, and the caravan chieftain's brow wrinkled.

Wynn was about to jump in when Chane said quietly, "We will take the night watch. Your own guards will be rested for daylight journeying."

A'drinô eyed him. "You've done night patrol? You know what is required?"

"Yes, as has the . . . wolf. She is well trained."

Wynn clamped her hand over Shade's nose, in case Shade understood what he'd said.

A'drinô finally nodded. "Well enough. My men can use more sleep, but you'll have to supply your own transportation and food. We've no room, and we leave at dawn."

Chane watched Wynn's expression change from relief to alarm as the caravan chieftain walked away. They had no wagon as yet, and the city would be closed up for the night.

"I will find a wagon and horses," he assured her, glancing back the way they had come. "You and Ore-Locks try to find more food at the nearest market— anything still available."

"Shouldn't I handle the barter?" Ore-Locks added, and crossed his arms, still gripping his staff in one hand, as if put out by his near failure.

Normally he would be correct, but Chane was not going to settle for just any wagon. They still had a potentially long journey ahead, should Wynn find clues among the Lhoin'na to the remains of the long-forgotten seatt. They could not afford to *buy* the type of team and wagon necessary.

"Fresh food is just as important," he told Ore-Locks. "Help Wynn barter for proper stores."

If this flattery affected Ore-Locks, he did not show it.

"Come on," Wynn said. "We have only tonight. We'll meet back here."

With one last glance at Chane, Ore-Locks followed Wynn and Shade toward town.

Chane waited until they were out of sight and then headed shoreward. A caravan station on the outskirts would not be the only place to land cargo in a port. He worked his way along the waterfront's southern end, watching for any sign of a major stable nearer the warehouses. It did not take long.

When he spotted a likely place up an inland side road, he looked all ways for anyone in the streets. Testing the wide stable doors, he found they would not budge. The fact that they were barred from the inside actually brought him some relief. This also meant there had to be another exit—or entrance. The stable master had closed up for the night and would need another way out.

The closest people were more than two blocks away, so he slipped around the building's side, down the cutway, reaching an alcove off the rear alley. The stable's rear door was padlocked from the outside. It took little effort, and a little noise, to dislodge the locking plate from the doorjamb.

Soft knickers greeted him inside, along with the scents of leather, hay, and dung in dusty-smelling air. Pitchforks and hay bundles lined the back wall to the open rafters, but a black gelding and a bay mare stood in the nearest stalls. Both were the youngest and healthiest among six others. He searched until he found harnesses pegged on the front wall and pulled down the newest-looking pair. As to a wagon, he had no such choice.

The only one inside was a large, two-wheeled cart, but it was not large enough. As the only vehicle, it made little sense for a place so near the docks, and there were six horses and multiple harnesses.

Chane stepped back outside and circled the stable all the way to the alley at the alcove's back. Just around the left side, he found a large wagon in the alley and hurried over to inspect it.

The seat was long and thick. The entire bed was walled with planks that had outer brackets for lashing a tarp over cargo. Folded canvas was stacked in the back. It was perfect, except for two things.

The front left wheel was chained down to an iron ring embedded in the alley's cobble. Chane decided to wait on breaking that until he was fully ready to leave. The other problem became evident as he walked back to the stable's rear door.

To harness the horses, he would have to lead them out to the wagon. He had expected to be able to do so inside, and then open the main front doors and drive off. Now he would have to harness two horses, one by one, in the open. If he was seen at this time of night, someone might question what he was doing.

He had no further options except to search elsewhere, hoping for something more accessible, but that seemed unlikely. Besides, once he was off, even if someone found the wagon and horses missing at dawn, they would not likely trace it to a caravan station with wagons and teams of its own. He simply needed to hurry and finish without being seen.

Chane piled the harnesses on the wagon seat and returned to lead the black gelding out. It followed him without protest, and he harnessed the animal quietly. When he hurried back into the stable for the bay mare, she nickered softly as he took her halter.

"Shhhh," he murmured, stroking her velvet nose.

She followed him out, and he backed her into position beside the gelding. As he buckled down the last of her harness, the barest creak carried through the quiet alley.

"Is someone there?" a masculine voice called.

Chane slipped around the wagon and flattened against the building's backside.

Footsteps followed, and a stocky man with a dark beard and tied-back hair, both traced with gray, came around the alcove's corner. He stopped, spotting Chane immediately. At first, he appeared more surprised than concerned. Perhaps theft was not common here.

"What are you doing?" he asked, and when Chane did not answer, his expression clouded. "Don't you move!"

In another breath, the stable keeper would shout for the authorities.

Chane bolted along the building's side, but before he reached the corner, the man ducked back out of sight. Chane rounded into the alcove, and the tines of a pitchfork drove for his face. He twisted to the side, though an outside tine slid along his temple.

A slight sting rose as the skin beneath his hair split. He grabbed the fork's base with his left hand, and another tine's tip scraped along his wrist. When he struck out, his right fist caught the stable keeper on the cheekbone. The heavy man toppled backward through the open rear door as Chane jerked the pitchfork away.

And the beast inside of him struggled to awaken.

Chane stood staring as the man stirred limply just inside the doorway. All he wanted was another kill, another true moment as it should be. Perhaps it would be his last chance. No one would know, even Wynn, except . . .

Even the beast seemed only dully piqued, as if groggy from dormancy. In its strange complacency, reason plagued Chane.

Once he returned to the caravan station, they would not leave straight off. A stolen wagon was one thing; a dead man was something else. It might bring a more thorough search for a perpetrator.

The beast inside of him suddenly became more aware, and wailed in frustration.

Chane bit down, but there was nothing between his teeth. He could haul the body away in the wagon, dump it along the shore where it would take longer to discover, and return safely to Wynn.

He still hesitated, for Wynn had forbidden him to kill any sentient being.

No . . . she had forbidden him to kill in order to feed.

Chane had struggled and fought with himself to follow her wishes. Even if he left the stable keeper alive but unconscious, the moment the man woke, he would raise the alarm.

The beast within him wobbled as it rose. Shaking off some lethargy, it lunged to the limits of its chains.

Chane reached down and grabbed the man's head in both hands. With one quick wrench, he broke the stable master's neck. The man's body tensed once all over and went slack upon the stable's straw.

The beast shrieked. Chane winced, as if hearing—feeling—its rage at being denied.

He hauled himself up the doorframe and dragged the body out to toss it in the wagon's back. He jerked a tarp across, took one last look around the stable, and grabbed a sack of oats, a bucket, and a pile of blankets.

Every motion was mechanical, but inside, Chane ached from what he had not done more than for what he had done. One brief chance at release, for his own need, and he had not taken it.

Finally, he picked up a heavy shovel leaning against one wall and slammed the sharp end against the chain holding the front wheel. It broke easily, but so did the shovel. He tossed the shovel in the wagon and climbed aboard, grabbing and flicking the reins.

Driving the wagon south out of town, he went even farther than where he judged the caravan station lay. He dumped the body over the rock lip above the shore, not bothering to watch it splash into the water, and tossed the broken shovel after it. When he turned inland over the rough ground, finding the road back toward the city, it was not long before he spotted the campfires in the night.

Chane had acquired what they needed. At least in part, he had done so as Wynn required.

Wynn was quite satisfied as she led the way back carrying three heavy skins of fresh water. Ore-Locks hauled a burlap sack nearly filled with potatoes, carrots, and some strange type of apple she'd never seen before. And, of course, there was more smoked fish.

They'd also found speckled eggs, a clay jar of olives in their own oil, and a little goat cheese sealed in wax. If Chane was successful, they could also scavenge seaside driftwood to bring, should they have trouble with dry firewood along the way.

When they reached the caravan camp, fewer people were up and about. Some had settled into bedrolls around the embers of dying fires. Wynn saw no sign of Chane anywhere.

What would they do if he couldn't acquire transportation that could be covered during the day?

"Here he comes," Ore-Locks said. "But why is he . . . ?"

Ore-Locks didn't finish as Wynn followed his gaze.

Chane drove a wagon along the dirt road. He wasn't coming from the city, but rather from the south. He pulled up, tied off the reins, and dropped to the ground. Two fine young horses in new harnesses were hooked to the large wagon with high sides and a thick rear gate. This was more than what Wynn expected, and her pleasant surprise turned to discomfort.

"How much did you have to pay?" she asked quietly.

"Nothing in coin," he answered. "I traded for it."

"Traded?" she echoed. "Traded what?"

Her discomfort grew when he didn't answer straight off.

"Some of Welstiel's rods," he said. "The metal alone is worth a good deal."

Wynn had never liked that Chane kept all of Welstiel's arcane possessions. Trading away any of them was fine with her, especially if someone was going to melt them down for their metal.

She smiled, patting the neck of a pretty bay mare. "Well done. You're getting as good at barter as Ore-Locks."

Then she noticed a dark line running out of his sleeve and down to the palm of his hand.

"Are you hurt?"

"It is nothing," he said, turning away. "We should get the wagon ready."

Just before dawn, Chane lay curled in the wagon's covered bed, listening to the bustle of team masters preparing the caravan to leave. Ore-Locks, Wynn, and even Shade were up on the front bench, ready to head out.

No one had come looking for the wagon or horses.

Chane still wore his heavy cloak and had put on the gloves and scarf, as well. The mask and glasses lay next to his head, along with both of his swords. Should the caravan be attacked during daylight, he would know it, hear it, and be ready.

He pulled the narrow, leather-bound box from Welstiel's pack and opened it, taking out a glass vial containing the violet concoction.

"We're off," Wynn said, though not to him.

Ore-Locks grunted acknowledgment as the wagon lurched forward.

Chane downed part of the vial's contents and then returned it to the padded box. He could already sense the burning rays of the sun just beyond the canvas above him.

It would be a long day.

CHAPTER 9

The monotonous creak of wagon wheels mixed with clopping hoofs still echoed in Wynn's head when they set up camp each night. One day blurred into the next until the caravan stopped for two days to repair a wagon wheel, and she realized that more than half a moon had passed.

The line of wagons traversed an expansive valley between high ridges, rocking along on a northeasterly inland path. Grass-covered stone hills flowed down into intermittent woods of wild green brush, and the trees marked the landscape difference most of all. There were fewer firs and pines, as in the Numan lands, and far more massive, leafy, deciduous growths. The hardened dirt road was so old that it often exposed packed stones uncovered by years of use and rainfall.

Like the seasons' rhythms, Wynn's daily life changed from her time aboard the ships. She drove the wagon all day while Chane and Ore-Locks slept in the back, under cover, and on opposite sides of the wagon. Then they woke to stand guard all night.

Shade napped only during the day, perched upon the wagon's bench with Wynn, but she never seemed to fully sleep. Often, she would suddenly lift her head, going rigid all over as she stared into the wild. It happened most when they passed through densely wooded regions. Her vigilance began making Wynn more nervous in having left civilization. And too often, Wynn began peering into the trees as well, waiting to hear a voice or voices of the Fay rise in her thoughts.

But the trees were silent, and the wagon rolled on. Soon the isolated woods thickened into even denser forests between the open fields and hills.

One day, as dusk approached, Chane and Ore-Locks were asleep in the back when Wynn spotted a side road beyond the wagon line's head. Another appeared shortly after on the other side. They'd come to a main fork.

The chieftain, A'drinô, shouted from ahead for a halt. He came striding back to Wynn's wagon, his heavy braid swinging as he walked, and he pointed to the left, northeasterly path.

"That leads to Lhoin'na lands and a'Ghràihlôn'na," he said. "Keep to the road, and you'll come to an open plain. Their forest proper is beyond it, and the capital not much farther."

A'drinô gestured toward the southeast fork on the right.

"We've a few stops along the valley's southern foothills." He glanced at Shade, then back at Wynn, and a wry smile spread across his mouth. "Tell your pale friend and the dwarf they might *not* be missed. Some of my men have grown lazy, sleeping through the nights."

"Thank you for everything," Wynn replied, though she was puzzled. Apparently the caravan wasn't bound for Lhoin'na lands; perhaps they had no cargo to trade there.

A'drinô nodded, still smiling, and turned away. But he paused, glancing northward with a frown.

"Lhoin'na patrollers are . . . strict about anyone crossing the plain."

"What do you mean?"

He shrugged. "Never understood it. They allow no blood spilled there, neither for hunting nor injury. Keep any weapons sheathed or stored, and take it slow, at a comfortable pace."

His words tickled something at the back of Wynn's mind—something about an open field on the way to an elven forest. She couldn't remember what it was, let alone where she'd heard . . . whatever she couldn't remember.

"You don't know why?" she asked.

"For any people, the reasons for some old ways can be long forgotten. All that's left is a tradition. But polite as the elves are in their way, they take this one seriously."

Wynn nodded, anxious without knowing why. A'drinô returned a curt bow and walked away. When the caravan rolled on and Wynn reached the fork, she guided the wagon out of the line and onto the side road.

Shade immediately rose on the bench, ears stiff as she watched the caravan leave them behind. She turned about, pressing her shoulder against Wynn and exhaling two sharp huffs.

—*stay . . . Wynn . . . people*—

With those words came another flash of the night the Fay had assaulted Wynn.

"This is the only way," she answered, but even she watched the trees closely.

The farther they went, the more Shade fidgeted, trying to watch everywhere at once. But in less time than expected, a break in the forest appeared ahead. Wynn pulled the horses to a halt where the trees stopped.

An open plain of tall grass gently undulated with tans and traces of yellow-green. Wynn thought she spotted hints of white wildflowers, but they were too hidden to see clearly. Farther out, the edge of a vast forest, more overwhelming than the one she left, stretched both ways beyond sight.

At first, the trees didn't seem too far away, but then Wynn realized why. Where the road entered between them, it looked like no more than a thread in width. The tallest of those trees were immense, ancient sentinels.

Wynn had never been here before, but the sight was eerily familiar.

Shade huffed again, looking off to the left as she shoved in closer against Wynn. A dull, distant pounding grew in volume.

Three riders came across the grassy plain at a full gallop. The rear pair held their reins one-handed, and gripped long, wooden poles in the other. The leader appeared to hold only a bow in his free grip. But as they raced nearer, the first thing Wynn noticed about the riders themselves was their hair and eyes.

Oversized and teardrop-shaped, their amber irises glowed in the falling sun's light. All three had their wheat- or sand-colored hair pulled up and back in high tails held by single rings, and the narrow tips of their tall ears were plain to see. They were garbed in tawny leather vestments with swirling steel garnishes that matched sparkling spaulders on their shoulders. Running diagonal over their chests, each bore a sash the color of pale gold. As they drew closer, slightly curved sword hilts became visible, protruding over their right shoulders.

Wynn grew relieved. These had to be the border guard that A'drinô had mentioned. At least as a sage, she might ask for escort.

The leader reined in his tall russet mare directly in front of the wagon's horses.

"*Veasg'âr-äilleach*," Wynn said, greeting him.

His stern expression relaxed as he quizzically raised a thin, slanted eyebrow. Wynn noticed a silver ash-leaf brooch on his sash, though the other two didn't wear one. He nodded and his thin lips parted, but a reply never came.

His gaze fixed on Shade, and he sucked in a hissing breath. Horror flattened his features just before they wrinkled in anger.

"*Valhachkasej'ä!*" he spat at her.

Wynn tensed at the foul utterance Leesil had often used. She'd even picked up his bad habit, but she'd never heard it aimed at her. Before she could speak, the leader reached over his left shoulder and pinched the notched end of an arrow in his quiver.

"Pull the wagon back, woman!" he commanded in Elvish.

"What? I don't—" Wynn started.

"Now . . . *despoiler!*"

"Blessed Bäynæ, what is the problem?" Ore-Locks growled from the wagon's back.

Wynn heard further rustling behind her but didn't take her eyes off the patrol's leader. Her wagon wasn't even onto the plain yet, and he wanted her to retreat?

"I don't understand," she finished in Elvish. "Why can't—"

The leader's hand flashed down across his face.

Wynn heard a crack close beside her, and Shade erupted into loud snarls. An arrow shaft vibrated between them, its head buried in the wood near her thigh.

"Force her down!" the leader shouted.

The other patrollers lowered blunt lances, and Wynn's breath caught as they kicked their mounts into a lunge. One lance slipped between her and Shade, separating them before she could move. Shade snapped it in her jaws as the rider tried to sweep it toward Wynn.

Wynn exhaled, "Oh, seven hells!"

This wasn't about her; it was about Shade.

"I can explain," she called, forgetfully slipping into Numanese. "Just let me—"

The other lance struck her shoulder.

Wynn tumbled off the wagon's side, slamming down beside it. She'd barely rolled over when she heard the canvas snap. Over the thud of two feet, she heard a rasping hiss.

Chane stood over her, gloved and cloaked, his face obscured by the leather mask and darkened glasses. She could only imagine what he looked like to the elven patrollers.

"No," Wynn groaned, "ah no!"

Chane heard Wynn speaking with someone but could not understand either of them. It was likely Elvish, as he had heard Wynn speak in the strange, lyrical lilt a few times. Though not dormant, he was groggy and barely aware. He had not taken a dose of the potion for several nights, and the last one was beginning to wear off.

His awareness increased when Ore-Locks had grumbled, "Blessed Bäynæ, what is the problem?"

Wynn shouted something more, and then a crack of wood cut her off.

Chane heard—felt—it through the wagon's frame. Something had struck the bench above his head. When Shade snarled, Chane frantically groped for his mask and glasses.

"*A'Jeann a-shéos è!*" shouted an angry, lilting voice.

"Oh, seven hells!" Wynn said breathily.

More shouts and scuffling hooves built as Chane ripped away the canvas. He vaulted the wagon's side, nearly landing atop Wynn. She was curled on the ground, holding her shoulder, and he jerked out both swords.

Three elven riders blocked the wagon's path. An arrow was stuck in the wagon's bench. Shade snarled and snapped at the trio.

This was all Chane needed to know.

"No . . . ah no!" Wynn whispered.

He did not look down, and rasped out one word: "Shade!"

Chane vaulted over Wynn as Shade leaped, her paws touching twice along a thick, protruding lance.

The instant Chane jumped over Wynn, she scrambled up the wagon's side, but Shade had already charged, as well. The dog bounded off the lance and rammed headlong into the patrol's leader. Both tumbled off the flanks of the panicked, rearing horse. Then Ore-Locks rolled out of the wagon's back, bleary-eyed.

"All of you! Stop this!" Wynn shouted. "*Èan bârtva'na!*"

The first lunging rider swept his lance across the bench and at her head.

Wynn ducked, and then someone grabbed the back of her cloak. She spun as she was slung around and barely caught herself on the wagon's rear wheel.

"Get back, and stay there!" Ore-Locks ordered.

A rider wheeled his mount around the wagon.

"Behind you!" Wynn shouted.

Ore-Locks twisted back as the lance's blunt tip came straight at his head. He slapped it aside, but the rider's horse barreled straight into him. Wynn's mouth gaped, and she lurched off the wagon's wheel, reflexively trying to reach for him. But Ore-Locks didn't go down.

The hulkish dwarf's heavy boots skidded across the packed earth and stones under the horse's momentum. Then they caught, and he rooted.

Ore-Locks's thick arms wrapped around the horse's shoulders, and he grabbed the saddle's girth on both sides. The rider dropped his lance and reached over his shoulder for his sword's hilt. Before Wynn shouted another warning, Ore-Locks heaved.

The rider went slack-mouthed as his mount's front hooves left the ground.

Ore-Locks let out a guttural growl through clenched teeth. He wrenched sideways on the saddle's girth. Rider and horse began to topple, and then both tumbled off the road in a crackle of branches and brush.

"Stay down, you *yiannû-billê!*" Ore-Locks shouted as his opponent thrashed in the tangle.

A clang of steel jerked Wynn's attention ahead. The third rider had dismounted, sword in hand, and was trying to drive Chane out of the plain's grass and toward the wagon. He was holding Chane at bay, at least, and Shade . . .

Wynn ran past Ore-Locks before he could grab her.

Shade had forced the patrol leader along the road into the plain. The man held out his sword, still sheathed, fending her off. Wynn saw only one way to end this quickly.

"Chane, no blood!" she shouted.

He ignored her and sidestepped, trying to get around to his opponent. The elven patroller shifted the other way, never taking his eyes off Chane, but he stalled at the sight of Wynn and exposed his side. It was a terrible mistake, and the only thing Wynn could hope for in a panicked moment.

Wynn ran headlong, ducking at the last instant as the patroller raised his sword.

"Wynn!" Chane rasped.

Wynn's small shoulder rammed into the elf's side. She tumbled more than rolled through the tall grass, and she kept tumbling blindly to get out of reach. When she regained her feet, her shoulder ached even more, and she wavered a little.

The elf rose out of the grass with his long, delicately curved sword in hand.

"Back off, Chane," Wynn called, and turned to face his opponent. "No blood! *Na-fuil!*"

The elf hesitated. Before he changed his mind, she spun and ran for Shade.

The leader stood three paces off, shifting at each of Shade's snapping lunges as she tried to find an opening. He gave her none and held his ground, though his sword was now out of its sheath.

Apparently, any tradition against spilling blood went only so far here when they thought a human had taken a majay-hì. But the leader held his blade at guard rather than readied to strike.

The patrollers appeared to think Wynn had stolen a sacred majay-hì from their forest. But if they'd stopped to think about the obvious, she might have had a moment to explain. She was entering, rather than leaving, their lands.

"Shade, stop it!" Wynn shouted, resisting the urge to grab the dog, and she looked to the leader. "I'm no despoiler—*na-re-upâr*! I didn't steal the majay-hì. She came for me . . . *â a'cheâva riam*—"

"I understand you, woman," the leader returned in clear Numanese.

Shade broke off her attack, circling back and rounding closely against Wynn's legs. The leader stared at her for a few seconds, and then raised his voice.

"*Na-bârt—a'greim äiche túâg!*"

Wynn glanced back as he ordered his men to hold their positions.

There was Chane right behind her, his back to hers. He had his shorter blade in his left hand, point down, with the dwarven sword at the ready in the other. His opponent stood beyond sword's reach, looking to his superior.

Back near the wagon, Ore-Locks stood in the brush, staring down, with one large fist clenched. Wynn could only assume he had the third patroller pinned under his foot.

This was a mess, and one she should've foreseen. She'd seen how the an'Cróan had first reacted to Chap traveling among humans. Here, by what little she knew, majay-hì didn't mingle among the Lhoin'na as they did among the an'Cróan, let alone outside their lands.

Wynn reached back to touch Chane's elbow. "It's all right. I can . . ."

Her voice failed when she felt the shudder in his arm, and he did not stop shaking at her touch.

"Chane?"

She glanced back again, and then lifted her gaze briefly.

In the west behind her, the sun had barely dropped into the treetops beyond the wagon. Chane's outer protection obviously wasn't enough for him to last much longer.

Wynn turned and grabbed his arm.

"Get in the wagon, quick," she whispered in Belaskian, so no one else would understand. "I can handle this, and—"

"No!" he rasped, though it came out grating under strain.

"Don't be an idiot." She jerked on his arm, though she couldn't pull it down. "Shade and Ore-Locks are here. Just do it, before this gets any worse and someone gets suspicious."

He stood there until she pulled on his arm again.

Chane half turned, lowering his head, but all Wynn saw was a featureless leather mask and dark, round lenses. He finally pulled away, slowly and widely sidestepping around his opponent.

Wynn turned back to the leader, not knowing how to explain Chane's disturbing appearance, so she didn't try.

"Look at me," she said, brushing a hand down her short robe. "I am a *sage*, come from Calm Seatt to deliver an official communication from my Premin Council to that of your branch. So either *please* escort me to the city . . . or get out of my way."

Shade stepped forward, growling at the patrol leader. He didn't even flinch, but as he looked at her, his brow wrinkled in confusion. A majay-hì, far from where it should be, was ready to turn on him for the sake of a human.

This was the last way Wynn could've ever wished to enter Lhoin'na lands for the first time.

*   *   *

Chane lay alone beneath the canvas in the wagon's back, listening. He heard the clop of horses to the left and the right, and he knew the patrol was still present as the wagon rolled along. But he could also hear his companions.

Ore-Locks whispered, "Why did they bother inspecting our horses for wounds before letting us onto the plain?"

"I don't know," Wynn answered.

Neither did Chane. He still puzzled over Wynn's instruction that no blood be spilled in this place.

"Wait!" Wynn whispered excitedly. "Stop the wagon."

The wagon lurched to a halt.

"What's wrong?" Ore-Locks asked.

"Look at all of this," Wynn breathed.

Chane frowned. This was no time for her to be taking in the view.

"Just flowers," Ore-Locks scoffed. "Strange enough, but nothing to—"

"Not just wildflowers," Wynn answered. "They're *anasgiah*, a sacred—"

"What did you say?" interrupted a third voice.

The strange accent and blunt tone marked it as the patrol leader, the one who had finally introduced himself as Althahk.

"The flowers," Wynn answered. "Why do you have *anasgiah* planted all over here?"

A long pause followed.

"You mean *anamgiah?*" he asked. "It is a healing and cleansing herb that grows wild, suitable to this plain's tranquillity."

Chane was already trying to get his mask and glasses back on. Premin Hawes had corrected him the same way when shown translated notes from the *Seven Leaves of Life*. If he had heard right, one of those seven was here, all around him.

"Yes, um, that's what I meant," Wynn answered.

Chane heard Ore-Locks cluck and then flick the reins. As the wagon lurched, Chane peeked out from beneath the canvas's edge.

The sun had not fully set, and he ground his teeth as the glasses darkened. He waited for them to adjust, hoping he would not miss what Wynn had seen.

As the wagon moved onward, a small bit of white appeared in the tall grass beyond the road's edge.

Chane's gaze locked as it slipped slowly by.

The dome of tiny, pearl-colored flowers was almost phosphorescent in the fading light. Their leaflike blossoms grew in clusters that shimmered like white velvet. The stems appeared so dark green, they were nearly black.

All Chane wanted was to climb out and snatch them up. Then they were gone. As the wagon rocked down the road, he searched the grass, though his view was far too limited. He caught only two more glimpses of white too far out in the deep grass to see clearly.

"Hand me the reins," Wynn said.

"Why?" Ore-Locks returned.

"We'll be entering the forest shortly, and I should drive."

This was not an adequate answer to Ore-Locks's question, but it said much to Chane. Wynn had told him of her experiences within the Elven Territories of the an'Cróan, and of what Chap had learned concerning the Ancient Enemy's hordes of long ago.

No undead could enter an elven forest. Or, specifically, by Wynn's reasoning, no forest protected by an ancient tree called Sanctuary, or its like offspring on Chane's own continent.

The forest itself would sense any undead and confuse it with madness and fright. Then the majay-hì would come to pull it down and slaughter it. In Chane's time with Welstiel, that cold madman had also mentioned this.

As an undead, how could Welstiel have known and survived to speak of it?

Chane stroked his thumb over the ring of nothing, fitted snuggly on his left third finger. Perhaps the forest had not known Welstiel was there. Chane braced himself, waiting.

He did not know what to expect, and Wynn had also worried about this moment. He lay there so long in hiding, wondering how close they were. He began feeling exhausted by tension, and at last his grogginess began to wane.

Had the sun finally set?

"Chane, you can come out," Wynn said softly. "We're there!"

Chane flipped the canvas aside and heard Shade, who was also in back, growl as its corner flopped over her rump. Darkness filled his view, and he pulled off the glasses and mask, immediately pivoting onto one knee. They were surrounded by the trees.

Wynn glanced over her shoulder, first at him and then beyond. He followed her gaze to the two elven patrollers still behind the wagon. They both took note of his sudden appearance and frowned slightly in silence.

Likely Althahk was out in front. This was not good. If Chane was wrong about the ring, the last thing Wynn needed was to be caught bringing an undead into their land.

Chane began to feel . . . something.

A nervous twitch squirmed through his body. Perhaps it was only some effect of the violet concoction amplified by his anxiety. He peered into the trees all around. They were everywhere. One passed by right next to the wagon, and he leaned away on instinct.

The trunk was as large as a small fortification tower, and at least so wide that the wagon did not reach its far side before the trailing riders drew parallel with it.

A tingling, annoying itch began swarming erratically over Chane's skin. There was no breeze in the forest, but the sensation was like streams of dust blown over his exposed face and hands.

The prickling grew.

It brought a memory of toying with an anthill as a child. Chane remembered speck-sized insects crawling over his shirtsleeve, looking for a way to get in . . . to find out what he was. He pivoted slowly, beginning to shake, until he faced Shade sitting on the wagon's far side.

She watched him silently, her large, crystalline irises too bright in the dark.

Chane turned away. He knew the forest's wards, or whatever guarded it, were no superstition. But even that told him more as his thumb rubbed nervously over the ring he wore.

His thoughts were still sound and clear beneath the fear.

"Are you all right?" Wynn whispered.

"Yes . . . I am fine."

Wynn pulled out a cold lamp crystal, rubbing it brusquely on her thigh until it brightened, and handed it off to Ore-Locks.

She'd been so eager to get here that she'd been careless and forgotten good sense. She hadn't thought of what Shade's presence might evoke from the Lhoin'na, let alone about running into any of them before reaching her destination. Now traveling with this armed escort, she couldn't shake all she'd learned in her time among the an'Cróan concerning the undead and their forest.

To complicate things, she'd just rolled Chane right into such a place.

There'd been no chance to let him test it cautiously. They'd both known this was coming, but reality was a far cry from anticipation. Bringing him here had been a blind gamble, for her as well as him, all the while hoping that tiny ring would protect him.

He seemed all right, though his eyes were wide and watchful. Then she noticed his left hand trembled as he fidgeted with the ring.

Ore-Locks remained silent, studying their surroundings, and Wynn turned her attention ahead.

Above them, the lowest branches of the largest trees were thicker than her body. Higher still, they had long since twisted and intertwined. Not a single night star showed through the canopy. It was all too quiet.

"What is that up ahead?"

Wynn flinched at Chane's rasp right behind her head. At first, she couldn't see anything beyond Althahk and his horse. A slight flicker appeared, followed by more. As they drew closer, those glimmers took shape as distinct lights. Some of them were too high above the ground.

"Dwellings . . . in the trees," Chane whispered.

Wynn couldn't quite make out what he saw. His vision at night was far better than hers. Shade huffed once, and Wynn twisted her head. The dog stared back and huffed once more—one single utterance, too startlingly familiar.

Wynn remembered Chap's system used with Leesil and Magiere. He'd used one bark for "yes," two for "no," and three for "unknown" or "uncertain." Had Shade seen this in some memory of Wynn's, and then added it to her own reluctant vocabulary?

Shade huffed once more.

Wynn frowned, turning forward again. Perhaps it was a good thing, but right now it was just unsettling.

"Not only domiciles," Chane added, and pointed upward over Wynn's shoulder. "That is a shop of some kind."

There was no sign of a city or any such large settlement ahead, but they must have reached its outskirts. Even Ore-Locks craned his head back in astonishment.

Wynn's eyes adjusted to those glowing points of light spread upward into the great trees' heights. The thickest branches were the size of normal tree trunks. A complex system of walkways stretched between various levels.

People went about their ways in early nightfall. Tall elves stood on or walked the paths, stairs, and landings, circumventing structures mounted around the trunks or perched out on the more massive branches. Of those few that Wynn could make out passing near glimmering lanterns of glass and pale metals, everyone moved without a care for the heights.

"Lunacy," Ore-Locks said. "One's feet should remain upon the solid earth, as intended."

Wynn wrinkled her small nose, remembering what he'd called the patroller during the confrontation.

"Don't you ever again call one of them *yiannû-billê*—'bush baby' again," she told him softly.

"Heat of the moment," he replied under his breath.

Dwarves were a curious and accepting people. Wynn had never expected to travel with one who might be a bigot. It was one more thing that separated him from his kind—and all the more offensive considering his disguise. He was still attired like a shirvêsh of Feather-Tongue, who was a wise and worldly traveler spoken of in dwarven sacred myths and legends.

Chane leaned past Wynn's side. She watched his gaze roam the heights in fascination. While he sometimes expressed arrogant attitudes and he could be coldly judgmental, new experiences always riveted him. If Chane hadn't been forced into death and beyond it, he would've become a true scholar, no doubt.

Homes and small-to-medium structures blended into the leafy upper reaches, making it difficult to distinguish where one ended and another began. All were made of plank wood, though Wynn thought some roofs might be covered in cultivated moss. The branches of these huge spruces and oaks and gargantuan maples dwarfed the trees she'd seen along the journey.

One wavering light, low to the ground, caught Wynn's eye. Not all of the settlement was built above.

Those lower structures were all dark but for a few lanterns somehow suspended along the paths between them. Perhaps these were for the more trade- and craft-related pursuits. How had all this come to be? Why did Lhoin'na choose these strange, high settlements, as opposed to the an'Cróans' wilder enclaves upon the earth and their homes *inside* of living trees?

Shade whined, nosing into Wynn's side. Wynn reached back, stroking the dog's cheek.

Sudden memories of the an'Cróans' wild Elven Territories rose in Wynn's head—but they were not her own memories. The Lhoin'na forest must seem dif- ferent to Shade, and Wynn hoped it didn't make the young majay-hì too homesick.

"Althahk . . . veasg'âr-äilleach!"

The patrol leader slowed his horse at the call of his name. Wynn drew in the reins as she searched the heights for the greeting's source. A tall elf stood at a walkway railing ornamented with swirls and ovals of trained, leafy vines. It was hard to make him out, but a nearby lantern sent white and silver shimmers through his long, unbound hair.

"And fair evening to you, Counselor," Althahk returned in their tongue.

"What brings you in so late, Commander?" the counselor asked. "And why do the *Shé'ith* escort visitors to . . ."

Wynn was too busy with that one unfathomable word to wonder about the long pause. That term wasn't in the Elvish she knew or the older dialect of the an'Cróan. The root *shéth* meant "quietude" or "tranquillity," sometimes "serenity." Perhaps what she'd heard was something older still.

"The old one is looking at us," Chane whispered from behind.

"It is odd, indeed," Althahk answered back, and turned a stern eye on Wynn.

No, not at her, but at Shade.

"I will speak with you tomorrow," the elder answered back.

By the time Wynn looked up, he was gone. Althahk clicked his tongue, and his horse moved on. Flicking the reins, Wynn guided the wagon onward.

In breaks between settlements, the forest's guardian trees overwhelmed any hint of civilization. Glimpses of dwellings soon came more often, to the point where long, extended walkways began joining one to the next. Build- ings among the massive trunks multiplied upon the forest floor, until Wynn couldn't follow the pattern of them in the darkness, even by the wispy lantern lights along paths above or below.

The wagon rounded a gradual bend where the darkness appeared to break beyond the trees.

A sea of light struck Wynn as Althahk turned a final sharp bend. Her eyes popped as the group rolled through a living arch of two trees grown together high above.

Wynn was still blinking at spots of glare when a'Ghràihlôn'na—Blessed of the Woods—filled her whole view.

Sau'ilahk materialized upon the road a stone's throw from the massive forest's edge. He had already backtracked to find the caravan along another route; Wynn was no longer with it. Alone in the full night, he knew that she had crossed into those ancient trees and was on her way to the Lhoin'na sages.

Sau'ilahk could not follow, but what of Chane?

The road was the only way the wagon could have passed. If Chane had been left behind, he would be waiting here. Or had he gone with her somehow?

Impossible—unless there was more to that strange little ring.

Sau'ilahk wavered, staring about the grassy plain. It was a bitter place he had heard of only in his living days. So much had begun and ended here. An age ago, a line had been drawn, marked by where autumn's dead grass met the ever-living green of that forest. The war's waves of victory had broken here. But that wasn't what had ended the war.

It had been as if Beloved had simply given in.

The time of victory would come again, and next time, the Children would not lead. Sau'ilahk would regain youth and beauty, awe and glory. He alone would dominate Beloved's forces. Their worship would feed him more than all of the life he had consumed in his altered existence.

But what of Wynn Hygeorht? What did she seek in this place? Where was an orb that would free him? Where was lost Bäalâle Seatt?

That he depended on this whelp of a sage, an immature infidel, ate at him. He was not foolish enough to pass the tree line and would have to follow her from afar once more. A servitor of Air or Earth would not serve his needs this time. He needed an emissary of consciousness connected to his own.

He needed eyes as well as ears, and perhaps more.

Again, Sau'ilahk blocked out the world, focusing inward, and then looked down. Within his thoughts, he stroked a glowing circle for Spirit upon the road's packed dirt. Within that came the square for Earth. Smaller still came another circle for Spirit's physical Aspect as Tree. Between the lines of these shapes, he stroked the glowing sigils with his thoughts.

Spirit to the Aspect of Tree, Tree to the essence of Spirit, and born of the Earth.

His energies bled into the pattern on the road that only he saw.

Sau'ilahk's form thinned to transparent in weariness, and then a shaft of wood cracked the dirt at the pattern's center.

It jutted upward as if an overly thickened branch suddenly sprouted there. That short, bark-covered limb bent over, far suppler than it appeared. Along its length, six tinier limbs sprouted to lift its body and rip itself from the road. Turning around, a small knot of ochre root tendrils twitched around its base.

Sau'ilahk bled even more energy into his creation.

Bark peeled back around the root knot. Those tendrils coiled tighter and tighter into a ball. And that sphere took on an inner limelight, growing severe, until it *blinked* at him.

Flexing lids of wooden root tendrils clicked over one glowing orb like an eye. The servitor spun and rushed toward grass at the roadside.

No! Sau'ilahk commanded.

He reached for his fragment of consciousness embedded within his conjured creation. It halted in its tracks. He held it there as it struggled in resistance, until it finally submitted.

Remain unseen. Follow the trio of human, dwarf, and wolf.

As he released it, the servitor skittered away and shot into the tall grass. Only a ripple among those blades marked its passing. When the trail reached the tree line, that legged branch with one eye in a root knot skittered up a massive tree trunk and vanished into the forest's canopy.

Sau'ilahk watched foliage shiver briefly and heard the faint click of its legs upon bark. His consciousness rode the servitor into a land where the dead could not walk. . . .

At least none but perhaps Chane Andraso.

* * *

Passing through the city's archway, Wynn wasn't given time for awe. Althahk pulled his horse sideways before the wagon, forcing its horses to stop. He pointed off to the right.

"In there," he commanded.

A large barn, perhaps a stable, was built on the ground. With the exception of smooth, rounded corners, it looked much like any barn in Wynn's homeland. She didn't care to be ordered about, but turned the wagon aside. Before the horses had stopped at the wide, closed doors, Althahk gave a shrill, trilling whistle.

One wide stable door slid aside. A bleary-eyed elven male of advanced years stepped out. Only a brief nod of acknowledgment passed between him and the commander. Then he turned to nod a greeting to Wynn—and he froze.

Unlike the commander's stern suspicion or the counselor's cold parting words, the stable master just blinked twice, eyes clearing at some wondrous, rare sight.

"Can you stable our horses and store our wagon?" she asked in Elvish, and climbed down.

The stable master almost couldn't turn his eyes from Shade at first. When he did, he looked Wynn up and down with a friendly smile.

"Most certainly, sage," he answered.

Everyone else disembarked as Wynn headed around back to retrieve her staff and begin dragging their packs out. But she paused at reaching for the chest.

"Will the rest of our things be safe here?" she asked.

"Certainly, sage," the elder elf said again.

"How much?" Chane asked, reaching for his money pouch.

Both Chane and Ore-Locks would have difficulty communicating here. Ore-Locks spoke only a smattering of Elvish, and Chane spoke none at all.

"No need," Althahk interrupted in Numanese, and both his men dismounted. "The guild will be notified and handle payment. Now, if you will follow—"

"I'm not going to the guild just yet," Wynn said, and even Chane froze at this.

"Where else would you go at this time of night?" the commander challenged.

"There's something I need to see for myself," Wynn answered. "Unless you have further doubts or reason for interference, I won't keep you from your duties."

Althahk raised an eyebrow.

Wynn started off before even Ore-Locks or Chane could ask where they were headed. Shade fell into step, and at the last instant pulled ahead, pacing a dead line straight at the commander.

Althahk hesitated, stepping aside at the last instant. Wynn never looked back, though she heard Chane and Ore-Locks's footfalls as they hurried to catch up.

All four of them headed down the wide lane into the brighter night lights. The stable might have seemed recognizable, but any semblance of familiarity ended as they walked into the "city" of trees.

Cleared stretches of paths slightly narrower than a common street were paved with packed gravel and natural stone slabs. Gardens and alcoves of flora flowed around made structures and up the tree trunks in tendril vines of glistening green leaves and night-closed flower buds. More earthbound buildings surrounded them than in the outer settlements. Their abundance was matched by tiers of higher structures above, all the way beyond sight in the canopy. In the street, there was a break in the trees above, like a matching road in the sky, where stars shone brightly beyond the haze of a nearly full moon.

Wynn slowed to barely a shuffle as she looked about. She had a sense of where to go from references on this city she'd found in the guild library. Somewhere on its northern side was another arch like the one through which they'd entered, but this exit would lead deeper into the forest.

"Where are you taking us?" Chane asked. "I thought we . . . Wait!"

He grabbed her arm, pulling her aside beneath the shadow of a hanging building wrapped around one great tree. Its underfloor spread out above, shadowing them. The few people about were all on foot, but Wynn spotted what had startled Chane.

More patrollers—the *Shé'ith*—approached along the narrow street in a line of tall horses. They carried lances, but these had long and narrow steel tips. Their attire was the same as that of Althahk's trio, and each bore another slightly curved sword in a shouldered sheath. A few had bows and quivers.

There were many more of them—more than a dozen at quick count. Unlike the commander, the one in the lead bore a pearl white leaf brooch upon his sash.

"They're all cavalry," Chane noted. "Do you not find that strange . . . for a tree-born race?"

"Yes," Ore-Locks agreed quietly.

"Domin High-Tower once told me they value speed," Wynn said, "being able to quickly traverse their forest or, rather, its surrounding lands."

At mention of his brother, Ore-Locks's expression darkened in silence.

Once the riders passed, Wynn took to the street again. She renewed her trek through this strange and beautiful forest-city, wondering how it would look by daylight. Some trees held multiple small structures up and around their trunks, like steps of giant, moss-roofed, shelf fungus with lantern light glowing through curtained windows.

What must it be like to live in a world that moved vertically as opposed to horizontally?

"Why do they live this way?" Chane asked, looking up.

Wynn shook her head. "Domin Tilswith couldn't trace its history back far enough to learn how it began, let alone why. Just another ancient practice that became a way of life."

But she still wondered. Even for elves, it seemed odd to her.

The an'Cróan's founders had originally come from this land; thereby they shared the same forebears as the Lhoin'na. But those founders of the far-off Elven Territories had left amid the great war's end. This way of life couldn't have started until after that.

Shade crept out ahead, though she remained within Wynn's reach. Again, although her home was a wild elven forest, these people were nothing like the more clan-based an'Cróan. And more than one passerby stumbled and froze, stunned as they watched a black majay-hì leading two humans and a dwarf. Wynn wondered if the majay-hì of this land remained barely more than living legend, even among the Lhoin'na.

A cluster of human merchants ambled out of a side path, all Numan, and one of them eyed Shade too long and almost tripped on the heels of his companions. Though he probably just wondered how a wolf—but too tall and lanky-legged—ended up as someone's pet.

"Where are we going?" Chane asked.

"Out of the city," Wynn answered, "and back into the forest."

Again, he raised his eyebrow. "What could be out there that you have to see so urgently?"

"Aonnis Lhoin'n," Wynn answered firmly. "First Glade."

CHAPTER 10

Staff in one hand and a glowing cold lamp crystal held high in the other, Wynn tried to illuminate their way. Shade was out in front, leading them down a narrow path of flat stones set in the earth. But the walk to First Glade took longer than expected, as the forest grew more and more dense around her.

Endless masses of twisting ferns and vines meshed tightly between the trees on both sides. The intertwined canopy overhead blocked out the moon and stars.

"This is foolish," Ore-Locks said from the rear. "We should have gone to the guild and taken rooms until morning."

"You're welcome to turn back and wait," Wynn answered.

A sharp intake of breath came from behind. No answer followed it.

In part, Wynn knew he was right, but she'd been too eager, and Chane couldn't come with her in daylight. Then she glanced back and realized that the sharp sucking of breath hadn't come from Ore-Locks.

Chane's face was so pale in the crystal's light that it bordered on gray. A mere ghost of brown remained in his irises. His eyes shifted rapidly as he peered into the dense foliage.

"What's wrong?" she whispered.

He jerked out the new sword in one swift movement and stiffened to a sudden halt.

"They're moving," he said. "Can you not see? The trees . . . are shifting when we are not looking!"

Wynn grew frightened, though not because of what he saw. She suspected this might happen the closer they came to First Glade—to Chârmun, the great tree called Sanctuary. Chane was succumbing partially to its influence flowing out through the Lhoin'na forest, even while wearing the brass ring.

Ore-Locks turned his head, following Chane's fixed gaze. "What is wrong with you?"

"There is nothing wrong with *me*!" Chane rasped, and pointed back the way they'd come. "That vine over the path . . . it was not there before. I would have had to push it aside if it had been."

Ore-Locks looked behind them, hefting his iron staff and perhaps expecting to see whatever had unsettled Chane. Wynn held the cold crystal with only her thumb and tugged on Chane's sleeve with her fingers.

"I promise you, the trees are not moving," she said. "Focus on me—only me—and you'll be fine."

Ore-Locks shook his head. "It looks the same as before."

"Let's move on," Wynn insisted, still trying to pull Chane around before . . .

Shade circled back and began snarling, her full attention locked on Chane.

Ore-Locks started at the dog's behavior, and then retreated two steps back from Chane and leveled his iron staff.

Chane ignored both of them and twisted about.

"I know what I saw!" he whispered to Wynn.

The light of her crystal showed his irises as colorless. His pale face was coated in a sheen, as if he perspired.

"What is happening to him?" Ore-Locks asked. "What is . . . he?"

This was all Wynn needed. Chane was succumbing to the elves' forest, and Ore-Locks was openly demanding answers.

The undead, especially anything akin to a Noble Dead, were almost unknown on this continent but for veiled references in forgotten folktales. Ore-Locks had probably never heard the word "vampire," let alone understood what it meant. But he certainly knew of the undead, as any stonewalker did; he'd helped destroy Sau'ilahk.

There was no knowing how a corrupt stonewalker might react to Chane's true nature. A rational guess led to the worst of conclusions. Anyone who thought a mere explanation would settle this was a fool. Chane had done horrible things without remorse that Wynn didn't like thinking about, but the situation wasn't that simple.

"Answer me," Ore-Locks said.

"When nothing else needs my attention," she returned. "And, Shade . . . be quiet."

Shade fell silent, though her jowls still quivered as she watched Chane.

Wynn didn't know if this place heightened the dog's natural instincts, or if Shade simply didn't like the idea of Chane going to First Glade. Or perhaps it was just Chane's obviously decaying state. Wynn could do no more than put off dealing with any of this.

"Lead . . . now," she said.

Shade reluctantly turned and slunk ahead.

"We are not going any farther," Ore-Locks stated, "until you answer me."

"Then leave," Wynn replied.

His threat was a bluff. Ore-Locks would never get what he wanted without her, and they both knew it. He'd never let her go on without him, nor would he challenge Shade and Chane just to stop her here.

He said nothing more, and Wynn took up Chane's free hand, placing it on her shoulder.

"Hold on, and you won't feel so lost," she assured him. "Chap did the same for me in the forest of the an'Cróan."

She'd been affected by that far elven land, for that place not only abhorred the undead, but anyone not of full elven blood. Even Leesil, with his mixed heritage, had fought to keep his wits there. Almost everywhere Wynn had gone in those wild lands, she'd kept her fingers clenched in Chap's scruff.

Chane's fingers gripped down, but Wynn didn't wince. He slid his sword back into its sheath. A bit of soft brown stained his irises once more, but Wynn felt him shuddering.

"Do you want to go back and wait for me?" she asked quietly.

"No," he answered between clenched teeth.

Wynn considered arguing, but turned and waved Shade onward. She was ambivalent at the sound of Ore-Locks's heavy footfalls following along. Then the path split in three directions.

Shade sniffed the air and craned her head, looking up into the branches.

Wynn waited in silence, for in this place, she put her trust in Shade's senses. The dog finally trotted along the center path, but Chane made another harsh sucking sound.

"Close your eyes," Wynn told him.

Her crystal cast eerie shadows in the wild underbrush, but something more stood out in the darkness overhead. She gazed upward, raising the crystal, and its light caught on tawny vines as thick as her arm. They wove their way through the high canopy, some of them paralleling the path ahead.

Wynn slowed, looking closer. The vines were smooth, perhaps glistening from moisture, and utterly unlike anything else in sight. She thought she saw grain in them, like polished wood.

—follow . . . tree—

At those broken memory-words, Wynn looked down at Shade. How could she follow a tree? Which tree? But Shade pressed on, and Wynn stepped after her.

The farther they went, the more Wynn noticed those strange, tawny vines—and they grew broader, thicker. Smaller ones appeared here and there, perhaps branching off from the larger ones. All were woven into the upper reaches of the trees, and now . . .

They didn't glisten as much as they appeared to faintly glow, as if catching the radiance of the moon hidden from sight.

Wynn traced onward by their faint radiance as she followed Shade, until another light appeared ahead, beyond the forest's tangle. Vines and branches, trunks and bearded moss were like black silhouettes between her and the nearing illumination.

Shade lunged ahead through a break at the path's end.

Wynn couldn't keep up without leaving Chane behind—which she would not do.

"Shade!" she called.

Within a few paces, Wynn stepped through the break and stopped.

She stood in a broad clearing wholly roofed by the forest and touched Chane's hand upon her shoulder, looking up at him. His eyes opened before she turned back.

Wynn looked across the moss-covered earth to the immense glowing tree in the heart of First Glade.

*   *   *

Sau'ilahk watched the forest floor rush past through the eyes of his servitor. The experience was disorienting.

He had caught only glimpses of tree-bound settlements in his creation's furious racing. It caught up to Wynn somewhere northeast of where he waited on the grassy plain. When thickening forest forced his servitor out of the trees and onto the path, Sau'ilahk caught only a glimpse of Wynn between Ore-Locks's thick legs at the rear of their procession. Worse, his creation's resistance grew the farther it went.

It began struggling to turn back.

Continue, he commanded, and he drew upon more of his consumed life and forced it onward.

Ahead, light rose beyond Ore-Locks's broad, tromping boots. It filtered through the surrounding low underbrush, and Sau'ilahk had one clear glimpse of Wynn leading Chane into that lighted place.

Where was she headed, and why at this time of night?

The servitor began to writhe.

Sau'ilahk's awareness spun with shattered sights and sound. Vertigo sickened him as he seized the servitor with all his will. A strange pressure built on him, as if he had suddenly become corporeal. He felt submerged as in mud, and forced down as it began to shift and push him back.

A sound—a feeling—like wood splitting apart stunned all thoughts in his mind.

Sau'ilahk lost all awareness as his world went pitch-black.

"*Vanâkstí Bäynæ*," Ore-Locks whispered from behind Wynn, as she gazed across the broad clearing at the faint glow of a tree too large to be real. An unnerving sensation spread through her, almost as if Chârmun watched her in turn.

She had heard some an'Cróan refer to its offspring in the Elven Territories as an ash tree, but it didn't look anything like an ash. Massive roots split the turf in mounds nearly as tall as she where they emerged from the trunk to burrow deep into the earth. Its great bulk, the size of a small tower, twisted and turned like a slow, serene dancing giant frozen in time. Though it was completely bare of bark, it hadn't grayed like dead wood. The soft glow emanating from its glistening and pale tawny form lit up everything in the clearing with shimmers.

It was alive, as impossible as that seemed, and Wynn looked up into its huge branches above.

They spread and mingled into the forest's canopy. These were the origins of the "vines" she had seen. She understood what Shade had meant by "follow the tree." Shade had been following the limbs of Chârmun, as if the dog knew what they were. Now that Wynn looked upon Sanctuary, that tree, she questioned that overwhelming drive to see it this night.

What had she expected to find here? She only knew of this place from ancient memories Chap had stolen from Most Aged Father.

Once called Sorhkafâré—the Light Upon the Grass—as leader of the westernmost allied forces in the great war, he had taken a cutting from Chârmun and left with any of his own people who would follow him. Some of the first Fay born into wolves, whose descendants would become the majay-hì, joined him, as well. He led them across the world, all the way beyond what were now called the Farlands, to establish the Elven Territories. There he had planted that cutting to become Roise Chârmune—the Seed of Sanctuary—at the heart of what would become their ancestors' burial ground.

Unlike here, that land barred anyone not descended from those first settlers. Whether it was because of the Seed of Sanctuary or the will of decrepit and undying Most Aged Father, or both, Wynn never learned. But only elven blood, or perhaps only an'Cróan—Those of the Blood—could enter that land unimpeded.

First Glade was—had been—sacred, a haven and sanctuary against the undead. In a time to come, this place where she stood might need to be so again, should she and very few others fail to stop another war from enveloping their world. Perhaps she'd simply needed to know that Sanctuary was real. It was like seeking to look upon a promise of hope, and she needed that so badly.

Shade padded slowly across the clearing, pausing beside one long mound in the forest floor where a great root pushed up moss-blanketed earth. The mound was almost the height of Shade's pricked-up ears as she stared up into the tree's branches.

Wynn was caught breathless by the sight, and she slipped her cold lamp crystal into her pocket.

"Wait here," she whispered, lifting Chane's hand from her shoulder. "Don't try to come closer."

She took only one step before Chane latched on to her shoulder again.

"No!" he rasped. "This is not right. . . . This place . . ."

Wynn pried at his fingers but was unable to move them.

"Let go and stay here," she told him. "I'm in no danger. Don't give in to what you feel. I won't be long."

Ore-Locks stepped closer, but never turned his back on Chane.

"What are you doing now?" he asked.

"What I have to," she returned, and then Shade huffed once.

Shade stood directly at the base of Chârmun—Sanctuary—and glanced expectantly toward Wynn. With hesitant steps, Wynn headed toward Shade, but looked only at the tree. With every step, Chârmun grew in her sight, until it filled her entire view at arm's reach.

—*Wynn . . . stay here*—

Shade's memory-words were soft but emphatic in Wynn's head. It was a comforting notion, though impossible. Wynn slowly reached out, eyeing the trunk's golden grain, and blinked against its close glow. In the last instant, she hesitated.

It suddenly seemed so wrong to touch it.

"Go on. It is all right."

Wynn twisted toward that lilting voice, just shy of a laugh, as Shade began to growl. She thrust out her staff in warning, seeing only a cowl at first. The shoulder of a long robe followed, its cloth pure white.

"Truly, you can touch it . . . if you like," the figure said.

Wynn heard a sword jerked from a sheath.

"No!" Chane rasped. "Wynn, get back."

Shade snarled and flattened her ears.

The figure leaned its shoulder lazily against the tree, as if lounging in a private garden. Long-fingered tan hands reached up to pull back the cowl. Golden brown hair streaked with gray curtained the figure's face. A tauntingly slow turn of head exposed creases at the corners of large, slanted amber eyes, and he smiled.

"Chuillyon," Wynn whispered in disbelief.

*　　*　　*

Night stars, tall grass, and white flowers, and the darker shapes of the forest trees faded back into Sau'ilahk's view. He hung there on the plain, clinging to returning self-awareness. For an instant, he had fallen into dormancy.

He reached out through his connection, the fragment of his will embedded inside his servitor. It was not there, not anywhere. This was impossible. He should have felt his creation at even a greater distance. How could it be gone, and why at the instant he was about to see where Wynn had gone?

Something in that clearing had not allowed the servitor to enter. Something had too easily taken it apart, banishing it into nothingness.

Sau'ilahk wanted to shriek, and, indeed, any living creature near enough would have fled from the wind of his conjured voice. Slowly, he reclaimed his self-control.

He needed a servant to be his eyes and ears, one capable of invading in the elves' forest. It now seemed he needed something more natural to that place. There had been that pressure he had felt, even without willing himself to a physical state. As if something in there tried to force him out.

Sau'ilahk had felt this before, though not with such force. And the last, too recent time had been . . .

"Chuillyon?" Wynn whispered again.

Anger drove the numbness of shock out of her, but she still couldn't believe her eyes. She'd seen him head off for the royal castle of Calm Seatt barely seven days before her journey began. No one could have reached the forest before her, let alone known where she would go first upon arrival.

All he did was nod, a curt bow of acknowledgment. And he was still smiling softly at her.

"What are you doing here?" Chane asked.

At a glance, Wynn saw the sword in his grip. Chane stood well away from Chârmun, as if hesitant to approach, but worse was the sheen on his face. She'd never seen him perspire, didn't even think it was possible for the undead. His eyes were utterly colorless again.

When Wynn looked back at Chuillyon, he wasn't smiling anymore.

"You are a never-ending source of perplexity, Wynn Hygeorht," he said, but his gaze was fixed on Chane.

No one could know what Chane was while he wore the ring . . . could they?

Ore-Locks stepped wide around Chane, but as he looked to Chuillyon, he grew visibly uncomfortable. He swallowed hard and lowered his eyes in a respectful bow. Clearly, Ore-Locks hadn't expected to see his master's comrade here, either.

Chuillyon clicked his tongue.

"Your sudden absence has been a great concern, stonewalker," he said in a parentlike tone. "Master Cinder-Shard would be quite shocked to learn of the company you keep."

Ore-Locks continued to look at the ground.

Wynn studied him. Hadn't he told Cinder-Shard or any of the Stonewalkers where he'd gone?

"Your penchant for unusual companionship continues," Chuillyon added.

Now he was studying Shade—and smiling again—leaving Wynn uncertain to whom he'd been speaking.

"What are you doing here?" she asked.

"Me? Just a brief retreat of rest," he answered, with obvious mock surprise. "It is my homeland, after all."

She examined his hair, free of tangles, as if freshly groomed. His pristine white robe and even the toes of his soft boots showed no sign of travel. He looked as if he'd just stepped from the royal grounds for a leisurely walk in the woods.

"Turnabout is certainly fair," he continued. "Why are you here, journeyor, other than for the peaceful welcome of Chârmun?"

"None of your affair. You have no authority over me."

"Chârmun's blessings!" Chuillyon said with a soft laugh.

What did he want? Had he followed her, or was his reason for rushing home a coincidence? She had long stopped believing in coincidence.

"Wynn, we should leave this place," Chane rasped.

He sounded manic, but he was right. She'd seen First Glade for herself, but the appearance of this *false* sage had ruined that one moment of unblemished assurance.

Ore-Locks barely glanced up at Chuillyon. The dwarf's broad face was a mask of urgency fighting reluctance, as if caught between explaining himself and simply leaving as quickly as possible.

Wynn decided upon the latter. She backed toward Chane, and Shade wheeled to follow.

"You came all this way," Chuillyon called after her, "but you leave without even one touch? Come, now, have you lost all of your curiosity?"

She wasn't about to let him bait her, and placed Chane's hand on her shoulder, turning to lead him out. Then Shade stiffened beside her and spun sharply, making Wynn stall.

Shade hadn't turned toward Chuillyon or Chârmun. She began twitching ever so slightly as she stared toward the clearing's far side.

A long, almost mournful howl rose out of the forest.

"What was that?" Ore-Locks asked.

Chuillyon released a long, exhausted breath. "Oh, not now."

That unguarded slip was like an annoyed boy's mischief interrupted—or another snide utterance from an aging deceiver hiding beneath tranquillity.

A single form burst from the trees at the clearing's rear side. Shade stood at full attention, but she didn't snarl.

Tall and leggy, a silver-gray majay-hì loped purposefully forward. Another dog leaped out of the brush, and then another.

By Chârmun's glow, Wynn watched a majay-hì pack appear one by one out of the forest, until nine paced and padded around the glade. They looked so much like the ones Wynn had seen in the Elven Territories of the Farlands . . . silver and gray, or dull brown to charcoal, though none were as near to black as Shade. And they were all silent. Crystal blue eyes shone clearly as they closed in, circling watchfully around the intruders.

Then something more upright pushed through the trees where the last two dogs stood waiting.

Wynn stared in surprise at the newcomer.

She was small for an elf, shorter than an average human male. By her deeply tanned complexion, she could have passed for an an'Cróan, if not for her darker hair. It was so dark that it could've been brown rather than the sandy blonds of the Lhoin'na, let alone the brighter tones of an an'Cróan. Still, those locks were lined with vivid silver streaks. Her hair was bound by a circlet of green cloth, perhaps raw shéot'a by its dull shimmer.

At a distance, Wynn couldn't see any lines in the woman's face, though her presence gave the impression of long years. Flanked by the pair of majay-hì—a female of steel gray and a mottled brown male—she moved smoothly in a felt skirt bound in pleats by leather thongs wrapped about her narrow waist. Her firm steps were purposeful, as if soft earth and moss, or even the fragrant air itself, would move to her aide if she wished.

She glanced once at the intruders, and then her eyes narrowed as they turned upon Chuillyon.

He offered her a half bow of his head. "Always a pleasure . . . Vreuvillä."

Wynn caught the veiled, put-upon annoyance in his voice as he addressed the woman called "Leaf's Heart."

"I felt something twisted within the forest," she returned pointedly. "I knew it must be you tampering with Chârmun . . . *again*."

Chuillyon raised one feathery eyebrow. "Then hardly a need to come and see."

"Unless something more vile followed you."

"Unlikely."

"Chârmun is not your tool! Go back to your guild of ranks and orders. The glade is not—and has never been—a place for your kind."

Wynn caught every implication. This woman thought Chuillyon was part of an official guild order, but that wasn't possible. There were only five orders, and none of them wore white.

"What are they saying?" Chane whispered.

There wasn't time for Wynn to translate, as Vreuvillä turned their way. The woman settled a hand upon the head of the steel gray female majay-hì.

Shade pressed into Wynn's thigh, her tall body trembling, and a barrage of images, sounds, and smells assaulted Wynn. All of them related to Shade's homeland; her mother, Lily; and her siblings. Shade was too young to be thrown into this foray.

—*Wynn . . . safe . . . here. . . . Wynn . . . stay here*—

Vreuvillä focused her large amber eyes on Shade, and then raised them to Wynn.

"Who are you?" she asked bluntly, and her tone implied no choice but to answer.

Chane's grip tightened on Wynn's shoulder, and he pulled her back. She saw his sword tip at her side. He didn't need a translation to catch the challenge in the woman's voice.

"My companions do not speak Elvish," Wynn said.

"How careless of them," Vreuvillä answered in Numanese.

Chane felt worse than on his longest day aboard the ship, testing his concoctions. Disoriented and sick from this place, from that unnatural tree, even the woman—all felt *wrong* to him. He was desperate to leave but could not show this to anyone but Wynn.

The elven woman was still studying him. Then she pointed back at Chuillyon.

"You are not with this self-righteous . . . *priest*?"

Chuillyon sighed caustically. "Vreuvillä, really—"

"Certainly not," Wynn cut in.

But the woman's last sharp word stuck in Chane's head. She spoke it with such derision that it might have meant "heretic" instead. So what was she? Regardless that she spoke a language he understood, he was too ill to clear his mind. He could not tell if either this woman or Chuillyon uttered any deceits.

And what was Chuillyon doing here? How had he arrived first?

Vreuvillä pivoted, heading off toward the glade's far side from where she had entered.

"You should all leave," she said, walking away. "Disturb this place no further."

All of the majay-hì turned likewise. One paced right past Chane, and he tensed. But the mottled brown male with the woman lingered, and then stepped toward Shade, stretching out its nose.

Shade leaned away with a quiver of her jowls. The male wheeled and was the last to hop into the brush, though the wild elven woman was already gone.

The glade was silent, and Wynn pushed down on Chane's sword arm.

"Let's go," she whispered.

"Back to the guild?" Chuillyon asked. "It would be my honor to escort you and assist in—"

"No, *thank you*," Wynn said, without looking back, brushing her fingers between Shade's tall ears. "Come, girl."

Shade whined again and reluctantly slunk along beside her.

Chane backed away as Wynn led him, keeping his eyes on Chuillyon. He waited until he heard Wynn's boots step onto stone and knew she had reached the path. Only then did he turn his eyes from Chuillyon.

The trees appeared to block Wynn's way, to catch and trap her, though she never faltered in a step. Chane sucked air into his dead lungs as she miraculously passed through. She reached up and briefly touched his hand upon her shoulder, and then retrieved her cold lamp crystal from her pocket.

"Close your eyes and hang on," she told him.

CHAPTER 11

Wynn drew relief in seeing Chane improve once they returned to a'Ghràihlôn'na. Still edgy and twitchy, he no longer shook visibly, and his eyes had regained their semitranslucent brown.

They stopped at the stable for their travel chest, which Ore-Locks hauled over his shoulder, along with his sack. He was quiet and withdrawn, asking no questions. Perhaps he had his own concerns after encountering Chuillyon. It seemed Ore-Locks had abandoned his sect and duties without a word to anyone. Like Wynn, he would face consequences upon his return, if he returned.

Wynn led them south through the city, with Shade close at her side. She had some sense of where to go, having looked up as much about the place as she could before leaving home. The city's narrow paths were quiet at night, but the trees' heights were still marked by the glimmer of lanterns, like mist-shrouded stars that settled among the branches. Some dark, ground-level buildings were constructed from stone as well as timber, and Ore-Locks slowed now and then to study them. One in particular baffled Wynn.

Each higher tier of pyrite-spattered granite was slightly narrower than the one below as it swept upward to seven levels, all terraced. The peaked front door with a tooled arch—shaped like an aspen leaf—was made from white wood to match its stone. Wynn had no idea what purpose the place served.

They passed gardens overladen with sleeping flower buds, but here and there Wynn spotted night-blooming jasmine. She'd never seen so many carefully nurtured enclaves that stood out only from the natural landscape by the density of crafted yet natural design. Even in darkness, it was all foreign, beautiful, and intimidating, and left her with a stab of regret.

Wynn finally looked upon a'Ghràihlôn'na—Blessed of the Woods—but not as a journeyor come to study or just as a visitor. She came as a nearly outcast sage at best, and a spy at the worst, hunting secrets to steal.

Then the buildings around her became immense.

Wynn halted and turned slowly. These giant trees, so much larger than any an'Cróan dwelling, were the buildings.

At any moment, she expected to see an an'Cróan round one of those living structures, or even one of the Anmaglâhk, those assassins clad in gray. No one had ever mentioned the Lhoin'na living within trees, aside from these ancient, great structures. If they could do so, why did so many live in constructed domiciles, even ones up in the forest's heights?

The street she stood upon ended before a broad park. Wide granite stairways rose gradually through terraces of green lawns and gardens around a small, placid lake. Every building—every ancient tree—surrounding that space dwarfed those she'd seen across the grassy plain. Great doors of white oak, scroll-carved brass, or colored with stain were set into shaped openings of living bark.

"What are those?" Ore-Locks said, pointing up and ahead.

Between the highest leafy branches of two buildings across the park, another structure loomed in the night. Barely visible by the lights upon or within it, where those lights shone, this structure had a strange, reddish tinge. It was only the hint of its shape that Wynn truly recognized.

"The Lhoin'na guild branch," she answered, a guess from what she'd seen in sketches of its exterior.

They rounded the park and the trees of what they thought must be the city's civic center. When they turned down a packed-earth lane at the far side, Wynn looked up . . . and up.

Sketches hadn't done justice to this place.

Perhaps as old as the Forgotten History, a ring of giant redwoods had melded into one massive form, one life. Hints of once-separate trunks bulged from its mass. Over a thousand years, the redwoods had grown so vast that they were now one great circle encompassing whatever lay within.

Wynn rose on her tiptoes, trying to peer over the surrounding hedge fence in both directions. She couldn't make out either side of the gargantuan structure's base through the surrounding trees.

High above, elongated teardrop windows dotted the guild's side, some lit up from within. At its top, barely within sight in the dark, parts of the structure rose higher than the rest, like lofty pinnacles upon a royal fortification. In place of pennants, their tops were likely graced with high branches. It had no battlements, for it was a place of contemplation and learning. Rather than a stand against enemy forces, this was a fortress against another loss of the world's knowledge.

Wynn led her companions to an iron archway and a gate through the high hedge fence. Beyond it, a wide shale-cobbled path wound through low shrubberies to a deep divide in the citadel's bark. Shaped like a teardrop's top half, it was four yards tall. In that dark entryway's back was a like-shaped lighter color amid night shadows.

It might be a door, but Wynn couldn't see it clearly. She grabbed the gate's handle and twisted. It wouldn't budge. In a place like this, she hadn't expected to be locked out.

"Here," Chane said, and a clanking tone sounded.

Wynn watched him pull the cord again, and a bell atop the gate's frame clanged. She looked toward the dark alcove and waited.

Her first task was to deliver the sealed message from her branch's council to the high premin here. But it was the middle of the night, and everyone was probably asleep.

"Perhaps we should have found rooms elsewhere?" Ore-Locks commented. "Then come here tomorrow?"

A heavy clack carried from beyond the gate, and light spilled from the guild's entryway. A silhouette appeared amid the glare, so tiny at first. But it was only the size of the doors that made it appear so. The figure wobbled out, paused where the path met the melded ring of ancient redwoods, and raised a hand.

A light grew there, where a tall, sleepy-eyed elf in a brown robe held up a cold lamp crystal. He squinted at the new arrivals as his feathery eyebrows cinched together.

If he carried a crystal, he had to be at least a journeyor, though likely not a master or domin if he tended the doors late at night.

Wynn raised a hand in greeting, calling out in Elvish, "Forgive us for ringing so late."

The elf drew closer. He was young by human standards, but there was no way to be certain of an elf's age after he reached early adulthood. He looked down at Wynn through the gate's ornate ironwork and then suddenly blinked, his eyes widening.

Perhaps he hadn't noticed Shade's dark form at first. He was still staring when Wynn cleared her throat.

"We've just arrived and need rooms . . . if possible."

The elven sage met Wynn's gaze, and then took in her gray travel robe.

"Domin Ch'leich âr Én'wir designates guest quarters," he answered. "But he has retired."

That name threw Wynn. Was it a title, a proper and family name, or what? It was something like "a ridge in a river's mouth."

"What is wrong?" Chane asked.

He must have sensed it from the elf's tone, and Wynn quickly reiterated the problem. Ore-Locks shifted the chest's weight on his shoulder.

"So much for Lhoin'na hospitality," he said.

"They are quite hospitable," Wynn countered, "but—"

"Please follow me," the elf returned, this time in Numanese. With the twist of a key, he opened the tall gate and stepped aside.

Startled by the sudden change, Wynn stepped through with a nod of thanks. But again, the journeyor watched only the black majay-hì. Shade padded by him without returning his notice. Chane followed, and Ore-Locks came last.

Halfway to the entry alcove, the elven journeyor stepped ahead on his long legs. When he pulled the handle on one door in that dark space, warm light again spilled from the split.

The double doors were made from polished redwood. They fit delicately within the entryway's shape, but were so tall and appeared so heavy that Wynn couldn't imagine how the elf opened them with only one hand. Among a pattern of carved and glittering green filigree that arced from one door to the other, she read the New Elvish rendered in Begaine symbols.

FHÉRIN TRIJ FHORUS . . . FHORUS TRIJ SHOLHUS . . . SHOLHUS TRIJ FHÉRIN . . . FÄIL-RÉUILACH ÂG ÄISH.

It matched the Numanese engraved in frame stones above the entrance to the new guild library in Calm Seatt.

TRUTH THROUGH KNOWLEDGE . . . KNOWLEDGE THROUGH UNDERSTAND-
ING . . . UNDERSTANDING THROUGH TRUTH . . . WISDOM'S ETERNAL CYCLE.

Wynn grew sad at the sight of the creed she had grown up believing. Truth
in this place would be well hidden, just like First Glade's ancient heritage. It
was a hoarded secret rather than a worldly treasure to be safeguarded for all.

Worse than that, Wynn was no longer certain which was right or wrong
in the details.

She'd never found drawings of this branch's interior, so she had no idea
how the place was laid out. As she stepped inside, memories of an'Cróan
homes didn't prepare her, and she slowed to a stop.

The floor was covered in grouted shale tiles of irregular shapes. But the
walls themselves were much the same as she remembered in the Farland's Elven Territories . . . except for their size.

She tilted her head back, which was the only way to see the high ceiling
above.

Like an'Cróan homes, the interior was bark-covered, rough and red like
the structure's exterior. In some places, bare wood showed through, although
those openings appeared natural rather than cut. They exposed wood still
glistening with life. Inside these openings, cold lamp crystals glowed outward,
mounted in brass fixtures with frosted glass globes.

The size of it all was unbelievable, even for what she'd seen of the exterior.
The entry chamber was easily three times the size of High-Tower's study in the
guild keep's northern tower.

The walls flowed organically upward to the ceiling, beyond clear reach of
light. To either side were wide, natural exits that might lead onward into the
ring of redwoods. Directly across from the entrance was a smaller pair of polished redwood doors. Even those were tall enough that any elf would've had to
reach up to touch the frame's top.

"This way," the journeyor said, heading straight for the second doors. He
opened one, holding it as he waited.

Wynn stepped through the door and into a massive courtyard inside the
redwood ring.

A few stone benches lined the pathways that she could actually see among
hedges and bushes, trees and vine-covered atriums. Their guide pushed on,
and she hurried to follow with the others. Along the winding way, the only

other thing of note that she saw clearly was located in the center of the sculptured, living courtyard.

A round depression rested at the courtyard's center, surrounded by stone steps or seating enclosing its open floor. At a guess, it could have held fifty or more. Perhaps it was a place for gatherings, not unlike the seminar rooms at the Numan branch.

At the courtyard's far side, the elven journeyor opened a single door, and they all reentered the redwood ring. Chane and Ore-Locks paused to get their bearings as Wynn went straight to wandering about the room.

It felt circular, though an archway at the back led into another chamber. She spotted two narrow passageways in the first chamber nearer the door to the courtyard. The one on the left curved downward, and the one on the right led up. Both had steps of living, shaped wood that was free of bark.

Brighter light shone out from the back chamber, and the apprentice crossed quickly. Wynn followed.

An open area with benches carved into the walls awaited her. A stone pit in the floor contained glowing orange crystals—dwarven crystals—that emitted light and heat. It left her wondering how these sages had acquired them, since nothing like them were used at her own branch.

"A welcome sight," Ore-Locks said, and Wynn found all of her companions close behind her.

Several freestanding benches stood on each side of the stone pit. This must be some type of common room. A wide shelf jutting from one wall contained glazed ceramic mugs, a pitcher of water, and a bowl of apples. Two tall openings directly on opposite sides led to smooth shale floor passages.

"Dawn is not far off," the journeyor said. "I will speak with the domin when he wakes. Can you take your comfort here until then?"

"This is just fine," Wynn said in relief, wanting to hold both her hands over the pit of crystals, but she glanced once at Chane. "Does the domin rise before dawn?"

"Usually . . . sometimes," the journeyor answered.

That could be a problem. But if need be, she could insist on housing Chane somewhere here in privacy.

"Thank you," she said.

The tall elf bowed his head and stepped out into the courtyard, perhaps returning to his vigil at the main entrance. Wynn turned back to find Shade snuffling along the base of a wall, her tail in the air. Chane headed for a table and dropped their packs on it.

"This is the best we can do for now," Wynn said. "I'll get Shade some jerky and try to heat some water for tea. Ore-Locks, maybe you could cut up a few of those apples."

He didn't respond, but he set the chest down next to the packs. Chane sank onto one bench, his expression strained.

"Are you all right?" Wynn asked.

"Chuillyon serves the royal family of Malourné," he said. "What is he doing here?"

She'd wondered that herself since they'd left the white-robed pretender leaning against Chârmun as if it belonged to him. She just shook her head.

"It may have nothing to do with us."

Chane frowned at her. Yes, it was a weak evasion.

"What is the next step?" he asked.

Ore-Locks looked over as he sliced an apple, waiting on Wynn's answer.

"I'll deliver the message from the council," she said. "That's my excuse for coming—even if the letter is nothing more than a warning against me, then I need to start searching their archives. If anyplace has information on Bäalâle Seatt, it is most likely here."

"You guess," Chane whispered.

"Yes, I guess. Every guild branch has its region from which it recovers lost information unearthed in various ways. We know Bäalâle Seatt was likely in the Sky-Cutter Range, considering its name was based in terms of tribal dialects once spoken in the great desert. This is the closest branch to the range."

"Anything that old should have been shared with all branches," Chane returned.

"Yes . . . it should have," Wynn echoed coldly.

Ore-Locks closed on her, holding out slices of apple. "If the premin here exposes the content of your branch's message, these sages might not be any more helpful than those of Chathburh."

"I don't need their help. I'm a journeyor, and guild branches share—are supposed to share—archives with all ranks of journeyor and above." She looked back to Chane. "So long as they don't learn what I'm really after, I'll find the information myself. All we can do is avoid Chuillyon until I dig up something useful . . . something to tell us where to begin searching an immense range that crosses an entire continent."

Thinking that, let alone saying it aloud, prompted Wynn to drop tiredly on the bench beside Chane. After so many days on the road, and switching back to being awake in daylight, she wasn't accustomed to being up all night. She was about to say more when she heard a soft rattle.

It carried through the archway from the main chamber nearer the courtyard. She stepped over to look out.

"What is it?" Chane asked, rising.

The outer chamber was empty all the way to the courtyard door.

"Nothing. I just thought I heard—"

The door's handle twisted and the door swung open.

It was shoved by the shoulder of a slender figure not tall enough to be an elf, dressed in a midnight blue robe. Dark hands juggled a small pile of books as the visitor stepped in, trying to keep the top book from sliding off. With another shoulder nudge, he shut the door and turned about.

Wynn saw that he most certainly wasn't an elf.

Dusky skin and kinky black hair inside the midnight blue cowl of a metaologer marked him as Suman, though certainly not as tall or distinguished as Domin il'Sänke.

He froze at the sight of her.

He looked about twenty, though his self-assured expression made him seem older. A triangular tuft of beard on his chin was so well manicured it could've been there awhile. He smiled, bowed his head without lowering his eyes.

Then he noted the sliced apples in her hand. His dark eyes rose to see Chane standing beside her, as Shade nudged her way into the arch between the chambers. The barest hint of surprise crossed the young man's face, followed by what Wynn thought was . . . an instant of recognition.

That brief change vanished, and she was certain she'd never seen him before.

"Apologies," he said in Numanese, and his accent was even thicker than il'Sänke's. "I did not know anyone would be here so early. I would have announced my presence properly."

"We arrived too early—I mean late—for room assignments," Wynn returned.

He bowed slightly again, still smiling. "I am Journeyor Mujahid il'Badrêyah of the guild branch in Samau'a Gaulb, il'Dha'ab Najuum."

Wynn knew little of Suman Empire culture, or, rather, its many cultures, but it was considered polite to make proper introductions right away. She stepped closer so that her companions could enter behind her.

"Pleased to meet you," she said. "I'm Journeyor Wynn Hygeorht of the Calm Seatt branch. This is Chane Andraso, and Ore-Locks Iron-Braid."

"Ah, so I am not the only one far from home," he replied.

"You are up very early," Chane observed. "It is not even light out."

If his rasp affected the journeyor, the young man didn't show it. Nor did he appear surprised by a dwarf's presence in elven lands. Instead, he glanced toward one stairway leading up on the left, and then back to Wynn, as if trying to reach a decision.

"Yes, I hoped for some quiet time to study," he said, and his expression filled with a sort of formal concern. "Perhaps I can assist you. I, too, came with companions. This is not the traveling season, and the guest wing is nearly empty. I cannot procure rooms for you, but you are welcome to rest in mine and the adjoining one, until something proper is arranged."

His offer struck Wynn as odd, but she had no idea why. He was just so amiable and eager to help. However, the thought of lying down even for a short while was tempting, and she needed to secure Chane someplace before he fell dormant at dawn.

"We're so tired that we may sleep all day," she said. "Will that be all right?"

"Most certainly," Mujahid answered. "I have a full day with no need to disturb you until after dinner."

Again, he was all too eager to help, but Wynn couldn't fault his generosity.

"Thank you," she told him, and then something more occurred to her. "I'm sorry to ask, but would you let the journeyor on watch know where we are? He'll be looking for us as soon as his domin awakens."

"You mean Domin In-Ridge?" Mujahid queried.

That answered Wynn's question on how to shorten the unknown domin's name in translation.

Mujahid nodded with a slow close of his eyes. "I will . . . as you would say, pass the word."

Still uncertain but aching for sleep, Wynn followed him to the stairwell leading up.

Sau'ilahk desperately needed life. Conjuring a servitor with consciousness and the long struggle to control it had drained him. When his creation had come upon that strangely lit glade while following Wynn, the black lash of its destruction had wounded him somehow. It was as if in riding the servitor's consciousness, he had stepped into the clearing himself.

Whatever had disassembled the servitor had partly reached him, and he had lost track of Wynn's whereabouts.

Sau'ilahk stood upon the road through the plain with no animate life within his awareness. The forest's trees were like a wall beyond which he could see or sense nothing. Worst of all, he did not have the strength to blink elsewhere by memory over a great distance.

He studied the tree line stretching in both directions beyond sight. Even if he found sustenance, even if he made another, more suitable servitor, how would he locate Wynn?

Sau'ilahk began to fade, sinking into dormancy, and cried out in that darkness upon the edge of his god's dream.

"*Beloved . . . help me!*"

Do you follow the sage? Does she still lead you?

"*I starve for my efforts!*"

Then find life, as small as it might be. Consume it in the hunt for a greater feast . . . so you may serve.

This was no answer, and frustration frayed Sau'ilahk's wits even more.

"*There is no life substantial enough for my need that I can reach here and now.*"

His patron's hiss sharpened like spit-upon coals—or the grind of massive scales upon sand.

A droplet of moisture from a corpse can be lifted from the desert, though it be barely enough for a burrowing carrion beetle.

"*Wynn Hygeorht is beyond my reach,*" Sau'ilahk argued. "*I cannot sense even the forest's own life. Even if I could, how am I to find her singular spark in such a place?*"

Where life is . . . death follows. Find the latter to find the former.

Sau'ilahk paused. In a land teeming with life that shut him out as unliving, perhaps "death" had walked into those trees if Chane had somehow followed Wynn in there. Beloved's cryptic retort seemed to confirm this, but Sau'ilahk had so rarely been able to sense Chane's presence. Perhaps that strange ring had also allowed the vampire to enter where no other undead could.

His interest in Chane's little brass ring grew.

"*I still . . . cannot,*" he pleaded. "*Please, my Beloved . . . I starve.*"

Unearth your need, like a droplet in sand . . . and then another . . . until you find means to serve. Dig and borrow for it, if you must, but do not pray to me to salve the wounds of your failure.

Sau'ilahk sank deeper into dormancy under Beloved's rebuke. The only source of life he could think of was the caravan. He did not have the strength to search for it, let alone any memory that would let him awaken at its constantly changing location. He remained lost in the black silence, not knowing for how long.

All that was left to him were the painful past memories of his god that made him seethe in silence. The Children had never been treated this way. Though he had earned Beloved's displeasure through disobedience, he had done all he could to regain a state of grace in his god's awareness. When trapped between faithful service and desperate need, he was treated like . . . an insect in the dirt, just short of a whim to step upon it.

And the world reappeared.

Sau'ilahk spotted the barest gray in the eastern sky, and panic set in. Had he remained dormant for too long? He could not bear a whole day in darkness amid such hunger, and he sagged like a limp scarecrow draped in black sackcloth.

All that filled his awareness was the road.

Not the sands of the great desert from long ago, but packed earth with stones exposed by decades of weathering and use. Drops of water were not what he needed, though they were more plentiful here than in the dunes. The sting of Beloved's rebuke ran through him like a wasp's poison in the veins of living flesh.

Where there was water, or just moisture, even in another's remains, it could sustain a tiny life. He had once been such sustenance at the end of his living days.

That old, old memory still haunted and sickened him.

All had been mysteriously lost at the war's end. Or, rather, the war had simply ended for no reason he had understood. Years had passed since the night that he received the "blessing" of eternal life. Then one night, the Children simply vanished.

Sau'ilahk went to the mouth into Beloved's mountain, and it was gone. Not as if blocked by a collapse or filled in with stone and earth. The opening simply was not there anymore . . . as if it had never been there.

Gone were the guardian locatha, those hulkish abominations like the offspring of a man and some monstrous reptile. The tribes and others of the horde began to disperse, but not before they turned on each other. Northerners and other defectors in the war turned against the desert tribes. Tribes turned on each other, no longer needing the excuses of old blood feuds. Packs and herds of the Ygjila—what would one day be known as goblins—tore into any but their own kind.

They massacred each other over what little spoils of war had been gained, and then fled into the peaks and across the sands. Amid it all, the Children's offspring from the battlefields hunted and harried the living in the nights. They slaughtered anything for as much blood, as much life, as they could gain so deep in the desert.

Sau'ilahk fled with the remains of his underlings among the Reverent.

In more years that followed, he searched for any trace of the Children. Each year, he grew more afraid and maddened by spite. For when he looked in his polished silver mirror, his own visage was too much to bear.

Lines had grown on his once beautiful face. His glistening black curls of hair steadily dulled with streaks of gray. His joints slowly lost their range of motion amid growing aches at every movement. Food consumed for its comfort became mud upon his tongue, devoid of all taste. And his days became as his nights as his sight began to fail. That last loss was almost a relief from ever looking into the mirror again.

Sau'ilahk had grown old.

He withered, cheated by the *lie* of eternal life. It was not until after his heart finally halted its weak beats that a *truth* made his fear grow all the more. When he finally died, he could see again.

Sau'ilahk lay in the tent upon piled rugs for a bed, amid the haze of funerary incense. All around him, the remaining Reverent in their black robes and cloaks murmured prayers for Beloved to welcome him into the afterlife. Sau'ilahk was little more than a withered bag of bones as he watched them, knowing he could not be dead if he could now see.

His followers bowed their heads and closed their eyes, though some faces appeared subtly relieved rather than mournful. He tried to take a breath to rebuke them for prematurely dismissing him.

Sau'ilahk could not draw air—nor could he move his mouth. He could not blink or close his eyes—or if he did so without knowing it, no one noticed . . . and he could still see them.

The nearest swiped a hand across his old face as if to shut his eyelids. Still he could *see* them, *hear* them.

Some of the lesser Reverent left in that last night of his "life." Three remained to whisper among themselves, until whispers became sharp words. They argued over whether or not to bother fulfilling his final decree concerning proper burial. In the end, two of the trio won out by using a hooked-point blade to tear out the throat of the third.

It brought Sau'ilahk no satisfaction.

He lay mute and paralyzed, unable to tell them he was not dead, even as they stripped and washed his withered flesh. They wrapped him in strips of black burial cloth, layer by layer, so suited to Beloved's most reverent of the Reverent. Even as they rolled the strips over his eyes, again and again, he still watched them. He screamed from within as they bore him off, though no sound escaped his still lips.

They lodged him in a small cave high in the great mountain range. As they crawled back to the opening, all he had left to see was a rough stone ceiling an arm's length above him, torchlight still flickering upon it. That light began to grow dim as he heard the stones being piled.

Until that flicker vanished altogether, and there was only silence.

Sau'ilahk's silent screams turned to sobs as he came to know Beloved's truth. He had his eternal life, but not eternal youth. All his beauty was gone, but not the prison of his flesh in its death.

How long did he wait until *they* came?

Something entered his awareness in the dark. Like a spark he could not see, it skittered around the space of his tomb. And then another—and another.

Something pulled, jerked, and tore at the cloth strips over his sunken belly. A small form scuttled over his face and burrowed into the cloth over his right eye.

Were they worms, beetles, flies? What had crept and flitted too many times, too close across his cloth-wrapped face, only to wriggle through the wraps over his desiccating flesh? How long had it taken for them to amass?

Was it days, moons, or even years in that dark silence, until all he felt and heard was their burrowing, their biting and gnawing? It became a distant thing to be eaten alive—eaten dead—like a wound so harsh, the mind shuts it out. Horror numbed any sensation too torturous to bear.

For slow ages Sau'ilahk lay there, eaten away in small pieces while the rest of him decayed, until . . .

Out of dark dormancy Sau'ilahk rose one night through the mountainside, his first utterance a scream that had built within him over a century. No longer anchored in flesh, dawn soon cut into his madness and drove him back down into a dormancy as dark as his tomb had been. But he rose again under the stars after the following dusk, still mindlessly wailing and unable to touch anything, most of all himself.

Even now, as he stood upon the road Wynn had taken, Sau'ilahk quaked under those endless years. Only the sound of scuttling in the dark had kept him company. That and the screams of his thoughts, so loud they could have cracked his dried bones if he had had a true voice.

Sau'ilahk lowered and thrust his incorporeal hands through the road. He sank his arms nearly to his shoulders, feeling in the earth for any *drop* of animate life.

Be it a worm, a burrowing beetle, or a grass grub, when he touched something, that small spark of life vanished into him. They were no more than that drop of water in a dune. But he persisted, sweeping his arms slowly through earth. He worked his way into the field at the road's side, blades of tall grass passing through him. And once he touched something else.

A sting of cold rushed through Sau'ilahk.

He jerked his hands out of the earth, still aching and burning from whatever his fingers had passed through. What was buried down there that caused him this discomfort? Even if he sank his cowl into the ground, he would not see it, and he had too little energy to solidify a hand with which to dig. But it had felt like . . .

That cold burning that had torn at him from within whenever his hand had passed through Chane Andraso.

This made no sense, and he returned to foraging carefully for more tiny lives. He reached deep this time, and worked his way farther into the field. He swept his way along through the grass, its blades not even bending in his passage, until . . .

Sau'ilahk's shoulder swept through a dome of flowers, and his shriek became a wind that tore the grass around him. In retreat, he nearly passed through another cluster of blooms before he lurched the other way. He burned inside, the sensation like shudders and dizziness, though he had no flesh.

He stared down at white velvet petals, shaped like leaves, as they began to darken, turning dull yellow at first. They withered to an ashen tan and died, crumpling to the earth and blowing away to catch in blades of grass.

Sau'ilahk slowly turned as he scanned the plain in all directions. What was this place with such hidden blights that could hurt him?

It was somehow familiar. Not as if he had been here, but perhaps something he had heard of once. As eternal as he was, his mind was no more immune to forgetfulness than that of any living being. Over a thousand years, no one continued to remember everything that they once had. Memories faded, particularly ones that seldom came to use.

Still starving, Sau'ilahk slipped carefully back to the road, avoiding any domes of flowers. There was no time left to ponder them, or what he had felt under the earth. Dawn was near, and with what little life he had gained, he still had to find the caravan. Once he had fed properly, he would have little trouble remembering this place to reawaken here after the next dusk.

He would lure and enslave a more natural servant—something that could move within the Lhoin'na lands. If he could not find the one life of Wynn from afar, the one *unlife* of Chane Andraso might more easily bring the sage back under his scrutiny.

Sau'ilahk fled up the dirt road like roiling streams of black vapors in the dark.

CHAPTER 12

Wynn opened her eyes at the sound of a nearby whine, and then she flinched to see a bark-covered wall a hand's length from her nose. She lurched upright and away, nearly falling off the bed shelf she lay on. She spun about, wrestling out of the blanket.

For an instant, she thought she'd awakened in an an'Cróan tree home. Shade sat fidgeting on her haunches as she whined, but Wynn was still lost for a moment.

The bed wasn't a raw shéot'a cloth mattress stuffed with straw and wild grass. It was fitted with heavy linen. She was in a room at the guild branch of the Lhoin'na. As she swung her legs over the bed ledge, her head filled with a rush of memories.

She saw the guild keep's rear grove, the forests on the way to Dhredze Seatt, and the wild woods they'd encountered on their present journey. More and more wild places popped up in Wynn's own perspective, showing Shade scurrying off into the brush.

"Yes, yes," she said. "Just . . . give me a moment."

Poor Shade needed to go out quite badly. But the next rush of memories showed a variety of meals.

First was the guild hall, then her room, complete with all the smells that didn't fit well together. A late breakfast of dried salt fish at the temple of Feather-Tongue mixed with a greasy sausage bought in a dwarven market.

—*outside . . . food . . . outside, outside—*

Wynn grabbed her head. "Shade, stop it. I'm coming, already."

A large umber-glazed washbasin sat beside the room's teardrop-shaped door. She'd set it there last night for Shade, filling it from its matching water pitcher. The basin was completely empty.

"Did you drink that whole bowl?"

Shade spun off her butt, and scurried to the door.

—outside, outside, outside—

With a groan, Wynn hauled herself up. A heavy gray curtain covered the room's small window, though a little light filtered around its edge. She wasn't certain of the time of day. At the room's far side, Chane lay stretched out on another bed ledge, completely covered, a blanket pulled up over his head.

Barefoot in only her shift, Wynn hastily wrapped herself in her robe and tiptoed to the other inner door. She cracked it open and found Ore-Locks snoring away in the adjoining room. He'd stretched out on the floor, likely unable to get his bulk onto a bed ledge. He'd been living on Chane's schedule since their caravan trip began and would likely sleep half the day.

Wynn quietly shut the door, and Shade's whine shifted to a discontented rumble.

"Hold on," she whispered as she reached for her clothes draped over the travel trunk.

She'd been too exhausted last night to do anything but crawl into bed, but now she took clearer notice of the room. Stacks of books, loose paper, and leather satchels were scattered about haphazardly. Mujahid wasn't particularly orderly for a sage. Two unlit, half-burned candles sat on the small table, along with a crucible and a mortar and pestle.

Wynn picked up one book. Its flaked, gilded title, written in exaggerated elven script, read *The Wells of the Elements,* by Premin Glhasleò ácärâj Jhiara-jua Avcâshuâ. She vaguely recognized the name.

Premin "Gray Light" or "Dusk Light" had been one of a few metaologers to become a high premin—and the only such among the Lhoin'na. About three hundred years ago, he'd been criticized and suspected by his peers for his manic interest in the arcane. He'd died in bed at only seventy-two, after eating a plate of mushrooms. It was recorded that he'd gathered them himself, so theories of foul play were dismissed.

Wynn lifted a finely crafted parchment from the desk and scanned its

Elvish writing. It was a conservative treatise on the hazards of thaumaturgical practices involving elemental Spirit. What, exactly, was Mujahid researching here?

Suddenly, Shade growled, bit down on Wynn's robe, and jerked, making her stumble back. Wynn dropped the book and page on the table. Shade's urgency also left her feeling a bit too nosy. Whatever Mujahid's reasons, he'd been generous with his rooms, and she shouldn't take advantage.

She pulled on her formal, full-length robe and retrieved the sealed message entrusted to her. Then she paused to scavenge a scrap of paper and a small charcoal stick. She scrawled a quick noted in Belaskian for Chane, telling him she'd try to be back at dusk.

"All right, come on," she said softly.

Wynn barely opened the outer door when Shade squirmed through and bolted out in a ruckus of scrabbling claws. Wynn rolled her eyes and followed, not bothering to call after the dog.

The narrow passage didn't exactly resemble a hallway—more like a strange, bark-covered, organic tunnel. Taller than it was wide, it burrowed through the place in a gradual curve ahead. Tall, teardrop-shaped doors, no two ever alike, were spaced sporadically along both sides. Wynn finished the arcing downward slope, reached the flowing stairs, and followed them downward.

When she reached the chamber where she'd met Mujahid, Shade already stood wriggling before the door to the courtyard. The instant Wynn opened it, Shade shot out, and Wynn followed more slowly.

The day was cold and clear outside, though the walls of the redwood citadel cast the courtyard in dusk as she waited on Shade. Hopefully, Shade wouldn't desecrate some labor-intensive shrubbery.

Wynn craned her head back, looking straight up. By the light of the circle of sky above, she guessed it was early afternoon. Perhaps lunch was still being served. If so, and if she could find the meal hall, she might find assistance with directions, as well.

Shade came back at a leisurely trot, looking much relieved, and Wynn opened the door.

Upon stepping back in, Wynn heard voices echoing from the next inner chamber. She shooed Shade ahead and followed the sound into a passage much wider than the one outside the guest quarters. She'd lost track of how far around the redwood ring they might have gone when she stepped into a cavernous chamber of flowing bark walls.

Light filled the busy place from crystal-paned windows that went up and up along the inner wall. Though the tree ring had to be quite broad, it wasn't as deep as the hall of Wynn's guild branch. Instead of spreading out, it spiraled upward.

A central, bark-covered pillar as big as a single redwood rose out of the shale-tiled floor into the heights. Anchored between it and the chamber's walls were at least five partial levels that she could see. Stairs of bare wood sprouted from the walls, leading from one level to the next. Sages and even others in plain elven clothing sat at tables on each level and chatted away in their lyrical tongue.

And, as usual, too many eyes looked Wynn's way, or, rather, at Shade.

Apparently, the sight of a majay-hì was almost as bizarre among the Lhoin'na as in Calm Seatt. More so, since such creatures were known to be real to these people—and this one kept company with a human. Many present stared openly, but not even the closest queried Wynn as Shade pressed against her leg.

Remnants of lunch were still spread on tables as young elven initiates busily cleared plates and bowls. Wynn tried to see where the food was being served from, but she noted two things instead.

First, while nearly all the occupants were elves, a small group of Suman sages—including Mujahid—were gathered around one table. He bowed his head politely to her, and Wynn nodded back. His cowl was down, and Wynn was a little surprised at his curly black hair hanging almost to his shoulders. Ghassan il'Sänke, whom she still counted as a friend, kept his quite short, like the few other Suman males she'd met.

She couldn't help noticing he was the only metaologer in his group. The others were robed in cerulean and teal, the orders of Sentiology and Conamology.

Second, there wasn't a single white-robed sage in the place, though she hadn't expected such. If Chuillyon belonged to some legitimate but unknown order, it had to be a small one, and that was a big if.

Ignoring quizzical glances amid sudden silences, Wynn hoped everyone would just go back to their conversations. Between her and the Suman contingent, one elderly male elf in a gray robe sat sipping a cup of broth. He had a serene countenance, and he wasn't staring at her or Shade.

"Pardon," Wynn said in Elvish, approaching him. "I have a message from the Calm Seatt branch for your high premin. Could you direct me?"

He glanced at Shade before looking up at her.

"Our high premin is on a mission of mercy," he said. "She is assisting other healers in combating the fever at a human settlement."

He said "the fever" as if she knew what he meant, though she didn't.

"Premin Gyâr of Metaology can take your message for now," he continued. "He is handling basic affairs in her absence."

Wynn hesitated. A high premin off grounds was unexpected; leaving the head of Metaology in charge was unprecedented. In a high premin's absence, the premin of Cathology usually stood in, if the two weren't one and the same. After that, the premin of Sentiology was typically next in line.

All Wynn wanted was to get rid of the message, and perhaps if she didn't treat it as urgent, it might be held unopened until the high premin returned. This might gain her a bit of time and willing assistance, if needed, should this message have a similar effect to the one she'd delivered in Chathburh.

"Where can I find Premin Gyâr?" she asked.

"I am heading that way myself," someone said. "I will take you."

Wynn turned at the thick accent, and Mujahid stood up among his companions. Sitting so close, he couldn't have missed her conversation. Something about his eager manner put her on guard again.

The elderly elven cathologer nodded, as if relieved of a burden, and Wynn couldn't refuse Mujahid's offer. He gathered up his short pile of books and gestured toward the hall's back and its courtyard door. Lips pursed, Wynn had started to follow Mujahid when a loud growl halted her.

Shade hadn't budged. She eyed Wynn and then a nearby table where people were still eating. Shade shook her large head wildly and sniffed the air with great drama.

"We'll eat soon enough. Now come," Wynn urged. "First things first."

Then she noticed the room had gone too quiet.

Even Mujahid stared at the human casually talking to a majay-hì, as if it were normal.

About to speak again, Wynn swallowed hard and cringed under all that scrutiny. She whispered through her teeth, "Come on."

Shade curled a jowl and slunk toward the door that Mujahid still held open. All three of them ventured outside into the courtyard's cool air, where there were far fewer eyes.

"Most premins and domins keep offices in the west side," Mujahid said matter-of-factly. "Metaologers prefer the south."

"I'd guess by your order that you know Domin il'Sänke," she said. "Have you studied with him?"

"Certainly," he answered. "All of my guild branch knows the domin."

That was puzzling. Metaologers were a reclusive lot and mixed sparingly with *all* of a guild branch.

"He helped me during his stay in Calm Seatt," Wynn added. "When you see him again, please give him my best."

Mujahid returned a deep nod. "Most certainly," he said, a phrase he used too frequently.

Wynn fell silent as they walked an outer path. The courtyard was even lovelier in its dusky daylight. She wondered how all of this growth thrived here, considering that direct light would enter only when the sun was at its highest point of the day.

Glistening ivy climbed the guild's bark walls. A few birds flew from tree to tree, peeping and rustling among the leaves. The entire courtyard was filled with life, and she couldn't count the varieties of flowers she saw. A large squirrel bolted across the path, into the shrubberies on the far side.

Shade's ears stood on end.

"No," Wynn said quickly, though Shade hadn't taken pursuit.

As Mujahid neared another door, Wynn again tilted her head back, staring upward. High overhead, the structure's upper reaches were not even. Marked with remaining branches and foliage, the ancient redwoods' tops had melded together in five places that rose well above the rest of the structure.

Wynn lowered her head to find Mujahid holding the door. As she stepped in, she genuinely wished he would stop being so helpful.

"The premin's office is higher up, at midpoint," he said.

This entry chamber was smaller than the one where she'd first met him.

He led her through a rear archway into a vast, open chamber. Elves favored light, space, and organic order, but none of those things existed here.

Dimly lit, the place was filled with a confusing array of colored glass tubes; mortars and pestles; small, shielded burners and tin plates; and bowls of all sizes on tables variously made from stone that was resistant to dangerous substances. Rather than benches, she saw light stools, much easier to move from place to place. Aging books and a multitude of wood, ceramic, and metal containers lined floor-to-ceiling shelves along the walls. Only one person occupied the chamber.

Dressed in midnight blue, he stood hunched over a book on a table at the far side. He raised his head, half turned it, and looked toward them. Mujahid stopped abruptly, forcing Wynn to do the same, and she thought she heard him swallow quickly.

"Forgive the intrusion, Premin," he said in fluent Elvish. "I thought to find you in your office above."

The dark-robed elf straightened, and Wynn squinted into the dim light.

Premin Gyâr was nearly seven feet tall, with broad shoulders and a muscular build—or at least for one of his people. His hair was more brown than gold.

"Journeyor Mujahid, is it not?" he asked.

"Yes, Premin. Again, forgive the intrusion."

"Do not concern yourself," Gyâr assured, waving them in.

Mujahid took a step back. "You have a messenger from Calm Seatt. I was merely showing a newcomer the way."

He bowed respectfully to the premin, adding a quicker nod to Wynn, and turned immediately to leave.

"We'll be out of your rooms by dinner," she called after him.

If Mujahid heard, he didn't answer as he stepped out. To her shame, Wynn found herself wishing that he'd stayed.

Premin Gyâr didn't come to meet her. He stood silently by the table, taking in the sight of Shade and then Wynn's gray robes. Finally, he looked her directly in the eyes, waiting.

Wynn was forced to cross through all the tables to him.

His face was triangular, like most elves', though slightly long of jawline. He appeared middle-aged, which might be considered young for a premin. His eyes became more disturbing the closer Wynn drew.

They were less slanted than a typical elf's, less amber, and glimmered with a shade of dark yellow.

"I am Journeyor Hygeorht of the Calm Seatt branch," she said, filling the unpleasant silence as she pulled out the sealed letter. "High Premin Sykion asked me to deliver this during my visit."

Premin Gyâr didn't move or hold out his hand. The ghost of a frown passed over his features, but he never blinked. Finally, he broke the silence.

"Premin Sykion sent a journeyor cathologer all this way to deliver a letter? Is something amiss?"

His tone was flat, the only inflection on "cathologer," as if the word were distasteful.

"Not that I know of," Wynn replied in feigned ignorance. She held out the letter again, and this time he took it as she added, "I also have research assignments to conduct . . . in your archives."

Again he said nothing, simply turning the sealed message under his gaze. His dark yellow eyes then shifted and locked on her. His expression altered in an instant with a welcoming nod and faint smile.

Wynn grew even more wary.

"Be sure to see Domin In-Ridge about a room assignment," he said. "Have you eaten?"

In spite of that smile, his voice was still cold—and jarring for the abrupt change of topic. Why would he use the domin's translated name, as if she wouldn't understand his native one?

"Not yet, Premin," she answered.

"Do so before making use of our archives. If initiates have cleared the meal, tell them I sent you. Something can be found in the kitchens."

"Thank you, Premin."

Wynn backed up two steps before turning.

There was nothing wrong with him that she could put a finger on. But she was eager to leave, and, hopefully, wouldn't need to meet him again. As she passed through the archway and out of that chaotic chamber, she noticed that Shade hadn't followed. Wynn glanced back.

Shade was the one staring this time—at Premin Gyâr. The premin watched her in turn, not a bit of shock or awe in his expression.

"Come, Shade," Wynn whispered. "Time to eat."

Shade turned, but not with any of her earlier urgency. Once they were back in the courtyard, Wynn took a deep breath, released it slowly, and put that odd encounter behind her.

Uncertain of her current position within the redwood citadel, she backtracked along the way she'd come. When she spotted a small group exiting into the courtyard, she grabbed the door to peek in. The meal hall waited inside, and Wynn felt a little more confident about finding her way around.

Better yet, the hall was almost empty.

Some dark bread, goat cheese, and late-season blackberries still graced the end of one table. Wynn made a beeline before someone cleared them away. Shade was satisfied with the bread and cheese. In the past she'd turned up her nose at anything baked, but these days, she'd even eat jerky and biscuits.

A few elven initiates looked at them—at Shade—but no one approached.

"Mind your manners," Wynn said, breaking off more cheese for Shade.

Shade snapped and gulped and then whined for more, sniffing at the table's edge.

"That's enough for now," Wynn said. "I need to find the archives."

The courtyard door slammed open.

Wynn stiffened on the bench when Premin Gyâr strode in, his midnight blue robe swinging around his booted feet. Two young initiates sucked in audible breaths and scrambled out of sight. Gyâr's gaze locked on Wynn, and her stomach knotted as he came straight at her.

"I am glad to have found you," he said, and the calm in his voice belied the hostility in his eyes. "I have been informed of a change of circumstance. Our guild is preparing for a complete restructuring of the archives. The work begins sooner than anticipated."

Wynn dropped a hunk of cheese on her plate.

"It is unfortunate that you traveled such a distance," he continued. "At present, no one besides the archivists and their assistants will be allowed to enter. I do apologize."

Wynn flushed cold with shock as she stood up and carefully asked, "How long will this restructuring take?"

"Indefinitely . . . as it involves a great deal of work," he answered, and turned immediately to leave.

Wynn was left standing there, staring after him. This was far worse than what had happened in Chathburh after she'd delivered the first message.

"I am in no hurry," she called after Gyâr.

"Then your stay will be a long one," he said, his back to her. "Of course, you are welcome to visit the public libraries in the branch's lower levels."

And he was gone.

Wynn was still numb, like the moment right after a sharp blow. It had never occurred to her that she'd be shut out. Not even her own superiors had gone that far. The frustration and the loss were overwhelming, and then shock burned away in anger.

What had that damned Sykion put in this message?

Wynn had sold a sacred cold lamp crystal for a more secretive passage than she'd told her superiors. Chane had suffered through the caravan ride to get here. Ore-Locks was still on her heels, trying to force her onward.

And she'd been locked out from afar by Sykion.

What was going on inside her own guild branch? It wasn't enough for them to just get her out of their way for as long as possible, much as they'd connived to keep her connected to the guild and under watch. It now appeared she remained a sage in name only.

Shade rumbled softly.

Wynn wondered whether the dog reacted to Premin Gyâr's demeanor or understood what had just occurred.

Two remaining initiates still stared at the courtyard door. They cast furtive glances at Wynn, as if she'd brought something fearful among them.

Wynn fled the meal hall, pulling Shade along. Once outside, she was panting in anger, frustration, and panic. This time the courtyard's serenity didn't help her. She wanted to hit something—or someone.

Had Sykion's unknown warning been so dire that Gyâr had closed down the entire archives? It didn't seem believable. Or were the archivists really engaged in such a vast reorganization while giving Gyâr a few moments' notice? That was just as far-fetched.

The sound of shuffling footsteps and sloshing water barely cut through Wynn's thoughts. A young initiate, perhaps fourteen, was hauling a bucket along the path in the other direction.

"Pardon," Wynn called, hurrying after the girl. "Could you point me to the archives?"

The girl blinked. The question appeared to confuse her as she looked over Wynn's gray robe. She pointed upward, above the courtyard.

"There," she said.

Wynn peered up, trying to follow the girl's finger. At a guess, the initiate pointed to one side of the redwood ring below one of its five spires.

"Thank you," Wynn said. "Shade, come."

They hurried around the courtyard's perimeter, leaving the elven girl staring after them.

Wynn kept looking upward, trying to gauge when they were somewhere below where the girl had pointed. When she thought they were close, she went for the first door she saw. She and Shade slipped inside a chamber barely larger than an alcove. It emptied into a wide passage lined with more doors that ran along the middle of the redwood ring. Almost immediately, she heard raised voices.

Wynn followed the sound. She hurried into the passage, saw a branch that sloped upward, and scurried onward.

"What is the meaning of this?" someone shouted in Elvish, but he had a heavy Suman accent. "You have no authority over the archives! I was here this morning, and there was no indication that it would be closed."

Wynn saw the top of a teal cowl over the passage's rise and crept a little closer.

Two Suman conamologers in teal robes, one a middle-aged man with peppered black hair and another, perhaps a journeyor, were raising a fuss. To the passage's left side stood a pair of armed patrollers, the Shé'ith. The first stood his place, staring ahead, as if the Suman sages no longer existed. He and his female counterpart blocked an opening.

Wynn shifted to the sloping passage's right side for a better look. Beyond the patrollers, inside the opening, broad steps curled sharply upward through the structure like a spiral staircase. She couldn't see where they led, but for an instant, she was distracted from the dispute.

There was no lockable door in the opening, as there were in the stairwells down to the archives of her branch. In part, that explained the presence of the

Shé'ith, though she'd never heard of armed guards placed inside any guild branch. Even when the threat of the wraith had come to her branch, there were limits upon what Captain Rodian had been allowed to do with his city guard contingent.

"Apologies, sir," the female patroller stated flatly. "The archives have been closed until further notice."

"Where was the first notice?" the elder Suman sputtered. "I will speak to the Premin Council about this breach of interbranch protocol."

The female patroller didn't even blink. Her male counterpart was equally silent and expressionless. With no response from either Shé'ith, the Suman sages turned away. The younger one spotted Wynn as they passed.

"Do not bother," he said in Numanese. "It would seem that not all sages have the full amenities in this branch."

The elder was muttering angrily in Sumanese as they headed downward.

Wynn knew those two would get nowhere if Premin Gyâr had any say. And he did, as one of the Premin Council here, as well as sitting in for the high premin. Was there something happening here beyond just hampering her? It made Wynn wonder what else was in Sykion's message.

Regardless, Wynn hadn't come all this way for nothing. She had to gain access to the archives if there was any chance they held some long-forgotten mention of an ancient fallen seatt. But without the means to even look for such, what was she going to do?

Chuillyon had kept the same rooms at the guild for nearly sixty years, though in the last thirty, he hadn't enjoyed them often. Most of his time was spent with the royal family in Calm Seatt, but he had no intention of ever giving up his quarters here. They suited him. Down in the earth beneath the base of the south spire—even beneath the giant roots of the redwood ring—he enjoyed nearly absolute peace and quiet.

Although his chambers in Calm Seatt's third castle were lavish, he preferred this place. Every item here was carefully chosen for a balance between subtle elegance and a monastic simplicity. In the main room, the desk and a small table had been shaped into flowing bentwood curves. A few shéot'a cushions of plain forest colors softened three basic chairs of polished mahogany. His more private room was in the back, beyond a pale blue, curtained doorway. That space was filled with only a bed covered in a cream quilt of duller raw shéot'a, a wardrobe, a cushioned rocker to match his outer furniture, and a modest collection of favored texts. Oh, but there were a few little amusing toys from his youth, as well.

One small, carved scene, which could fit in his lap, had a twist crank in its bottom. When wound up, a woodsman hacked away at a tree until it toppled. The tree would bounce repeatedly off the woodsman's head, pounding him into the ground like a peg until only his head peeked out.

Nature had a wicked wit.

This toy had been a gift in his boyhood from what humans would call a favorite aunt. If only she had known what mischievous notions it would inspire over a lifetime. If nothing else, Chuillyon loved his jests. Or perhaps that was his refuge against what he hated most: sadness. There had been too much of that.

He sat at his desk, awaiting two visitors, hoping they would bring him more news than he had gleaned for himself. Why had Wynn traveled all this way? What was she up to now?

"Chuillyon . . . are you in?"

The deep voice was not one he had expected. He rose, stepping into the masoned passageway between the guild's great roots.

"Premin?" he called back, glancing toward the stairwell leading upward.

"May I come down?"

"Please do."

Despite knowing the caller, Chuillyon was perplexed at the sight of Premin Gyâr descending the stairs, bowing his head to avoid the ceiling. By necessity, they had been closely connected over the decades, but they did not visit each other's private chambers.

"Forgive the intrusion," Gyâr said.

To Chuillyon's further surprise, his tone *was* almost apologetic—and quite out of character. Gyâr's dark yellow eyes were troubled or angry, which was not out of character. A stray strand of light brown hair hung forward over one of his eyes, as if he was too distracted to notice it.

"What is wrong?" Chuillyon asked.

"A journeyor arrived from Calm Seatt with a message for the high premin."

Chuillyon took a deep, slow breath. "You mean young Hygeorht?"

"You know her?"

"Yes. What has she done now?"

Gyâr took a folded paper from inside his dark robe. Its wax seal had been broken.

"High Premin Sykion of Calm Seatt sent this," he said, holding it out.

Chuillyon hesitated. "What is it?"

"Read it."

"Really," Chuillyon scoffed. "Is all this drama necessary?"

But he took it just the same. It was double wrapped, and he unfolded both enveloping sheets to view the letter within.

Dear T'ovar . . .

Chuillyon stalled at the informal opening, but he read onward.

The bearer of this message poses a threat. She has proven herself without conscience or reason, and is set on a course that will undermine guild efforts, safeguards, and preparation for what may come. For her own goals, she risks exposing hard-won knowledge to the masses. We cannot allow this before we are fully prepared for the panic and backlash that will come if what we learn leaks out. I believe she comes to scavenge your archives in the hope of finding support for her interpretations and theories concerning the ancient texts still being translated.

Although she is under my authority, and is my responsibility, I have no further way to keep her from the texts other than to let her go abroad. I will not tolerate further interference with our efforts, yet I cannot expel her, and thereby lose limited control over her.

You have my leave to do what is necessary—and to do so now.

May you live in wisdom's eternal cycle.

Your friend, Tärtgyth Sykion

Chuillyon stared at the note's end and grew suddenly anxious over what Gyâr had done. He lifted the letter to look at the two enveloping sheets. The outer with the broken wax seal was unmarked, but the inner was addressed only to *T'ovar*.

Chuillyon could barely catch his breath. "This is—"

"A personal letter, not a guild communication," Gyâr finished.

The admission was not an explanation.

Chuillyon scanned the letter twice more, his thoughts turning over the varied truths and lies, as he knew them. Wynn was certainly in full possession of both her reason and her conscience, though she had a reckless penchant with information best kept secret. Now things were so much worse.

One high premin secretly asked another to cut off Wynn. One of the three who sat on the entire guild's High Premin Council had stepped beyond protocol into personal manipulation and favors. Gyâr, in the absence of their own high premin, had illicitly intercepted that communication, suspect as it was, and taken action with his temporary authority.

A deceit wrapped in a collusion just to block the efforts of one young sage.

Chuillyon worried where this would lead the guild as a whole.

"T'ovar will know this was meant for her eyes," he said.

Gyâr pulled the letter's addressed inner wrap out of Chuillyon's hand and slowly crumpled it into a ball.

Chuillyon shook his head in disbelief. If Gyâr thought that was enough to claim he had not known it was private before opening it . . .

"I have closed the archives," Gyâr said.

Chuillyon swallowed hard. This was not just about Wynn. Gyâr was using her as an excuse for something more.

"Considering your rare, present residency," Gyâr went on, "I want your support to convince the council my decision was correct. T'ovar has long-standing doubts concerning the two human branches of our guild, but she has been too hesitant—"

"Fair-minded," Chuillyon corrected.

Gyâr glared at him and continued. "Too overly empathetic where they are concerned."

"Do not do this," Chuillyon warned.

"You have expressed like concerns, as well. You *know* we must maintain safeguards and secrecy."

"It is too far . . . and too soon!"

"Better than too late."

Gyâr paused for several breaths, perhaps trying to regain calm. Chuillyon had never been one to respond to a forceful persuasion.

"I cannot see how this journeyor ever came to even know of such writings," Gyâr said, "much less try to access them. Sykion and Hawes have become lax in their protection of the recovered texts. For all of il'Sänke's faults, at least he keeps his people under control."

"Yes, he manages that," Chuillyon returned dryly.

Either Gyâr ignored the sarcasm or he did not notice. Chuillyon had his own estimation of Domin Ghassan il'Sänke, and of the influence metaologers tried to wield in any of the guild branches.

"This will also cut off il'Sänke's minion in that Suman contingent among us," Gyâr added.

Chuillyon tried not to swallow, to sigh, or to wince as his peer, his superior, went on.

"If all is settled before T'ovar returns, she will not balk at what was done. It will simply be a relief that the decision was made, one that she's put off time and again. May I count on you?"

Chuillyon knew things about Wynn Hygeorht that would drop Gyâr's jaw. He had kept everything that had happened in Dhredze Seatt to himself. He had worked so hard to guide Malourné's royal family, as had his subordinates assigned to the Numan nations and territories. It was a duplicitous game of aid balanced against subtle control, and he had fought to keep his superiors from taking things too far.

His life had been spent perched upon a pin tip, trying to keep any faction of a future alliance from trampling the others in blind panic. Now it appeared he had not paid enough attention to how easily someone closer at hand could suddenly flick that pin out from under him. And just as unexpected, it had come riding on the robed skirt of Wynn Hygeorht.

Chuillyon should have laughed at his own foolishness, for he had overlooked the most likely possibility. And now . . .

"May I count on you?" Gyâr repeated pointedly.

Chuillyon looked his old comrade in the eyes and feigned a serene smile. "Always."

"Good." And Gyâr turned for the stairs. "I will convene the council first thing tomorrow morning."

Chuillyon waited until the premin's footsteps faded up the outer stairs. He then backed into his chamber, sank into a chair, and pressed his fingers to his mouth.

He could not openly oppose Gyâr and risk weakening his own position and the standing of his suborder within the Order of Metaology. His support had hastened Gyâr's rapid rise to authority and, through the tall premin, he had often influenced the council to a degree. He had held off their suspicions, their fears concerning the humans and their two branches of the guild. All the while, he had labored carefully to retain faith in his counsel from all sides that would be needed one day. For even the Numans had their own doubts about his people, as well as one another's nations.

Then Wynn Hygeorht returned with those ancient texts, still a secret to all but one nation among the Numans.

Everything was unraveling too quickly, and it had started from within the guild itself. He saw a day to come when he might be an enemy to all of the sides he had tried to hold together.

"Master?" a female voice called from above.

This was one he had been expecting, and he called out, "Yes, come."

Two robed elves appeared at his chamber entrance. One was an overly slender young woman in a midnight blue robe, and her male companion wore white. Hannâschi and Shâodh—"Within a Consecrated Space" and "Care-Tender"—were among the few people he trusted. Or at least among those he trusted mostly, if not completely.

"What kept you?" Chuillyon asked.

Hannâschi bowed slightly. "We saw Premin Gyâr enter the stairwell and thought it best to wait."

She was shorter than a human male, and so slender her closest friends sometimes called her Fohk'hannâ—a play on her name meaning "little female corn sprout." Her hair was a deep shade of gold, and when uncoiled hung a ridiculous length down her back to her knees. She had overly expressive eyes, especially for a metaologer.

Chuillyon was unaffected by her lovely appearance, though it had proven useful more than once. The way she listened, as if with her whole being, loosened the stiffest of tongues. She was a good judge of character in general. And though she had no intention of ever leaving the main Order of Metaology, she had quickly attached herself to him more than to cold-blooded Gyâr. Chuillyon valued her for that, as well.

"Did he tell you he closed the archives?" Shâodh asked quietly.

"Yes . . . he did," Chuillyon answered, eyeing the rare journeyor among his own suborder.

Shâodh was a much different story from Hannâschi. His eyes were a bit small and closely set. Not exactly slender, he was tall enough to make it appear so, and stood a full head above his companion. Somewhat stoic and private, Shâodh disliked bothering with personal appearance. He kept his sandy hair cropped short.

"And?" Shâodh added. "How did you respond?"

He rarely spoke unless necessary. Bland as a river stone on the surface, he was intelligent, careful—one might say sly—and fiercely loyal to the Order of Chârmun. He was also ambitious and ethically pliable, but these characteristics had their uses.

"I will support Gyâr before the council gathering in the morning," Chuillyon answered.

Shâodh's brow puckered, the closest thing to dissatisfaction he would show a superior. Hannâschi's slow shake of her head was more disapproving, a gesture that Gyâr would have considered insubordinate.

"Have you learned anything?" Chuillyon asked.

"The metaologer among the visiting Sumans gave them his room," Hannâschi answered. "So far, only Journeyor Hygeorht and the majay-hì have ventured out."

"Long enough to instigate closure of the archives," Shâodh added flatly.

"So, how do we learn what she is after if she has no access?" Hannâschi asked. "She will not get past the Shé'ith, or not for long, even with her armed human and dwarven escorts. The black majay-hì is, of course, another matter."

Chuillyon clenched his jaw and exhaled sharply through his long nose. Hannâschi was slightly tainted by her premin's attitudes toward humans.

"She would never go that far," he countered. "But you cannot imagine the lengths she will go, if given the slightest chance . . . and a drop of assistance."

Hannâschi cocked her head, and her voice took on a taint of suspicion. "Master . . . you have something in mind."

"I do." Chuillyon smiled impishly. "With some simple thaumaturgical assistance."

Hannâschi closed her eyes and slumped. "Oh . . . not again."

Shâodh was trying very hard not to smile.

Domin Ghassan il'Sänke stood near the bow of a Numan merchant vessel headed south along the coast. Harsh sea winds snapped his midnight blue robe as much as worries tugged his thoughts.

Before leaving Calm Seatt a day after Wynn Hygeorht had gone to the Dhredze Seatt, he had finished a more proper translation of fragments she had gleaned from Chane Andraso's strange scroll. Of course, Ghassan had kept his own copy, but he had wrestled with how much of it, if any, he should leave for Wynn. In the end, he had given up trying to decide. At least in her undisciplined way, she had uncovered for him many things her Numan superiors could or would not. He prepared a letter and the translation, leaving both for her, if she returned home.

His forced exit from the Numan branch had come sooner than expected, and with too little gained. He had only one thick journal's worth of surreptitious copies from whatever pieces of the ancient texts he had been allowed to work on or view. It was galling the way the Numan Premin Council, especially Sykion and her underling High-Tower, kept everything hidden away. Those texts should have been transferred to the Suman branch. Hints of the earliest assaults from the Ancient Enemy's forces seemed to have come out of the great desert.

Even without such hints, Ghassan already had his reasons for both knowing and believing in which corner of the world the next war would begin. If he had been able to find those texts, he would have taken them at all costs. There was too much at stake not to do so. But nothing could be done for the moment.

Frustration left him anxious for his journey's end. He had been away from his homeland and his guild branch for a long while. It would not be long now, maybe a few days more at best.

A sudden warmth built on his sternum.

Ghassan pressed his hand against the front folds of his robe. He glanced about the deck as he felt heat from the copper medallion he wore inside his robe. There were too many sailors close at hand.

Trying not to rush, he stepped down the forecastle's ladder and headed belowdecks to his cabin. Once there, he settled on the bunk's edge, pulled out the medallion, and let it rest upon his palm. He closed his eyes, waiting.

A voice rose in his mind, dull at first, but sharpening as he fixed his will upon it.

Master?

Yes, Mujahid, he answered.

She is here. I do not know how or why, or how you knew . . . but she arrived last night.

Indeed, Ghassan had half expected this, for he knew her general location. He had his own way of tracking Wynn, one she would never suspect. As long as she carried the staff, he would know her whereabouts by direction and approximate distance. He could always find the staff with his mind if he focused. He had helped to make the crystal and imbued it with a fragment of his will.

Ghassan knew Wynn had left the Numan branch of the guild, traveling south at first. Much later she had turned east. He had never been completely certain where she headed, but the direction pointed toward very few places she might go. It was pure chance that Mujahid had been on assignment at the Lhoin'na branch. Ghassan had notified the young journeyor under his tutelage, who was also a prime future candidate for his inner sect.

Was she alone or with others? he finally asked.

Three companions. A tall human male, a male dwarf, and a wolf . . . or what the Lhoin'na call—

A dwarf?

Yes, Domin, but I know nothing about him as yet.

Ghassan moved on to details over which he had more control. *Is the human called Chane?*

Yes.

This troubled Ghassan deeply. Wynn Hygeorht's choice of companions had always been a concern and an unpredictable influence. How in all of Existence had Chane Andraso walked into the Lhoin'na forest?

Do not allow yourself to be alone with that one, Ghassan warned, and then paused in thought. *Do you know why Wynn is there?*

Not yet, but . . . the Lhoin'na Premin Council has shut the archives.

What? Why?

The territorial Shé'ith—their Serenitiers—guard all entrances rather than sages. Domin Safir and Journeyor Marwan were physically barred from entering.

This was too much, so drastic it could not be about Wynn alone. No branch dared deny access to ranking sages from another branch, at least not in such an obvious way. Something else was happening in the upper ranks of elven sages.

They claimed it is for restructuring, Mujahid went on, *but I have not seen one archivist or assistant enter access points that I have watched. Only once did anyone pass the guards . . . only premins.*

Ghassan had no notion of what purpose this severe action served or what had caused it.

When did this happen?

Mujahid paused before answering. *I took Journeyor Hygeorht to see Premin Gyâr, as she had an official communication for High Premin T'ovar, who is not present. I left her there, as I did not think it pertinent.*

Likely neither had Wynn. Ghassan's suspicions were already working. There was little chance to learn what that letter contained, but it must have come from the Numan Premin Council if it was for T'ovar—perhaps directly from Sykion. Was there something developing between the Lhoin'na and Numan sages? If so, would they leave Ghassan's own branch out?

Domin . . . how am I to continue if I cannot access the archives?

Ghassan slouched upon the bunk's edge. Mujahid's assignment was critical, but more critical was why Wynn had shown up at the Lhoin'na branch. Likely she sought those same archives for good reason, but the message she had brought had cut off both her and Mujahid.

What should I do? Mujahid asked.

Keep me appraised of Journeyor Hygeorht's activities. Without access to search for what we need, you will continue reporting to me, and only to me, so long as your group remains there. You will report anything you learn concerning the Lhoin'na Premin Council.

Yes, Domin.

And especially, Ghassan added, *everything you can learn concerning Premin Gyâr.*

Mujahid fell silent.

Is there a problem?

The journeyor of Metaology did not answer immediately. When he did, Ghassan felt the trepidation carried by two words.

No, Domin.

Ghassan let the medallion fall against his chest and sat silent.

Mujahid was frightened of Gyâr, as he should be, though there was no real danger. The Lhoin'na premin of Metaologers was manipulative, ambitious, cold, and cunning, and a bigot. But Gyâr would never overstep guild protocols too far if he caught a "foreign" journeyor snooping about.

Ghassan tucked away the medallion and returned to the open deck. He leaned over the rail, looking ahead for any sign of a harbor along the coastline. As yet, there were none, and he traipsed back toward the aftcastle.

"Captain," Ghassan called out. "Please make landfall at the first opportunity. I must disembark."

CHAPTER 13

Chane awoke to scuffling and hushed voices. He swatted off the blanket and sat up.

Wynn and Ore-Locks were busy about the guest quarters, gathering belongings. Shade watched from the other ledge bed with her nose on her paws. At Chane's sudden movement, Wynn glanced over.

"We have our own rooms," she said. "I told Mujahid we'd be out by now."

Before Chane even straightened his rumpled shirt, Ore-Locks grabbed the chest. Chane hefted his packs and swords. He was still groggy and beginning to wonder what had happened while he lay dormant. Wynn's manner was not only brusque; her expression and whole demeanor had changed.

He saw no relief in her face in gaining their privacy, let alone in having reached her destination. She looked strained, and her brow suddenly furrowed over some unknown thought. A trace of anger marred her soft features.

"I am hungry," Ore-Locks said.

Chane realized it had been more than a day since the dwarf had eaten anything besides apple slices. Hopefully, Wynn had found something for herself and Shade.

But then he found himself distracted as he stepped out into the passage.

Since entering the Lhoin'na forest, he had felt watched, continually prodded, as if something unseen sought him out. Now he stood inside of a *living* place. Much as the ring dulled his awareness and hampered his heightened senses, he dared not take it off until they left this land.

Wynn nodded ahead down the passage and looked to Ore-Locks. "Those two doors on the right. Soon as we're settled, I'll show you the meal hall."

She opened the nearer door and held it for Chane. Ore-Locks seemed about to argue, but dropped the chest by the door and headed off to the next one. Chane entered and found the room identical to the one they had left—minus Mujahid's paraphernalia. After Wynn and Shade followed, he waited until he heard Ore-Locks's door close. He then dropped the packs, quickly slid the chest inside, and closed himself away in privacy with Wynn.

"What's wrong?" he asked.

Wynn sank on the far bed ledge. Shade crawled up beside her, though it was a tight fit, and nosed Wynn's hand.

Chane's head had not fully cleared, and perhaps the nagging prod of the forest's presence wore on his patience, as well.

"Wynn?"

She raised only her eyes to him. "The archives have been shut."

Chane took a quick step. "What?"

She recounted everything from when she awoke to the two Shé'ith expelling a pair of Suman sages. Chane turned aside and dropped down hard on the opposite bed ledge.

"Armed guards? You told me it is impolite to openly carry weapons inside a guild branch."

"It is," she answered dryly. "And yet."

No doubt something in Wynn's delivered message had caused all of this, though it seemed extreme to cut off everyone just to keep her out.

"Has this ever happened in Calm Seatt?" he asked.

"I don't know of this *ever* happening at *any* branch," she answered. "Domin Tärpodious oversaw categorical restructurings, when holdings in some sections outstripped space. But he closed off one section at a time, not the whole archive. . . . And no city guards or constabularies were called in."

Wynn appeared to grow weary before Chane's eyes. She ran her hands over her face, pushing back her hair, looking small and defeated. Even the anger drained from her features. Chane began to fume in her place.

Why did Wynn's own superiors keep going to ever greater lengths to hinder her? The twisted world at large had never been worth Chane's concern. Now he saw the same taints inside the guild. If not for Wynn, he would have had no part of it anymore. That dream of a better life in her world almost died within him.

"When did this happen?" he asked.

"Just after lunch."

"What did you do all afternoon?"

She got up and went for her pack, digging out a new journal.

"Their public library was open, so I took a look, for the sake of it. Sometimes things don't get put back where they belong, out of sight."

This was the Wynn that Chane knew, never leaving any possibility unexplored.

"Did you find anything?" he asked.

"No." She laid the journal on her bunk and began turning pages. "But I copied bits of an old map. It's crude, but might be useful. I don't dare ask for a scribed copy, or request to take it off grounds for the work to be done elsewhere. I'm probably being watched."

Chane got up to join her, standing to one side as he looked down at the journal. It was a simplistic line sketch of the region at large. It showed general areas south all the way to the nearest part of the Sky-Cutter Range separating Numan nations and free territories from the southern desert. Wynn pointed to a blank vertical strip between columns of inverted wedges for unnamed mountains.

"This is called the Slip-Tooth Pass," she said. "It ends at the northern side of the range. It isn't enough to go on, but if I can't gain some hint to Bäalâle Seatt's whereabouts, it's the shortest and clearest path to the range."

Chane shook his head. "That range is at least a thousand leagues long, probably much more. It would take a year to search even that nearest part of it. We must get into the archives."

Shade hopped off the bed, rumbling in agitation as she squatted. Perhaps she understood and did not care for Chane's suggestion.

"How?" Wynn asked. "I've gone over everything I can think of, including you drawing the guards off for me. All notions lead to you getting arrested . . . and all of us being expelled."

"Ore-Locks could slip through one of the walls."

Wynn shook her head. "I don't think stonewalkers can pass through wood—only earth and stone, maybe metal. And Ore-Locks isn't as skilled as his elders. When I was taken to the texts in Dhredze Seatt, he stood guard, but he had to wait for another to retrieve me." She paused. "Besides, I don't trust him in there on his own."

Chane scowled at this. He trusted his own newfound instinct for deceit, though of late, it seemed to vanish at times. But at their first real meeting with Ore-Locks in the Chamber of the Fallen, his sense of deception had been acute. Chane had not sensed a lie when Ore-Locks had denied Wynn's insinuation that the dwarf served some traitorous ancestral spirit.

Ore-Locks had his own agenda, unknown as it was, but the wayward stonewalker was the closest thing they had to an ally with necessary skills. Any help should not be so quickly dismissed.

"Show me where the guards are," Chane said. "Perhaps we—"

A quick, triple knock sound at the door.

Chane heard Wynn's breath catch, and she rose and hurried over, not yet opening it.

"Yes?"

"Journeyor Hygeorht?" called a light voice outside. "A message for you."

Wynn pulled the door open as Chane approached behind her.

A metaologer in a midnight blue robe stood outside. Chane had seen few elves in his life before coming to this continent. Even he was a bit startled at the sight of *her*.

Stunning, even for an elf, she was like something out of his land's fables and folklore. She was so slight she might break under a strong breeze, and so beautiful she couldn't be real. She smiled and held out a folded and wax-sealed sheet of paper.

"Who is it from?" Wynn asked as she took the message.

The young woman simply shook her head, as if she did not know, then turned and walked away. Wynn closed the door, flipping the message in her hand.

The cream paper was thick and of fine quality, its folded edge locked down with a green wax seal impressed with the shape of an ivy leaf. Wynn broke the seal, unfolded the paper, and revealed a sharply stroked script. Chane assumed it was Elvish.

Wynn dropped her hand so fast the paper crackled, and she jerked the door open, rushing out to look down the passage.

Chane leaned out, looking both ways. "What is it?"

Wynn pushed him back, stepped inside, and shut the door. She stood staring blankly at the sheet of paper.

"It's a pass . . . into the archives," she answered without the slightest relief or joy.

"Who would send you this?"

Wynn shook her head and studied the letter again. "It's unsigned, but the council seal makes it official. I just show it to the guards and . . . and I'm in."

Chane distrusted sudden changes of fortune, and it was clear Wynn had equal doubts.

"I don't care who sent it," she said firmly. "We go now, before someone finds out and takes it back. Shade, come!"

This time Shade growled more sharply.

If the dog truly understood what had happened, Chane could not disagree with her warning. But what choice did they have?

Sau'ilahk rose from dormancy and materialized after dusk on the plain bordering the Lhoin'na forest. He had sated himself after finding the caravan before the previous dawn, and now brimmed with consumed lives. He would need that power tonight.

Drifting nearer the tree line, he kept to the road, shying from those little domes of velvety white flowers and whatever lay beneath in the earth that had filled him with painful cold. He stopped when he felt the slight tingle of the forest's presence reaching out to find him.

Sau'ilahk looked down on the road's stone-packed bare earth at a spot that would serve his need. There he crouched. This time, he would use the externalized trappings of ritual to aid his conjury.

Solidifying one hand, he scraped a double circle in the hard earth with one black, cloth-wrapped finger. Once he had filled that border ring with sigils, he rose and shut out the world to focus his thoughts on that pattern.

The lines in the earth began glowing with pale chartreuse in his sight.

Sau'ilahk drew upon his stores of life. He formed a clear image of a small creature in his mind. In a long existence, he had learned of many things, even of creatures that lived in places from which he was barred. He shaped that image, seeing that creature as if it stood there in the circle. Lost in the summoning, he did not notice it leave the forest until grass along the tree line rippled in its passing.

It broke from the plain's grass and bounded up the road.

Sau'ilahk immediately shifted focus, and the luring image in his sight vanished. He looked on the animal as it halted within the circle. No common beast would serve his purpose as well as this one.

About the size of a common barn cat, it had a ferretlike body as well as some of that animal's coloring. A stubby tail, darker than its bark-colored fur, quivered once before it rose on its hindquarters. Large, round brown eyes peered around a pug muzzle in a face masked with black fur. Twitching, wide ears made the tufts of white hairs on their points blur in vibration. But most useful of all were those tiny forepaws.

Almost like small hands, their stubby digits ended in little claws. A tâshgâlh—"finder of lost things"—stood mesmerized before Sau'ilahk.

A natural-born thief, the tâshgâlh possessed dexterous paws that exceeded a raccoon's for getting at whatever it became obsessed with. A trilling coo vibrated from its throat, for it was still entranced by the summoning; it did not actually see him yet. Tâshgâlh were found only in elven lands. Wherever he sent it, no one would give it notice other than to hide any shiny baubles that might catch its attention.

In a smooth flash, Sau'ilahk solidified one hand and snatched the tâshgâlh by the back of its long neck. Its trance broke, and its pigeonlike purr became a squealing, screeching chatter. He let it thrash, its tiny rear claws hooking nothing as it tried to tear at his incorporeal forearm.

It was the most perfect selection for a familiar.

With this beast Sau'ilahk could hunt for Wynn Hygeorht within a land forbidden to him.

Wynn paused at the courtyard door and looked back into the meal hall.

Ore-Locks's reddish hair badly needed brushing, as it was looking wild and tangled even when pulled back with a leather thong. As he gulped large spoonfuls of stew, nearby initiates stood dumbfounded, eyeing the other plates they'd brought him moments ago, which he'd emptied. They obviously had no idea how dwarves could feast at a moment's notice, though why Ore-Locks did so now was puzzling. Dwarves could store up food and go without for three times as long as a human.

"We should bring him," Chane whispered.

Wynn shook her head. This small venture was best kept from Ore-Locks; she'd told him nothing about the mysterious letter. Instead, she told him that she would look into how else she might gain access to the archives. He'd been too hungry to argue.

She might not be able to get rid of Ore-Locks, but she would keep the upper hand in whatever they did—by what she learned and he did not. The more dependent on her that he was, the better. For whatever he wanted at Bäalâle Seatt, she couldn't have him leaving her behind and getting there first.

Wynn turned to hurry out, shivering once in the cold air as they emerged in the courtyard.

"Which way?" Chane asked.

"North."

She trotted ahead, still gripping the unsigned letter and wondering who had sent it. Was someone here actually trying to help her? Or was the letter merely bait to trap her, complete with grounds for her expulsion? If the latter, it wasn't very effective. She would still have the pass with which to implicate whoever had sent it.

"Do you have any plan?" Chane asked. "Besides showing the pass to the guards and waiting to see what happens?"

She shook her head. "They'll let us through, and then it's a matter of time. Whoever arranged this is at odds with Premin Gyâr. We can only hope this comes out too late for him to stop us."

Wynn was even more uncertain than she sounded. They headed along the courtyard's paths, reaching a spot beneath the northernmost spire. Upon reentering the great redwood ring, her uncertainty turned to dread.

What if Gyâr had sent the pass? He was acting high premin and could simply claim it was forgery, no matter how legitimate it looked. He could've even used the council's official seal. She'd be trapped, and he would simply misdirect all others in a hunt for whoever had illicitly used the council's seal.

When had she become this paranoid? Steeling herself, she pressed on. What other choice did she have?

The entrance chamber was empty, and Wynn took a long breath before leading the way. Finally, she pointed up the sloping side passage where she'd seen the Suman sages expelled.

Chane looked positively grim, and Shade had been rumbling intermittently along the way. The dog had even once wrinkled a jowl at Wynn, expressing displeasure at all of this. Wynn pressed onward and upward.

They emerged to face the same two shé'ith standing before the opening to the spiral stairs. She'd forgotten how intimidating they were—tall, armed, and expressionless. She stepped leisurely forward with as much confidence as she could muster, and held out the letter.

"I'm here on assignment," she said in Elvish. "The Premin Council granted me this pass to enter the archives."

The female shé'ith looked down—not at the letter, but at Wynn.

Wynn couldn't help a flash of anxiety. She stood waiting, still holding out the letter.

When the woman took it, she snapped it open and scanned its content. A flicker of surprise on her triangular face washed away under a frown. She looked beyond Wynn at Chane and Shade.

"Is something amiss?" Wynn asked, extending her hand for the letter.

The female shé'ith turned over the letter, taking in the wax seal on its outer wrapping sheet. Still frowning, she finally returned it to Wynn but didn't move. All the while, her companion watched out of the corner of his eye, as if waiting for her to decide what they would do.

"This is an order from the council," Wynn said. "Stand aside."

She considered threatening to get a premin but feared the woman might agree. If the pass was some kind of bait, that would end her attempt to gain the archives right here and now.

Finally, the woman stepped aside.

Wynn avoided the smoldering uncertainty in the female shé'ith's large eyes. She strode by up the stairs, never looking back, and hoped Chane and Shade would follow quickly. When she glanced back, Chane blocked the view down the steps, but she heard the guards whispering. Then Wynn heard the sound of boots rushing off.

"Hurry," she whispered. "I think one of them went to verify the pass."

Chane waved her onward, and they quickstepped upward.

The stairway's living wood walls narrowed, until they had to climb single file. The stairs curved sharply around and around, but then suddenly leveled off into a more gradually arcing and rising passage.

Wynn passed a teardrop-shaped opening filled with a glass pane in the right wall. Through the window, she saw the tops of trees and knew she was looking beyond the guild's confines to the open forest. A soft light suddenly glowed beyond the passage's curve above.

When Wynn finally saw the cold lamp mounted on the wall, she paused on the landing. The lamp's cream-colored base likely contained alchemical fluids, just like those of her guild branch. The fluid produced enough warmth to keep a crystal lit instead of friction by hand. Then she spotted the door on her left, and it suddenly struck her that the guards weren't the only obstacles.

She'd been so focused on getting past them that she hadn't considered any archivists waiting beyond a door. If she ran into some counterpart to Domin Tärpodious, would the letter be enough?

Wynn reached for the door lever but didn't press it. There were two key-holes in the lock plate; two keys were needed to open the door. That was why only the entrance below need be guarded.

"What are you waiting for?" Chane whispered.

She looked up the passage to another set of stairs leading farther into the redwood ring's heights. If this door was locked, were there more above? The ring's thickness wasn't nearly the breadth of the Calm Seatt catacombs. Perhaps the Lhoin'na split their archives between multiple levels, but she had to start somewhere.

Wynn pressed the lever, and to her surprise, the door opened easily. This was unexpected, after the fuss over closing the archives. Perhaps she'd come to expect that nothing she tried would ever be without obstacles. She peeked in, thinking she would find someone waiting.

The main, northern entrance to her own branch's archives emptied into Domin Tärpodious's main room. Here she saw only rows of shelves beyond a smaller open space with three small tables. No one was present.

Standard cold lamps glowed on two tables, one of which had a pile of open books upon it. Someone had recently been working in here and left that work lying out. By the low light, Wynn spotted bound volumes and sheaves, as well as scroll cases, filling the nearest casements beyond the tables.

There was no sign of any restructuring in process.

Her anger returned for an instant, but she'd managed to gain the archives—even if under suspicious circumstances. Now she had to hurry.

Wynn rushed in. Chane couldn't read Elvish, or many other languages found in archive holdings, but that didn't matter. She pointed to the end of one freestanding casement where the faded etching of a lone triangle was still filled with remnants of paint.

"Look for Fire by Spirit, a triangle above a circle," she instructed. "That's for material on myths and legends in historical context. If you can't find that, search for a circle above a triangle for direct myths and legends possibly categorized by culture, region, and time frame."

The guild's orders were often represented by geometric symbols associated with the prime Elements of Existence: Spirit, Fire, Air, Water, and Earth. In turn, any works that fell into an order's fields of endeavor were filed in libraries and archives by those symbols. Columns of symbols on casements, individual shelves, and on some works themselves, were used to classify, subclassify, and cross-reference subject matter.

Circle, for Spirit and Metaology, indicated works on metaphysics, philosophy, religion, and folklore. Triangle, for Fire and Cathology—Wynn's own order—marked history and the organization of knowledge and information. The square of Air and Sentiology was for politics, law, government, economics, and so on. A hexagon for Water designated works of Conamology, including mathematics and applied sciences. The last was the octagon for Earth and Naturology, with its emphasis in natural and earth sciences, as well as prominent trades and crafts.

"I will start over here," Chane answered, heading off to the left.

Wynn passed him the spare cold lamp crystal before she took off the other way with Shade. She fingered along casement ends, scanning their etched symbols, but she found only octagons alone or as the top symbol in pairs and trios. Works about earth sciences and crafts wouldn't include what she sought. She wandered between the shelves, twice spotting Chane doing the same on the room's far side.

Most guild archives were much larger than what was placed in their common libraries. She'd heard that the one in the Suman branch dwarfed those of the Lhoin'na and Numan. Still, one could get lost wandering the dark catacombs of her own branch. This place appeared considerably too small, and all the casements so far held only works of various subdivisions under Naturology.

It made no sense. Where were the texts for the other emphases of the guild?

Wynn stumbled upon a narrow, steep stairway in the room's rear-right corner. Sparked with hope, she climbed into an even smaller room. Making her way through its maze of casements, she found its single central table. But all shelves along the way were marked with a leading octagon, though the columns of symbols were now three, four, or even five deep.

Wynn grew anxious. Something was wrong here. Shade huffed twice, and not from nearby. When Wynn turned about, she couldn't spot the dog.

"Shade?" she called out, and the dog barked. She followed the sound and found Shade at the top of the narrow stairs.

"Wynn, where are you?"

Chane's soft rasp carried from below, and Wynn hurried down the stairs.

"Chane?"

"Here."

She followed his voice around the end of a casement to where he stood scanning the shelves and slowly shaking his head.

"I have found only octagons as lead symbols," he said. "The only triangles are lower symbols in the columns. I have seen no circles at all."

Wynn's worry increased. How was this even possible? The elven archives couldn't be entirely devoted to the order of Naturology.

"We've missed something," she whispered.

"Perhaps there is another level farther up. We might—"

Chane stopped so suddenly that Wynn looked around in alarm. Then she heard the voices grow louder.

"I swear, Domin, the books were on my desk!" one said in Elvish.

Another voice, crackling with age, replied, "New acquisitions do not just get up to shelve themselves."

"I unwrapped them with my own hands," the first returned. "It is not often that the Suman branch sends anything our way. When I saw how old they were, I locked my chamber and came for you."

"Yet no one else knows of a delivery," the old one said sharply. "And your desk is bare of even the wrapping paper. Someone has been—"

"Where is she?" demanded a third voice.

Wynn shivered in the following pause. The newcomer's voice, filled with such cold disdain, was familiar. She covered Chane's hand, closing his fingers over his crystal as she smothered her own.

"Premin?" the old one replied. "For whom are you asking?"

Wynn scurried silently between the casements toward the light she'd seen upon first entering. When she peeked around the last shelves into the open space of tables . . .

Premin Gyâr stood inside the entrance, and a pair of gray-robed elven sages faced him, their backs to Wynn. In the open door behind Gyâr stood two shé'ith that Wynn had never seen. Just how many of the patrollers had the premin requisitioned?

She pulled back to find Chane behind her, his hand on his sword. In the half darkness, he mouthed something at her.

Another way out?

She shook her head and leaned close to whisper, "Let me do the talking."

Chane's eyes widened as he grabbed her arm.

"You, look to the next level!" Gyâr commanded. "And, you, start searching in here."

Chane began to pull Wynn away, but she shook her head at him. There was no way to escape. The longer they dragged this out, the worse it would end. Gyâr had come so urgently—and yet late. That meant he hadn't been the one to draft the letter to bait her. Otherwise, he'd have been waiting and watching to catch her before she got in.

Someone else had sent her the pass.

Wynn barely finished that thought when she stepped into the open, feigning bafflement as best as she could. She never got out any falsely innocent question as to what was going on.

"You are under arrest!" Gyâr spat immediately, his tight features breaking into a mask of rage. "Shé'ith, here . . . take them!"

An elderly cathologer spun about, along with his younger counterpart. The old one stared, stunned, at the sight of Wynn. She recognized him as the elder sage who'd advised her in the meal hall. Was he the master archivist?

Wynn heard Chane's blade slide from its sheath. Before she could turn, both shé'ith drew their sweeping blades in the same swift motion. Shade's snarl rose behind Wynn.

"Wait!" she cried out, sidestepping into Chane's way and grabbing Shade's scruff. "What is this about?"

"Do not confound your offense with more deceit," Gyâr answered. "One of the guards below came to ask about the pass you showed them, since they were never told of such."

"Yes, I have a pass . . . with a council seal on it," Wynn confirmed. "It was delivered to me this evening. I assumed—"

"Give it to me," he said, striding forward. "I do not know how you forged it, but—"

"I forged nothing," Wynn countered, fishing the letter from her pocket. She'd barely extended it when he snatched it from her hand.

"I would never have entered without proper authority," she added.

Gyâr's expression dulled as he studied the letter. His gaze hung the longest at its bottom, where the council seal was stamped. Confusion briefly broke the anger in his near-yellow eyes. He flipped the letter, glancing once at the wax seal on the sheet that had enveloped it.

Wynn knew one thing.

The council's imprint at the letter's bottom was no forgery. Whoever had sent it to her had—or had gained—access to the council's official seal.

"How is this . . . ?" Gyâr began weakly, then his voice sharpened as he fixed on her. "Who issued this for you?"

"I assumed it came from you," she lied. "Since an apprentice metaologer brought it to our room."

The premin's tan face appeared to pale, and he closed another step. Wynn felt Chane's hand settle on her shoulder, his fingers tightening. Both shé'ith tensed.

"A metaologer . . . to your room?" the premin asked. "Which apprentice?"

"I don't know your people," she answered. "I don't know who it was."

Wynn became reluctant to mention that it had been a woman—probably a journeyor—or to provide any description at all. Whoever had made that pass, possibly someone in Gyâr's order or the premin of another, may have used the young metaologer as an unwitting tool. That person might be a hidden ally or just another enemy trying to further hinder and malign Wynn. She wasn't about to risk incriminating the wrong person until she was certain.

Gyâr's anger surfaced again as he glanced at the elderly archivist watching

all of this closely. Some inner frustration seemed to keep the premin from getting out whatever he wanted to say. If the pass was real, the premin certainly
couldn't have them arrested—or worse—in front of witnesses.

"Journeyor," the old archivist said to Wynn, stepping forward. "What are
you seeking in the Naturology archives? For your calling, I would think you
would want the southwest of our five spires."

"The southwest spire?" she echoed.

"Yes . . . for the Cathology archives."

Wynn felt ill.

She'd asked the young initiate in the courtyard for directions to the archives, and the girl had pointed around the redwood ring to the closest way
to the closest spire. There was a reason why every casement here had symbols
that all began with an octagon.

Five orders and five spires, or five archives for each order, and she'd picked
the wrong one.

"Witless" Wynn Hygeorht, the madwoman of Calm Seatt's guild branch,
had done it again.

Even now she didn't know which of the other four held the archives for
Metaology, marked with a circle for Spirit. She wasn't about to ask, for they
were all beyond her reach. Her mysterious pass had been confiscated, more of
the Shé'ith would be guarding every spire's entrance, and she'd again drawn
too much attention.

Her stomach began to hurt.

"Tell me who brought you this letter," Gyâr demanded. "What did he look
like?"

Wynn feigned confusion. "I only remember a dark blue robe. I was too
surprised when I saw the letter, thinking it had come from you."

Gyâr took a long, slow breath, and froze in indecision.

"Put those swords away," the old archivist admonished, gesturing to the
guards, and then turned his disapproval beyond Wynn. "You, too, young
man. There has been enough irreverence here for one evening."

Wynn felt Chane's hand leave her shoulder as he sheathed his blade. The
elder archivist stepped past the premin toward Wynn.

"All right, now. Back to your rooms," he told her, as if she were a child up past her bedtime. "And mind the premin concerning the archives. We will handle the rest of this nonsense ourselves."

But as he reached toward Wynn, she saw a pleading in his gaze that spoke louder than his fatherly words. He was giving her a way out, a way beyond the premin's immediate reach, and she'd better take it.

"Of course, Domin," she said quickly. "And our apologies for this upset."

To Wynn's relief, Chane followed her with only one last glare at the elven guards. Shade scurried ahead, rumbling at the younger archivist until he back-stepped in shock.

Gyâr reluctantly let them pass, but his eyes never left Wynn.

Her relief was short-lived. They may have escaped the premin's anger, but they had nothing to show for it.

Chane did not say a word all the way back to their room. Much as he would prefer to let this failure drive Wynn toward home, his thoughts raced else-where. He searched wildly for some way to get her into the correct archives. For certainly if he did not, what would *she* do next, and thereby place herself in even more danger?

None of his abilities, his arcane tools or books, or even his recently mas-tered concoctions offered a single way to help her. There had to be something, though he could not yet see it.

Wynn shuffled ahead of him through the small common room and up to the passage to their quarters. Only once did Chane catch her profile. He expected to see defeat, but instead her features were tense, eyelids half-closed in some deep thought. This made him worry even more.

He wanted to say something, to *do* something, to make her feel better or divert her from whatever drastic scheme she would try next. Still, he could think of nothing, and it was driving him mad under the constant prodding of this place, this forest, all over his flesh.

Wynn opened the door to their room and stepped inside.

"Where have you been?"

Chane looked over her head to see Ore-Locks standing inside their room. Without answering, Wynn walked past him and sank down on her bed ledge.

This penchant of hers was also beginning to worry Chane. More and more, she often shifted between suffering in defeat and rushing into thoughtless action.

"We had a chance and we took it," she sighed.

Ore-Locks crossed his arms. "What *chance*?"

Wynn looked up at him, hesitating, and then told him everything up to the point where Gyâr had come for them.

"We were in the wrong archive," she finished. "Now I have no way to gain the right one."

Ore-Locks grimaced, his anger no better contained than the premin's, though his reason was exactly the opposite. Whatever his ultimate motivation might be, his goal was for Wynn to succeed in finding the lost dwarven seatt.

"We cannot stay here doing nothing," Chane finally said. "Yet we cannot continue until we learn where to go. We are without options."

"I know that!" Wynn nearly shouted, and then shut her eyes. "Sorry," she said more softly, "but I'm well aware of our situation."

Ore-Locks glanced sidelong at Wynn, his broad face thoughtful. His resentment had vanished, which left Chane wary. Dwarves were not quick to real anger, but once it came, it did not fade easily.

"If you cannot access written words," Ore-Locks said, "then turn to *truer* spoken ones."

Wynn lifted her head, looking at him in puzzlement. Then she dropped her chin back into her hands.

"Oral tradition may be your people's way," she said, "but not for the guild or the elves."

"The elves are long-lived," he went on. "They may not be as oral as my people, but more so than humans. Someone here must know something of use."

Wynn sat upright. Something in Ore-Locks's words must have sparked another wild notion.

"No one here will talk to us," Chane interrupted. "They have been warned against us by now."

"Then find someone who disagrees with them," Ore-Locks stated, looking only at Wynn. "We have already met one such who finds the guild quite distasteful . . . because of Chuillyon."

Wynn lifted her eyes to him and whispered in astonishment, "Vreuvillä!"

Chane's chest tightened the instant that name crossed her small lips, for Ore-Locks might be correct. That wild woman—priestess, whatever she was—might tell them whatever she knew simply out of spite, if she knew anything useful at all.

Chane could not bear the thought of going anywhere near First Glade again. The first night had been horrible.

Wynn's soft brown eyes shifted to him, concern and questions on her face, as if she'd read his thoughts. Chane knew it was too late now to stop her, but he raised a hand before she spoke.

"We have no idea where or how to find her in this . . . forest."

The anticipation on her face faltered. It crushed him to crush her hope. Yet Wynn would still push blindly forward, now that Ore-Locks had prodded her.

Chane simply hoped he could stall a little longer—long enough to find a better answer. Only then did he notice an oddity from the only silent one in the room.

This time, Shade had not protested at all.

CHAPTER 14

S au'ilahk observed a'Ghràihlôn'na through the tâshgâlh's eyes. Not one elf walking the city's paths noticed the animal darting between sculpted shrubs and bushes. The beast was easy to control, but once it reached the guild's living structure, it paused under Sau'ilahk's own astonishment.

He had never searched the Lhoin'na lands before. Sight of the guild left him briefly stunned before sending his new familiar clawing up the thick bark. It peered through crystal-paned windows in search of Wynn, but found no sign of her. When it scaled the structure's heights, slipping through a tight saddle between treetop spires, Sau'ilahk looked down into a deep inner space.

The guild was not a solid mass, as he had first thought. It was a ring, its inner space left open between them. The tâshgâlh took longer than the upward climb to skitter down into the courtyard's green growth. It ducked in beneath a rhododendron's bulk and hid beneath the large purple blossoms.

Tall elves robed in various colors walked the shale pathways, but Sau'ilahk was looking for any way into the structure. Then he spotted Wynn by pure chance.

She emerged from a door with Shade—and Chane.

A glint from Chane's left hand caught the tâshgâlh's attention, and it began to croon. Sau'ilahk eyed Chane's brass ring with unsettling envy.

The ring had to be how Chane had breached the forest. No other explanation would justify a mere dabbler in conjury achieving such a feat as an undead. The ring became all the more desirable.

Ore-Locks came out behind the trio.

Sau'ilahk exerted will upon the tâshgâlh, stopping it from chasing after the object of both their obsessions. He held the creature back until certain of Wynn's destination, another door across the courtyard. To follow, the animal had to do so at the correct instant.

He directed it ever closer from bush to bush. As Wynn pulled open the door, the animal bolted toward the wall to the portal's right, ducking behind a hedge. When Ore-Locks stepped inside last, the tâshgâlh slipped through before the door closed. It darted into the dim entry chamber's nearest corner and curled in the shadows, waiting to follow unseen.

Chuillyon paced his outer room beneath the southern spire's base. He was not precisely worried. He was simply waiting—and waiting—for news.

Too much talk had spread among the domins and masters concerning an illicit entry into the Naturology archives. For such quick gossip, there were very few useful details. Naturology was the last branch of the archives Chuillyon would have guessed Wynn would seek. What, by Chârmun's grace, was she doing in there?

"Domin?" a lilting voice called from above.

"Yes, come!"

Hannâschi appeared at the chamber's entrance.

"What have you learned?" he asked immediately.

"The journeyor and her companions left the grounds and headed north, out of the city. They eventually took the Birth Path, likely all the way to First Glade."

Chuillyon was dumbstruck. There was no telling what Wynn Hygeorht might do next.

"Wait, go back," he said. "What happened in the archive? Have you learned anything new?"

For a mere journeyor of Metaology, Hannâschi's skills were exceptional. She could bend light by her thaumaturgy, creating simple illusions, or twist what it did or did not illuminate. She never attained the complete elimination of light, but her abilities made eavesdropping much easier.

"I could not get close enough," she answered. "I waited nearby in an unoccupied side passage. Premin Gyâr is furious about the letter. He believes someone broke into his office and used the council's seal."

Hannâschi offered Chuillyon the most irritated glare her elegant face could portray. He forced himself not to smile.

"I caught up with the premin," she continued, "as he closed himself inside his office with the master archivist. I amplified any sound within the wall's wood. His first instinct was to suspect you."

Chuillyon almost rolled his eyes. That much would be obvious.

"But there was doubt," she added. "He still believes you are his ally, yet he assumes none of the other premins would dare such an act. He is frustrated in not finding an answer."

"Good enough for now."

"He will not let this go," she warned, as if shocked by his satisfaction. "Tomorrow morning's gathering will be difficult."

Hannâschi had a polite way with euphemisms. "Difficult" would hardly describe it. Chuillyon would not be at all surprised if Gyâr called an emergency meeting tonight.

"What about Journeyor Hygeorht?" he asked. "What was she after?"

Hannâschi shook her head. "I suspect she did not realize that the archives are divided by the orders into five separate locations."

Chuillyon digested this notion. At least it explained Wynn's baffling choice of destination in using the pass. However, not only had she used up her chance, and a hard-won chance at that; she had wasted his capability to assist her further.

"And she is heading for First Glade?"

"Yes."

It was not difficult to guess why. The place itself held nothing useful for Wynn, even in seeking Chârmun's grace. As a somewhat typical human sage, she would have only scholarly wonder and curiosity in the tree.

Something—someone—else had been present there on Wynn's first brief visit.

Chuillyon let out a tired exhale. "Oh . . . rotted roots!"

Hannâschi's eyes blinked rapidly at his near obscenity.

"I had better follow her," he muttered, more to himself than to Hannâschi. "I should make certain—"

"Chuillyon!" a deep, angry voice called from above.

Hannâschi jumped slightly at the sound, her eyes popping wide, and Chuillyon's neck muscles tightened.

"Yes, Gyâr," he called back. "What may I do for you?"

Wynn pressed on along the narrow path to First Glade. With the sun crystal staff in hand, she followed Shade's lead, and Ore-Locks brought up the rear. Chane once more held on to her shoulder under the forest's growing influence, and she felt him tremble through his grip. When she glanced up, his eyes were closed. His face was covered by the same sheen as the last time they'd come this way.

Chane's gaze darted about. He flinched twice, as if something had jumped out of the dark at him.

At the rear, Ore-Locks was watching him closely.

"Almost there," Wynn whispered.

Chane's grip tightened briefly.

She wished she knew of a way to help him, but had he possessed an ounce of sense, he would have stayed behind. Really, how much protection could he provide in his current state?

They reached the path's strange three-way split, only this time Shade came to a dead stop. Her ears pricked as she raised her head high, nose in the air.

"What's wrong?" Ore-Locks asked.

Shade turned a tight circle and lowered her head as she appeared to search the forest. She suddenly huffed, and Wynn heard something in the distance.

A lone howl carried from far off.

Chane's grip tightened again.

A second howl rose, a little longer than the last. Wynn was still uncertain where it had come from.

Shade turned, looking between the trees. As another howl came, she wheeled around, and a single word sounded in Wynn's mind, in her own voice.

—*Follow*—

Shade bolted into the underbrush.

"What's she doing?" Ore-Locks called.

Wynn grabbed Chane's belt to pull him along, but he gripped her wrist and hauled her back. His colorless eyes shifted in every direction.

"Not into the trees!" he rasped. "You are not going in there."

Wynn couldn't see Shade. She heard the dog huff twice and that was all as she peeled off Chane's fingers and took his hand.

"Close your eyes and trust me," she said.

Sau'ilahk watched through his familiar's eyes as it scampered along the upper branches in pursuit of Wynn—or in pursuit of one shiny little ring fixed in its instinctual obsession. Its eyes offered a much better view at night than those of his conjured servitors.

Chane did not look well.

The vampire might have breached the forest's safeguards, but clearly he suffered for it. Wynn led onward ahead of the dwarf as they followed the majay-hì. When they came to a three-way split in the path, a loud howl carried from a distance.

The tâshgâlh froze, backing away along the branch. Sau'ilahk seized control to keep it still.

The dwarf muttered something, but Sau'ilahk was too distracted to catch the words. After a few more distant howls, Shade darted off the path, followed by Wynn and the others in a stumbling gait through the underbrush.

Sau'ilahk forced the tâshgâlh onward, choking off its whimpers of fright at those howls.

Chuillyon waited tensely as Gyâr's heavy footfalls descended the stairs outside his chambers. Hannâschi sidestepped away from the entrance. This was not a good time for a visit from the tall premin. Chuillyon snapped his fingers.

Hannâschi went rigid, her eyes locking on him. He pointed at the curtained doorway to his sleeping chamber, and she rushed through, trying to still the curtain in her wake.

An instant later, Gyâr pounded through the entrance, the letter held high in hand.

"We have a problem," he announced, as if the presumption that Chuillyon would share the weight of it was not debatable.

Chuillyon raised his feathery eyebrows. "And that would be?"

Gyâr held out the letter. "A sympathizer . . . and traitor in our midst."

Chuillyon took it, scanning its content as if he had never seen it before. Of course, he had not seen it since the council seal had been added.

The fact that no one had sought out Hannâschi meant that Wynn had given no description of the courier. This was no surprise. The errant little sage, so accustomed to persecution, would never give up another who had tried to help her.

"I assume you did not issue it," Chuillyon murmured, looking up with a carefully baffled expression. "Where did it come from?"

"From that Numan journeyor," Gyâr snapped, "standing in the north archive!"

Chuillyon feigned a gasp. "What premin would issue this? Perhaps Viajhuijh? Wynn, though from another branch, is a cathologer and of his order."

"I've already challenged Viajhuijh. He seemed as surprised as you . . . and would never dare go against me, let alone steal into my study to use the seal without consent or council approval."

"Well, someone did," Chuillyon said, "and someone gave Hygeorht extensive assistance."

This was not exactly true. No one had broken into Gyâr's quarters, and Wynn had been given minimal assistance in entering the archives.

Hannâschi's only direct thaumaturgy had been to trick Thrûchk, the master archivist's apprentice, into thinking he'd received rare tomes from the Suman branch. Thus he was lured out of the archive to his office, and Wynn had walked in unhindered. It had taken a bit more than twisted light to fake the books on Thrûchk's desk, but Hannâschi had managed.

Creating the pass with a council seal had been a little more mundane.

Chuillyon possessed a few sheets of the high premin's stationery and had written the letter himself. In the past, he'd more than once gotten his hands on documents with the stamped council seal. Sometimes those documents took a little longer than usual for their final delivery.

Hannâschi would apply an alchemical mixture to a wood block, press it on a document's stamped seal, and lift off a reverse imprint. The captured ink could then be revitalized once or twice, and the block used to reimprint another document. The covert stamp was not perfect, but neither was the original. However, it was the original image—with the original ink made for use only with the seal.

Gyâr paced to the entrance arch, braced a hand upon its edge, and glanced back, a predator's glint in his dark yellow eyes.

"How is this possible?" he demanded. "That Numan journeyor said one of *my* apprentices delivered the letter. I have spoken to all of them, and none claim any knowledge of it." His eyes narrowed. "What of the Suman entourage? Could they be responsible?"

"Why bother giving the letter away? They could have used the pass themselves."

Gyâr exhaled. "At the very least, someone may have acquired a metaologer's robe from our stores to play messenger. Do you trust everyone of your order? Would any of yours have reason to do this?"

Chuillyon frowned in manufactured resentment. "I assure you, no one under *me* has any interest in assisting Journeyor Hygeorht."

"Then we are back to our other three premins?"

"Really, Gyâr. Why would they help some wayward sage from Calm Seatt?"

"Then who else?"

Chuillyon raised his hands in feigned exasperation, although at tomorrow's council gathering, he knew exactly whom the others would suspect: *him*. Oh, he had been the prime suspect of lesser mischief, though nothing had ever been proven. At present, Gyâr was the only one who mattered.

The premin of Metaology, sitting in as high premin, held all the power for now. Gyâr's trust and need of an old ally outweighed casting suspicion the same way. The premins might be troubled over this subterfuge with the pass, but ultimately that would be the least of their concerns. All would disapprove of Gyâr's rashness in petitioning the people's council to bring in the Shé'ith—the Serenitiers, as humans might call them. Exactly what had he done to convince the Premin Council for that?

Gyâr dropped into one of the simple chairs. "Order some tea," he said. "We must reason this through . . . until a path to the answer is found."

Chuillyon gazed toward his chamber's entrance. He was not getting out of here any time soon—and neither was Hannâschi.

"Keep your eyes shut tight," Wynn told Chane, pushing leafy branches out of her face.

Her sleeves were soaked through from moisture clinging to foliage as she trailed Shade. Ore-Locks followed, but it took all Wynn's effort to drag Chane blindly onward. It seemed too long that she'd been fighting through this underbrush, but the howls and yips grew steadily louder and nearer.

Wynn broke into a small clearing and found Shade poised at its center with her ears upright. Something had stalled the dog, but as Wynn reached out to touch Shade's haunches, two furred forms burst from the underbrush on the clearing's far side.

Both majay-hì were long and lanky like Shade, with equally narrow muzzles and tall ears. One was a mottled brown. The other was a more traditional silver-gray. The pair split, rounding opposite sides of the small space.

Rustlings rose in the brush all around the clearing.

"Watch your backs," Ore-Locks warned.

Wynn looked about frantically. Noise in the underbrush sounded as if an entire pack had surrounded the clearing, but only two dogs had shown themselves. She spun back at a clack of teeth.

Both newcomers froze. The mottled one held a forepaw up in midstep, as Shade snarled at it with her ears flattened.

Wynn had placed her trust in Shade. The last time she'd encountered a majay-hì pack had been in the Farlands' Elven Territories. Only the presence of Chap and his mate, Lily, had made them tolerate her. She hoped the same would work here with Shade.

The silver majay-hì turned and lowered its head. Shade snapped the air before it.

Chane's hand slipped out of Wynn's and latched onto her wrist. Before she even turned, she heard his sword sliding from its sheath.

"Chane, no!" she said, grabbing his sword arm.

Another snarl erupted, pulling her attention. The sound hadn't come from Shade.

The mottled one's jowls quivered around bared teeth as it raised its head and sniffed the air in Wynn's direction. It snorted, as if expelling a foul smell caught in its nose.

Wynn wondered why it needed to smell her at all. It should've picked up her scent without such effort. Then the reason dawned on her—perhaps it wasn't her that the newcomer smelled.

Chane was the one who didn't smell right. The brass ring could do nothing about that.

Ore-Locks pushed past Wynn into the clearing, his long iron staff at the ready but his blade still sheathed. The silver majay-hì swung its head toward him.

"Everyone be still," Wynn said. "They aren't animals. They're as intelligent as you are."

Shade still rumbled, and the silver one eyed her as if puzzled by Shade's actions. It stretched out its muzzle toward her, and Shade bared her teeth.

"Easy, Shade," Wynn whispered.

Shade was caught between two opponents and swung her head back and forth to keep track of them. When the silver majay-hì was a head's length away, Shade turned fully to it.

There came the briefest touch of noses.

Shade flinched back and fell completely silent. The silver-gray dog turned and dashed back into the brush the way it had entered. The mottled brown one wheeled and followed. Shade, still frozen in place, looked to Wynn.

"Go," Wynn told her.

Thrashing onward, Wynn could hear the pack on all sides in the forest. Their hidden potential threat made the way seem longer, so that when she finally broke into the open, she bent over, panting behind Shade. She was light-headed, and her breath still caught when she looked ahead.

Strange, bulging lanterns of opaque amber glass hung in the lower branches of maples, oaks, and startlingly immense firs. The trees loosely framed a broad gully with gently sloping sides that stretched ahead. Decades of leaf fall had hampered undergrowth, leaving the gully clear of underbrush. But ivy climbed over exposed boulders and around and up evergreens. Bushy ferns grew here and there, but these were all that broke the mulch, aside from the crackle of paws on fallen autumn leaves.

A dozen or more majay-hì paced in the view before Wynn.

They dashed past each other, rubbing heads, cheeks, or shoulders. Wynn could only imagine the memory-speak passing rapidly through the pack. She wished she could've listened in, as she did with Shade. All of them paused intermittently, looking at the black majay-hì, before wheeling toward another of their own in whatever they shared so rapidly.

Shade's presence had caused trepidation or excitement or both.

"What is this place?" Ore-Locks asked. "It is not overgrown, like the rest of the forest. But the trunks . . . they are too large for these kinds of trees."

"Ahead . . . slightly left," Chane whispered. "Look to that fir."

Wynn looked down the gully.

The fir tree's trunk was almost as wide as a guild keep tower in Calm Seatt. The barest hint of a dark opening showed in its base. Some kind of hanging, perhaps aged hide or dyed wool, filled that entrance and made it seem part of the bark until Wynn looked right at it.

After the structures in a'Ghràihlôn'na, she would've never imagined that tree. But there it was, a living tree home, like those in the an'Cróan's wild enclaves. It looked almost out of place in this forest.

"What are *you* doing here?"

The warning in that lilting voice made Wynn turn quickly, shifting her gaze. And then there *she* was, coming from the trees, down the slope, walking right through the pack of majay-hì.

Vreuvillä stopped, tensely poised like some wild spirit manifested in elven form. A circlet of braided raw shéot'a strips held back her silver-streaked hair. In place of the skirt draped to her feet, she now wore pants; high, soft boots; and a thong-belted jerkin, all made of darkened rawhide.

"I told you," she said, "your presence disturbs Chârmun."

Her Numanese was too perfect for someone who lived an isolated life so far from foreigners, let alone her own people.

Ore-Locks watched her closely but held back. Releasing Chane, Wynn took a step up behind Shade.

"We need to speak with you," she said.

Vreuvillä moved toward them, barely disturbing the fallen leaves beneath her narrow feet. The mottled bark brown majay-hì paced her.

"Where is your friend, that white-robed heretic?" she demanded.

"He's no friend or anything else to us," Wynn answered. "We came all the way from Calm Seatt, and I have no idea how he beat us here."

"No, I am sure you do not."

Wynn was too tired of being played at every turn to care what that meant. But she didn't care for the taunt itself. Then the silver majay-hì from the first small clearing circled into Vreuvillä's path and passed close along the woman's side.

Long, tan fingers combed between the dog's tall ears.

Vreuvillä slowed for an instant. Only her large amber eyes lifted to gaze beyond Wynn. And her nostrils flared.

A chill spread through Wynn. Not because it looked like Vreuvillä could smell what the majay-hì had. Not because the woman might suspect what Chane was. It was that touch that left Wynn shocked in disbelief.

The only reason Wynn could memory-speak with Shade through a touch was because of the taint left by a mistake with a thaumaturgical ritual. Even the an'Cróan and their Anmaglâhk couldn't do this with majay-hì.

But had Vreuvillä just done so?

"From Calm Seatt?" the woman repeated, and glanced at Shade. "With a majay-hì? I do not think so."

Wynn tried to recover. "Shade came for me. She's from what is called the Elven Territories on the eastern continent. Its people are called the an'Cróan— Those of the Blood."

Vreuvillä closed within reach of Shade. Shade remained quietly watchful, though the woman of the woods didn't looked down again.

"So, you have met our wayward kin of old?" Vreuvillä said.

"Yes. Several of them are . . . my good friends."

Vreuvillä's large eyes narrowed. Little enough was known throughout the Farlands of the xenophobic an'Cróan. But almost no one on this continent had ever heard of them until Wynn had returned. Yet Vreuvillä knew of them and their ancient link to her own people.

What else might this woman know of older ways and times? Perhaps things the guild could never uncover from lost scraps of the Forgotten History.

Vreuvillä took a long breath and instantly turned up the broad gully. "Come with me."

Wynn was still shaken, but she grabbed Chane's arm. His whole body was trembling.

"Can I help?" Ore-Locks asked, though his offer sounded forced.

This entire venture had been his suggestion, but he now appeared to regret it.

"No, I've got him," Wynn answered.

Chane might be sick and disoriented, but he was still aware enough to act. Wynn didn't know what he might do in this state if Ore-Locks touched him.

The pack parted as Shade led the way, but majay-hì paced them on all sides. Ahead, the paired silver and mottled bark brown ones flanked Vreuvillä all the way to the great fir's draped entrance. The woman slipped inside without even glancing back.

When Shade reached the entrance, she hesitated, eyeing Vreuvillä's escort at guard on either side. Wynn pushed past, pulling Chane inside the tree. She grabbed a stool she spotted nearby.

"Sit and rest," she said, guiding him to the seat. Perhaps with the forest out of sight, he might calm down.

Ore-Locks stepped in, followed by Shade. When the hide flap closed over the entrance, Wynn looked about.

Vreuvillä crouched before the flickering embers of a freestanding clay hearth at the rear. With a stick, she lifted a char-stained kettle out of the flameless coals.

The interior was bark covered, like the guild's redwood structure, but the walls here were lined with living protrusions at all possible levels. Those shelves were filled with ceramic pots and jars. The chamber wasn't as big as the tree from the outside, and Wynn saw another opening at the back draped with a wool cloth.

Someone had guided this tree's growth, like the Shapers of the an'Cróan. But it was not as old as the greater trees in the city. Wynn turned back as Vreuvillä reached up to retrieve a gray porcelain jar with a wooden stopper.

As before, Ore-Locks remained silent, and Chane seemed beyond speech.

Vreuvillä crouched before the hearth, pulling a bit of yellow root from the vessel and dropping it in a rough wooden cup. She immediately doused it with the kettle's scalding water. She rose and came at Wynn, but thrust the mug out at Chane.

"Drink it," she ordered. "Some humans are *too human* for the forest . . . though I have never seen one so affected."

If Vreuvillä thought Chane was a mortal, Wynn had no intention of altering that assumption. But she doubted the root tea could do anything for an undead.

"He's my guard . . . and companion," she explained. "He would not stay behind."

"At least he is not another white-robed schemer."

Wynn hadn't come to discuss Chuillyon, but she couldn't help asking, "Why do *you* dislike him?"

"Dislike?" Vreuvillä hissed.

Her head dropped forward but her narrow gaze remained on Wynn. Strands of silver-laced hair shifted across her left eye and exposed the tip of one tall ear.

"Sages and their orders!" she said; it seemed to rise from her throat like one of Shade's rumbles. "They title themselves masters, domins, and premins to seek stipends from their kind, for their own purpose. The whites, so-called order of Chârmun, are a consumption in their midst . . . as if they bear any love or reverence for the one tree in all things. But do they teach? Do they bring the people back to what is sacred? No. They hide and manipulate among . . ."

Vreuvillä's voice caught as she looked Wynn up and down, studying the gray robe.

"Even among *your* kind," she finished. "That heretic and his sycophants are deviants, fallen from the true way of the Foirfeahkan. They serve themselves, with Chârmun and its children as their tools."

"That's not why I'm here," Wynn said. "There are greater concerns to me."

Vreuvillä raised her head slightly and cocked it aside. Her one exposed eye glanced toward the draped entrance. Shade sat vigil there, as if she could see through the hide drape, and watched the entrance with no apparent concern over Vreuvillä.

"Perhaps so," the wild woman answered.

Chane caught Wynn's wrist. She looked down as he set aside the emptied mug. Wynn watched in astonishment as his irises began regaining their lost hint of brown. He nodded to her, looking suddenly fatigued in his relief.

Whatever Vreuvillä had given him had helped, but Wynn reflected on that one strange term—"Foirfeahkan."

She knew it only from histories learned in early education, though she couldn't remember how to translate it. It was from some lost dialect of Elvish even more obscure than that of the an'Cróan. The Foirfeahkan were—had been—a spiritual sect, though their origins and their supposed end couldn't be traced. Wynn had never heard there were any left.

Animistic in ideology, they believed in the spiritual—ethereal and sacred rather than theistic—that existed within this world and not in a separate realm. Not quite like the dwarves, and they considered the center or nexus of it all was in one tree.

Wynn had never considered that that tree had to be Chârmun.

If Chuillyon was some pretender priest in the guise of a sage, then Vreuvillä's disdain made perfect sense. But Wynn was uncertain concerning the reference to using the tree known as Sanctuary as a "tool." And what had the woman meant about its "children," as in more than one? Did that include Roise Chârmune, Seed of Sanctuary, in the an'Cróan's hidden ancestral burial ground?

No wonder Vreuvillä despised Chuillyon's order as heretics and traitors. They had potentially turned an ancient belief system into an organized profession.

"What does bring you here . . . *sage*?" Vreuvillä asked.

Wynn ignored the thin disdain in that final word. She wondered how to gracefully lead into her request. But there was no polite way to broach the subject, and she was tired of subtleties. It seemed this unknown Foirfeahkan preferred directness.

"I believe an enemy from forgotten times is returning," she said bluntly.

"And?"

Wynn faltered. That should've been enough to pique concern or at least interest from anyone who knew even the scant myths. Obviously, Vreuvillä did know.

"I've learned it had powerful devices," Wynn went on. "It used them in the mythical war some speak of. And the devices still exist. They may be the first hint of how—"

"Not the first," Vreuvillä cut in. "Devices are not how things begin . . . but sometimes the means by which they end."

Wynn fell silent. Did Vreuvillä know more clues—signs—of what was coming? More questions nagged at Wynn, but further hints of what she already knew wouldn't help with what she sought. Wynn neither wished to tax Vreuvillä's patience that much nor give Ore-Locks anything more to serve his own hidden desires.

"One device may lie hidden at a place once called Bäalâle Seatt," Wynn continued. "I need to find that place before the device falls into the wrong hands. If it was a tool of this enemy, it cannot be used again for whatever purpose it served."

Vreuvillä frowned.

"We're trying to stop a war," Wynn went on, all the frustration of recent seasons rising within her. "No one will help! My superiors and others seem obsessed with hindering us." She drew in a long breath. "Please, if you know anything of Bäalâle Seatt . . . then tell me."

Wynn could feel Ore-Locks's eyes upon her.

Vreuvillä stood silent, as if waiting for more, but then her expression softened slightly. "And what makes a child like you believe the Enemy is returning?"

"Because I saw the beginning of the end a thousand years ago."

Wynn began with what she'd learned through Chap and Magiere's experiences within the memories of Most Aged Father, leader of the Anmaglâhk. Speaking so in front of Ore-Locks was the last thing she wanted, but she kept to only events in general.

Wynn recounted the flight of Sorhkafâré—Light upon the Grass—with the last remnants of his allied forces at the war's end. Once they reached First Glade's safety, he and some of his people took a cutting from Chârmun and left this continent. Some of the first Fay-born, those born into varied animals, including wolves who would become the majay-hì, had followed him, as well.

"Sorhkafâré still lives," Wynn said. "He is now called Aoishenis-Ahâre—Most Aged Father—and I have stood as close to him as I now stand to you. He believes absolutely that the Enemy is returning. I wouldn't trust him for an instant, but I trust his fear of that."

Vreuvillä's voice was strangely calm. "Sorhkafâré, like the great war, is a legend . . . a myth among my people. If he truly lived, he would have died long ago."

Was that some sort of challenge?

"He lives," Wynn said plainly. "And for his unnaturally long years, he remains convinced the Enemy will return. There are others who've come to believe this, as well . . . even when they've denied so to my face!"

She stepped forward.

"We have to reach Bäalâle Seatt before anyone else learns what we're after. If you can't help us, I won't waste your time anymore."

Wynn turned away. About to step past Shade and out of the tree, a soft chuckle halted her and she turned.

Vreuvillä smiled at her and sighed tiredly.

"Child, you speak of things too openly, as if . . ." and she trailed off, looking about her chamber. "But if nothing else, obviously you do not follow in that heretic's footsteps."

"No, I don't."

"There are proper ways . . . for speaking of such matters."

Vreuvillä reached for a bowl and pitcher on a shelf, and then began gathering pinches from varied jars. The chamber's air filled with a cacophony of herbal scents.

"You will wait here while I go for more water," she instructed. "Do not utter another word about this purpose until I return."

She slipped past Shade and outside. As the entrance drape settled, Chane struggled to his feet.

"What are you doing?" he whispered. "We know nothing about this woman. Why did you tell her so much?"

His face was still covered in a sheen, and the fingers of his right hand flexed over his left forearm, as if just barely refraining from peeling off his skin. Whatever Vreuvillä had given him hadn't lasted long.

"She already knows," Wynn answered. "Weren't you watching her? She knows of the an'Cróan. Even when she challenged me about Most Aged Father . . . she already knew about him."

"A guess," he snarled. "And now what? We wait in some unknown place for some unknown woman to do . . . what? Make us an herbal tea before giving us any information at all, let alone something of use?"

"Sit down and be silent," Ore-Locks told him.

Chane spun on the dwarf, but Wynn grabbed his arm.

"This forgotten priestess might well have what we need," Ore-Locks continued. "If she serves us a feast of stones, you will swallow every pebble and thank her. We have nowhere else to turn."

Wynn hesitated. "He's right, Chane."

This was all they had. And now that they were alone, she needed to know if Shade had picked up anything from . . .

"Oh, not again!" she breathed.

Shade was gone. She must have followed Vreuvillä, though why was another unanswered question.

"Stay here," Wynn ordered Chane. "I'll bring Shade in and—"

"No," Ore-Locks and Chane said in unison.

Chane took hold of Wynn's belt, adding, "Not without me."

She jerked around, trying to break his grip, and failing. "Shade has figured out . . . certain *things* for us. What makes you think the pack couldn't do the same for that woman? You're not going anywhere, and I am going after Shade."

She looked to Ore-Locks and pointed her finger at Chane. "You stay in here and watch him. Sit on him if you have to."

Before Chane could react, Wynn pulled the cinch on her belt, and it slipped in Chane's grip. She slapped the entrance drape aside, but as she ran into the gully, she stalled.

Not a single majay-hì remained in sight.

The place was completely abandoned. Then Wynn spotted Shade's charcoal black tail disappearing through a shuddering bush at the gulley's far end. She thought she heard other rustlings out there, as well.

If Shade had left to go after the pack, then was Vreuvillä up to more than just preparing herbal tea?

Wynn glanced back once at the tree dwelling, and then ran down the gully and thrashed into the underbrush.

The tâshgâlh hung upside down from the lowest branch of the great fir tree— right above its draped entrance. And Sau'ilahk watched, as well, through its inverted perspective.

Wynn bolted into the forest's undergrowth.

He had heard every word the little sage had recklessly expelled. All his scantest hopes had been revealed, spilling from her lips like the sweetest pomegranate wine of his lost, living days. She was convinced that an anchor—an "orb" as she called it—lay hidden in a place called Bäalâle Seatt. She had actually found someone who might point the way.

For all Wynn's tight-lipped secrecy, even with her own companions, she had told this pagan priestess of false ways more than any of Sau'ilahk's servitors had ever acquired. How astonishing were the things this one troublesome little sage knew? Still, there was more waiting.

Once he learned the location of what he desired, a pause would come. He would linger long enough in the plain beyond the forest to greet Wynn Hygeorht properly. She would pay with her life for all of her interference. That joyful appetizer would initiate the greater sustenance for his long-held desire—the key to reclaiming flesh.

Chane Andraso would pay as well, by watching her die.

But that hidden undead and the wayward stonewalker were still within the tree.

For an instant, Sau'ilahk was uncertain of losing track of all those involved. Then the tâshgâlh shot along the forest branches, as it raced after Wynn.

CHAPTER 15

Out in the forest, Wynn pushed through thick brush with both hands. The farther she got from the open gulley's strange lanterns, the darker it became. She didn't dare take out a cold lamp crystal, for fear of being discovered, and she couldn't call out to Shade for the same reason. There was no telling how Vreuvillä or the pack would respond to being followed.

Shade was one thing, but an interloping human was another.

Wynn clambered over a toppled tree trunk blanketed in moss and then halted. Stifling her panting, she listened for sounds ahead and glanced upward. Scant moonlight showed beyond the black silhouettes of needles and leaves.

A sharp rustle rose from somewhere nearby.

Wynn froze, wishing for that sound to come again. When it did, she stumbled on, tired, damp, and cold as she navigated by those brief sounds. That closer noise had to be Shade, and Wynn certainly didn't wish to encounter other majay-hì instead. Even being disoriented by the night forest, she guessed they weren't headed toward First Glade. Her direction seemed more southeast.

Droplets upon vine leaves glittered in the darkness. And then, somewhere ahead, she spotted more illumination than just errant moonlight. Quieting her breaths, she slowly advanced, worming far to the left until she gained a clearer view.

A dozen paces off, a low light exposed a clearing's edge. That light didn't seem to come from a torch or fire or even a lantern, as in the gulley. She'd barely taken three more careful steps when . . .

Vreuvillä passed into sight within the clearing and headed straight toward a broad circle of slender aspens at the far side. The trees looked perfectly normal, if perhaps too pristine for a wild place. When Vreuvillä breached their circle, her hair began to glisten as if she'd stepped into a spring dawn. Silver streaks in her locks turned almost white, and her amber eyes sparked as she raised her face upward, for the light seemed strongest within the aspen circle.

Majay-hì hopped out of the forest to pace softly around the aspens. When one of them passed the clearing's right side, Wynn noticed a shadow shift suddenly in the underbrush beyond it.

Shade hid there, silently watching the clearing.

Within the aspens' circle, the priestess spread her arms low to the sides, palms forward, and spoke a stream of Elvish difficult to follow. Wynn was hard-pressed to decipher the words. In her time among the an'Cróan, she'd grown accustomed to dialects long forgotten, but this was older still.

Vreuvillä spoke again, and this time, Wynn made out the beginning of the utterance, but not the end: "Heed me, guide me, here and now . . . *cräjh-bana-ahâr.*"

It sounded like a prayer or invocation, but seemed composed of pure root words. Wynn didn't catch any conjugations or declinations into verbs and nouns, and the structure scrambled in her head. She struggled to translate all that she'd just heard.

I am at the end where you are at the beginning . . . to speak between this moment and Existence. Heed me, guide me . . . here and now . . . Pain Mother.

The last of it turned Wynn cold. To what or whom had Vreuvillä called out?

A breeze began to build in the forest. Mulch on the clearing's floor churned around the priestess's boots. She curled her arms forward and inward, one after the other, as if pulling the air in upon herself. Fallen leaves between the aspens began rising in a column that turned around Vreuvillä.

Wynn braced against a young redwood as the forest shuddered under a growing wind. She swiped strands of hair from her eyes and stood mesmerized by what she saw. Then the back of her cloak jerked hard. The force nearly pulled her off her feet, and she twisted in panic.

Shade half crouched behind Wynn, biting down on her cloak's hem. But an abrupt scratching, fluttering sound in Wynn's head made everything grow dim.

Her stomach clenched as her mind filled with the sound of a thousand chattering leaves. Or was it more like swarming insect wings beating about in her skull?

The dark forest spun before Wynn's eyes. She toppled forward, and her shoulder struck the young redwood.

—*run . . . run . . . run*—

Those memory-words erupted inside her head as Shade jerked her cloak again. But Shade's effort only made Wynn crumple, sliding down the redwood to her knees. She barely raised her head, her fingers biting into the tree's bark.

Amid the whirlwind in the aspen ring, Vreuvillä stared back at her.

Majay-hì wheeled and charged across the open space, but Wynn couldn't take her eyes off the priestess. The last time she'd heard—*felt*—that torrent of buzzing in her head had been with Chap. This time wasn't the same as when he spoke into her head in every language she knew. Nor was it like the memory-speak she shared with Shade.

Still, you spy upon us . . . abomination!

Those words formed within from the crackle of a thousand leaf-wings in Wynn's mind.

Vreuvillä's lips hadn't moved, although she shuddered, as if she'd heard the words, as well. Something had come to this place through the priestess.

Wynn began shaking as Shade's broken memory-words screamed in her head.

—*run . . . Fay . . . run . . . Fay . . . run*—

Chane grew anxious in waiting and glanced toward the tree's draped entrance.

Ore-Locks immediately blocked the way, gripping his iron staff. "She will be back when she finds the dog."

Chane fought the urge to charge. "Too long!" he hissed back through clenched teeth.

Ore-Locks did not move, but his eyes widened a fraction.

Chane knew what the dwarf saw.

No doubt his irises had lost all color. He fought to control his shudders under the crawling of his skin. The longer he stood within this tree, the worse he felt. This living domicile, like the rest of the forest, probed him, trying to uncover his true nature.

The forest knew he did not belong here, and Wynn should have found Shade and returned by now.

"Sit down," Ore-Locks ordered.

The dwarf always seemed ready to protect Wynn in his search for whatever he hoped to find at Bäalâle. But now that she was close to answers, he had let her go alone into this forest. The situation had gone too far.

Without a flicker of warning, Chane snapped out his right fist with full force. To his dull surprise, Ore-Locks's chin twisted aside under the blow.

Chane might not be as strong as a dwarf, but he was faster. Grabbing the entrance's edge, he pushed through the drape and rushed out before Ore-Locks regained his wits. He stopped after only three steps.

The gully was empty. Nothing moved in his sight, and then something snagged his cloak between his shoulders. Chane lashed back with a fist as he spun.

His forearm smacked painfully against the iron staff that blocked it. Before he could strike again, he saw the dwarf's face. Ore-Locks was slack-jawed in alarm as he too stared into the empty gully.

"What did I tell you?" Chane rasped. "That woman did not go after any—"

"Enough! Can you find Wynn, locate where she is?"

At the very least, the stonewalker had guessed Chane possessed some unnatural abilities. Chane looked about the clearing, the amber glow of lanterns nearly blinding in his night sight.

"Can you?" Ore-Locks demanded.

"Quiet. Go and get Wynn's staff."

Ore-Locks hesitated, but he appeared willing to try anything as he turned back into the priestess's home.

Chane closed his eyes. What he could not see, he might hear or smell. Wynn could not have gotten far. A mix of panic and suffering raised his hunger, and his senses widened. He did not hear one rustle of a bush, yip or bark of a dog, or even someone struggling in the underbrush. He heard nothing but . . .

Wind in the trees rustled branches . . . somewhere.

He opened his eyes and saw none of the lanterns was swaying. Not one leaf fell to the mulch-covered gully floor. The crackling wind blew farther off, but it seemed impossible such a noise would not show any effects here.

Chane bolted down the gully as Ore-Locks's pounding footfalls closed on his heels.

*   *   *

Sau'ilahk could not clearly see what was happening. Though his familiar had perched high above Wynn on a branch, he had barely glimpsed the barbaric elven woman sweep her arms through the air. The woman should have told Wynn something by now. The whirling breeze raised a column of leaves around the priestess as the wind began ripping through the forest.

And the tâshgâlh went mad with fright.

It spun and tried to bolt back along the branch. With the pack so nearby, whatever was happening was too much for it.

Sau'ilahk's sight blurred through his familiar. He heard growling below, the breaking of branches and brush, and all was drowned out by the wind. A throaty, terrified trilling erupted from the small beast carrying his awareness. Rage and frustration took him.

He tried to subdue the tâshgâlh, to crush its will to nothing, but the small beast only clamped its limbs around the branch and froze. The forest grew darker before its eyes—and in Sau'ilahk's sight. He thought he heard thrashing in the forest's underbrush. It seemed to come from farther off, back the way Wynn had entered.

The branch beneath the tâshgâlh began to waver. The last thing Sau'ilahk heard was Wynn's weak shout, but he never caught her words.

A rapid series of snarls and snaps erupted from below, followed by a yelp, and darkness surged over the tâshgâlh's senses. Sau'ilahk felt its fear peak and its body go limp.

He flinched each time the beast hit a branch as it tumbled down through the tree in a sudden faint.

Out upon the plain beyond the forest, a black-robed form shrieked in a rage that rose in yet another wind. Truth had been within Sau'ilahk's grasp, only to be blotted away yet again.

Wynn tried to clear the cacophony of leaf-wings inside her skull. The pack was closing in, and there was nothing to stop the Fay from reaching her. Even the forest's trees could soon come at her under their influence.

Her cloak jerked hard again, but not toward Shade this time.

The sudden tension pulled Wynn toward the clearing. She twisted and fell facedown through the vines. Lifting her head, she began trying to crawl backward when Shade suddenly leaped over her.

Shade landed on a dark gray majay-hì that still gripped Wynn's cloak's edge in its teeth. The majay-hì yelped, releasing its grip, as both dogs tumbled in a snarling mass toward the clearing's edge.

Wynn scurried back to claw up the young redwood.

Shade rolled up in the torn brush, snapping with her jowls pulled back.

Her opponent frantically wheeled and darted away into the clearing. A handful of majay-hì beyond veered off, pacing uncertainly beyond the tree line. Even Vreuvillä pulled up short, eyes wide as she looked at Shade. The sight of a black majay-hì attacking its own stunned them all.

Wynn's stomach lurched under leaf-wing words in her head.

You atrocity . . . you end here!

She saw Vreuvillä stiffen.

Pull her down . . . remove this thing from our presence.

The priestess looked up and around the clearing through the whirlwind of leaves. A flash of confusion swept across her dark features.

Wynn heard the sound of breaking brush beneath the wind's racket. In despair, she thought the rest of the pack must be surrounding her. Even shock over Shade's actions wouldn't hold them off much longer. A branch crackled and snapped behind her.

She turned, reaching behind her back for Magiere's old battle dagger.

Chane burst out from the forest's depths, his colorless eyes glistening. Branches and leaves shredded under his reckless charge. Ore-Locks surged through behind him and swerved away before Wynn could call out.

The dwarf had her staff in one hand, and his own iron staff in the other. With that long bar cradled under his armpit, he swung its free end into a bush between two tree trunks. Leaves ripped away until it jerked suddenly. A peeling yelp erupted from something hiding in there.

Chane reached Wynn, his sword drawn, but his gaze was locked beyond her, on the clearing. Bloodshed would only make things worse.

Wynn lunged into his way, shouting, "No! No killing!"

A set of jaws clamped on to her right hand. She tried to jerk her trapped hand free as she grabbed Chane's shirtfront. Her skin began to tear, but those teeth didn't bite down any harder.

A memory filled Wynn's head.

She saw a great, barkless tree of tawny, glistening wood in an open, moss-covered clearing. It looked more gargantuan than she remembered, as if she were crouched between the mounds of its large roots.

The teeth released her hand and memory-words filled her head.

—*Sanctuary* . . . *Chârmun* . . . *run*—

Shade raced out into the forest's underbrush.

"Follow Shade. Now!" Wynn called to Ore-Locks as she heaved on Chane.

Frustration made Sau'ilahk's hands solidify as he crushed them into fists. He could still feel his familiar, though its awareness was strangled by terror. Through its large ears he barely heard nearby rustling beneath the tearing wind, but there were no voices.

The tâshgâlh just lay quivering where it had fallen.

Fear was all Sau'ilahk had to make it respond to his will. He fed that fear with those scant sounds heard through its ears. Tearing brush, low pants and growls of the pack—all of these he sharpened within the tâshgâlh's awareness. . . .

It began to twitch with returning awareness.

Move . . . or die.

It could not have truly understood him, but the intention behind the words made the little beast thrash in terror on the ground. It opened its eyes, and its ears stiffened, and then it saw the sprinting legs and paws of majay-hì racing past.

The tâshgâlh scrambled around behind the tree's wide base.

Climb . . . you cowardly little thief!

So it did with its small, handlike paws. From its perch above, Sau'ilahk watched wolflike dogs race through the underbrush. That barbaric elven woman came after them. He did not spot Wynn, but all those he did see headed in one direction.

Sau'ilahk drove the tâshgâlh, leaping from tree to tree, until he gained on those below struggling in the forest's lower thickness.

Chane's mental focus dulled under the forest's prodding, but fear for Wynn's safety cleared any lingering effects of his last draught of the violet concoction. In its place, rage-driven hunger began awakening the feral beast inside him, so that it mingled with the one purpose in his clouded mind.

He forced Wynn on ahead of himself, so that nothing could reach her. Somewhere out front, Shade led them. But they ran toward a place his instincts told him not to go. Shade's insistence that they reach that horrid tree made no sense.

If the Fay had come for Wynn—if that elven woman had done this, then the tree of her worship was the last place they should flee.

Only two things kept Chane from picking Wynn up and running away.

He could not navigate under the forest's influence, and only Ore-Locks's effort to clear a path behind Shade gave Chane any sense of direction. And second, the pack might catch them, in part or whole, before Shade reached the place she sought.

The beast within Chane lunged to the limits of its bonds. It shrieked and howled, wanting him to turn . . . to kill whatever hunted them . . . to hunt it instead.

"Faster!" he urged Wynn as they ran.

Anything that tried to touch her would die—anything at all.

Wynn burst into the open behind Ore-Locks. Shade wheeled and began barking at her, as the dwarf turned and set himself facing the forest. One stolen memory-word kept echoing in Wynn's head.

—*Sanctuary . . . Sanctuary . . . Sanctuary*—

And there it was, merely a stone's throw away. The whole clearing was filled with the low shimmer of Chârmun's barkless form, as its glowing wood spread light like the moon.

Why did Shade believe this place was safer than anywhere else? The Fay could invade anything growing in the forest. That tree, by its pervasive nature, was more akin to them than any other.

Ore-Locks glanced at her—then just beyond her. He suddenly dropped her staff to the ground and leveled his long iron one in both hands. He swung the thick bar back and up over his head.

"Get away from the trees!" he shouted.

Wynn was about to bolt when a rasping snarl rose behind her. Someone grabbed her, nearly throwing her out beyond Ore-Locks's swing. When she regained her footing and turned, Chane stood between her and the trees with his back to her. Branches of an elm beyond him twisted in the air, reaching toward where she'd stood.

Chane raised his sword, but never got to swing, as Ore-Locks's staff ripped downward.

Leaves exploded in its passing. Twisting branches broke into splinters. But a dark form shot out of the forest over the top of Ore-Locks's downed staff. The mottled brown majay-hì went straight at Chane as Shade charged two more of the pack rushing from the underbrush.

Wynn grew frantic in trying to think of a way to end this before blood was spilled. At any moment, Vreuvillä would catch up, and she was the one who'd started all this chaos. Wynn whirled around, looking to the great tree glimmering in the clearing.

Why had Shade wanted them to come here?

Wynn looked back and spotted her staff lying behind Ore-Locks, who now whipped his long iron bar back and forth, warding off three majay-hì. She ducked in below his backswing and snatched the butt end of her staff.

One quick burst from the sun crystal might stun everyone without harming Chane too much. This was all she could think to do as she raised up the staff and backpedaled. But she stumbled as something lashed around her calf and jerked her leg straight.

A thick root sprouting from the moss-covered ground coiled around her knee.

Wynn reached behind her back for Magiere's old dagger.

"Pull back!" Ore-Locks shouted.

The moss-covered earth split again at Wynn's feet. A second earth-stained root shot upward over her chest.

"No!" was all Wynn got out as she toppled.

*   *   *

Sau'ilahk saw light ahead as the tâshgâlh raced through the forest's heights. The farther the animal had gotten from the aspen clearing, the more the wind had subsided and was left behind. Yet the nearer his familiar closed upon the light, the more the surrounding trees wavered and shuddered under some other influence. Sau'ilahk could not make sense of this.

A slight break in the trees ahead gave him a filtered view. He thought he saw Wynn standing in the clearing. Chane and Shade and the dwarf stood before her. The rest was a wink as the first of the pack broke into the clearing.

Ore-Locks went at them, as did Shade. Chane rushed forward to the tree line, and Sau'ilahk lost sight of him, his familiar too high above. Then the earth broke at Wynn's feet.

Something dark writhed up to coil around her leg.

The tâshgâlh leaped to a tree on the clearing's edge—and the world went black.

The last thing Sau'ilahk saw was something glimmering, tawny, and pale in that space—a massive, ancient tree, bare of bark but still growing in the earth. In the darkness that swallowed everything from his senses, Sau'ilahk again heard a sound like splintering wood.

That crackling cascaded through him, as if he had flesh and bone—as if he were that green wood being ripped apart. All of his awareness went as blank as his sight through his familiar. But he did not fall into dormancy like the last time.

The plain beyond the forest slowly returned to his sight.

Sau'ilahk stood there, shuddering in the aftermath.

Another familiar had been severed from him by the one place he could not follow Wynn. Again, so close—again, so lost—but this time it brought panic instead of outrage. Something assaulted the sage—something in the forest itself. Had that barbaric woman summoned an influence he could not identify?

If Wynn died in there, what became of his hope to follow her to his one desire?

What became of Sau'ilahk's dream of flesh?

*   *   *

Chane chopped downward with his sword as the mottled brown majay-hì tried to bite into his calf. The animal lunged away, and his blade gouged up moss and earth.

"Pull back!" Ore-Locks shouted.

Chane glanced over—and then a leafy branch slapped into his face. He lost sight of everything, and on instinct pulled the sword upward, trying to slash and clear his view.

A tan hand gripped that branch. Chane quickly tipped the blade down.

A sharp clang sent a slight shiver up his sword. He sidestepped as he thought he saw a long, white blade strike for his abdomen. Hunger flushed through him as his gaze snapped upward.

Chane stared into angry amber eyes among the tree's leaves. He groped for the elven woman's hand or blade, and leveled his sword to slam its edge into her head.

"No!"

Wynn's cry made Chane falter. He twisted away with a wild slash to fend off the priestess and heard his cloak tear. A sharp pain filled the left side of his chest. Hunger ate away the agony as fear cleared his thoughts, and then he saw . . .

Wynn was on the ground, and something dark coiled around her throat.

He ran straight toward her, as she gripped the dark tendril with one hand and slashed through it with her dagger. Another one coiled around her left calf and knee, squirming up her thigh.

Earth-stained roots were somehow moving on their own.

Chane slashed through the second root's base as Wynn ripped away the piece she had severed from her throat. She groped for her staff as he reached down for her, but at the same time, he glanced over his shoulder.

Ore-Locks backed toward them, farther into the clearing, whipping his iron staff in a wide arc as he tried to keep the pack at bay. Shade darted around his circumference, harrying anything attempting to go around. But more of the pack poured from the forest as Vreuvillä stepped into the clear. The priestess held a long, curved white dagger in her hand.

"To the tree—now!" Wynn shouted.

Chane balked as he pulled her up. The crawling on his skin had grown worse since entering this place.

Another root erupted at Wynn's feet. She lunged away, pulling from Chane's grip. The root writhed and twisted toward her, growing thicker at its base as it extended.

Chane hacked down. The instant the root severed, another tore up through the moss and lashed at his face. He stumbled away, and it swerved toward Wynn.

How could it know where she was? Even though it moved, it could not so precisely target her. Either something directed it or its sense of its target was not natural.

The smallest notion broke through Chane's faltering reason.

So long ago, he had crouched in hiding with Welstiel, as they were hunted by Magiere. That night, neither Magiere nor Chap had sensed or tracked Chane's presence—not while Welstiel had a grip on him. And Welstiel had been wearing the ring.

Chane spun and rushed at Wynn. Twisting behind her, keeping everything in his sight, he wrapped his left arm across her front. Grabbing her far shoulder, he closed his left hand hard upon it, until the brass ring bit into his finger.

Chane dragged Wynn backward, hoping this would work, as rage-fed hunger washed over him again.

Wynn struggled to keep her feet as Chane dragged her. She kicked at the root, trying to fend it off as it reached for her ankle, but Chane's grip crushed her shoulder so hard, she gasped.

"Still," he snarled in her ear. "Quiet."

Wynn did as she was told and watched the root.

It rolled and lashed the earth and whipped to the left. Mulch and moss tore at its base as it coiled and snaked about. Suddenly, it rolled over and lashed her way.

Wynn cringed, flattening her body up against Chane's.

The root flipped and twisted to the right, snaking beneath old, decayed leaves.

Wynn swallowed hard, trying to breathe as quietly as possible. The root had lost track of her, though she stood only a staff's length away. How was that possible?

More roots erupted all around the clearing's edge. Majay-hì scampered away from those twisting tendrils. Vreuvillä quickly stepped clear, and then froze, staring at them.

Each thick, earth-darkened tendril felt about the ground, searching for something—for Wynn.

With their adversaries distracted, Ore-Locks and Shade retreated to a position just shy of those roots. Not one root sprouted farther in than the clearing's edge. None emerged within reach of them, as if . . .

Wynn struggled to twist her head around and look to Chârmun.

"Back up," she whispered.

Chane didn't move, until Wynn nudged him with her elbow. He retreated, hauling her along, but Wynn felt him shuddering harder and harder, his sternum pressed between her shoulder blades.

Skulker . . . do you think you can hide from us forever?

Vreuvillä stiffened, and Wynn cringed at the scratching leaf-wing chorus of the Fay in her head.

Hide? How could she hide in plain sight?

Her shoulder throbbed, and she glanced at it. The brass ring on Chane's left hand was biting into her shoulder through cloak and robe. She tapped his hand with her dagger's butt, and he slackened his grip.

Every tree around the clearing began to crackle as wind grew among them. Branches shook and writhed, joining the search of the roots. Even the trunks began to creak and waver.

Vreuvillä watched the trees, horror twisting her face, smothering any other emotions.

"*Cräjh-bana-ahâr!*" she cried out, and Wynn barely caught the meaning of the rest. "You have told me what to do. Why . . . why do you violate your own child to reach your enemy?"

Even a part of my child may be sacrificed . . . to save it from the decimation that abomination will bring upon it!

Wynn couldn't fathom what any of that meant, let alone Vreuvillä's connection to the Fay. Tears rolled from the elven woman's eyes, which were so filled with shock that the whites showed around her large amber irises. A breaking point had been reached, though Wynn wasn't certain of what.

Some of the majay-hì eyed the humans and the dwarf as they spread around the clearing's circumference. Only the silver-gray and mottled brown kept watching the forest, staying close to Vreuvillä. But the longer Vreuvillä was stalled by what she saw, the more her doubts might grow. That meant keeping the pack at bay as long as possible.

Wynn wasn't about to give them another instant to recover. She dropped the dagger and grabbed Chane's ring hand.

"Cover up!" she whispered to him.

Wynn twisted out of his arms but kept her own fingers on his and the ring. There was no time to wait for him or to dig out her glasses. She thrust the staff upward, its crystal held in her mind's eye as she ducked her head. She envisioned the patterned shapes around the crystal, hoping she could ignite it without holding it in her sight line. This was something she'd never tried before.

Only the last line of il'Sänke's instructed recitation raced through her thoughts, with no time to cross her lips.

Mênajil il'Núr'u mên'Hkâ'ä—"for the Light of Life."

Nothing happened. Not one bit of sudden brightness filled the clearing.

Vreuvillä pivoted suddenly, as if something had caught her eye. She didn't look at Wynn, but rather *up*. Wynn quickly followed that gaze.

Above her, the long sun crystal burned within, fully aglow. It was almost too painful to look upon. But not a single ray of light spread along Chârmun's tawny branches above. The crystal had answered her intention, growing bright within, but its light of the sun hadn't spread.

Cold astonishment knotted in Wynn's throat, and her focus broke. The crystal's imprisoned glare winked out. She was at a loss, and panic set in. When she lowered her head again, Vreuvillä had set herself, her strange white blade held at ready. The full pack of more than a dozen large majay-hì circled in from all sides.

Then Wynn spotted Shade.

Shade stood her ground, snapping and snarling just beyond Ore-Locks with his iron staff raised for a strike. Vreuvillä's two guardians, the silver-gray female and the mottled brown male faced them. Strangely, though the male bared his teeth in weaving paces back and forth, the female remained poised in silence.

She was watching Shade and took one soft step forward.

"Look at her!" Wynn called to Vreuvillä, though she pointed at Shade and not the silver-gray majay-hì. "Think about her!"

Vreuvillä held her ground, only briefly turning her eyes upon Shade.

"Why would she defend me . . . turn on her own kind?" Wynn demanded. "Why . . . if what your 'Pain Mother' says is true?"

Vreuvillä scowled with disdain at that translated title.

Wynn wasn't certain what it meant, but it gave the priestess further pause. She needed to stall a little longer for what she thought might happen.

The silver-gray female inched another step. Shade lunged partway and snapped at her, and then froze as the mottled brown male wheeled in, returning Shade's threat.

"Shade, no!" Wynn called.

The silver-gray dog shouldered the mottled brown aside and took another step.

Do not listen to this spy! Truth and lies—she will use both to delude you!

Wynn tried not to shudder under the Fay's denouncement. At least she'd turned their focus onto their own emissary, and this confirmed Wynn's suspicion.

The Fay couldn't enter First Glade. They were afraid now, and Wynn knew it was the truth they feared more than any lie.

"Look at *them*," she told Vreuvillä, pointing to the silver-gray female, as even the brown male stood in tense watchfulness. "They want to know. . . . Don't you?"

"Know what?"

"Ask them," Wynn answered.

The female came nose to nose with Shade. Even as Shade snarled, the female thrust her head forward. Shade's spittle spread across silver-gray fur as they slid muzzle against muzzle.

Shade instantly quieted.

Her hackles began to settle, though the mottled brown male stood a half length behind the female, ready to lunge. These two of the pack, or at least the female, wanted to know why one of their own, foreign and strange as Shade was, had turned against them for a human.

Shade would tell them, and Wynn could only imagine the flurry of memory-speak.

Whether it was her own remembrance or that of Shade's mother, Lily, Shade among all majay-hì was more gifted at passing on the memories of others. The silver-gray female would see that one dark night, halfway across the world.

In a clearing within the an'Cróan's forest, Chap had gone to commune with his kin and learn why they'd left Leesil's mother to suffer in isolation. He learned something more, as well. When he'd chosen to be born into flesh as a majay-hì pup, he was fully aware of the task that lay ahead in his life. But he was not aware of everything he should've been.

His kin had stolen most of his memories from his time among them.

There were secrets the Fay kept from him in his newly taken form, his new life. Even now, like Chap, Wynn wondered what he was missing. When he had denounced them for this, they had caught Wynn unintentionally listening in.

If not for Chap, or more especially Lily, a true majay-hì, Wynn would've died that night.

Lily's faith in Chap made her dive in to defend a human, and her pack had followed. But the Fay hadn't relented. They turned upon the majay-hì who tried to help. The Fay invaded through a large downed tree, making its roots and branches lash at Lily's pack.

They killed a majay-hì that night—without hesitation—in their attempt to kill Wynn.

All of this must've passed from Shade to the silver-gray female in less than three blinks. The female wheeled, rushing back around Vreuvillä's legs. The mottled brown male joined them as Vreuvillä crouched down and lowered her head.

As both of the priestess's companions nuzzled her face, Wynn heard the torrent in the trees whip to a frenzy. It was so suddenly violent that it pulled her attention from the trio.

"What is happening?" Ore-Locks called out, turning every which way.

Shade backed up until her rump hit Wynn's legs. She was trembling as she looked about. As the wind shook the trees, Wynn thought she saw something move among them.

It was only a glimpse . . . a large form that walked just beyond the closest thrashing trees at the clearing's edge. Or, rather, Wynn thought she saw branches bend and spring back in something's passing. What it was, she couldn't tell, for it was little more than a darker shadow. Something made of whirling wind, swirling leaves, and mulch torn from the earth stalked through the forest.

Again, Wynn wanted to look to Chârmun, but she couldn't take her eyes off the forest.

"Aovar?"

Vreuvillä cried out that one root word in her tongue. It meant "reason," or even "cause" or "impetus," but her anguished inflection made it something else.

"Why?" the priestess shouted again.

Standing upright between her companions, she glared into the trees. Her tan cheeks glistened with smeared tears. The silver-gray female and mottled brown male raced out among their pack. Brief touches of heads and muzzles passed quickly among them.

Because that thing listens! She steals . . . our hope, our knowing . . . that which no mortal should have, more so a tainted one!

Again, Wynn heard those words in her mind.

"Answer me," Vreuvillä returned, her voice growing raw. "Why did you kill one of your children?"

The wind quieted only a little and a long pause followed.

Regretful . . . tragic . . . necessary.

Wynn had no pity for their regret.

With tears flooding, Vreuvillä shrieked at the immense shadow beyond the trees like some animal too enraged for the power of speech. When she regained her voice, Wynn followed her strange dialect more easily.

"Your descendant of flesh, a majay-hì, guards this Numan woman . . . even against its own kind! You killed one of them to get to her? Would you do so again, here and now?"

She is a tainted piece of Existence, too twisted and dangerous.

"You gave birth to Existence, no matter the form of its parts!" Vreuvillä snarled back. "Is this now what you make of the bond that I serve . . . that all Foirfeahkan have nurtured for ages?"

Wynn glanced aside. The pack circled chaotically, but mostly toward Vreuvillä. What they'd learned had left them confused and wary.

"How can I," Vreuvillä went on, "or any others left of my way, serve to maintain the bond of parent to child . . . if this is the price?"

No answer came.

Every root around the clearing went limp upon the earth. The wind died in the trees in all but one place. Wynn thought she saw a form hidden partly beyond the branches. Larger than any living being she could imagine, it was not as tall as the trees themselves. That shadow of whirling air and leaves beyond the branches was the only spot Vreuvillä focused on.

Necessary . . . mournfully necessary.

That answer made Wynn long to shout her own denial at the Fay. They were insanely set on a course of enforced inaction, deterring anyone's efforts against what might come. That included Magiere and Leesil and Chap, even more than Wynn herself. But Chap hadn't agreed with his own kin, even in ignorance of what they truly hoped to accomplish at any cost.

Neither did Wynn.

She kept her tongue, letting the priestess's tension mount. The Fay were sacred to this woman in some way, and this conflict was costing her. Wynn had to shape that outcome to her need, even to creating a crisis of faith for Vreuvillä.

"Whatever would be gained is not worth this," Vreuvillä said. "Whatever would be made by it will never replace what is lost. I see no price or loss in what this woman seeks . . . not for what you have done."

The wind died instantly.

Wynn heard a disquieting sound in her head. The leaf-wing chorus made it hard to be certain. It could've been a shriek of either rage or suffering.

Leave the fallen dead of the Earth where they lie.

Wynn tensed. Was this a reference to Bäalâle Seatt? Did the "dead of the Earth" mean the dwarves who had perished there?

Leave that of the Earth in hiding . . . that of ours, no longer a slave to a slave.

Wynn turned sick with revulsion at more insistence for inaction. But there was something that didn't match up. What was this nonsense about a "slave to a slave"?

The dwarves were slaves to no one. Their people would rather die than submit. But she glanced sidelong at Ore-Locks, wondering about the descendant of Thallûhearag, that so-titled "Lord of Slaughter"—Lord of Genocide.

Vreuvillä's brow creased, but she uttered no reply to the Fay's last demand. In the clearing's silence, Wynn saw nothing more hidden beyond the trees as their branches settled.

Chane had remained silent, though Wynn could feel his shudders through his hand, as he was still gripping hers. Ore-Locks was watching Vreuvillä in confusion, and then he looked to Wynn.

"Whom was she speaking to?" he whispered.

No one answered him. Wynn didn't even know how.

The Fay were gone. All that was left were limp roots among the branch fragments on broken earth as scattered leaves settled to the clearing's floor.

Shade whined loudly, and Wynn looked down. The dog was still trembling against her leg.

Vreuvillä turned her head, one eye peering around her dangling, wind-whipped hair. "Who are you?"

Her voiced was strained with suspicion.

"Just a sage," Wynn answered, "thrown into the middle of all this . . . who does what her conscience tells her."

She released Chane's hand and took a step. Shade growled in warning and tried to cut her off. Ore-Locks lowered his staff in front of her. Wynn stepped around Shade and pushed aside the iron bar.

"What are you to them?" Vreuvillä whispered, an edge of anger returning to her voice. "They tried to take your life, to have me do so . . . and they have tried before."

"So have many others, and I'm still here."

Shade remained tight at Wynn's side, eyeing the pair of majay-hì framing the priestess.

"My purpose isn't as far from theirs as you might think," Wynn added. "Though they want you to believe otherwise."

Vreuvillä studied her. Strong as the priestess was, it was not an easy thing to have what one believed suddenly transformed into something else.

"I've nowhere left to turn," Wynn suddenly begged, and the fear and reality of the last few moments sank in. "Do you know anything of a place called Bäalâle Seatt, a forgotten dwarven city or stronghold in the mountains bordering the desert?"

Several of the pack tentatively closed around Shade, sniffing at her from a safe distance. Wynn ignored this, focusing only on Vreuvillä.

"There are some writings left by my forebears," the priestess finally answered, taking a long, haggard breath. "Mentions of dwarves who once mingled freely among the people . . . my people. They came from the south. If these are true, the surest path would have been what is now called the Slip-Tooth Pass."

Something—perhaps hope—began growing in Wynn. "Yes, I've seen it on a map."

Vreuvillä looked away, glancing toward the trees before she dropped her head.

"Where?" Ore-Locks asked, his voice too eager. "Where, exactly, did they come from?"

"I do not know," Vreuvillä answered. "But if it was a seatt that fell in the war . . ."

She trailed off.

"Anything might help," Wynn urged.

"There is a place one of my forebears found in wandering and labeled it 'the fallen mountain'," Vreuvillä said quietly. "It was too odd to be called anything else, as if a peak amid the range had been sheared off, crushed, or collapsed. A flat, sunken plain one would never find amid such mountains. I have not seen it for myself. I cannot direct you more than this."

Wynn's mind was racing. She had a crude map of the region already in her possession. If they were to trust in Vreuvillä, they simply had to follow the Slip-Tooth Pass between the smaller, northbound ridges all the way to the Sky-Cutter Range. After that, finding this so-called "fallen mountain" was another matter, but it might be closer than she had ever hoped.

A thousand years had passed, even for mountains that ran across an entire continent. Who knew what changes to the landscape had come and gone since the time of war? But at least this was *something* to go on.

"Thank you," Wynn said.

"Do not thank me. Chârmun gives me no guidance in this . . . as I had wanted in calling up those who birthed it."

Wynn had little guidance, either. But mention of the tree called Sanctuary raised so many questions as to what had happened here.

"What was that out there?" she asked. "What is this Pain Mother you spoke of?"

"Not *pain*." Vreuvillä corrected, scowling again. "The Pained Mother . . . though it is a weak meaning in your tongue. It is the manifestation of *them*— what your kind calls Fay—that represents what first made all of *this*."

Vreuvillä swept her arm wide as she turned to the stilled trees all around her. At first Wynn wondered if the priestess meant the clearing or the whole forest surrounding it.

"It is all from them, from 'she who suffers and mourns,'" the priestess went on. "Like a parent whose child grows, goes its own way, and forgets what birthed it. I am . . . the Foirfeahkan were . . . all that remain to hold that ever-thinning bond, reminding 'mother' and 'child' of each other."

Wynn knew varied creation myths of some cultures, both living and dead. These, in turn, had contributed to the notion of the Fay and the Elements of Existence used metaphorically by her guild. Some sages had even taken on a foundationist's perspective, combining the core pieces of long forgotten belief systems, believing there was some primary force that had initiated everything, Existence itself. It didn't often sit well with current formal religions or the guild itself.

Wynn had her doubts about such things, preferring what could be reasoned. Of course, she had no doubt that the Fay were real, whatever they—it, the one and the many—ultimately were. Beyond all this, whatever the Fay or Vreuvillä thought or believed, the core of Wynn's being told her that what she did was right. It had to be right, no matter the cost, because she couldn't face the alternative.

She'd turned against the guild, deceived and lied, and even stolen revered cold lamp crystals and used them like currency. She had done—would continue to do—all these wrong things for the right reason.

"I do thank you," she told Vreuvillä.

But she turned away to find Chane fixated upon Vreuvillä. He was shuddering, and his eyes seemed dead, their irises like circles of crystallized ice upon white marble orbs. He looked nothing like himself . . . or perhaps as if there was nothing left of himself inside.

"Chane?"

Only then did Wynn realize something. Whenever questions had been asked of someone unknown or untrustworthy, Chane had stood right behind her. By a whisper or a squeeze upon her shoulder, he'd guided her through the truths or deceptions of those who gave answers.

Wynn had heard nothing from Chane through the entire exchange with Vreuvillä.

Now the priestess watched him alone, her grip tightening on the white, curved blade.

"Chane?" Wynn whispered.

Fear-fed hunger, the screeching beast within, the prodding forest upon him like an army of insects . . .

This was all that Chane felt, all that filled his head, until he could do nothing but hold himself in as he stood behind Wynn.

The barkless tree behind him felt like a cold fire on his back, its suspicious chill penetrating his dead flesh. It might not know what he was, but it wanted him gone—not just from this place, but forever. Amid this, all Chane could cling to was what he wanted: Wynn, safe and always within reach.

This was the only clear desire left in place of his reason.

Fear of any threat to him—to her—grew too much. It wrapped around that one desire as the forest prodded him without mercy, trying to uncover what he was. And that wild woman now eyed him, as if some living beast within her sensed the unliving one within him.

He saw her hand clenched on her white blade's hilt. The beast inside him howled to face this threat. But Chane saw only the threat to Wynn.

Chane lunged around Wynn, and she sucked air so fast, her throat turned dry. Snarls erupted from the pack and even Shade, as well. Wynn instinctively grabbed for a hold on any dog she might get.

Shade swerved in and rammed Chane's knee with her shoulder. His sword jabbed and stuck in the earth as he toppled over the dog.

Wynn was still confused as to what had gone wrong with Chane. She was about to rush in before he and Shade turned on each other.

He pushed up with his hands to all fours, and Wynn saw his face. He looked like some pale beast gone mad.

Vreuvillä's eyes seemed to glow in shock. She raised her blade and took a step toward Chane as the mottled brown male bolted around her legs, trying to come at Chane from the far side.

Shade spun, charging at Chane.

"No!" Wynn shouted.

But Shade pushed off with her hind legs, and Wynn had to duck away.

Shade went straight over the top of Chane. She landed and threw herself straight at the mottled brown male.

A horrendous thump hit the earth. Wynn felt the impact through her feet and spun toward the sound.

Vreuvillä landed in a backward hop as earth, mulch, and moss splashed up around where Ore-Locks's staff had struck. Ore-Locks jerked the iron staff back up, lashing its end when Vreuvillä tried to advance.

Stunned that Shade had tried to both stop and defend Chane, Wynn didn't know to do. She didn't understand what had driven Chane into this sudden assault. But Shade was being harried by two more of the majay-hì. Ore-Locks spun his staff, the butt end swinging out at a third dog. They were all outnumbered, and the pack would be on them far quicker than the last time.

Chane came up on one knee and reached for his upright sword. Ore-Locks whirled the staff around overhead and took a thundering step toward Vreuvillä. Wynn looked at only Chane.

His eyes were on the priestess, and his face twisted into the mask of a monster. When his lips curled back, she saw his teeth had changed.

Wynn could see only one choice.

"No—at Chane!" she shouted to Ore-Locks. "Put him down!"

Ore-Locks blinked once, slack-faced. In a second blink, fierce determination tightened his broad features. Wynn had an instant of frightful doubt when the iron staff changed directions midswing.

The iron bar struck Chane's head off-center, glancing downward with full force on his shoulder.

The crack and ringing sound wrenched the breath out of Wynn.

Chane wobbled like one of those wind-whipped branches. He dropped onto both knees but didn't go down, and the staff's end struck the ground. Wynn again heard—felt—thunder in the earth.

Ore-Locks turned the staff over, stomped forward one step, and brought the staff's other end down with his full weight. Wynn whimpered as she thought she heard bones break, and Chane crumpled to the ground like a sack of stones.

The whole clearing went silent except for Shade's threatening snarls and ragged breaths. All the other majay-hì held their positions. Ore-Locks stepped in, his eyes on Chane, the long iron staff poised in his large, tight fists.

"Enough," Wynn gasped, trying to push him off.

Vreuvillä was watching them all, and Wynn feared if the priestess got closer, she might see Chane bleeding something other than red blood.

"What is this?" Vreuvillä demanded.

Wynn needed to get Chane away from here. "I'm sorry. It's the forest. You know it can affect some humans."

It was a feeble lie, as Wynn well knew. The Lhoin'na forest would not turn any human into a mad beast.

"He's ill," she added. "We should get him back to the city."

"Clearly," Vreuvillä returned.

"I won't forget your help tonight," Wynn said.

"I will not forget you."

It was a sharp ending, as the priestess turned away. The pack was slower in following her. The last to pause at the clearing's edge were the silver-gray female and mottled brown male. The female lingered an instant longer, watching Wynn as her mate dove into the underbrush.

"Did you learn anything else?" Ore-Locks demanded.

He hadn't heard everything that she had. Only she—and for some reason Vreuvillä—could feel and hear the Fay speak. All he cared about, still flushed from battle and hovering over Chane, was whether she could better serve his own ends.

"Pick him up," she said shortly, looking in panic at Chane's limp form. "We're leaving."

Sau'ilahk still hung on the plain, pushed so far through rage and fear that he had grown ignorant of what might have happened with Wynn. He would not allow himself to sink fully into dormancy's comfort. Only just so far that the night around him appeared darker than it should.

Sau'ilahk . . .

At that thundering hiss in his mind, he answered.

Yes . . . my Beloved.

Why do you leave the sage beyond your sight? Dog her, drive her, at any cost. Serve—if only to serve your one desire.

Sau'ilahk grew so very still in that half slumber upon the edge of his god's dreams. He could only do as commanded if Wynn still lived. And being so ordered, did his Beloved know so? It brought him thin relief, though he wondered how, even for a god, Beloved knew this. Wynn's life was still for his taking, when the time came.

But there and then, he was so weary and depleted. He doubted that he could conjure another servitor or even summon some beast to bind as another familiar. Certainly not—not unless he fed yet again.

Sau'ilahk wondered at his god's determination, but he dared not argue nor reveal doubt or suspicion.

Yes, my Beloved.

CHAPTER 16

Wynn reached her room at the guild and opened the door, and Shade trotted in. She held it while Ore-Locks carried Chane inside, and then breathed a short sigh of relief at having completed their rush through the redwood ring.

Even late at night, there had been too many sages about. Wynn had urgently clanged the outer gate's bell and then hurried in when the attendant came. She'd quickly dismissed his offer of aid or to fetch a physician when he saw Chane hanging limply over Ore-Locks's shoulder.

At least now they were behind a closed door.

"Lay him on the far ledge," she said.

Ore-Locks nearly dropped Chane onto the ledge. Chane landed with a thud, but his eyelids didn't even flutter.

"Careful," Wynn yelped.

Ore-Locks backed away, not bothering to straighten Chane's skewed limbs. Wynn pushed past and tried to make Chane comfortable, but as she lifted his dangling left arm onto the bed's edge, she stalled.

A dark stain—not red, but black—had spread around a slash in the side of his shirt. It was still wet. She tried to think of what to do as she tucked his arm against his side to hide the stain. How did one tend the wounds of a vampire?

"Yes . . . I saw it."

She didn't jump at Ore-Locks's low voice. Perhaps out in the dark, Ore-Locks hadn't noticed the stain's true color.

"It's not serious," she said, pulling part of Chane's cloak from under him to cover the evidence.

"Truly?" Ore-Locks returned. "No serious *blood* loss . . . or any crippling bone breaks?"

Wynn stiffened and then turned slowly about.

Had Ore-Locks tried to kill Chane in the clearing? Was this some test to confirm the dwarf's suspicions? Regardless that a living man might have died under the dwarf's iron staff, did he now think he had been wrong?

Shade sat on the bed ledge nearer the door, her eyes fixed upon Ore-Locks's back. Twice she glanced toward Wynn.

"You saw what happened to him out there," Ore-Locks insisted. "What *is* he?"

And there it was. Ore-Locks could no longer pretend to look the other way, and Wynn could no longer hide that Chane wasn't a living being.

"Why should I answer, if you think you already know?"

"That black thing, that . . . *wraith*, as you called it," he went on, "came among our honored dead. You brought it, as well."

"No, I didn't."

"How many of these creatures do you—"

"You were there in the tunnel when I destroyed Sau'ilahk," Wynn cut in. "And you know Chane was just as desperate to kill that wraith. Don't you ever compare Chane to Sau'ilahk." She paused. "He protects me. I thought that's what you wanted."

Ore-Locks didn't answer.

"He's the same man you knew yesterday," Wynn continued quietly. "The same you've sailed with, who has slept across the wagon bed, who has fought beside us. Nothing has changed."

"Yes, it has," he returned. "Everything has changed . . . except our destination. What else did you learn in the clearing?"

The shift of topic caught Wynn off guard. "Nothing," she answered.

"I could see it in your face! You heard more out there than I did."

Ore-Locks took a step toward her.

Shade hopped off the bed ledge and growled at him, but he didn't acknowledge her presence. Ore-Locks seldom made open demands. This night's events had clearly shaken him.

"You tell me, or—"

"Or what?" Wynn challenged, but she wasn't as unafraid as she sounded.

Only the monumentally naive wouldn't shake to their bones in facing the threat of a dwarven warrior, especially one as tainted as Ore-Locks. But Wynn knew she had the upper hand, and certainly he knew it. He simply thought he could scare her, which was equally true.

"I'm the one who uncovered your lost seatt," she said. "I'm the one who can find it—not you. Even if I told you more, you wouldn't understand it. You need me, but I don't need you . . . and I never did."

Looking into his face, for an instant Wynn saw the dark figure of Ore-Locks in his sister's smithy. As she tried to pick herself up after being thrown out of his family's home, literally, Ore-Locks had closed on her. He loomed over her now as then, like a massive granite statue caught in a forge's red light.

Still, whatever Ore-Locks hadn't figured out about Chane, or the unfathomed hints Wynn gained from the Fay, she wasn't giving these to him. He would do nothing to her as long as she was his only way to find the burial place of his traitorous ancestor.

Ore-Locks hadn't moved. Wynn kept her eyes on him but waved Shade off.

"Get out of the way," she said.

"Where do you think you are going?"

"Water, food, bandages—"

"Bandages for what?" He jutted his chin toward Chane. "He is not even alive."

"I don't have to explain myself to you."

He hesitated, caught in indecision, as his gaze shifted between her and Chane. A gravelly exhale escaped him.

"I will get them," he said, though he paused again before turning away. "You will not leave this room until I return . . . shortly."

Again, he seemed worried about leaving her unguarded, even here at the guild. Or perhaps he didn't wish to let her out of his sight. She didn't care either way, as long as she had breathing space to gather herself. As Ore-Locks left and the door closed, this night brought one thing to clarity.

Each of Wynn's companions tried too hard to keep her safe for their individual reasons. At the moment, Shade seemed the only one with whom Wynn could reason fairly—and that in itself was ironic because of their difficulties in communication. Ore-Locks was no longer the one who worried her most, and his harsh words were not unwarranted.

Something had happened to Chane out there in the forest.

Whatever . . . however that tainted toy of Welstiel's, the brass ring, allowed him to walk into elven lands, it wasn't enough. He'd lost himself in that last moment, when he'd tried to assault Vreuvillä, nearly shattering a tense truce. Even that worry wasn't the worst of it.

Wynn had tried to put aside what Chane was for so long. It was easier, more convenient, and even a relief to have him at her side. Some might have thought it flattering, perhaps enamoring, akin to a dark-natured stranger who always appeared to save her. Chane was more dangerous than that, and Wynn was no juvenile girl with her head clogged by myths and legends coated in misguided romanticism.

Her purpose put her at great risk. Despite the harm she'd caused along the way, in the end the price of failure—or success—could be her life, but the alternative for so many others was too great. The path ahead terrified her compared to the life she'd known and wished she could take back.

Wynn accepted this, but Chane didn't.

Not even the whys and wherefores entered into it for him. He didn't believe in the absolute necessity of her mission, not on any level that mattered beyond his own desire. All that mattered in this world to Chane, beyond himself or his vision of the guild, was *her*.

Something had to be done.

Chane opened his eyes. At first the ceiling above looked unfamiliar. Anxiety rushed in, followed by pain. He could not remember where he was or how he had gotten there.

Apprehension increased as his sight cleared. The entire ceiling was covered in bark that flowed down the wall on his right. He rolled his head to the side.

Wynn sat cross-legged on the floor, writing in a journal—or perhaps she was crossing something out. Shade lay on the bed ledge across the room, watching him, as usual.

Chane realized that he lay upon a bed ledge in their room at the guild.

This did not take the edge off his discomfort. His head throbbed, as did his side and left shoulder, but worse were the scattered and disconnected fragments of memories as they began to return.

What had happened in the clearing around that barkless tree?

"Wynn?" he rasped.

She looked up, dropped the journal and quill, and crawled toward him.

"Are you . . . are you all right?"

He swung his legs over the bedside. The room swam before his eyes, and the pain in his skull and side sharpened. He had been badly damaged somehow. Hunger followed too quickly, and he forced it down.

"What happened?" he whispered.

"I had to . . . had to have Ore-Locks stop you. We brought you back, and you've been dormant all the way to this evening."

Chane glanced toward the curtained window and then stared at her. "It is the next night?"

"Yes. But I think I know where to start searching . . . sort of."

Her words barely registered.

Chane tried to stand up, and winced as something tightened around his stomach. His shirttail hung out, the left side stained with his own fluids. When he lifted the edge, a linen bandage was wrapped around his midriff. When had he been cut?

"I didn't know what else to do," Wynn said. Then she repeated, "Are you all right?"

Chane let hunger leak slightly through his cold flesh to eat away some of the pain.

"I will be." Bits and pieces of the night before started coming back. "You ran off alone," he said, unable to keep the accusation from his tone.

"And I told you to stay in Vreuvillä's home," she countered. "You were foolish to go running around in that forest . . . no matter how it worked out in the end."

Chane sat silent at that. Try as he might, he remembered so little beyond the moment he had found her—and then after he had pulled her away from those moving roots.

Wynn watched him closely, with the hint of a frown. She was biting back something more, perhaps not wishing to argue. What else was wrong?

"I'm fine," she said, perhaps reading him. "I've got information that might help us find the seatt . . . and other pieces I don't yet understand."

The situation was more than disconcerting. He had never lost time like this before. The last thing he remembered clearly was pressing the ring against Wynn's shoulder in blind fear of losing her.

Wynn sat back on her knees.

"Let's just move onward," she said evasively. "I think we need to get you out of this land as soon as possible. Everything will be better, will be all right, after that."

It was not—would not be so. It was all broken in his head. And the beast began to rumble and whine inside him. He pushed his hair back with both hands and clenched at the sharpening pain in his head. Glancing once toward Welstiel's pack in the room's corner, he thought of what he needed in there. In the moment, he had a greater concern.

"You learned the location?" he asked.

"Not precisely. No one could possibly know that. I have a direction and something to look for."

Wynn related what Vreuvillä had told her and what else she had surmised. When she mentioned the Fay's scratching "leaf-wing chorus" in her head, Chane was uncertain what to think. Had she truly heard these nature spirits, or could she have imagined this?

"If dwarves visited among the Lhoin'na forerunners in ancient times," she went on, "then the Slip-Tooth Pass would've been the most direct route. We'll head south down the pass to where it meets the Sky-Cutter Range. I believe the seatt is on its far south side, closer to the desert, but if we travel in a straight line from the pass's end, we'll have the best chance to spot any 'fallen mountain.' At this point, it's the most sensible way to begin."

"What makes you think it will be on the south side?"

"Something Domin il'Sänke told me. When spoken in Sumanese, 'Bäalâle' is pronounced *min'bä'alâle*, which is an ululation of praise for a desert tribal leader. That suggests the seatt was near the desert. Perhaps the dwarves of old were friendly with some desert tribe or people."

Taking in Wynn's oval, olive-toned face, Chane saw a hint of her old, blind confidence there. But he pondered the strange duality of what she said she had heard from the Fay. What was the difference between "the fallen dead of the

Earth" and "*that* of the Earth?" What did "a slave to a slave" have to do with any of this?

None of it mattered against the mounting danger to her. It unsettled Chane that she had managed to gain enough information to head into what sounded like a correct direction.

"We need to restock supplies," she said, "and prepare for at least a moon's worth of travel, if not more. I don't know if there are settlements along the way. Certainly not once we head into the range."

Which meant that she had no intention of turning back, no matter what.

Chane swallowed hard, though his throat had gone dry. At least her plans offered two immediate solutions.

"Do you . . ." he began, and faltered. "Is there anything more you need here at the guild?"

She looked at him in puzzlement. "I don't think so. But it may take a few days to prepare before leaving."

"Then we should lodge elsewhere in the city—find an inn; be on our own."

Before he even finished, he saw agreement flood her expression, and perhaps relief. It would not surprise him if Premin Gyâr was having them watched. Chane had not forgotten the menace on the premin's face in the archives.

"Yes," Wynn said, nodding. "On our own again."

Shade lifted her head, ears pricked at full attention. She hopped off the bed ledge and padded to the door, sniffing at its bottom crack near the floor.

Chane rose, clenching his teeth against the returning pain. "Take hold of her."

Wynn started at his words, and then saw what Shade was up to. She pulled Shade back as Chane jerked open the door.

He looked both ways, seeing no one along the passageway's gradual arc. Someone had been there. Even with the ring on, the starving beast inside him sensed this as much as Shade had smelled it. And there was something more that he sensed.

A thin and strange scent lingered in the passage. Partly cinnamon, but with another spice or two he did not recognize.

Chane backed into the room and shut the door.

"Take Shade and find Ore-Locks," he said. "Make sure he gathers everything. We are leaving immediately."

Wynn studied him for an instant and then looked to the door. Her eyes narrowed just before she nodded. Without a word she got up, passing her small fingers over Shade's head, and they both left. As soon as the door closed, Chane rushed to the corner.

He slumped down the wall, digging furiously into Welstiel's pack, and pulled out a brown glass bottle wrapped in a felt scrap. Fumbling from exhaustion, he managed to open it, and he downed what was left of its contents. In his rush, a single dribble rolled out the side of his mouth to his jawline. The fluid was so dark red, it was nearly black.

That stolen life, taken by Welstiel's filthy little cup, burned down Chane's throat to the pit of his stomach. He buckled over, shuddering and clenching as life flooded through his dead flesh.

It seared him, and he suffered all the more for his broken state. It would heal him somewhat, though it would not bring back his memories of what had happened in the clearing.

And this made Chane feel more powerless than ever in protecting Wynn.

Ghassan il'Sänke sat in his small camp among the thin palm trees along the coast. He required time to think. His instincts had once told him to silence Wynn forever. He had chosen otherwise, and even assisted her in translating part of an ancient scroll alluding to a place called Bäalâle Seatt.

Had he chosen wrongly? He could not count how many times he had second-guessed that decision since he had last heard from Mujahid.

The medallion against his chest began to grow warm.

Ghassan jerked it out by its chain and squeezed it in his hand, and Mujahid's voice filled his mind.

Domin?

Yes, I am here.

She leaves soon, a few days at most. I am sorry I did not learn more. I was outside her room, and their voices were uneven. I picked out only a few words.

Do you know her destination?

The young journeyor's grasp of thaumaturgical alchemy was sound, perhaps beyond his years, but he showed less aptitude for . . . more subtle skills. He was forced to rely on stealth and his above-average hearing.

I do not. Only that she will follow the Slip-Tooth Pass. Does this assist you, Master?

Ghassan closed his eyes.

What he had translated of the poem in Chane Andraso's scroll, with its mention of Bäalâle, had combined with other bits and pieces he had gleaned over a lifetime. During the great war, word had spread to the westernmost forces that a dwarven seatt had fallen. For that message to have reached them, the seatt in question had to have been somewhere on the western third of what the Numans now called the Sky-Cutter Range.

Ghassan had never learned a name for that lost seatt until Wynn had tampered with that scroll. And now, knowing her penchants, she had to be seeking that mythical fallen seatt. But for what purpose?

Master, do you wish me to follow her? If so, I should find a map and—

No. Where possible, complete work assigned by your group's leader, Domin Nahid. When it is time, return home as if nothing is amiss. I may not be reachable again for some time.

Good fortune, my domin.

And to you . . . to all of us.

As the medallion cooled, Ghassan rose and stood gazing down into the small fire. So little light tried to push back the dark. How ironic that in darkness was where he had always learned what would be needed in the coming days.

Wynn slipped down the passage but hesitated at knocking on Ore-Locks's door. If only he hadn't been there in First Glade to hear even the smallest part of where they would go next. She might've taken Shade and Chane and slipped away before Ore-Locks knew. But he had been there.

And if he hadn't, what would've happened when Chane went mad? No matter who might've died in that moment, she wouldn't have gained anything from Vreuvillä either way. Still she couldn't help wanting this tainted stonewalker gone.

The wraith had once followed her to the ancient texts. She'd unwittingly led it right to the dwarven underworld and a hidden prince of Malourné. But even these mistakes, not of her own choice, seemed paltry compared to leading Ore-Locks to Bäalâle Seatt.

What did he want there? If only she knew.

Shade sat down beside her in the passage. Steeling herself, Wynn knocked. She heard heavy footfalls. The door cracked open, and Ore-Locks looked out at her.

His long, reddish hair hung past his shoulders. He'd removed the burnt orange vestment and wore only breeches and a loose shirt. There was a shadow of beard stubble on his face.

"We're being watched," she told him. "Pack up. We're moving to an inn until we're ready to leave."

She turned away.

"So you intend to continue, as before?"

The question stopped her. Had there been any doubt? Why would he, of all people, even ask, since this search was all he wanted? Wynn glanced back at him, saying nothing.

"You will still travel . . . with him?" Ore-Locks asked. "Accept protection from him, even after last night?"

Wynn had hidden herself away for so long in a place of denial regarding Chane. Now Ore-Locks was determined to force the truth before her eyes. He might not know Chane's true situation, but Wynn did. Chane had killed countless people so that he might survive. He'd changed himself for her sake, but nothing could be forgotten.

"Don't be so pious," she answered. "You want him protecting me."

"I can protect you."

Wynn had no idea how to respond to this. Instead, she stepped slowly down the passage until she heard his door close. She stopped and slumped against the wall, and Shade pressed up against her.

—not . . . go . . . Wynn . . . stay—

Shade's growl sharpened in emphasis.

—not . . . go . . . Wynn . . . stay safe—

"Stop it," Wynn whispered. "Not now."

All three of her companions were shoving her over the edge of reason. Everything was coming apart from the inside. The pressure of it all pushed tears from Wynn's clenched eyes.

Chuillyon's day had not been easy.

Gyâr was furious at being unable to uncover who had given Wynn the pass. During the morning's council meeting, when the premin of Conamology questioned Gyâr's judgment in closing the archives, Gyâr had turned on her, nearly accusing her of collusion. The meeting did not end well.

Chuillyon had no desire for further discord among the council; rather, the opposite. He needed them pacified, so he could remain intimately aware of all activities at the highest levels. Like young Wynn, he, too, believed the Ancient Enemy would return. It was essential that he knew at all times exactly who was doing what, when, and where.

Should the worst come, he would require a powerful voice in the outcome of political and military decisions for the entire Numan lands. In this, he served the royals of Malourné as counselor and quietly influenced his own branch of the guild. He might in time become high premin himself, working closely with both his own government and that of Malourné. It would put him in the best position for whatever would happen.

But until recently, Chuillyon had never bargained for the antics of one headstrong human journeyor.

Wynn Hygeorht was like a wild boar crashing through a crystal shop. She distracted everyone from his careful misdirection. She drew too much attention, and yet she always seemed to get through to her goal. He had to know exactly what she was up to before anything else was broken.

"Master?" Hannâschi called from above.

"Yes, come."

He was not surprised to see Shâodh enter first. These two were most often found together. Chuillyon could not quite fathom what Hannâschi found appealing in the company of stoic Shâodh, but he never gave it much thought. Hannâschi entered next, lovely and composed as always, but a few strands of her hair appeared tangled.

"Journeyor Hygeorht has left the guild," she said immediately. "She is preparing to seek out this Bäalâle Seatt. I apologize for having learned so little, but I was behind a tree in the courtyard and only able to pick up a few words as she and her companions headed for the gate. I could not follow farther for fear of being seen."

Chuillyon stared at her, barely hearing anything after "Bäalâle Seatt."

Hannâschi smoothed her hair and waited for some response. Chuillyon sat numb, until she and Shâodh exchanged a concerned glance.

"Domin?" Shâodh asked.

"Yes . . . yes, I am listening."

"Again, I only picked up bits and pieces," Hannâschi went on. "It appears the journeyor did go looking for Vreuvillä. I can only assume that lone Foir-feahkan told her something of use."

Chuillyon let out a weary breath and looked away. Wynn's antics had frequently piqued his curiosity, and death often followed in her wake. But this was the first time her conscious choices had made him deeply nervous.

Bäalâle had fallen long ago, burying its dark secrets of how and why. Was she purposefully trying to rush events forward in seeking that place, if she could find it? What did she know that he did not?

"Where is she now?" he demanded, his voice sounding hard to his own ears.

"They are relocating to an inn somewhere in the city," Hannâschi answered, sounding distressed that she could not tell him more.

As of yet, Shâodh had said little, but he stepped forward. "Do not be concerned. We will locate her."

Chuillyon's thoughts turned inward. "Yes, you do that."

"And I will be ready, when it is time, to follow her," Shâodh added firmly.

Chuillyon looked up at his subordinate, slightly surprised by Shâodh's certainty of what would come next. Hannâschi eyed her companion with an almost dumbfounded expression on her lovely face.

Shâodh nodded in respect to Chuillyon as he turned away. But as Hannâschi followed, she jerked on Shâodh's sleeve and whispered something in his ear.

Chuillyon called after them. "Both of you be ready . . . for a long journey."

CHAPTER 17

Before the first bell of full night, Wynn stood in the entry room of a ground-level inn. Her tears were used up, but she felt no better at leaving the guild. Now she waited silently with Shade for the inn's proprietor to return. Chane and Ore-Locks had both remained outside.

Chane still looked a mess, his pale face battered, although not as bad as earlier. He'd claimed he shouldn't be seen in good light, causing anyone at the inn to wonder what trouble had walked through the door. Ore-Locks said nothing to this and backstepped three paces behind Chane to wait. Wynn had ignored them both.

Now she reached down to stroke Shade's head as the elderly, sleepy-eyed innkeeper reappeared through one of the room's two tall wooden doors.

"All three rooms are ready, miss," he said in Elvish.

Stooped by age, he was still much taller than she, and his thin, silvery hair was pulled back in a frizzy tail. His shock upon first seeing Shade remained, but overall he was so kindly that a majay-hì's presence couldn't be the only reason.

"Thank you," Wynn replied, and counted two silver pennies into his hand.

"If you need anything, there is a small bell outside of each room. Ring it sharply, and I will be along."

"Thank you," Wynn said again.

She stepped out to find Ore-Locks and Chane exactly as she'd left them.

"Around back," she said, and they headed off.

Being on their own again brought no relief to Wynn; it only seemed to make things worse. Chane and Ore-Locks weren't speaking to each other, and Wynn fought against her rising sense of guilt in denying the price of Chane's companionship.

She knew—had known—what he was, but kept seeing the *other* Chane, until he'd utterly lost himself in First Glade. That undead monster of his hidden nature was all that had remained. And it had been caused by more than just the forest's influence.

It was also because of her.

Someone could've been needlessly hurt, or even died, for nothing. He would sacrifice anyone, anything, for her.

Shade kept to Wynn's side as both men followed them to the back of the inn. Wynn unlatched the door to the first room and peered inside. Only then did it dawn on her that she hadn't needed a key.

It was strange to be in a place where concern over security or privacy wasn't given any thought. The place looked simple, comfortable, and perfectly clean, but what would they all do now? Sit in their separate rooms until morning, when Chane fell dormant and she would go out seeking supplies?

"I need a new shirt," Chane said, breaking the silence.

He stood before the next door, watching her quizzically. Perhaps her affected calm wasn't as convincing as she'd thought. But his suggestion that they go out to buy supplies tonight was not unwelcome. Dinner was long past, though some shops might still be open. At least it gave them something to do rather than talk—or think.

"Let's stow our things first," she agreed quietly.

Stepping just inside, she unloaded her pack around the door's edge and then faltered, the sun crystal staff still in hand. She didn't like going anywhere without it, but carrying it might become troublesome if they found enough supplies tonight. She tucked the staff in the corner behind the door and stepped out.

Ore-Locks stood before the third door, the chest on his shoulder.

"You don't have to come," she told him.

Ore-Locks opened the third room, slid in the chest, and then shut the door and stood waiting.

*   *   *

Chane had not expected mention of a new shirt to result in a group excursion. He had wanted to go off by himself. Yet here they all were, walking a manicured lane and looking for open shops.

Tension between him and the others was too thick. Worse, he still could not remember what he had done in First Glade. Wynn avoided any mention of the subject, and Ore-Locks watched his every move.

Chane did not care what Ore-Locks—or even Shade—thought of him, but Wynn was another matter. She appeared strained and was more distant than ever. He wanted to pull her aside and demand she tell him what was wrong.

Part of him knew better than to try that; another part was afraid of her answer. So he did nothing.

Ore-Locks pointed toward a shop ahead with pale green melons in a wooden bin out front. The sight took Chane back to his living days. Melons, though bulky and heavy, would be a good food source while they had a wagon to carry such. They kept well and provided fluid as well as nourishment.

Ore-Locks stepped up to engage the shopkeeper sweeping the front porch.

"How much?" he asked in Numanese, gesturing at the melons.

The rather stocky woman, or stocky for an elf, eyed him before returning, "In coin or barter?"

She obviously knew dwarven customs.

As the bartering began, Chane whispered to Wynn, "I have other errands. I will meet you later at the inn."

She looked up, and the veneer of calm on her face did not hide the sadness in her eyes. He wavered again, longing to pull her aside, but she nodded and turned back to watching Ore-Locks.

"I pity that shopkeeper," she said quietly. And then said softly, "Go."

Chane flinched.

Fear of losing her, even before this journey ended, tortured him. He had one chance to procure something rare and important—a slim hope of finding another way to keep her alive, should the worst come. That was all that mattered. He silently backed away and ducked off the road between the widely spaced buildings.

Chane began running as soon as he slipped from Wynn's sight.

*   *   *

Wynn sighed, tired of waiting on Ore-Locks's stubborn bartering. The poor shopkeeper looked worn and exasperated. Wynn turned about, looking down the road at the few people still out for the evening. Chane was nowhere in sight, but she guessed where he'd gone.

He needed to mend himself—to feed. The thought only made her more aware that she'd chosen to keep company with an undead. She closed her eyes tightly, opening them again as a sudden worry struck her.

Hopefully, Chane had gone after wild game. He knew better than to touch anyone here after her warning—didn't he? How he'd managed to feed on livestock so far without being seen, after moons of travel, was another question she'd pushed aside. He never talked about it, never would, but this populated place wouldn't offer him many options for privacy.

Would he go after the local livestock? What if he was discovered?

Wynn took a step, peering between the buildings and great trees. She touched Shade's head and a memory of Chane's face passed between them.

"Find him—now!" she whispered.

Shade loped off, sniffing the ground, as Wynn hurried after.

Chane pushed himself too hard, and the pain in his side returned. Stolen life gathered by the brass cup had not mended him enough. He ignored the discomfort, but at least his fluids had stopped leaking from his side. Soon he passed through a grove, emerging near the stables where they had first arrived.

Wynn might keep at her preparations all day tomorrow while he was dormant, and then suddenly announce that they were leaving at dusk. She had sprung such things upon him before. These lands offered something he might never find elsewhere. He had to finish one task and return before she began wondering where he was.

He ignored the stables and jogged out of the city. Even as he passed settlements along the way, where a few elves stopped in the night to watch in puzzlement, he kept to the road as the fastest route.

Wynn was gasping when she broke out of the trees behind Shade and spotted the stable across the way. Had Chane gone there?

She couldn't believe he'd be so foolish as to feed in the stable. They had to come here to get their horses and wagon. What if someone spotted him or found a wounded animal in the morning, let alone a dead one?

Wynn stumbled across the road, looking about in panic, and hoping no one appeared until she could retrieve Chane. Shade huffed sharply, and Wynn almost jumped as she spun around.

Shade stood midroad but no longer sniffed the earth; she sniffed the air instead. She lunged past the stable and a few paces up the road toward the city's huge tree archway. Before Shade breached the arch, she stopped to look back.

Wynn looked down the road beyond the city to its first hard turn among the trees.

She didn't doubt Shade, but what was Chane doing? Where was he going to hunt? Or was he just leaving? Had his memory of the night before come back, horrifying him? No, that wasn't like Chane. He'd followed her across half the world. Even if she chose to be rid of him, it would take effort to shake him loose.

Shade lunged another three steps and barked. A memory of the open plain beyond the forest surfaced in Wynn's mind. She stared into the dog's eyes.

How could Shade know this? She couldn't dip into Chane's rising memories while he wore the ring. Had he headed beyond the forest? That was at least some relief. Out there he might be alone, unseen as he fed.

Relief vanished quickly—there were Shé'ith patrols out there.

The instant Wynn started running, Shade dashed ahead, leading the way.

Chane reached the forest's edge in agony. The pain in his side would've taken his breath away—if he'd had to breathe. He leaned against a broad tree trunk and didn't even care that the contact made his skin crawl. As he fully widened his senses, he peered out across the open plain.

He heard no hoofbeats nor smelled anything made of flesh in the low breeze. There was only the grass shifting softly in the dark, and hidden within it was what he sought. He crouched, looking again in all directions.

As he crept beyond the tree line, that sensation of a thousand insects crawling over him faded. His eyes half closed as he stalled. He had become so accustomed to the forest's fear-laced prodding, trying to seek out what he was. Its absence was bliss.

He moved on, spreading the tall grass with his hands.

Sau'ilahk instantly sank halfway into the earth. The shock of Chane's lone appearance blotted every thought from his mind. He had not felt Chane's presence before the pale undead appeared, so Chane still wore the ring. . . . And he was alone. What was he doing out here?

Perhaps he simply foraged for a kill, trying to find some wild animal to feed on? That did not make sense; the forest or enclaves of the Lhoin'na were better places to hunt.

Sau'ilahk refrained from rushing forward. He had no physical possessions, as such required continued use of energy to carry. He would have to leave them behind each dawn as he slipped into dormancy. But that ring offered so many possibilities.

Chane had gone into a place Sau'ilahk could not. Chane's true nature was hidden from any unnatural awareness, even Shade's. With that ring, neither Wynn nor her majay-hì would know when Sau'ilahk finally came for her.

It was too much to let pass.

Sau'ilahk slid through the dark, and not a single stalk of grass caught as they flowed through his black robe and cloak.

Chane flinched and squinted at a sudden glare of white before his eyes. It was almost too bright to look at where it caught the moonlight.

A dome of white flowers sprouted between the tan stalks of wild grass. Tiny pearl-colored petals—or leaves, by their shape—looked as soft as velvet, as delicate as silk. They appeared to glow, though the stems and leaves beneath them were so dark green, they were nearly black where moonlight could not reach them.

Their true use, hinted at in *The Seven Leaves of Life*, was still a mystery. Chane knew only that their name meant everything concerning Wynn.

Anasgiah . . . Anamgiah . . . the Life Shield.

He had to learn the secret of that thin text, one more step toward preserving her, if he ever failed in protecting her.

Chane slid his hand along the earth. He reached under with his fingers for the stems, not wishing to even bruise those precious petals. Like his need, they filled his awareness, until he neither smelled grass nor felt the hushed breeze, nor even heard a footfall.

Wynn stumbled into a broad tree trunk at the plain's edge as she caught up to Shade. Dizzy and exhausted, even in the cool air she'd sweated through her undergarments. She tried to swallow away dryness in her mouth as she looked beyond Shade standing at the plain's edge.

There was no one out there as far as she could see in the dark.

Where was Chane? Had he gone across to the woods beyond? She couldn't even see the far trees at night. If he'd crossed, she'd never find him. This was wasted effort, and more than likely she'd be the one to stumble right into a patrol.

She pushed off the tree trunk, but Shade still stood perfectly still, staring out across the plain. Her head didn't move. Her tall ears stood upright and poised. Her whole attention fixed in one direction.

Shade began to rumble low in her throat.

Wynn tried to follow Shade's focus, but she still saw nothing.

A dark silhouette suddenly rose out of the tall grass.

It had to be Chane—just him. Who else would be on foot out here at night?

Wynn grew cold, shivering in her damp clothes now that she'd stopped moving. Something about the plain had nagged at her the first time she crossed it. Chane's lone, dark silhouette stood silent in the grass, and Wynn remembered. . . .

So long ago, Magiere—or perhaps Chap—had told her of a memory stolen from Most Aged Father. Once called Sorhkafâré—the Light upon the Grass—he had led the remains of his forces in desperate flight toward the only safe haven. So very few made it to First Glade, and Sorhkafâré had wandered in grief and rage to the forest's edge.

And he had seen *them*.

Scores of undead had raced about the night plain, trying to find a way in. With nothing living within reach to feed upon, they turned on each other in frenzy. Their fluids matted the grass with stains of liquid darkness. All of those risen remnants of the enemy's horde, as well as fallen allies who'd fought against them, had torn each other apart.

Chane stood in the grass as if he'd risen from that earth still stained black in Wynn's imagining. He, one of the undead, stood amid the ghost memory of ancient hunger that couldn't stop until it consumed even itself.

Wynn realized that very plain of madness was right before her eyes.

"Chane?" she whispered.

Shade's rumble grew to a sharp snarl. Her voice twisted until it became something like the threatening mewls of a cat. Even then, Wynn couldn't take her eyes off the dark silhouette in the grass. She began to take a step.

Shade instantly wheeled and snapped at her leg.

Wynn lurched back, but Shade wouldn't stop. The dog lunged again with a vicious snarl.

—*Wynn . . . back . . . Wynn . . . stay*—

"Not now, Shade," she said. "Stop trying to—"

A shriek upon the plain smothered the last of Wynn's words. It hadn't even died before she screamed out, "Chane!"

Chane shook and convulsed—though only one white petal had fallen upon his palm.

He had stood up, holding his precious find by the stems, only to pause and wonder. They were just flowers, as strangely shaped as they were. In curiosity, he could not help pinching one petal with the fingertips of his free hand. Indeed, it felt like silk-thin velvet, though it stuck to his fingertip. He quickly pushed it off with his thumbnail, and it dropped into his palm.

It was so fragile, like Wynn.

The petal in his palm quickly darkened—first to dull yellow, and then to ashen tan. As it withered, black lines spread from beneath it, twisting and threading through the skin of Chane's palm. He whipped his hand to shed the tiny husk, but the lines did not stop. They wormed up through his wrist.

Chane dropped the flowers and grabbed his wrist. He thought he felt his skin begin to split beneath his grip, but instead, the veinlike marks were worming up his forearm, beneath his shirt's sleeve.

He began to grow . . . cold.

He never felt cold—not after rising from death—not even when his hands had frozen solid in the mountains. Paralyzing, icy pain filled his black-veined hand, quickly following those worming lines into his arm. The cold carried agony to his shoulder and into the side of his throat and face.

Chane shrieked, the sound deafening in his own ears.

He began to fall, darkness thickening before his eyes, as his widened senses collapsed. Someone—somewhere—called out his name.

Was it Wynn, or did he only wish it so?

Sau'ilahk slowed at a scream carrying across the plain.

Chane vanished into the grass, and before his scream faded, Wynn's cry spread over it. She was here, looking for him. Most certainly the dog would be with her.

Everything changed in an instant for Sau'ilahk. He heard the dog's snarls, and then someone thrashed farther off near the forest's edge.

Sau'ilahk could not bring himself to flee into dormancy. Frustration was unbearable with the temptation of Wynn so close, and Chane had been alone with that ring so close within reach. Sau'ilahk hovered in the dark, caught in indecision, until . . .

The thrashing in the grass kept coming closer. It was now well beyond where Chane had stood, and the sound of snarls and growls came with it.

—*Wynn . . . stay back!*—

Shade's command erupted in Wynn's head as the dog charged into the grass toward the last place they'd seen Chane. Wynn wasn't about to stand there, and she bolted after Shade. All she could do was follow the grass parting in the passing of Shade's black form.

It was only moments until she realized they should've reached Chane. Shade didn't stop there. She charged onward into the plain as Wynn slowed for an instant.

"Shade?" she called in a hushed voice. And then, louder, "Shade, get back here!"

Shade's snarls grew more distant by the moment. All Wynn could do was hurry onward, until she nearly tripped over a fallen form writhing in the grass.

Even in the dark, she could see Chane curled up and convulsing. He gripped his right wrist, silently choking and gagging as if . . . as if trying to breathe.

Wynn dropped to her knees beside him, not daring to risk igniting a cold lamp crystal. That would only alert anyone else out here. She grabbed his face, trying to turn it toward her, and his flesh felt damp and icy, as if he'd been out in a winter storm.

"Chane?" she whispered, but he wouldn't focus on her. "Chane! What's—"

A massive hand clamped over her whole jaw and mouth. It smothered her voice as something hulkish wrapped her in thick arms and jerked her back. Before Wynn began struggling, an iron staff toppled and flattened down the grass beside her.

"Quiet!"

Ore-Locks's gravelly hiss was too loud next to Wynn's ear.

"Riders . . . across the plain," he whispered. "Do you want them to find you . . . or *him*, like this?"

Ore-Locks removed his hand. As he released Wynn, she spun away on her knees, but his attention was fixed into the distance along the forest's tree line. She didn't even wonder how he had found her.

"I don't hear anything," she said urgently. "Now help—"

"I can feel hoofbeats on the earth," Ore-Locks answered, "long before a human can hear them."

Wynn was too frantic to answer back. Shade had run off, and she didn't know what was wrong with Chane. If Ore-Locks was right, they had to leave before the patrol stumbled on them.

"Get *him* out of here," Ore-Locks ordered, hefting his dropped staff. "I will delay the riders long enough."

"No! I can't lift or drag him by myself. You have to help."

Wynn finally heard the hoofbeats, more than one set. The Shé'ith were coming.

Ore-Locks hissed something under his breath as he reached down to grab hold of Chane's shirtfront.

*   *   *

Sau'ilahk blinked through dormancy. It was a half-blind shift.

Uncertain where he would awaken on the plain, it would be enough to baffle the majay-hì. That beast had somehow sensed him. The instant Sau'ilahk reappeared, he heard the rapid pound of horses—two, perhaps three—and he whirled to find his bearings.

The road was far off to his right, so he must have shifted north, maybe a hundred yards more along the plain's midline. He traced the road to where it met the forest's edge and the nearby place where he had spotted Chane.

There were two shapes there now, but he was too far off to be certain who they were. The hoofbeats pulled his attention. The shapes of three riders were farther along the forest's edge in a direct line toward those two waiting figures.

Sau'ilahk panicked. How much more downfall could come atop a missed opportunity? He had heard Wynn call out Chane's name, so what had the undead been doing out here? He could not afford to have Wynn delayed—or arrested. Perhaps she and hers were finally prepared to move on, out of that cursed forest to where he could track her once again.

The very thought that he would have to save her burned Sau'ilahk within as he skimmed the grass and blinked once more through dormancy.

Wynn looked out across the night plain as Ore-Locks hefted Chane over his shoulder. The dwarf headed toward the tree line, but she didn't follow him yet. Shade was still out there on the plain.

"The dog knows where to find you," Ore-Locks whispered.

He was right, and she couldn't afford to call out for Shade.

Another shriek broke the quiet, and Wynn stiffened.

Even Ore-Locks spun about, staring along the tree line, as the sound of something heavy hit the earth in the distance. The rhythm of hoofbeats broke amid the frightened whinny of horses. Thrashing in the grass followed as someone shouted and cursed in Elvish.

The riders had stalled, run afoul of something, but what? That thought had barely finished when Wynn heard Ore-Locks snarl under his breath.

"Be still!"

Chane was struggling, clawing at the dwarf's back.

Wynn rushed toward them, but before she reached out, Ore-Locks dropped his staff again. He latched both hands on Chane's torso and heaved. Chane hit the nearest tree trunk, and the impact twisted him midfall.

His shoulder struck the earth first, and his arms and legs whipped down across the base of large tree roots. Almost immediately, he began clawing the earth, as if he hadn't felt the impact. He couldn't seem to get up, and he started crawling toward Wynn.

Ore-Locks closed on Chane, cocking one clenched fist. Wynn threw herself onto the dwarf's back, wrapping her small hands over his face to obscure his sight.

"Enough," she said directly into his ear.

When Ore-Locks froze, Wynn slid off his back and ducked around him to drop beside Chane.

Chane wasn't lying at the dwarf's feet. He was still trying to crawl off and kept whispering something as Wynn grabbed him, trying to pin him down.

"Flowers . . . my flowers."

Wynn looked to the grass plain. Chane hadn't been trying to crawl to her. A memory of white petals came to her.

"What have you done?" she breathed.

Magiere had once been seized by the an'Cróan while in their land and taken before their council of elders to be tried as an undead. Fréthfâre, who had acted as prosecutor, had pulled a vicious trick in front of everyone. She'd held up the white flowers and proclaimed . . .

"*Anasgiah*—the Life Shield. Prepared by a healer in tea or food, it sustains the dying, so they might yet be saved from death. It is vibrant with life itself, and feeds the life of those who need it most."

Wynn remembered every word like it was yesterday, for then Fréthfâre had slapped those flowers across Magiere's face. Magiere was not an undead, but her father had been one, and she shared some of their nature through him. When the flowers struck her, their effect was so damaging that she'd nearly collapsed.

Chane was a true undead, and he'd touched the same white petals. Why?

His hand clamped down on Wynn's thigh. She felt its icy chill through her pants, and though he tried to squeeze, his fingers convulsed too much.

"Flowers . . . for you," was all he said.

His eyes closed, and he stopped moving.

"Chane?" Wynn whispered as she shook him. "Chane!"

She looked wildly over his body lying facedown in the dirt. Was he gone? Had the *anasgiah* finished him? How was she to know with no way to check for . . . someone who wasn't alive?

"Move aside," Ore-Locks said, stepping in over Chane. "I will bring him, but we must leave—*now!*"

Chane's body flinched at the sound of Ore-Locks's voice. Wynn gasped, not realizing she'd been holding her breath.

"Get him deeper into the trees," she whispered to Ore-Locks. "I'll come in a moment."

"No, you will—"

"Go! Now!"

Wynn ran onto the field, crouching low. All of this was mixed up in Chane's obsession with her. Whatever purpose he had for those flowers might've cost him even more in his ignorance. When she reached the place where he'd fallen, she barely spotted the dropped flowers in the dark. They were crushed by his fall.

She spun on her haunches, spreading the grass as she crept about, looking for more. As she saw another dome of white and grabbed hold of its roots, a rumble from behind pulled her around.

Shade stood there, jowls still quivering.

"Where have you been?" Wynn whispered.

She immediately wondered if Shade had been scouting for the patrollers. There was no time to ask as another notion came to her. She took Shade's snout in her hand and tried to remember useful images to pass as she spoke.

"Riders are coming. Lead them away. Then find me." She released Shade. "Go!"

Shade rumbled once and took off through the dark.

Wynn ripped out the dome of flowers, roots and all, and ran for the trees.

Sau'ilahk remained far off, uncertain if his ploy had worked. As much as he had wanted to take the chance to feed, he had not. He had only slipped through the dark and nestled in the grass along the riders' path. When the horses cantered nearer, moving too quick to see or sense him, he lashed his arms through the lead one's legs.

It had screamed and fallen instantly, and he had blinked away before its rider hit the earth. When he rematerialized, he could see the three elves moving about in confusion. It was not long before they regained their wits and the horse recovered, but it was longer still until they gathered themselves and continued on.

They reined in short of the place where he had first spotted Chane. He thought he saw one of them point back the way they had come. They remained there, their horses stamping the grass, and Sau'ilahk finally risked rising to look.

Back along the way the riders had come, something raced away that left a trail of whipping grass. Not one of the riders took chase, though neither did they race on toward where Wynn had vanished.

For the second night in a row, Wynn stood in a room while Chane lay worse than broken and unconscious. Shade had barely caught up before they reached the inn, and now sat poised near the door.

It hadn't taken much for Wynn to get Ore-Locks to leave the room. Perhaps he thought Chane was finished and no longer a concern to his own goals. But Wynn saw the occasional shift of Chane's closed eyes, and the intermittent twitch of his one unmarred hand.

From what little Wynn knew of the ways of the Noble Dead, Chane didn't appear to be in true dormancy. She couldn't stop staring at his face.

Dull black squiggling lines like veins ran through his other hand, up his arm, and into the same side of his throat and face. She'd found more across his chest on the same side, as if something had wormed through him just beneath his pale skin. He was so cold all over, and she couldn't think of any way to help him.

She carefully wrapped the flowers and stowed them in her own pack. She thought again of Fréthfâre's words that *anasgiah* could hold off death. Had Chane inferred this from scant notes in her journals and made the connection when he saw the flowers?

Wynn realized why he'd wanted the flowers so badly . . . for her.

Chane suddenly gagged and rolled onto his side. She pushed back several strands of hair sticking to his eyelids. She let out an exhausted breath, sick with worry. This all had to stop, one way or another.

*   *   *

Two nights later, Wynn pulled the wagon's horses to a halt on the road at the forest's edge. She looked out across the grassy plain.

Chane was conscious but lay in the wagon's back, wrapped in his cloak. The black lines in his face and hand were fading but still visible. He'd claimed to be able to travel, and she hadn't argued with him.

It was time to move on . . . almost.

Ore-Locks had wanted to head directly south, through the forest. She'd told him that the branch road that the caravan had taken would give them easier access toward the south and the Slip-Tooth Pass. But that wasn't the real reason she'd come here again.

Wynn needed to see this plain—this place from Most Aged Father's memory—one final time.

The Lhoin'na called this the Bloodless Plain, though the origin of that name had been long forgotten. It wasn't that no blood was to be spilled here, but rather that those who'd perished here had no blood to spill. Their bones had been long buried by time and nature.

What bothered Wynn most was that glimpse of Chane, an undead, a Noble Dead, standing in the dark amid the grass. A connection tickled the back of her mind between what lay in the earth and him.

Magiere had once severed Chane's head, yet somehow he'd come back from a second death. Welstiel had done *something*, but Wynn had gotten no more than that from Chane. Aside from wondering if he really didn't know . . .

She stared across the plain, thinking of the horrors that lay buried and forgotten here, where only a blind tradition forbade the spilling of the blood of the living upon this place.

"What are we waiting for?" Ore-Locks asked.

Wynn didn't look at him, though he sat at the bench's far end. Shade rested her head over the bench's back between them.

Yes, it was time to go, since nothing more could be learned here.

Wynn snapped the reins. The wagon lurched forward along the road through the plain before her eyes and the other one in her memory.

*   *   *

Chuillyon sat on a horse amid the trees far off from the road. He waited beside Hannâschi and Shâodh, sitting on their mounts.

When Chuillyon had requested Hannâschi accompany him abroad, Gyâr had fumed until Chuillyon explained. Even Gyâr would want to know what some "covert" little Numan sage was up to. Not that Chuillyon would share all he learned of Wynn's pursuit.

"Why are they traveling by night?" Shâodh asked.

Chuillyon put a warning finger across his lips. He still had not spotted Wynn's wagon pull out of the forest onto the road.

"Her tall guardian is likely an undead," he whispered. "Though it would seem he has some method of hiding his nature."

Hannâschi, sitting on a white gelding, leaned forward to glance at him around Shâodh.

"And you neglected to mention this?" she said.

Chuillyon rolled his eyes and shushed her. "Either you or Shâodh can detect the others. The stonewalker will be the greater problem, if they actually locate the seatt. He can travel in ways that we cannot follow."

He waved both of them to silence as movement caught his eye.

Wynn's wagon pulled out of the trees along the road, heading slowly through the plain. Chuillyon waited until it had nearly reached the plain's far side. He could stop Wynn at any time, but he had no plans to do so—not yet.

"There's the patrol," Shâodh said, pointing.

Indeed, the Shé'ith guards emerged from the trees to the north and galloped along the forest's edge. They pulled up in the grass, waiting. All three nodded in respect to him, and Chuillyon returned his acknowledgment as he urged his mount forward.

Formalities mattered to maintain an image of authority.

"Let them pass unimpeded," he said.

The patrol leader nodded again. "As you wish, Domin."

Chuillyon did not want to get too far behind tonight—just enough to let Wynn have her unwitting relief at being free to follow her purpose.

CHAPTER 18

Wynn stirred in the wagon's back and sat up, feeling groggy. A whole moon had passed since they'd left Lhoin'na lands. She rubbed her eyes and crawled out of her lean-to canvas shelter. Two facts hit her instantly.

First, she'd overslept. It was fully dark, and they'd normally be on the move by now, traveling during Chane's waking hours. They'd made good time so far, as winter nights were longer than the days.

Second, she was alone, but this didn't worry her. The others were likely out foraging again, as their supplies were more than half gone.

Even if Wynn hadn't had her makeshift map, they couldn't have missed the head of the Slip-Tooth Pass. Once inside the pass, navigation became unnecessary; they simply pressed south by southeast between the tall ridges on both sides.

No one appeared to use this pass anymore. There was little path to speak of, let alone an actual road. Their way was occasionally interrupted by a depression, a boulder field, or having to locate a place to cross the broad stream that ran along parts of the pass's floor. Eventually this route would lead them to the northern side of the Sky-Cutter Range. Beyond the leagues and leagues of those immense mountains lay the vast Suman desert.

And they were nearing the end of the pass.

Crawling to the wagon bed's back, Wynn looked around, hoping to spot Chane or Shade returning. She didn't, and her thoughts drifted to the previous morning.

The wind had kicked up shortly after nightfall, channeled down upon them by the pass's high sides. The gale was so strong that the wagon rocked and rain began pelting them. Then the rain turned into hail.

Chane spotted a stone outcrop on the leeward slope and drove the wagon in beneath it. They lost part of a night and the next day but were grateful for any shelter. After Wynn's companions had gone to sleep, she'd stayed awake past dawn, listening until the patter abated. Then she crawled out in daylight to see what lay ahead.

In the hazy distance were the vast peaks of the Sky-Cutter Range. She'd studied those mountains, so great in size that it was difficult to judge how far they had to go. Finally, she'd settled down, curling up beside Shade in the small shelter on their side of the wagon's bed, and slept away the rest of the day.

Now she'd awakened alone in the dark.

"Shade?" she called tentatively.

The dog didn't answer. Hopping out, Wynn spotted pots and pans already laid out near a lit campfire, and both horses were munching oats from their buckets. She stumbled toward the fire, stretching out her aches, and her movements loosened an odor from her clothing.

Wynn wrinkled her nose as she picked up the teapot. She could barely remember the last time she'd had a decent bath.

Chane and Shade had taken to hunting as a team. Wildlife wasn't abundant, and Wynn knew what they'd likely bring back. She should've been grateful, but she didn't look forward to yet another roasted wild hare. That's all they seemed able to catch. What she wouldn't give for an herbed lentil stew with tomatoes, celery, and a bit of onion.

She dug through burlap supply bags in the wagon's back. All the melons were long gone, though they still had some small apples and dried jerky. She was saving those for when they entered the range, where nothing else might be available. Pulling out another sack, she found their last few potatoes and a couple of limp carrots. Maybe she could try making a quick soup?

Wynn paused, pondering the fire.

It was already lit, and the horses had been fed. Ore-Locks wasn't a hunter, so he'd taken to foraging for necessities like firewood. Had he already returned and was here somewhere? Bending over, she looked under the wagon.

He wasn't resting there. Straightening, she looked about, and then spotted a flicker of light halfway up the sheer slope on the outcrop's southern side. She barely made out a hulking form by that small torchlight.

"Ore-Locks," she called. "What are you doing?"

He didn't answer. She noticed how high he held the torch, its flame well above his head, but she hesitated at being alone with him up there. Curiosity won out when he began climbing higher, and she raced for the slope and scrambled upward to follow him.

"What . . . are you . . . ?" she panted, closing as he reached the outcrop's top. "What are you doing?"

Up close, he didn't smell any better than she did. A focused intensity covered his face.

"The top did not look right," he said absently, not looking at her. "This is not natural. . . . Too level."

Wynn followed his gaze.

The hang of the rutted ledge they'd seen from below was indeed level on top. By torchlight, she made out a pile of huge stones near its outward end. She was still staring when Ore-Locks headed out over that unnatural level toward the stone pile near the precipice.

Chane followed a few paces behind Shade as they made their way back to camp. Though he carried a large hare from a successful hunt, he wished they could have found something—anything—else to bring back from this wild, rocky land. Wynn never complained, but he knew she was probably dreaming of lentil stew.

Creeks and streams were plentiful enough for water. A few were large enough to support fish, if he was given time for the lengthy act of catching them. Wynn normally wanted to forage and move on as soon as possible. Between him and Shade, the quickest meal they could catch was a flushed rabbit, or maybe a partridge, if they caught it asleep.

Chane was walking at a good clip when Shade suddenly stopped. Her ears pricked up, and at first he thought she had lost her way.

But Shade never lost her bearings.

He followed her eyes to beneath a sparse pine tree downslope. A downed deer lay there, and Chane stepped around Shade to check out their find.

When their supplies were still plentiful, he had replenished his stores of life with the feeding cup by dragging down a few deer or wild cattle. He had not seen either in nearly a moon. An animal this size would provide food for some time, and venison might be a welcome change for his companions. But how long had the beast been dead? Would its flesh still be safe to eat?

Shade rumbled softly.

"What?" he asked, as if expecting an answer.

She remained where he had left her and wouldn't approach the carcass.

Chane dropped to his knees and found that the carcass was still warm to the touch. That gave him hope that it had not yet spoiled, but it felt boney and gaunt. He could not see it clearly and grabbed its hind legs to drag it out beneath the moonlight. It weighed almost nothing.

Once Chane saw it clearly, disappointment set in.

At first, he thought the creature had died of old age. Its skin was shriveled and stretched tight over its rib cage. Then he noticed that its antlers were short, barely nubs, where tines would eventually grow. The deer could not have been much more than a yearling, yet it looked old.

He rose to his feet and backed away. He had no reason to fear disease, but he did not want to carry any taint back to camp.

"Come. We're late," he told Shade, and she loped ahead as he stepped onward.

Even as he reached camp, something about the carcass still bothered him— until he realized the camp was empty, and all thoughts of the deer vanished.

"Wynn?" he rasped.

The black gelding nickered, and he saw that the horses had been fed and the fire was lit. He leaned down to look under the wagon. Ore-Locks's bedroll was empty, though his iron staff still lay there. Shade growled, and Chane straightened.

Shade sniffed the air, perhaps searching for Wynn in her own way, and Chane grew tense as the dog began ranging about the camp and peering out into the dark. Had Ore-Locks decided to drag Wynn off on his own in search for the seatt? Then why leave the wagon, horses, and weapons behind? Why bother building a fire?

"Wynn!" Chane called.

His maimed voice didn't carry far. Shade threw back her head and howled once.

"Up here!" Wynn shouted. "Come quick."

Chane looked up and saw light above the outcrop's top, perhaps thirty or more yards overhead. His relief faded under annoyance. What was she up to now?

He dropped the hare by the fire and ran to catch Shade scrambling up the slope along the outcrop's southern side. When he ascended to a height where torchlight reached his eyes, Shade was beside Wynn and Ore-Locks out on the outcrop's strangely level top. They were climbing over a pile of large stones—practically boulders—near the outcrop's end.

Chane was about to call Wynn back, not caring what brought her up here, when Ore-Locks dropped to a crouch beside one large, erect stone.

"Get over here," Wynn called, waving.

Exasperated, Chane stepped outward, but his curiosity did not take hold until Ore-Locks stood back up. The stone next to the dwarf was about his height and half that in width. Roughly weathered, it seemed too square. It was raggedly sheared at an angle, as if it had once been quite tall, but had broken off.

"What is it?" Chane asked.

Neither Wynn nor Ore-Locks answered at first. Perhaps they had not yet discussed this.

"A pylon?" Wynn suggested. "Like the ones in Dhredze Seatt, used to show directions?"

Uncertain as he was, her notion made him uncomfortable. By its worn and shattered state, it was very old, perhaps ancient.

"Why?" Ore-Locks ventured, for once so focused that he seemed open to discussion. "My people do not need pylons outside our own seatt."

"Unless . . ." Wynn began, "unless it's from a time when there was more than one seatt."

Ore-Locks's frown began to fade. "Or when more of my people once traveled well-used ways."

Reluctantly, Chane asked, "Is there writing?"

Wynn and Ore-Locks exchanged a look, and then both crouched and pawed at the erect stone's surface.

Chane hoped they found nothing—hoped Wynn might have grown weary by now and notions of giving up were in the back of her mind. When they reached the great range, and perhaps after days and nights on foot in those peaks with no sign of a "fallen mountain," he might finally take her home to relative safety. There were fewer threats that would risk following her among her own kind.

"Here!" she breathed.

That one word almost extinguished Chane's hope. Ore-Locks crouched beside Wynn near the squared stone's base.

"Can you feel them?" Wynn asked. "There's not much, but these might be worn traces of old engravings."

"Perhaps," Ore-Locks said at first. "Perhaps, yes . . . yes."

He rose again, torch in hand, and peered southward in the direction of the stone's face. Wynn looked up at him, her dust-smudged face faintly hopeful.

"This must mean we're on the right track," she said.

Ore-Locks tilted his head, appearing thoughtful now. "If the seatt is on the range's southern side, this marker is much too far away. Pylons, as you call them, point to the next closest location or subsequent marker in the direction from an engraved surface."

"Like what?" she asked.

Ore-Locks fell silent for a moment. "Perhaps the seatt is not as far as we thought."

"No, it has to be on the far side. Its name is derivative of an old desert language."

Ore-Locks paused, as if uncertain. "Then a way station . . . perhaps."

Chane's discomfort increased.

Wynn stood up. "A what?"

"A land-level entrance to a seatt or its settlements," Ore-Locks continued. "Like those of my people's stronghold, Dhredze Seatt."

"A passage?" Wynn asked. "All the way through the range to a seatt? That's not possible even for your people."

Ore-Locks gazed southward. "Something is out there, along our path."

He strode off past Chane and down the sheer slope. As Wynn passed, following the dwarf, Chane saw thoughts working hard upon her face. He just stood there, tired and frustrated, as Shade passed him, as well. When he turned to follow, Shade had paused at where the overhang met the slope.

Her ears pricked up and she stood rigid, facing northward.

Chane tried to follow Shade's gaze but saw nothing. The rushing night breeze made it impossible to pick up a scent. Then he heard a low rustling in the scant trees. A low branch swayed, but nothing came bustling out. Shade had likely sensed a hare or perhaps a thrush attracted by the torchlight.

"Come," he said.

Shade scurried off downslope, and Chane climbed down. When he reached camp, he went straight for the fire to skin and spit the hare.

"Couldn't you find anything tonight?" Wynn asked from behind the wagon, a nearly empty burlap sack in her hands.

Chane looked to the fireside and then all about the camp. The hare was gone. He glanced upward to the outcrop above. Perhaps Shade had not sensed another hare, but something else scavenging for an easy meal.

"Chane?" Wynn asked.

What could he say? He was not about to alarm her over some fox or wildcat that had outwitted him and Shade.

Sau'ilahk hovered in the shadows of a fir tree just above Chuillyon's camp on the pass's western slope. He'd discovered the elves trailing Wynn many nights ago. Unlike Wynn's group, these elves had no majay-hì to sense his proximity. He sometimes floated in the darkness, listening for bits of information they might unwittingly share.

Tonight was more difficult.

For one, the deer he had fed on provided so little life that he was still hungry. The sight of Chuillyon only thirty paces away was a nagging temptation. He had not forgotten how the old elf had hampered him, helped to trap him back in Dhredze Seatt.

But Sau'ilahk could not risk a vengeful feast just yet.

The old elf traveled with two others. By what Sau'ilahk had overheard from them, one was possibly another white-robed sage, though all three were dressed for travel. Tonight, only Chuillyon and the one called Shâodh were present, both looking a little worse for wear. They had not stocked supplies as carefully as Wynn, and had been sleeping on the open ground. There was no fire, only a glowing crystal resting on the boulder they leaned against.

The elves had always kept pace with Wynn, so why had they not packed up to ride out?

Chuillyon closed his eyes and leaned back, half sitting on the waist-high boulder. However, Shâodh glanced southward through the slope's trees a little too often.

Where was their third companion, the woman called Hannâschi?

"How much longer will the human journeyor continue?" Shâodh asked tonelessly. "They must be in a similar state to us."

Sau'ilahk sensed dissension between them as he caught the almost imperceptible tightening of Chuillyon's mouth as the old elf's eyes opened. These two had had this conversation before.

"As I have said," Chuillyon answered, "I believe she is looking for a seatt . . . which are always built in mountains or a high vantage point."

"You do not think she will turn back?"

"I do not."

Sau'ilahk wondered if perhaps against only two, he might take the old one and leave the younger alive enough for questioning.

Shâodh suddenly stood up and stared southward. Tree branches wavered and snapped back, as if something had passed through them. A strange ripple in the night formed three steps inward from that disturbance on the camp's southern side.

Hannâschi stepped out of the warped air as if from water, the colors and textures of the trees and earth flowing off her.

Sau'ilahk had not seen her do this before. It confirmed she was a thaumaturge, a metaologer among the sages. And she was fairly skilled, if she could bend light to hide herself at night.

"Well?" Chuillyon asked, straightening. "Are they moving? How far are they?"

Sau'ilahk realized the female had been spying on Wynn's group.

Hannâschi hesitated before answering. "No, they have not yet broken camp, but they will soon."

"Not yet?" Chuillyon echoed. "It is long past dusk."

"Come, sit," Shâodh interrupted, waving Hannâschi forward.

Of the three, she was the most exhausted by far—growing worse over the long nights. Sau'ilahk had noted this was another contention point between the two men. Chuillyon's annoying jovial nature had turned serious over this journey. However, he politely but more pointedly insisted that they continue.

"The pale one and the dog were out hunting," Hannâschi said, settling against the boulder at Shâodh's insistence. "The journeyor and the dwarf found a pile of stones high up on an outcrop. They seemed quite interested."

"Why?" Chuillyon asked, his brows creasing.

"I could not get close enough to hear. The majay-hì appeared to sense me or pick up my scent." She paused. "But if we can risk a small fire, I brought something back."

The two males exchanged quizzical glances.

"Supper," Hannâschi explained with a smile, opening her cloak to pull out a dead hare.

Chuillyon smiled back, a trace of his former demeanor returning.

Sau'ilahk anticipated when he would catch that old elf alone and unaware. That one would never stand in his way again.

Ghassan il'Sänke had traveled for more than a moon. He stood on a craggy foothill, gazing across the shallow depression before him at what appeared to be a fallen mountain.

The first part of his trek had taken him northward along the coast to the vast range's western end. There he had turned eastward along the foothills between the peaks and the desert's northern fringe of dried, dusty earth.

Tracking Wynn by the staff's sun crystal was limited, for he gained only a sense of her general direction and distance. But she was coming south from the Lhoin'na. By a map copied from the ship captain's records, Ghassan guessed she was nearing the end of the Slip-Tooth Pass. She would soon enter the range from the northern side, but he was not concerned. He had ample time, and she had a long, hard trek ahead of her.

With his copy of the poem fragment translated for her and the clues that it bore, Ghassan was certain he would find the seatt well before she did—if it existed.

He still wore his midnight blue robe with its cowl to protect him from the bright sun and the freezing nights. But he hadn't found ample firewood for the past eight days. All he had left to eat was dried flatbread. Water was not so much an issue.

Ghassan had grown up near the desert before joining the guild. Interaction with tribal people who still ranged the dunes taught him the ways to find water where others would see none. Even weary as he was, ever since translating that poem fragment, Ghassan often lingered in memories of his youth.

Allowed to sit "silently" at the evening fire with his grandfather when tribal elders came to visit, he heard many an entertaining though frightening tale—including one about a headless mountain. It was said that for any who found it, the last thing they heard in this world were whispered rumblings in the dark. Then the head of the mountain took form again, but as fire instead of stone. All there were consumed, leaving only ash that blew away in the next dawn's wind, and the mountain remained headless once again.

That tale had not been so entertaining or frightening to eight-year-old Ghassan. If such noises were the last thing one heard before the peak's missing head reappeared as fire, then . . . ?

"How could anyone have lived to tell of it?" he had whispered to his grandfather, not daring to speak openly, impolitely, before the hosted tribal elders.

Grandfather had smiled brightly. With a wink and pat on Ghassan's hand, he placed a finger over his wrinkled lips.

Ghassan had not thought of that tale again until after he met Wynn Hygeorht. Now he looked up the base slope of a headless—or "fallen"—mountain beyond, hidden from the desert below by the jagged hills and lower crags.

It must have once been as immense as any other peak in the range. He could almost not see from one side of its base to the other. About halfway up, the entire top half seemed to have caved in. He wondered, if he climbed all the way up, would he find a flat plateau, crumbled hillocks of boulders, or a crater?

"I am here, Wynn," Ghassan whispered in the cold evening breeze. "I have found it first."

He rushed downward through the depression to the mountain's base.

If this was where Bäalâle Seatt had once existed, climbing to its top would avail him nothing. Any higher entrance would have collapsed if the mountaintop had indeed fallen. But if the tales of the "headless mountain" were based on fact, anyone who had come here and lived had never mentioned anything below it. Lower entrances, if they existed, surely would have been found. So did they even exist?

Yes, he was here. He believed he had found the location of the lost seatt.

"But how do I get inside?" Ghassan whispered again on the wind.

CHAPTER 19

A few nights later, Chane was out foraging on his own. He took relief in being off by himself for a while.

In his mortal days, he had needed a share of solitude. That penchant had increased since the night he rose from death. Though he cherished Wynn's company, the last two moons in close quarters with others had begun to take its toll.

He still had some acquired life in one bottle, so he was not concerned for himself, but he strode the pass's western slope, looking for firewood or anything edible for his companions.

They had made good time in the last few nights, and mountains loomed close ahead. But even in darkness, the landscape was bleak, a rocky terrain spare of trees.

He wandered into an open area at the base of a shorn slope where no trees grew among the scattered, loose stones. Only the sharp angles of embedded boulders showed in the dark. He headed toward the straggly trees at the far side, for no game would linger here.

Chane's boot toe caught on something.

Stumbling forward before righting himself, he looked down at a square edge protruding from hardened ground. He found himself standing on a flat area, and an exposed patch of smooth stone showed where his boot had scuffed away the dirt. He bent over, studying it.

It was smooth—too smooth—and level versus the surrounding slope of dirt. Crouching, he began brushing away more dirt, and soon exposed an edge.

Though the stone was pitted with wear and age, the small patch appeared to be cut square. He began using his old shortened sword to break more of the hard earth. When he had cleared five paces' worth, he stopped to examine what he had exposed. The entire edge of stone ran straight and square for the whole distance. It might have once been the foundation of a small but heavy building set into the gradual slope. He stood up, scanning the ground around him, and let hunger rise a little to sharpen his night sight.

Those other shallow, angular protrusions were not embedded boulders. He could see the outlines for what they were—the bones of long-forgotten buildings at various points up the shallow slope.

Had there been a settlement here long ago? That was strange for the middle of nowhere.

Chane walked back along the edge he had exposed. He noticed a fallen tree, weather grayed, lower down the slope. Hacking off pieces, he gathered what he could before turning back the way he had come. But he paused, glancing back once at those ruins' remains, and remembered what Ore-Locks had claimed at the shattered pylon.

Something is out there, along our path.

Chane was tempted not to mention this place at all.

Before dawn, they had found a decent spot to camp between two ridges up the pass's western slope. A tiny, if somewhat clouded, stream trickled down a rock crevice to replenish their water casks. Walking into camp, Chane found a fire burning with the remains of last night's wood. Wynn was bent over a pot at the fireside.

"I'm telling you, they are edible," she said emphatically. "As long as they are thoroughly cooked with enough water."

Ore-Locks frowned, almost to the point of disgust, showing more emotion than usual. Lying nearby, Shade grumbled, her head on her paws.

"What is edible?" Chane asked, dropping the wood beside the fire.

Wynn looked up, and he noted her dust-laced hair. She wore it loose tonight, and instead of wispy and light brown, it looked flat and dull in the firelight.

"Oats," she answered.

Both surprised and dubious, Chane leaned over the pot. "The stone-rolled ones . . . for the horses?"

"It's the most abundant foodstuff we have left. Domin Tilswith and I were forced to live on them several times. They are perfectly edible if cooked down enough . . . but a pity we have no honey."

Shade made a little retching noise and squirmed around to face the other way.

Chane regretted the lost hare from a few nights back, more so when he studied the cream-colored goop Wynn was cooking. Fortunately, *he* would not have to eat it.

"Did you find anything else?" she asked.

"Nothing to eat," he returned. "Only . . . only a place."

Wynn stopped stirring. Ore-Locks was still slightly aghast, watching the pot. He blinked and looked up.

"A what?" he asked.

The look in Wynn's eyes made Chane clench his jaw, wishing he had said nothing at all. But it was too late.

Wynn held her crystal over the half-buried stone remains. Excitement—even hope—slowly built within her.

"Well?" she asked Ore-Locks.

He'd done some digging and unearthed a forearm's height of a stone wall's base. He was crouched, examining it.

"This was cut by my people," he confirmed. "Humans do not fit stone like this without mortar, but . . ."

"But what?"

"I see proof of only three dwellings. My people do not live in small villages in the middle of nowhere."

"So what was this doing out here?" she asked.

Wynn twisted in her squat and spotted Chane a few paces off with his arms crossed. For some reason, he'd been resentful about bringing them here. Shade sniffed the ground all around but didn't seem any happier than Chane. Wynn ignored them both.

Ever since finding the broken pylon and Ore-Locks's mention of a ground-level entrance into the mountains, her thoughts hadn't stopped churning.

"What do you think it was?" she asked Ore-Locks.

She couldn't keep the tremor from her voice. When she saw her own hesitant hope mirrored in his face, it made her falter for an instant.

"Perhaps a way station for overland travelers," he said slowly. "My people have constructed a few such north of Dhredze Seatt, along the coast toward the Northlanders' territory. But those were built on a well-traveled route and—"

"Then Vreuvillä was right!" Wynn cut in excitedly. "Dwarves once used this pass to interact with the Lhoin'na ancestors. But we are nowhere near the range's southern side and the seatt itself. Where were the dwarves coming from, going to, that they'd require a layover here?"

No one spoke, but Chane's expression grew darker. What was wrong with him?

Wynn scurried over to join Ore-Locks. "Are you certain your ancestors might be capable of building a passage all the way through the range?"

"If you sages believe much was lost in your Forgotten History, then there is no telling. . . . But I wonder what knowledge and skills my people may have once—"

"No!" Chane nearly snarled.

Wynn stiffened in surprise as Shade's head swung toward him.

"Even if you find such a thing," Chane went on, "we are not wandering down some tunnel beneath mountain after mountain, with little food, nothing to hunt, and only hope of fresh water. If we travel for days and nights and reach only a cave-in, do we walk back out, only to find ourselves worse off than before?"

Chane crossed his arms tighter.

"*Pohkavost!*" he hissed, anger making him slip into his own language.

Wynn didn't know what to say. He wasn't wrong in calling it "lunacy." Everything he'd said was valid, but he was not in charge here.

To make matters worse, Shade normally growled if Chane took that kind of hostile tone. She hadn't, and instead she got up and sat right in front of Chane, glaring at Wynn.

Ore-Locks remained crouched in silence. Wynn didn't need to glance back to know he was waiting for her to end this rebellion.

She was tired, hungry, filthy, and had no wish to fight with the two companions she trusted—and she certainly had no wish to side with Ore-Locks.

It suddenly occurred to her that while Chane and Shade had both remained at her side, aiding her, the more she gained hope in her purpose, the more reticent they'd become. Did they want her to fail, to abandon this desperate task and just go home—to be the dutiful little sage, finally obeying her superiors?

"If we found a passageway on this side," she said calmly, "we would not even have to search for the seatt. It would lead us right there."

Chane took a step forward, his mouth opening to argue, but she stood up in the same moment.

"We *have* to try," she told him. "We have to at least look. It's better than facing another moon or more wandering in the mountains, trying to find the remnants of a lost seatt on the edge of leagues and leagues of desert."

The words building in Chane never left his parted lips. Maybe now he would finally accept that no matter what, she would still follow her own path.

Shade rumbled at her softly and began walking over. Wynn wasn't about to tolerate a heated argument of chopped memory-words, either.

"No," she said, holding out her hand. "We're doing a search. Maybe I'm wrong and there is no passage, but these ruins, this place, existed for a reason."

She turned away, facing south, though it was too dark to see the foothills of the pass's end, let alone the mountains. Then she looked down at Ore-Locks still crouched at the base of the exposed wall's remains.

It felt wrong to hurt those close to her by turning to him, but whatever his motivations, he was the only one willing to help. If she could find a passage built by the ancient dwarves that led directly into the seatt, half this battle would be won.

"Well?" was all she said to him.

Ore-Locks simply nodded.

Ghassan il'Sänke was no closer to finding a way inside the seatt. He had given up counting days or nights. He searched the lower reaches of the headless mountain until exhaustion took him, and he simply dropped where he was to sleep. When the rising sun, or a sharp wind, or the night's chill woke him, he searched again.

A small voice in his mind began to taunt him. Could he be wrong? Was it not possible that this mountain had eroded on its own?

Perhaps there had once been a high lake up there, and it had simply dried out and filled in. Who was he to claim otherwise? A natural disaster, such as a volcanic eruption ages past, could have collapsed the top once it had cooled. Even that would have fit the legend of the mountain's head returning as fire. And again, nature would have taken care of the rest over centuries.

But Ghassan denied his self-doubts.

What natural disaster could collapse an entire mountain from the *inside*? A volcano would have blown the top outward, leaving sharp, pocked stones, if not hardened paths of cooled lava, in the aftermath. Many small ravines would have formed following the erosion of softer material. But it was not so.

The seatt was in there, beneath the headless mountain. He had only to find his way in before Wynn reached it. But he was no scout or guide, wise to these barren wilds. He needed to start relying on his strengths.

He was a metaologer.

Movement caught his eye where he lay exhausted on a gravel slope. At first he did not bother to look. It would be another tiny dust twister kicked up by wind curling through the peaks. When it came again, he heard gravel tumbling overhead.

Ghassan rolled his head, raising a shielding hand, and looked upslope.

It was only a barrel-chested lizard skittering away as a few specks of gravel tumbled down. The creature's scales were mottled brown and gray. Perhaps it had been there all along, blending with the landscape. He lowered his hand, too tired to even hunt it down for food.

But his mind came fully awake.

How or why had this ugly little creature come all the way out—up—here? But for protruding boulders and loose stones, there was little cover in this area, and yet he had not noticed the creature before. In its rush, it had sent gravel *down*slope. It would have done so whether it had climbed down or up to get to his level.

Ghassan rolled onto his hands and knees.

The lizard froze on a boulder beyond the gravel slide's edge; it had noticed him.

His thoughts galvanized as he blinked slowly. In that sliver of darkness behind his eyelids, he raised the lizard's image in his mind. Over this he drew the shapes, lines, and marks of blazing symbols stroked from deep memory. A chant passed through his thoughts more quickly than it could have passed between his lips.

He felt the lizard's tension, poised in the baser response of fight or flight. He wanted the latter as he opened his eyes and still kept the little beast's presence fixed in his mind. When he hissed at it, feeling the flight response seize it, he fed its instinctual fear with his will.

The lizard bolted.

Ghassan scrambled upslope after it, slipping and sliding on loosened gravel. The lizard must have someplace that it holed up; it was too far from the lower reaches to have merely wandered all the way up here.

The lizard was faster, or he was slower, than expected. By the time he reached the boulder, it was gone from sight, but he still felt its presence in his mind. He followed that blindly.

An immense rock protrusion jutted outward just around the slope's bend. Years of erosion had built up above it, creating a dangerous outcrop of loose material. He did his best not to make the slope's material slide as he worked his way toward the outcrop.

The closer he came, the more the presence felt as if it came from below. He did not care for traversing underneath that much amassed loose gravel and earth. Angling down toward the overhang, he inched along with many upward glances.

A flash of brown-gray darted in under the outcrop, and Ghassan froze. He could still feel it in there.

He carefully stepped farther down as he sidled around below the outcrop, watching those tons of dirt and rock atop it for any sign of shifting. Then he saw the hole and dropped on his knees in despair.

The lizard had simply run inside its den, a slit beneath the great stone, barely large enough to reach into. It was certainly no entrance into the mountain. But he had learned one thing.

Ghassan did not need to search alone.

He released the connection to its limited instincts, as it did not have the necessary mental function that he would need. A mammal of some kind would be better. He carefully hauled himself up, sidled along the slope, out of the outcrop's path, and then turned downward. Once panicked into running, the lizard may not have dived for a true entrance. But other forms of wildlife existed here.

Some might use other hiding holes here to take cover against high winds, cold, rain, and sleet. And perhaps one of their refuges was not naturally formed, something large enough for a dwarf, or him, to enter.

Chuillyon stood in the remains of what appeared to be some sort of small dwarven settlement too small to even have been a village. Apparently, Wynn and her companions had spent a good deal of time here shortly past dusk, and then had moved on toward the foothills into the range.

"What was it, do you suppose?" Hannâschi asked, crouching to finger the edge of a half-buried foundation stone by the light of her cold lamp crystal.

Her face looked too pale, her cheeks slightly sunken, and her gold-brown hair hung dull. Shâodh was faring only a little better.

Chuillyon cursed himself for being a fool, and not for the first time in recent nights. If he could find a way to go back in time for one moon, he would have managed all of this differently. Upon leaving his homeland, he'd decided they were better off traveling light. He had requisitioned horses instead of a wagon to ensure greater mobility, should they need to bypass Wynn or shadow her more closely. They had brought water bottles, blankets, crunchy flatbread, dried fruit, and limited grain for the horses.

In his younger days, he and Cinder-Shard had traveled long distances with far less. They'd always managed to forage for themselves, and he had not foreseen why following one small, human journeyor would be any different. But it was different, and in his zeal to discover Wynn's true goal, he had not calculated the possible outcomes carefully enough.

Although he had seen an ancient map showing the Slip-Tooth Pass, the distance had been difficult to gauge. They had traveled toward the mountains longer than expected, and though he had intellectually known they would enter some barren terrain, he had not fathomed quite how barren. The closer they came to the range, the less there was to forage for themselves or their horses.

He had handpicked Shâodh and Hannâschi long ago for their skills and quick wits. They were both journeyors, and so of course they had undertaken tasks of their own abroad. But Shâodh had gone with two other elven sages to help map sections of the great jungle to the east of their homeland, while Hannâschi had spent a year at the Chathburh annex aiding in an exchange of Elven and Numan texts—and to read and account the Numans' newest metaology holdings for comparison.

Both had performed well and returned home with useful information, but neither had ever faced conditions like this. Sleeping on the ground in winter was beginning to take its toll, and though faithful Shâodh had believed Chuillyon knew a great deal about Wynn's final goal, this was not exactly true.

If and when Wynn could find Bäalâle Seatt, Chuillyon knew nothing about what she sought there. Shâodh was growing more and more aware of this, and it did not sit well with the young journeyor. Worse, Chuillyon may have underestimated Wynn.

In spite of her surprising deeds at Dhredze Seatt, she was still only a small human. It never occurred to him that her physical constitution might outlast that of his own kind. The journey down the Slip-Tooth Pass had to be longer than she anticipated, and her supplies must be dwindling. Yet she showed no sign of giving up or turning back.

Chuillyon should have paid more attention to the fact that she'd trekked all over the eastern continent—even to one of the highest points in the world there. She was hardier and more tenacious than anticipated, and that admittance embarrassed him.

Shâodh crouched next to Hannâschi. "It is dwarven? You are certain?"

"Yes," she answered. "Not a trace of mortar was used."

His brows knitted. "So, they examined these remains and then headed straight south?"

Hannâschi merely nodded.

"Did you hear them say anything?"

"No, this area is too exposed. I could not get close enough, even by bending light and shadow."

Through all of this, Chuillyon remained silent. Shâodh looked up at him, a slight touch of disgust in his usually stoic expression.

Shâodh's demeanor was becoming an issue—not that Chuillyon entirely blamed him. The young one was loyal to the Order of Chârmun and to the guild. When given a clear mission, he would do anything to succeed. But they had no clear mission here except to tag along in secret without a known destination or ultimate purpose.

Only Chuillyon could feel the desperate importance of following Wynn, of finding out what she sought. That blind purpose had sunk into the core of his old bones. His fears of failing were not something he cared to verbalize for Shâodh. For now, he required assistance and obedience, and nothing less.

Hannâschi stood up. Back home, she often chided him for his methods. Out here, she never complained or tried to get him to explain their current purpose. But she was exhausted, and he knew it.

"On to the foothills?" she asked. "Once they are forced to go on foot, I might be able to get closer."

Chuillyon nodded once, and Shâodh looked away.

CHAPTER 20

With little choice, Chane spent the entire night helping Wynn search for some hidden entrance to a passage beneath the mountains.

To his silent relief, they found nothing.

He preferred that she head into the open range, aboveground, where he could better protect her. Let her look for the "fallen mountain" among hundreds of other peaks until she finally gave up and let him take her back into civilization.

Less than an eighth night before dawn, Wynn called a halt for the night, and they returned to their camp. After a meal of boiled oats, she sat near the fire and began repeating a ritual Chane had observed her doing more and more in her scant spare moments along this journey.

She and Shade would sit by the fire, and Wynn would open two or three worn, shabby journals. She placed them on the ground, and then opened a newer one directly in front of her. She would glance at pages of the old ones, write in the new one, and then close her eyes and touch Shade.

Once, he had summoned the courage to ask what she was doing. She had shifted uncomfortably and told him she was simply reorganizing her notes. His feelings toward her journals were so mixed that he did not press the point.

In nights past, Chane had recognized several of the shabby journals she copied from . . . because he had read them. In essence, these were also copies. Wynn told him she had recreated some journals from memory after a number of them were lost in a snowstorm during her journeys with Magiere, Leesil, and Chap. One of their packhorses had been dragged over a cliff by a snowslide.

Of course, upon returning to Calm Seatt, she had lost all her journals, recreated or otherwise, to her superiors for the better part of a year. Now that she had them back again, she seemed to be using spare moments to recopy them yet again. Chane wondered why.

Tonight, Wynn had two journals that seemed even older lying on the ground. Their covers were faded blue. He had seen them in Wynn's small stack but had not read these. She also had a faded brown one lying open that he had read. It was the one that covered her encounter with Vordana in Pudúrlatsat, when Chane had saved her from the undead sorcerer. The omission of his name in that particular journal still hurt him.

Chane moved toward her, as if to walk past. Wynn instantly took her hand off Shade, picked up the aged blue journals, and closed them.

"What are those?" he asked casually, as if they did not matter.

"Some older notes. When I was in Stravina with Magiere and Leesil, I managed to send Domin Tilswith a few journals before the rest were lost. He returned them to me later. I'm just copying and reorganizing."

Same excuse. She appeared to be doing a lot of copying these days, but he did not press her.

"I am going hunting," he said. "Shade can stay with you."

She nodded, but waited until he walked away before resuming her task.

Chane did not go hunting. Instead, he slipped into the shadows of a small outcrop and stood there, hidden and watching her. Again, she laid out the three old journals. She would glance at them, write briefly in the new journal, and then close her eyes and touch Shade.

After a while, she was turning pages of the old journals faster than the newer one. As little as she wrote, she was writing less and less as she went on.

Suddenly, she turned the final pages of the two blue journals, and then the final page of the brown one he had read. She touched Shade for a long moment, sat straight, and sighed as if in relief.

"All right. I think that's it—we're done."

Wynn stroked the dog's ears and slipped the new journal into her pack, which rested a few paces from the fire. And then, to Chane's shock, she picked up all three of the old journals and dropped them in the fire.

He wanted to shout at her to stop, but he braced himself to keep from running forward and kicking the journals out of the fire. Mixed feelings or not, those were her scholarly accounts! She could not have fit the contents of all three into the new journal now stored in her pack.

Chane did not know what to do and kept fighting his instincts to rush forward.

"Wynn, can you see to the horses?" Ore-Locks called out. "I will look for more firewood."

"Of course," she called back, and with one last look at the now smoldering journals, she walked away.

Chane waited only an instant more, until she was out in front of the wagon, where she could not see him. He dashed out of the shadows and grabbed the journals out of the fire, quietly stomping out their smoldering edges. Since he had already read the brown one, he quickly opened the blue ones—the oldest ones.

To his astonishment, he found numerous references to himself as he flipped through the pages. He was lost in trying to wrap his thoughts around this revelation.

Looking up, making sure she was still off with the horses, he quickly retrieved the new journal she had shoved in her pack. When he opened it, he found that he could not read it at all.

The symbols were dense, more complex than anything he had seen before written in the Begaine syllabary. The few he could discern by slowly deconstructing their combined letters and marks made no sense to him at all. Wynn had filled very few pages with these symbols, as if she had written condensed, encrypted notes—intentionally difficult to read.

Chane tucked the journal back into her pack, exactly as he had found it, and pondered this puzzle.

In her earliest work, she had included the stories of his involvement with her. Then, in her first rewrites, she had omitted him for some reason. Now that she was boiling *all* her journals down to encrypted notes—and far too few to hold all that she had originally recorded—she was burning anything readable.

He heard her humming, a little off-key, as she finished with the horses. She would return soon. A part of him desperately wanted to keep the three singed journals. The thought of a sage, his Wynn, destroying knowledge was like witnessing a fall from grace by one who truly mattered in this world. The thought of these journals burning felt like one of the last of Wynn's connections to scholarly pursuits would turn to smoke and ash.

How many old journals had she burned so far? And why did she stop in her reading and writing to touch Shade in silent stillness before continuing?

Chane rose in the dark as the only possible truth came to him.

Wynn could be doing only one thing with Shade—passing memories. Shade remembered everything once it settled in her strange mind. Wynn was not copying all that she had previously written into the new journal. She was copying encrypted symbols . . . and then mentally sharing the contents of the old journals with Shade.

To his shame, he envied their closeness.

He flipped open the brown journal. There were newer, small notes she had made in the margins beside names like Sorhkafâré. One read, *Omit anyone who might have lived during the war.* She was actively working to hide information from the wrong eyes. But foremost in his mind was still the question: Why had she omitted him completely in her first round of recopied journals and the much-later ones that had not needed to be re-created? She had mentioned all vampires but him.

Chane returned to his first revelation that Wynn was hiding knowledge. Another realization changed everything, and his hands began to tremble. She had not been trying to blot him out of her life.

Wynn had been hiding . . . *protecting* him.

And he could hear her coming back.

He could not risk her seeing him like this. He desperately wanted to keep the journals—especially the blue ones—to save a part of her for himself. But she had gone to great lengths to hide his existence, along with any possible information their enemies might acquire.

Wincing, Chane dropped the old journals into the fire and fled back into the shadows. He did not look back, as he could not bear to watch them burn.

Several nights later, past dusk, Chane watched Wynn and Ore-Locks climb higher up one of the foothills. Occasionally, they both used the ends of their staffs to pound the ground and listen for any hollow sounds echoing beneath.

Shade paced beside Wynn, sniffing dirt and rocks. Like Chane, she was a reluctant partner in this current task. The choice had been to either help or do nothing; the latter would have destroyed any illusions Wynn might still harbor that they wished for her success.

Until now, they had both tried to help despite their reservations. But Chane's recent discoveries through Wynn's journals did not make him any more bound to her mission. They made him only more determined to protect her, even from herself.

By this fourth night after stumbling upon the way station, they had found no further clues to a hidden entrance beneath the mountains. Their supplies were almost gone, and game was even scarcer here than along the ridges of the pass. There was nothing for Shade and him to hunt. Chane had been taking note of Wynn's demeanor, watching for any growing hints of uncertainty.

It was time to move on.

"This is ridiculous," he said. "We are wasting time."

When Wynn looked down from her higher vantage point, he expected her to argue, but for the briefest instant, doubt crossed her pretty, dusty face, as if she partially agreed. And he knew he had her. He required only the tiniest crack in her armor.

"One more night," she said, not sounding confident. "We'll look for the rest of tonight, and if we don't find anything, then tomorrow we'll return to the pass and move into the mountain range."

He could see the pain in her eyes as she spoke these words. Looking for a fallen mountain in a vast range was like seeking a single, special pebble in a rushing river. Shade looked up from her sniffing, swinging her head back and forth between Wynn and Chane.

"Do you want to waste another whole night looking for something that does not exist?" he challenged, crossing his arms.

This drove the doubt from Wynn's face, and she stepped toward him.

"Chane, you are not making the—"

"The decisions?" he cut in. "Apparently, neither are you. We have wandered in the foothills, wasting nearly four nights."

Her eyes widened. He rarely spoke to her like this, but he was not going to back down, not this time. Ore-Locks stopped and watched them both.

"So you think you found a way station?" Chane asked Ore-Locks. "Could it not be there for some other reason?"

Ore-Locks looked away. He never spoke to Chane anymore unless absolutely necessary.

"Perhaps it was built there as a rest stop for dwarves," Chane went on, "or it was just a lone settlement placed well off the pass to remain hidden from foreign travelers."

"Not likely," Ore-Locks said. However, like Wynn, he appeared less than certain.

"So your people are the exception among all others . . . and no dwarves would live any way other than the way you believe they should?"

No one answered, and Chane took a step closer to Wynn, softening his tone.

"It has taken so long to get this far, but there is nothing to be found here. It is time to move on."

Shade huffed once in clear agreement. Wynn looked down at her and then closed her eyes.

Chane knew the crushing disappointment she must feel. They had lost the hope of a possible path leading them straight to the seatt, and now they were back to a blind search in the mountains.

Wynn opened her eyes again, looking to Ore-Locks.

"They're right," she said bitterly, sadly. "If we're to find the seatt, we should head into the mountains now. Too much time has passed already."

Chane waited for Ore-Locks to argue—and then he would handle the dwarf. But Ore-Locks only began descending the hill with a similar expression of defeat. His obsessive goal was to find the seatt, and they were making no progress here.

Shade gazed up at Chane in what appeared to be surprise, and then she trotted beside him back toward the wagon—as if rewarding him for this victory. Indeed, he felt as if he had just won an important battle. Wynn's chances inside the range were almost nonexistent. In less than a moon, he might yet coerce her into giving up entirely.

The chances of this were certainly better now than they had been three moments ago.

Wynn drove the wagon down the pass for three more days before they completed traveling through the foothills and reached the base of the mountains.

Her heart was heavy, and all along the way she'd never stopped looking for hints or clues to the elusive entrance Ore-Locks had placed in her mind.

If only it existed. If only she could find it.

Tonight, Shade lay beside her on the bench, and Chane and Ore-Locks sat in the back on opposite sides of the wagon bed, both looking forward. The base of the range's first ridge loomed above them. In the night, Wynn could not see all the way to their tops, but Chane pointed ahead.

"The end of the pass," he said. "We may have to leave the wagon behind."

Wynn squinted, but he could see so much better in the dark than she could, at least from a distance. She'd known this moment was coming. They couldn't take a wagon into the range, and, eventually, they might even have to abandon the horses. She knew firsthand the dangers of bringing horses onto narrow cliffs.

"Pull up over there," Chane said, now pointing off to the left.

She sighed and pulled the wagon over. Chane jumped down to unharness the mare and the gelding. They would serve as packhorses now. Both were calm and gentle, and she hated the thought of eventually leaving them in the wilderness. She'd face that task when it arrived, as she had faced so many unpleasant tasks to get this far.

While Chane worked on the harness, Wynn climbed in the back with Shade to take down their makeshift tents, folding the canvas up with their blankets. If she packed things properly, the horses could still carry all the supplies that remained.

"Wynn . . . ?" Ore-Locks called from somewhere.

She could not see him.

"Wynn, come up!"

He rarely used her name, and she'd never heard him sound quite so agitated—or perhaps animated. Looking around, she spotted him to her right, partway up the base of the mountain.

"What is he doing?" Chane asked.

Shade rumbled softly.

Wynn jumped from the wagon's back and scrambled upward after Ore-Locks. Chane rasped something after her, but she couldn't make it out. She was too busy climbing as quickly as possible, sending small stones downward with her feet. Shade dashed up after her, and then she heard Chane cursing, as he only had the horses partway unharnessed and couldn't leave them in a tangled state.

"What?" she panted upon reaching Ore-Locks. "What is it?"

"Look," he said.

Pulling a cold lamp crystal from her pocket, she rubbed it and held it out. The light illuminated fragments of what appeared to be cut stone lying against the slope.

Wynn's heart began pounding from more than exertion.

"What are you doing?" Chane asked, coming up behind them. "I had to leave both horses loose down there!"

Wynn leaned slightly forward holding out the crystal. "These stones aren't natural."

"There," Ore-Locks said, moving up and to the left. "More of them."

Shade rumbled again, and Chane now appeared more unsettled than angry. Ore-Locks climbed further with surprising speed.

"And here," he said, pointing.

Wynn hurried after him, spotting more fragments of cut stone along the way. Soon the fragments became slightly larger, and then . . .

She glanced back and saw the pattern. It might never have been noticed if she hadn't first spotted them one by one along the way. There were two lines of those barely noticeable stones with open ground in between, as if . . .

"A path," she whispered, willing herself not to hope too much. "Are we walking an ancient path?"

Ore-Locks didn't answer. By the crystal's light, his eyes were wide and intense as he scanned the slope. He went onward and upward, and Wynn hurried after, barely aware that Chane and Shade came behind.

"I left the horses loose," Chane repeated.

"Then go down and tie them up," she said without looking back.

She didn't hear him turn back as she kept climbing after Ore-Locks.

The path began to curve and snake. Occasionally Wynn lost sight of any stones with telltale signs that they weren't natural. Ore-Locks would wave her and the others to a stop and begin clambering over the slope, searching. Again and again, he finally straightened up and waved Wynn onward. Soon they were passing through wind-bent trees, jagged outcrops, and rougher terrain. Pauses became longer, but Ore-Locks always continued.

"How far will we climb?" Chane asked.

Again, Wynn didn't look back. "To the end."

Shade growled, but kept on as they made their way out onto the crumbled base of a cliff. It was covered in heavy brush that had grown so tall it reached above Chane's head. Ore-Locks stopped, his gaze searching the rocky ground and the sheer rise of rock above them.

"I've lost the path," he said. "It just leads into the brush."

"It must go farther," Wynn returned, peering around at the heavy brush covering the cliff's base. "It wouldn't just stop here unless . . ."

She whirled around but pointed into the brush. "Shade, search! See what is behind there."

Shade's ears flattened.

Wynn didn't understand her reluctance, but as back in the foothills, neither did the dog refuse. She trotted to the thick brush, sniffing at its scraggly branches. Ore-Locks went to try to bend some of it out of Shade's way and looked to Chane.

"Help me."

Chane strode over, and with one final pause, dropped down to grip handfuls of the thick brush, bending it aside so Shade might crawl through.

"I do not know what you expect to find," he rasped. "We are wasting more time."

Wynn ignored him.

Shade crawled through the underbrush toward where the cliff's face must meet the slope behind the brush. Unable to stop herself, Wynn closed the crystal in her hand and dropped to all fours to follow Shade.

"What are you doing?" Chane asked in alarm, almost letting go of his branches.

Wynn scrambled in before he could stop her, keeping her eyes on Shade's tail . . . until she realized Shade should've reached the wall of the cliff by now. She raised the crystal, but all she could see was Shade's haunches.

"What do you see?"

—*Dark*—

Darkness, and that was all? Shade wormed into the brittle branches to one side, and a strange, soft shift of stale air blew over Wynn. She crawled into the space Shade had left and found herself in a barren area beyond the brush. Wynn held up the crystal again.

Light shone upon a stone archway directly above her. She stood and her head almost touched the top. Shade stood beside her, and Wynn turned around, holding the crystal forward.

Wynn almost couldn't believe what she saw. They were in the mouth of a tunnel, and every stone in the walls was perfectly set without a trace of mortar.

A short while later, Chane crawled into the tunnel after Wynn—with a knot in his stomach. In addition to his packs, he now carried heavy burdens of water, three blankets, and their remaining food supplies. They had abandoned the wagon and their travel chest, and let both horses go.

During the busy moments of final packing, when no one was looking, he had gulped down the last of the red-black life in his final brown bottle. After a moment's hesitation, he also took another dose of the violet concoction as well.

Shade was now leading the way, and Ore-Locks brought up the rear. But once through, Chane could not stand fully erect and had to hunch in the tunnel.

"It was foolish to abandon the horses and trust this passage to take us through," he said. "We do not know where it leads."

Wynn turned her head and gave him a resolute look he had come to know well. She carried her staff in one hand and her cold lamp crystal in the other.

"Ore-Locks says it is common for his people to build a back way out of their seatts," she said. "Though this one would be much longer than any he's heard of. Why else would this tunnel be here in the middle of nowhere?" She turned back around. "No, this tunnel has to lead to somewhere else."

The knot in Chane's stomach tightened, as he could not fault her reasoning. Why else *would* the dwarves build a tunnel that led to the foot of the Slip-Tooth Pass?

Wynn pressed on behind Shade, and Chane began to wonder how long he could walk stooped over like this. Then an opening appeared ahead in the light of Wynn's crystal, and they all emerged into a large, open area.

"What in the . . . ?" Wynn began, and she quickly pulled out the spare cold lamp crystal, warmed it, and handed it to him.

Chane held up his to match hers and he saw openings in the walls at ground level. The knot in his stomach eased slightly. As his light shone on Wynn's face, he could see doubt and even fear in her eyes. This was clearly not what she'd expected to find.

"Ore-Locks?" she said, her voice wavering. "What is this?"

The dwarf stepped around her. "I do not know. It looks similar to the entrance chamber at Cheku'ûn Station, in my seatt, but . . ."

Ore-Locks pointed up.

Chane followed his finger to see large dead crystals embedded high on the walls. In his mind's eye, he envisioned the rushing, busy entrance caverns that he and Wynn had visited at Dhredze Seatt, with glowing orange crystals offering warmth and light. Vending booths had filled the cavern air with the scent of sausages, smoke, and livestock amid the sounds of dwarves in avid barter.

Yes, he could see the similarities in this lifeless place, but it was somewhat smaller than the market cavern he had visited. Had they simply wandered into the remains of an old settlement? Perhaps they could still go back and he could catch the horses.

Wynn headed at a fast clip for a large archway at the chamber's far side. Chane and the others were forced to quickstep to catch her. In spite of himself, Chane began to wonder what they had found here.

Holding his crystal high as they passed through a short tunnel to the next cavern, he immediately spotted the large tunnel beyond. Three lanes of grooved tracks stretched into the dark passage. At the tracks' near ends were triple platforms. But what troubled him more was the sight of long-dead trams at all three docks. Whatever happened here, all trams that once served this unknown route had arrived and been left abandoned.

Did any of the trams still function? If so, he hated this prospect even more, for that would hasten Wynn's rush toward whatever lay at the route's end. He was losing any remnants of control here, with no way to stop her. If he openly argued now, she might realize his true intention and dismiss him.

Shade glanced up at Chane and rumbled, as if this was all his fault, as if he should have somehow prevented it.

Perhaps he should have.

"Come look at this," Wynn said quietly, standing beside the far end car of one tram.

Chane joined her and found her studying a cylindrical, dead crystal about the size of his torso. It was secured at the front of what had once been some form of engine to push and pull the tram.

"Do you remember?" she asked.

Of course he did. How could he possibly forget the sight of these crystals bursting into light and then the tram lurching until it raced down the tracks? The determination on Wynn's face was increasing by the moment. This must be so much more than she had hoped to find.

"Ore-Locks," she called. "Can you make these work?"

The dwarf was examining a long-decayed car. "I have no knowledge of such engineering, but even if I could, the tram cars are not sound." Then he looked ahead down the tram's tunnel. "I think I may see . . . wait here. I will be back."

Before anyone could speak, he trotted off at a fast pace.

"What is he doing now?" Chane asked.

Wynn just gazed down at the tram's crystal. "I wish we could make one of these work. Imagine how quickly we'd make it under and across the range."

But that was the crux—the trams did not, would not work.

"Can you not turn back?" he said suddenly, unable to stop himself. "Have you not tried hard enough, suffered enough, only to walk into dangers we cannot even guess?"

Wynn blinked in surprise. "Turn back? Chane, you don't really want to . . . ?" She trailed off, as if struggling for words. "You know we can't fail. You're *with* me here, aren't you?"

Chane hesitated, glancing aside, and he found Shade watching them both.

"Always," he answered.

He could see Wynn about to press him further, but Ore-Locks came trotting back, no longer carrying his iron staff.

"What did you find?" Wynn asked.

"Give me a moment, and I will show you."

To Chane's surprise, the dwarf leaned over and used his broad hands to bend the brackets holding down the crystal engine. Both brackets broke easily, and he lifted the heavy crystal off its base.

"Follow me," he said, trotting off again.

With little choice, they hurried after him. He led them a short way down the tracks to find two good-sized carts made of solid metal. Wynn walked quickly to the one farthest down the tracks.

Its platform was thick, but a large metal "box" with high sides had been attached on the top, as if the cart had once been used to transport materials for short distances. Ore-Locks's staff was already stowed inside. A bare section of the platform at the back sported a two-man pump.

Wynn looked to the large crystal in Ore-Locks's arms. "Do you think you can—?"

"No, I cannot make the crystal drive us, but this crystal may still absorb and reflect the power of another."

Chane did not follow the dwarf's intention. He watched as Ore-Locks laid the large crystal on a bare section of the platform at the cart's front, and then lashed it in place with a length of rope from his sack.

"What are you planning to do?" Chane asked.

Ore-Locks reached out to Wynn. "Give me your crystal."

With some hesitation, she passed it off to him.

"Step back," he said.

Ore-Locks looked away from the engine crystal and touched it with Wynn's cold lamp crystal.

Light instantly exploded from the front of the cart, illuminating a good distance down the track. Chane put his hand up to shield his eyes, and he pushed Wynn behind the cart, out of the engine crystal's sightline.

"Your sage's crystal does not provide enough light for safe travel with speed," Ore-Locks said. "The larger crystal can amplify its light, with the cart's box shielding us in back from too much glare."

"Good," Wynn said, nodding. "Chane, can you pump this cart?"

He could, but his despair began growing again.

"We will take shifts," Ore-Locks said.

His sudden willingness to work together only irritated Chane. The dwarf was nothing if not single-minded.

"Shade, up," Wynn said, tossing her pack into the walled box and climbing onto the platform. "Chane, we can put your packs and our supplies here in the box."

With one final, accusing glance at Chane, Shade jumped aboard after Wynn. Chane began passing blankets and water to Wynn. Every action, every movement, felt wrong, and as Shade blamed him, he could not help but blame Ore-Locks.

Wynn had both a route and means of transport beneath the range.

Nothing would make her turn back now.

*   *   *

Sau'ilahk had come to depend more and more on the elves who followed Wynn. No one in their group was able to sense his presence, yet they had their own method of tracking that had proven more than adequate so far.

Although he longed to feed on them, he had come to view their presence as necessary. They served him unwittingly, and he never needed to risk exposure. In the foothills with all the outcrops, trees, and brush, it was never difficult for him to hide close to them and listen without being detected. But his confidence in their abilities fell apart as they dismounted their horses and stood beside Wynn's empty, abandoned wagon.

Chuillyon picked up an empty harness, his face filling with confusion.

"You saw nothing?" he asked Hannâschi.

"No." She shook her head, equally troubled. "When I arrived, they were gone. Their horses were still here, set loose. All their belongings but the chest and tents are missing, and I could find no sign of the journeyor or her companions."

Sau'ilahk longed to kill them all right now. How could they let Wynn slip away?

Tall Shâodh approached the slope, his dirty cloak swinging over the top of his boots.

"It is clear they entered the mountains," he said, and turned about. "Will we do the same?"

His tone was almost challenging.

"Of course," Chuillyon answered. "Can you sense for their life shadows again?"

Sau'ilahk had become familiar with the abilities of these elves. He was not surprised when Shâodh turned to face the slope and closed his eyes, chanting softly under his breath. He stood there for long moments, and then raised one slender hand.

"There," he said quietly, pointing upslope and to the right.

It seemed Shâodh could sense the lingering tendrils of life and was capable of separating people from wildlife. At least he was doing *something*.

Sau'ilahk remained hidden behind an outcrop near the bottom of the pass as he watched all three elves begin to climb. It felt too long before he heard Hannâschi's voice echo down the slope.

"Look, Domin! A path."

He longed to blink up beside them, but there was little cover where they stood. Soon they started off again, snaking and curving up the mountain until he lost sight of them.

Sau'ilahk allowed himself to fall slightly dormant, to dematerialize and blink up the mountain. At first, he could not see them, but he heard voices again. He drifted ever so cautiously around the sharp slant of a sheer cliff face.

The last of the three elves was disappearing into the brush at the base of the cliff wall.

When they did not come out, anxiety began to trickle through Sau'ilahk. Rather than blink into the unknown, he drifted nearer, slowly following where he had seen the elves vanish. Within moments, he found himself looking out of a tunnel into a vast cavern with dead crystals lining the upper walls.

The elves were crossing the cavern, looking about in wonder. A large, open archway filled a good section of the far wall. The three were debating something, but Sau'ilahk had missed the first part.

"We cannot leave the horses saddled down there," Hannâschi said. "And we need what is left of our supplies."

"Go quickly," Chuillyon answered. "We cannot let the journeyor get too far ahead."

"I will go," Shâodh said.

Before the slender elf came straight toward Sau'ilahk, he blinked out, focusing on the archway at the vast cavern's far side. He was not at all surprised when he rematerialized and hurried onward to find a tram platform.

His anxiety changed to hope. Wynn had found an ancient tram station on this side of the range, but did it lead to the seatt? He dared not believe it yet. He had been disappointed too many times.

Drifting past the tram, he spotted an old metal pump cart out on the tracks, and he stilled his mind to listen. Far ahead, he could hear the rhythmic creak of heavy wheels in the tunnel's stone grooves for tracks. Wynn was already well ahead, leaving the elves behind.

Sau'ilahk glanced back, hearing Chuillyon's muffled voice in the tunnel leading to the tram station. He no longer needed these elves, and Shâodh was outside. Could he risk attacking the girl and the old elf to replenish himself before going after Wynn?

He remembered how Chuillyon alone had almost bested him once in Dhredze Seatt. He might spend more energy than he gained, and even in hunger, it was not wise to take such risks when he was so close to victory.

Sau'ilahk turned back toward the tracks in one last instant of indecision. Then he blinked down the tunnel after the sound of those wheels in the deep stone tracks.

Ghassan il'Sänke was not a man easily disheartened. But day after day, night after night, of searching this fallen mountain for an entrance had left him questioning his abilities. In addition, he'd been tracking Wynn's rough position. By her distance from him, she had to be inside the range. Although she had a long way to go before reaching this side of the mountains, she was moving more rapidly than he thought possible. *How* was the question he could not answer.

Tonight he searched the upper regions of the mountain's northern base, stopping once for a supper of flatbread—which was almost gone. He should have been glad for anything to eat out here, but when closing his eyes, all he saw were lamb kebabs, honeyed yams, and herbed rice. He had been away from home for so long now.

Ghassan was also not a man given to any kind of sentiment, but he could not help missing his rooms at the Suman guild, eating properly prepared food, and partaking of the companionship of his peers there. He had been too long among the Numans, with their tasteless vegetable stews and open, unguarded chatter.

And now he was alone, sitting on a fallen mountain, and looking for a way inside.

He shook his head, admonishing himself. His task to intercept Wynn, to learn what she was doing, took precedence over everything.

When Ghassan opened his eyes, he started slightly.

The sparks of two unblinking eyes looked back at him from around the side of a rock. Thoughts of self-defense flooded his mind first, but the eyes were small and curious. He focused in the darkness and made out the shape of a ground-dwelling creature remembered from his youth.

A geufèr, with light brown fur, round ears, and rotund body, was a harmless small animal that lived on grubs and insects.

Ghassan remained still, careful not to frighten it off, while his mind turned inward. He had rarely seen a geufèr above ground. Something about the sight of it here felt like a sign. Closing his eyes again, he raised the image of the small creature in his thoughts. Over this, he drew the shapes, lines, and marks of blazing symbols stroked from deep in his memory, and he chanted silently.

Once again, he drove a sense of fear into the animal. He focused hard on the need for the creature to go deep, deep down. When he opened his eyes, it was gone. There had been no chance to lock its presence in his awareness.

Ghassan scrambled up the slope, looking about for the geufèr. He glimpsed a light brown form as it shot between two boulders taller than him. He rushed up to the boulders but saw no way to get between them, and he stifled a cry of anguish.

He quickly rounded the left boulder, trying to see if it had shot out the narrow gap on the other side. What he found instead was a broader space between the bases of the two boulders.

Ghassan pulled out his cold lamp crystal and crouched down. Within the gap, he saw a pile of rubble and a pure darkness beyond it so deep that the crystal's light did not illumate the back of the space. Drawing a sharp breath, he wriggled inside. As the top half of his body passed into that darkness, he reached out, holding his crystal as far into the space as possible.

He saw a smooth surface above him.

He dared not hope too much, for this could simply be a shallow cave long filled with rubble. He crawled forward, and the rubble beneath him began to decrease as the space grew larger. He held his crystal up to the wall and ceiling, which were smooth, and knew then that he was inside what must have been a passage that had not caved in when the mountain collapsed. Still crawling, he reached a side passage on his left that was nearly clear. He scrambled over the last bits of broken stone and stood up, holding his crystal high.

There was no sign of the geufèr, but Ghassan still whispered his thanks. The tunnel he stood in stretched far beyond his light, leading straight into the mountain. Remnants of long-dead dwarven crystals were still embedded in the walls.

He had found the seatt.

CHAPTER 21

Wynn leaned against her pack aboard the cart, listening to the never-ending creak as Ore-Locks pumped them farther down the tracks. He and Chane had spelled each other for seven days and nights. She almost couldn't remember the scent of fresh air or the sun on her face.

Shade loped along the track beside the cart. Much as Wynn wanted her to stay onboard, after three nights, the dog had fallen into a depression and begun passing Wynn forlorn memories of open forests and fields. The only option was to let her run for a while until her spirits lifted.

Chane sat beside Wynn, leaning against the outside of the back of the metal box. He'd been watching Ore-Locks ever since he'd awoken. Even down here, he fell dormant, which was the only way they knew of dusk and dawn. When the sun presumably set in the outside world above, he was instantly awake. Not once did Wynn have trouble rousing him midday if they had to stop to clear debris from the tracks. It was strange, for he'd never come out of dormancy so easily during their time under the mountain of Ore-Locks's people.

In this way, they traveled as much by day as by night, only stopping for brief periods to eat or to gather water from scant trickles running from cracks in the tunnel walls.

"That is long enough," Chane said to Ore-Locks. "I will take over."

The dwarf was sweating as his thick arms pumped, sending the cart racing down the tracks. Wynn sometimes attempted to help him, thinking two could pump the cart more easily. She doubted she was much assistance, but it felt better to do *something*.

The worst part was not knowing how far they'd come, let alone how far they had to go. At times it seemed the tram tunnel was on a slight downward slant, and likely they traveled deeper as well as farther beneath the range.

Chane got up and stepped to the pump's other side, timing his grab of the opposite handle so as not to break Ore-Locks's rhythm. Keeping their momentum saved effort, for whenever they slowed or stopped, it took time to regain speed. Once Chane took hold, instead of letting go, Ore-Locks only pumped harder.

"I said that is enough," Chane repeated.

"I am good for a while," Ore-Locks panted back.

The cart did travel faster when they worked together. Wynn suspected Ore-Locks was bothered that Chane never became visibly tired, but Wynn knew how much this exertion cost Chane. He'd grown paler and quieter than usual, and there was nothing for him to feed on down here.

For Wynn, the endless darkness, broken only by artificial light and the monotonous walls racing by, was taking its toll. She began to worry what would become of them all if they didn't reach the end soon. Only Ore-Locks seemed at ease in this dim underworld.

The cart picked up speed, the tunnel walls rushed by faster than before, and Shade began barking.

Wynn sat up to see that Shade had fallen behind. She turned toward Ore-Locks and Chane at the pump. Were those two idiots engaged in some petty contest of stamina?

"Slow down and let me get Shade back inside," she called, peering ahead to where the engine crystal lit the tunnel. She realized that Shade was not barking because she couldn't keep up.

"Chane!" Wynn cried. "Brake now!"

On instinct, he looked ahead over his shoulder.

"The brake!" she nearly screamed.

Chane released the pump and grabbed the brake lever, pulling it with all his weight. A shriek rose from the cart's wheels.

Ore-Locks tried to reach Chane to help, but the cart's sudden lurch threw him forward over the pump handle. Wynn toppled, slamming into the back of the iron box. She struggled up to peer ahead over the box's short wall.

The cart was slowing, but not quickly enough, and a mass of rubble and stones blocked the tunnel ahead.

"We're going to hit!" she shouted, and then she felt a jerk and looked back. Ore-Locks had his arms around Chane's sides, and he'd grabbed hold of the brake, both of them pulling hard. The lever cocked back another two notches, and the cart jerked and bucked beneath Wynn. She ducked down and braced herself against the box's back side.

The cart's wheels shrieked as it skidded to a final stop, but Wynn never felt a collision. Everything went quiet but for her rapid breathing as Shade leaped onto the cart and scurried toward her, sniffing her face.

"Everyone all right?" Chane asked.

No one answered, and Ore-Locks released his grip, backing away from Chane to look beyond the cart. Wynn pulled herself up by the box's wall.

Now that they were safely stopped, her relief vanished under a new fear. The blockage filled the tunnel from top to bottom and all the way to both sides.

Chane was already on the ground, trotting forward. He crouched before the mass of rubble, and then hung his head. Snatching up a small stone, he tossed it sharply aside.

"We cannot pass through this," he said.

Wynn clambered out, rushing in beside him. "We have to."

"We do not know how far this collapse reaches," he answered. "It could go on for yards—or more. This is the end. We have to turn back."

Shade was sniffing the rubble, but she looked up at Chane.

"Turn back?" Wynn said, gasping. "No."

"The tunnel is impassable. Just as I thought it would be. It will not lead you to the seatt."

Wynn couldn't accept what he suggested. It would take another seven days and nights to return, and then what? Start from scratch and head into the mountains?

"We cannot turn back," Ore-Locks said, coming up behind them. "Our rations are low, and we will need to find more, perhaps by going out of the seatt's far side."

His expression was dark, like a storm about to break.

"We have enough," Chane countered. "It will be difficult, but Shade and I can hunt as soon as we are out. You will survive . . . which is more than I can assure if we try to dig through *this*."

Wynn couldn't bear turning back, not now.

Ore-Locks strode back behind the cart to the open tracks.

"If you do not care that we starve, then come feel this." He placed his hand against the stone floor. "Put your hands on the tracks."

Wynn frowned in confusion, but both she and Chane joined Ore-Locks. She put her hand down into the wide groove. She felt a faint vibration in the aged steel in the track groove's bottom, but she wasn't certain if it was just her own lingering shudders from their close call with the cave-in.

"I felt it through the tunnel's stone last night," Ore-Locks said.

Wynn looked up at him, unsure of what he meant.

"*They* must be a good distance behind us," he added. "But we are being followed . . . and cannot turn back."

At this, Wynn dismissed Chane's attempt at a rational argument. But Chane stepped straight toward Ore-Locks.

"You knew this last night and said nothing?"

Wynn moved between them. "Stop it, both of you."

Ore-Locks's revelation rattled her as much as it did Chane. They were trapped between a cave-in and . . . who? Who else knew where they had gone and how?

Ore-Locks walked past them and grabbed his staff off the cart. "Give me one of your crystals. I will see how far the cave-in reaches."

Handing him a crystal, Wynn looked at the rubble, densely packed all the way up to the ceiling.

"Can you pass through this?" she asked, for that option hadn't occurred to her.

Without answering, Ore-Locks stepped to the cave-in and vanished through the debris.

Chane looked down at Wynn and then at the cart. For one horrible moment, she feared he might pick her up, toss her in, and leave Ore-Locks behind. Would Shade even try to stop him, or would she side with him, as she had when they forced her to abandon searching the foothills beyond the dwarven ruins?

Wynn found herself uncomfortably alone with Chane and Shade. This unlikely pair seemed to have joined forces in a mutual goal to turn her back somehow. What a bizarre state of affairs that Wynn now had to look to Ore-Locks as her only support in her purpose.

She backed away from Chane, gathering all the determination she could muster into her voice. "Don't you even think—"

Ore-Locks lunged out through the rubble. His red hair and orange vestment were coated in dust as if he had rolled in the rubble.

"The cave-in does not reach far," he announced. "It is much less packed on the other side. Digging from there, we could clear a crawl space in a shorter time."

While this brought Wynn relief, she didn't relish the delay if they were being followed.

"Can't you try to do what Cinder-Shard did back in the underworld?" she asked. "Could you try to take us through stone?"

Ore-Locks shook his head. "Not you or Shade. I cannot take anything *living* with me."

As his words sank in, Wynn swallowed hard and looked at Chane.

Chane tried not to grimace as Ore-Locks took hold of his wrist and stepped into—through—the cave-in. He had only an instant to panic before the light from the engine crystal vanished and he found himself in total darkness. He was not afraid, not exactly.

He did not fear enclosed places, but even for an undead, the prospect of passing through stones, through earth, was overwhelming. He felt crushing pressure, the cold, and an odd sense of suffocating all at once. He did not need to breathe, but the lack of air, feeling trapped and immobile, enveloped him. Pressure seemed to build until it felt as if it might crush his bones.

All Ore-Locks needed to do was let go and leave Chane buried in a grave of stone.

Chane tried to shout, but could not open his mouth.

Pressure suddenly released. Chane inhaled stale air out of fear alone and collapsed onto all fours, feeling the edge of one track groove under his left hand.

"It will pass," Ore-Locks said coldly.

Chane remained on all fours, trembling a few moments longer. Turning his head, he looked back at what he had passed through. This side of the cave-in was looser, sloping further down the tunnel than on the other side. A part of him became determined to dig his way back to Wynn—as he had no intention of passing through stone again with Ore-Locks. Another part was reluctant to do anything that might allow her to continue.

"Get up," Ore-Locks said.

Chane had never cared for Ore-Locks one way or another, but a flash of true hatred grew as he rose to his feet. What would happen if Ore-Locks simply disappeared? Could Chane convince Wynn that the stonewalker had left them and gone ahead on his own? Without Ore-Locks's meddling, perhaps Chane could coerce Wynn away from this place . . . perhaps.

Ore-Locks met his gaze. Chane saw the reverse possibility, as it had come to him in that moment within stone. He might be the one to simply vanish, leaving Ore-Locks alone with Wynn and Shade.

Ore-Locks might be stronger, but Chane was not easy to kill. The dwarf would learn that the hard way if he tried anything.

A silent, cold moment stretched on, until something lying on the tunnel floor beyond Ore-Locks's large boots caught Chane's eye.

"What is that?" he asked before thinking.

Ore-Locks half turned, holding up Wynn's crystal. "There are more . . . many more."

A skeleton of stout bones lay across the tracks, covered in the decayed and hardened remains of leather armor. Shadows of others stretched on down the tunnel, as if dwarves had tried to escape this way, only to reach the cave-in before death caught them.

Chane stepped wide around Ore-Locks to crouch over the first bones. He touched a calcified forearm and scraped it with his fingernail. Black and brittle coating flaked away, as if this dwarf had died by fire. When he looked up, patches of the walls were dark and marred, as well.

They were much closer to a destination than Chane had realized. With so many remains along the tunnel, they must be very near a settlement . . . or a seatt.

"And you want to bring Wynn in here?" he challenged, rising.

As with so many times before, any emotion on Ore-Locks's face faded, and he became unreadable.

"She will not turn back," he said quietly. "Nothing you do can force her."

Yes, and that suited Ore-Locks perfectly.

"What is it *you* want down there?" Chane asked, fighting the urge to grip his sword's hilt.

Ore-Locks turned toward the loose rubble. "It will take less time if we both dig. We should start as high up as possible to avoid rubble sliding, but be mindful of another collapse from above." He paused, and his voice grew even quieter. "I do not know what we will find in that seatt . . . but she may well need us both."

Chane stood stiff. Without Ore-Locks, he could not pass through stone and would be forced to dig his way back to Wynn by himself. Once a path was opened, no matter by whom, Wynn would continue on. Perhaps she would need Ore-Locks down there. Chane hated that thought but could not ignore it. He looked up the sloping cave-in to the tunnel's high ceiling.

"Near the top."

Wynn heard scraping sounds long before she saw stones tremble amid the rubble. She had unpacked the cart and sat on its forward corner with Shade at her feet, wondering how Chane and Ore-Locks fared on the other side.

She wished she could somehow convince Shade that retreat was not an option. With undeads like Welstiel and Sau'ilahk willing to murder to find these orbs, the few like Wynn, who knew the truth, could not stop, no matter the cost.

Shade whined and put her nose against Wynn's hand but didn't pass any memories or words. Perhaps she had nothing to say.

"Wynn, move back."

Wynn stood up at Chane's barely audible rasp coming from the rubble. She quickly backed along the cart's side, calling Shade along.

A bulge broke in the cave-in. Stones and earth tumbled down. Chane's dirt-caked hands began carefully pushing out more debris until he squirmed through an opening and slid downward on his stomach. He stood up before her, filthy from head to toe.

Wynn saw no victory in his faintly brown eyes.

"Start passing me the supplies," he said. "I will bring you two through last."

Wynn noticed his right hand was bleeding, black fluid turning dirt into dark mud stains on his fingers. Regardless of his doubts on this journey, he always managed to get her through to the other side.

Wynn held out her sun crystal staff and one of the packs, and he took them.

Sau'ilahk waited down the tunnel until Chane pulled Wynn and Shade through the cave-in. He managed to remain patient only long enough for safety, and then blinked himself through. He was too eager to learn what lay ahead beyond the cave-in, and drifted forward at a distance behind Wynn heading farther along the tunnel. The sight of dwarven bones along the way filled Sau'ilahk with hope.

Large, dead crystals in the walls grew closer and closer to each other, and the skeletal remains grew more numerous, until he saw one dwarf piled on top another. In places, rubble partially filled the tunnel, half burying some remains. Finally, he grew rash and closed the distance enough to hear the faint voices of his quarry.

Sau'ilahk froze when he spotted Wynn ahead, and quickly pulled back. The last thing he needed was for the dog to sense him.

"We're close to the seatt, aren't we?" Wynn asked.

She sounded distraught, and Sau'ilahk wondered if all the bones upset her. These dwarves had died long, long ago, and her feeble pity was wasted.

"Yes, we must be," Ore-Locks answered.

Sau'ilahk swelled with relief. *Yes*, he agreed so vehemently that he could no longer wait. He slipped to the tunnel's other side, looking ahead around its gradual curve, and let himself fall into dormancy. As he winked out of existence, he held that glimpse of the tunnel's distance in his consciousness, though he was as blind as Wynn regarding what lay ahead.

He rematerialized somewhere beyond her and rushed on before the dog might sense him. Quickly enough, he found himself inside what must have been the tram station at the tunnel's far end. Of course, there were no trams here; they had all been abandoned centuries ago at the range's northern side. He briefly looked at the empty, grime-coated stone platforms before seeking an exit.

330 · BARB & J. C. HENDEE

Rather than the multiple tunnels leading from the stations at Dhredze Seatt, here only one huge archway led Sau'ilahk into another tunnel straight ahead.

Chuillyon's arms felt like lead as he pumped the handle. After so many days of powering this dwarven cart, every muscle in his body hurt. His thoughts kept drifting back to his days of travels with Cinder-Shard.

The two of them had tromped the countryside or rowed boats for days without stopping. But that time was long past. He had spent too many years dabbling in politics and diplomacy. However, though much younger, Shâodh was not faring much better on the pump's other end. His long face and high forehead were flushed from exertion.

When they had first come across this cart, realizing where and how Wynn's group traveled, Chuillyon had cautioned against moving too quickly, for fear of revealing themselves. He soon realized that overtaking Wynn was less of a concern than keeping up with her.

Ore-Locks was a dwarf, and Chane was quite possibly an undead. Between those two, they outdistanced Chuillyon at an incredible rate. Hannâschi often offered to spell Chuillyon or Shâodh. Though her offers were genuine, she could not provide much help.

In his life to date, Chuillyon had known a number of elven women who were quite strong. But Hannâschi was not one of them. Her strengths lay in other areas, so Chuillyon worked with Shâodh to keep from falling too far behind.

Upon spotting the engine crystal removed from a tram back at the station, he realized what Ore-Locks had managed. Chuillyon had found no way to break another crystal loose for his own cart. He and his had to rely on superior vision and cold lamp crystals for light.

His arms were nearly giving out, and he reluctantly decided to call for another rest. Hannâschi turned from looking ahead—over the top of the metal box—before he said a word.

"Slow down," she said. Looking forward again, she shouted, "Shâodh, the break!"

Without hesitation, Shâodh released his pump handle and grabbed the break lever, pulling back hard.

Ahead, Chuillyon saw what had alarmed Hannâschi. Before they would even hit the packed rubble, they were going to smash into another cart on the tracks. He struggled to reach Shâodh, but the pressure of the cart slowing so rapidly forced him to keep hold of the pump handle.

Shâodh strained, crying out once with effort, and the cart slammed to a halt. Its platform's rear end bucked upward, and Chuillyon fell across the pump handle. He heard another impact against stone before he could right himself. Upon impact, the other cart had rammed forward into the rubble.

Shâodh jumped away from the brake, taking hold of Hannâschi and pulling her up.

"Are you all right? Were you hurt?"

"No . . . I mean, I was not hurt," she answered, sounding a bit shaken.

Chuillyon dropped off the cart and left them both for a moment. There was a hole through the top of the cave-in.

"Shâodh, can you sense any life?" he called back.

With one last look at Hannâschi, Shâodh climbed off the cart and came forward. He briefly examined the cave-in, and the skin over his cheeks tightened. He closed his eyes, a soft, thrumming chant rising from his throat, and then he fell silent.

"I sense nothing," he said. "They must have passed here too long ago. They have a good lead on us." He glanced sidelong at Chuillyon. "You wish to press on, to crawl through to the other side?"

Chuillyon walked back to the cart for his pack. "Certainly," he said, attempting to sound cheerful. "They have already done the work for us."

Ghassan il'Sänke had been inside the mountain for at least eight days, possibly more. There was no way to be certain as he searched. From one dead end or cave-in to another, he had tried to climb higher into the seatt's upper remains. He soon realized this was impossible.

All levels above the one he entered had been lost when the peak collapsed. As of yet, he had not discovered any passable tunnels downward. A few times he had been hopeful, only to reach another cave-in and then work his way back up. Tonight he stumbled onto a broad passage, easily as wide as a city street.

Broken fragments of pylons lay all along the way, but there was room to pass or climb over the debris. Though he made good time, it was difficult to keep his bearings in this ancient maze. He was almost certain he was near the center of the mountain when he saw a large archway ahead, and quickened his pace. Upon stepping through, he was not prepared for the sight that waited. The word "vast" was so insufficient.

The massive, sculpted cavern could have held a sizable village, perhaps a town. He walked forward slowly, looking around in wonder. At this depth, he was standing in an architectural impossibility. Enormous, crumbling columns some ten or more yards in diameter held the remnants of curving stairways on their exteriors. Three of eight columns were still fully erect, reaching to the high, domed ceiling perhaps sixty to seventy yards above.

There were several massive cracks in the ceiling, though the light of Ghassan's crystal was not strong enough to fully illuminate those heights. Walkways ran around the walls at multiple levels, and broken landings at certain points showed where causeways had once spanned between the columns.

He passed the ruins of a great stairway that had once led upward into stone. Perhaps it had joined to levels above connected to the tiers of walkways. Losing all sense of time, he strolled on until he came to his senses at another huge archway on the cavern's far side.

With no wish to leave yet, he climbed one of the countless piles of broken stone to the top of a column fragment lying on its side. In frustration, he crouched and looked about.

So far, Ghassan had found nothing of significance to explain Wynn's desperate trek here—besides the astonishing fact that this place was not a myth. But she was not seeking some archaeological wonder.

Something about this cavern offered him comfort. He could not place his finger on exactly what until he realized that it was the only place he had seen that reminded him that other people had once lived and breathed here. Even the calcified, tragic skeletons scattered about served as reminders. Some appeared to have been too wounded or trapped by falling rubble to have escaped.

Poor souls. He could not imagine what horrors had happened in this place.

He looked around from his vantage point, still in awe of his surroundings. This seemed a good spot to wait—the only one, really. This was not only the heart of the seatt . . . this *was* the seatt, or all that was left of it. Whatever path Wynn traveled, it would lead her here.

He had earlier sat in meditation to track her position. She was closer, but her speed had slowed, possibly stopped, and he wished he knew why. He still had not decided what to do when she arrived. Should he join her on the pretense of offering aid, or simply give her complete freedom and then follow to watch what she did?

The first option offered more control. No doubt he could convince her that he had learned enough from the part of scroll he had translated to find her here. Wynn did not trust many people, but she trusted him, to a degree. He alone had helped her when no one else in her own guild branch would. He had made the sun crystal staff for her and fought at her side.

But joining her meant she would be guarded in her actions. Perhaps the second option was the one to more quickly uncover her secrets.

He was so deep in self-debate that at first he did not notice the disturbing sensation creep over him. Like an uncomfortable tickle, when it broke through, he knew he had felt it before. He slipped over the column's far side, crouching on the rubble he had used to climb up.

Darkness in one far archway shifted suddenly, as if those shadows awoke to life.

A black figure drifted from the opening, garbed in a flowing robe and cloak. Both garments shifted and swayed, though the cavern's air was still and stale. Ghassan saw only more darkness inside its voluminous, sagging cowl where there should have been a face.

It raised its arms in some sort of silent salutation or in triumph, and its sleeves slipped down, exposing thin arms, hands, and fingers all wrapped in black strips.

Ghassan did not want to believe his eyes. He and Wynn had burned this thing to nothing in the streets of Calm Seatt.

And yet here it was.

Sau'ilahk rematerialized in the tunnel before a huge archway at its end. He slipped through to find himself in the half-destroyed remains of a great cathedral cavern. Its immensity left him startled, as did its depth beneath the range.

Column fragments larger than cottages and piles of rubble lay everywhere.

There were fewer remains here than in the tunnel. He suspected some dwarves on this level had made it to the trams and escaped before whatever had happened that shattered and burned this place. The bones on this side of the cave-in must be from stragglers trapped by the catastrophe that had come.

He looked up, imagining the crushed levels above. Judging the seatt's possible population by this central cavern's size and the openings around it, tens of thousands must have perished up there. But Sau'ilahk gave them no thought.

His shifting, incorporeal form wavered, as if shivering with excitement as he raised his arms. At least Beloved had not lied in this. He was inside Bäalâle Seatt, and after all these centuries, he would find his heart's desire.

Ghassan struggled with what he saw. In his mind, the wraith had been destroyed and was long gone. That failure now changed everything.

What did it want? If it wanted Wynn dead, she would be. Ghassan forced himself into a calmer, better-reasoning state. It must have followed her and then slipped ahead. Then a greater fear crept into his thoughts.

He had been tracking the sun crystal's position, but that did not mean Wynn was still carrying it.

Fear turned to panic. What if someone else possessed the sun crystal, and he had been tracking the wrong person? Worse, what if he had been tracking Wynn, and the reason the crystal had stopped moving was because the wraith *had* killed her?

The black-robed creature began wildly searching the cavern, racing from place to place. Ghassan just watched. At the moment, there was little else he could do.

CHAPTER 22

S au'ilahk raced through downed columns and all about the cavern, uncertain what to look for. Where would the orb have been hidden?

Several archways in the east wall all led to cave-ins. Flying back out, he drifted up into the heights, following the multilayered upper walkways. Nothing came of it. He began to realize that although he had reached Wynn's destination first, he possessed no knowledge of this place. He wanted to weep when the only option taunted him.

He would have to wait on Wynn yet again.

In truth, he had no idea if she was any more informed than he. But the insipid little sage always wormed her way forward, inch by inch. The prospect of being so close and still dependent on her made him writhe.

Sau'ilahk settled to the cavern's floor.

The dog might sense him more easily in this open place. He could not allow that, so he drifted to the cavern's far side. Slipping behind one remaining, erect column, he peeked around its immense base.

Sau'ilahk watched the entrance, sickened by his hope that Wynn would come soon.

Ghassan closed his eyes, raising sigils amid patterns in his mind. Any noise might betray his presence to the wraith, and he focused inward. As he lifted one foot from the rubble, his will held him up, and he floated silently to the floor behind the toppled column.

Hiding was not difficult among the debris, and he slipped along to crouch behind the remains of the broad steps he had passed. Peering out, he spotted the black spirit behind another great column, but the creature's attention appeared focused on the archway through which it had entered.

If the wraith was here, hiding and watching, it could only be waiting for Wynn. Hope fueled that belief, as Ghassan could not battle the wraith alone. He needed to stay alive to counter any further damage Wynn might unleash in coming here. Again he considered revealing himself to her if—when—she arrived.

They had confronted the wraith together once before. If he could hold it, she could burn it, but obviously that had not lasted the first time. Remaining hidden still offered the better chance of uncovering her purpose.

Without warning, the wraith began moving again. It drifted back into a passage on the cavern's southern side. Within the span of a few breaths, Ghassan heard voices coming, and his gaze locked on the great northern archway.

Wynn stepped into a massive cavern, and her gaze slowly rose into the heights.

The dome's sheer size and the level of destruction were overwhelming. Her companions were equally stunned. Even Ore-Locks turned in a circle, as if trying to take in everything at once. How could this enormous place not have collapsed when the mountain fell?

Chane and Shade kept close to her as they moved inward. Wynn was so mesmerized that she stepped over piles of shattered debris without seeing them.

"Look," Chane said, pointing down. "These are better preserved."

Not catching his meaning, Wynn glanced down.

Thick skeletal remains lay to her right, half-covered in remnants of decaying armor and corroded blades exposed by rotted sheaths. One still wore an ax on his back, and a tarnished *thôrhk* lay among the shattered bones of his neck. Another skeleton, perhaps a woman, lay a few paces ahead, her bones still bearing a ring with a dark blue stone and a necklace of metal loops.

As when Wynn had walked the long tunnel from the cave-in, she suffered a returning sense of loss and sorrow. The scale of death here was too much to hold in her thoughts for long, and she wondered what Ore-Locks felt—thought—standing amid what his genocidal ancestor had done here.

Did he feel anything? He appeared merely entranced by the daunting visage of this lost city of his people's forebears.

Wynn couldn't help asking, "How can this be intact if the entire upper peak collapsed?"

Still gazing upward, Ore-Locks answered, "We are deep . . . much deeper than I realized. Thousands must have lived here, but why would so many choose to live this far down?"

Chane started to speak, but Wynn held up a hand to stop him. Ore-Locks wasn't looking at either of them, as if he'd forgotten their existence. For once, his guard was down as he absorbed the mysteries here. She wanted to hear more from him.

"They must have excavated deeply between levels," he went on. "So deep that the stone between them helped shield the lowest levels. The peaks on either side may have dispersed some of the downward force." His voice became almost too quiet to hear. "But whatever happened shook the entire mountain."

Wynn began to feel ill. None of his speculations changed anything. Pushing away the horrors of a forgotten time, she focused on her purpose in coming here. There was an orb to be found, but where would it be hidden in a place of this size?

As far down as they were, she believed the orb would have been placed even deeper—at the lowest place possible. How were they to find a way down in this much destruction?

Chane had crouched, examining the skeleton with the ax and the *thôrhk*; it was an odd, morbid sight watching his passive and silent study. Before she could call him away, he whispered to himself.

"The ends are not spiked . . . this was not a thänæ under one of the warrior Eternals."

His eyes turned to the ax, and his brow wrinkled. For a moment, Wynn was startled that he even pondered such things, but her own curiosity was piqued.

"Are there marks on its end knobs?" she asked. "If so, can you make them out?"

Chane looked back to the heavy *thôrhk's* two open ends. "They are too blemished, tarnished. But it does have end knobs, rather than being plain and unadorned."

Wynn looked at him in surprise. Only one type of *thôrhk* for one of the Bäynæ, the Eternals, had no end knobs of any kind. It was the one given to those honored under Bedzâ'kenge—Feather-Tongue. Although she knew of this practice, she had never seen a thänæ who wore such in her few visits to Dhredze Seatt. How had Chane ever learned such a thing?

Wynn started slightly when she realized Ore-Locks was watching her.

Straightening, she said, "We need to go lower."

He glanced away, and then he nodded and took the lead, heading south. "In Old Seatt, for my own people, the underways have tunnels out of places like this. Those headed north led to upward connections, while those to the south led to downward ones."

Wynn blinked. She'd never heard nor read such a thing. Then again, she'd seen nothing of Old Seatt besides its surface atop the mountain that held all of Dhredze Seatt. The newer settlements, like Bay-Side and Sea-Side, had spiral tunnels at the end of all mainways leading both up and down.

Motioning to Chane and Shade, Wynn hurried after Ore-Locks. For once, the dwarf might be truly useful. It bothered her that she was forced to follow someone with his hidden agenda, who could walk through stone and was a potential puppet of some traitorous ancestral spirit.

But it didn't bother her enough to stop her. It didn't even slow her down. She had to find the orb.

Ore-Locks headed into a large tunnel in the center of the south wall.

"You think this is the best tunnel?" she asked.

He half turned. "It leads down."

"Wait," Chane called, and began pulling blankets, canvas bags, and water skins from his back to pile them on the floor.

"What are you doing?" Wynn asked. "Those are all our supplies."

"I will bring some food and one water skin," he replied. "But I need to be able to move more freely, for whatever we encounter. We can retrieve all of this on our way out."

She was tempted to argue, but realized he was right. He kept both his own packs, but their weight was nothing to him. Ore-Locks waited and watched until Chane was ready, and then he headed onward.

Without hesitation, Wynn followed into the broad tunnel.

Still crouched behind the crumbled stairwell, Ghassan had watched Wynn and her companions enter the cavern. Even from a distance, the sight of her surprised him. She looked different, almost beyond travel worn. Her oval face was thinner than when he had last seen her, and she moved so surely, easily scrambling over loose debris. Not once did she accept assistance offered from Chane.

Ghassan remembered Chane and Shade well. In spite of himself, he had some respect for Wynn's choice of protectors. Ghassan had fought beside the undead and the dog. They were both formidable. The presence of the dwarf, however, made little sense.

Had Wynn hired him as a guide? That seemed unlikely, as this place was well more than a thousand years old.

As the four came closer and passed by, Ghassan studied the dwarf, thinking he bore a resemblance to Domin High-Tower. But where High-Tower was visibly aged, even for a dwarf, the one leading Wynn looked much younger, not as thick, and was clean-shaven . . . or at least had been before this journey.

Too many unknown variables convinced Ghassan that he should remain hidden, follow behind, and yet still shield Wynn from the wraith. At present, he did not believe the black spirit would harm her if it had followed her this far.

Soon he lost sight of Wynn's group as they entered a southern archway. He was forced to creep after, staying out of their awareness. But he struggled with indecision. He could not expose himself to the wraith, so he couldn't follow Wynn yet and let that creature come behind him. And still, he had no desire to lose track of her now that she had finally arrived.

The wraith drifted out from its hiding place.

The folds of its immaterial black robe shifted in the still air, even as it lingered near the passage Wynn had entered. It waited a long while before suddenly vanishing into the same wide and tall opening.

With the choice made for him, Ghassan quietly followed.

*   *   *

Wynn held her staff in one hand and a cold lamp crystal in the other as she followed Ore-Locks down . . . and down.

Chane and Shade brought up the rear, with Chane carrying the second crystal. To Wynn's relief, neither of them openly argued with her plan to go lower. They were tense and overly watchful, and Chane continually looked behind.

Wynn, as well, wondered if they were still being followed and by whom. She hadn't forgotten Ore-Locks's warning when they'd been halted by the cave-in.

The wide tunnel made a slow, curving spiral downward with main exits leading off to various levels, but along the descending way, many other smaller openings and stairways led up or down. Yet Ore-Locks always kept to the curving mainway.

Wynn hoped he had some notion of what he was doing. He was certainly succeeding in taking them to the lower levels, but beyond that, she was at a loss. They continued to step over more decayed remains along the way, and she steeled herself against being lost in sorrow or pity. Beyond taking care not to disturb the bones, she did not look right at them.

Her crystal's light suddenly exposed a black patch on the wall, and she instinctively flinched and swerved away from it. Chane's hand settled on her shoulder as Ore-Locks stopped and turned.

His gaze fixed on the black spot as Wynn finally saw what it was.

"Charred," she said quietly, "like it was burned."

"Look here," Chane said.

She spun about and found him on one knee beside a skeleton. Its bones were too long and narrow for a dwarf.

"Human?" she whispered.

Shade whined, and Wynn glanced over to see the dog nosing another set of remains. Wynn could see something covering its rib cage. Chane moved over to crouch beside Shade, and he frowned.

"This one's leather armor is almost intact." He looked up at Ore-Locks. "These remains are not nearly as old as the others, but there is char just the same. We are not the first to find this place, but these others never made it out. They only got this far. . . . And what killed them?"

Ore-Locks's black irises seemed to swallow any light from the crystals. "Perhaps they argued and killed each other," he said quietly. "Is that not the way of greed among humans?"

"With their weapons sheathed?" Chane rasped. "And they somehow burned the entire wall first?"

"We don't have time for this," Wynn said. "Since we don't know how they died, we should get moving again . . . with our eyes open."

In spite of her confident words, she pondered Chane's questions. Ore-Locks turned away and continued onward. Wynn stroked her fingers over Shade's head.

"We're close," she whispered. "We have to keep going."

To her relief, as she stepped onward, Chane and Shade followed without argument. But she was well aware that Chane was near the breaking point in his zealous overprotection. Perhaps he'd never expected her to get this far, and she had no idea what might happen when he snapped.

The tunnel soon stopped at a wall, with a sharp turn to the right leading down. At the bottom of a stone ramp, they exited into a larger, open tunnel.

"Is this it?" Wynn asked in alarm. "We've reached the bottom?"

She could see only one archway ahead and hadn't expected their descent to simply stop like this.

Ore-Locks moved quickly toward the archway, looking up. She followed with Shade at her heels. There was something carved over the archway in its topmost frame stones. Holding her crystal high, Wynn spotted the remnants of symbols made of complex strokes.

"Are those *vubrí*?" she asked.

Certain Dwarvish words weren't always written in separate letters. The sages' own Begaine syllabary used symbols for whole syllables and word parts, and might have once been inspired by such symbols. The harsh strokes of Dwarvish letters could be combined into a vubrí, a patterned shape. These emblems were used only for important concepts or the noteworthy among people, places, or things.

Ore-Locks's eyes narrowed as he tried to see marks that were higher than Wynn's light would reach.

"Chane, hold your light as high as you can," she said.

He did as she asked, and she squinted up once more. The symbols were worn and faded.

"I think that one is Wisdom," she said, pointing. "And that one might be Virtue, but I'm only guessing. The strokes are different from the vubrí I know."

Ore-Locks appeared to be chewing the inside of his cheek as he started forward again, walking through the archway. Now curious, Wynn didn't try to call him back, and stepped through.

She'd barely taken three steps inside when Chane rasped, "More."

They were in a small tunnel now, wide enough for two to walk abreast. Chane held his crystal toward the left wall.

Dwarvish characters and more vubrí filled the wall in multiple columns, just like in the room of "stone words" Wynn had seen in the temple of Bedzâ'kenge—Feather-Tongue—at Dhredze Seatt. Those engravings had chronicled exploits of that saintly dwarven Eternal of history, tradition, and wisdom.

A sense of hope began growing within Wynn. Had they found a temple deep in the bowels of the mountain? If so, what did it mean?

Every few paces, she or Ore-Locks stopped to try to read the symbols, but many of them were too etched by grime and age to make out. Then she spotted one small, clear section and almost gasped.

"Stálghlên . . . Pure-Steel!" she whispered. "And look there . . . that has to be for Arhniká—Gilt-Repast."

"Bäynæ?" Chane said. "References to the Eternals? On the walls?"

Wynn's thoughts raced over the implications. Dwarves practiced a unique form of ancestor worship. They revered those of their own who attained notable status in life, akin to the human concept of a hero or saint. Any who became known for virtuous accomplishments, by feat or service, might be graced with a thôrhk and become one of the Thänæ—the honored ones. Though similar to human knighthood or noble entitlement, it wasn't a position of rulership or authority.

After death, any thänæ who'd achieved renown among the people over decades and centuries, through continued retelling of their exploits, might one day be elevated to the Bäynæ—one of the dwarven Eternals. These were the dwarves' spiritual immortals, held as honored ancestors of their people as a whole.

"Is Feather-Tongue mentioned anywhere?" Chane asked.

At that, Wynn almost stopped trying to decipher more symbols. Why would Chane ask that?

"No, but give me a moment on this next one." She couldn't make it out. "Ore-Locks, can you see any reference to . . . ?"

He was already heading down the tunnel at a fast pace.

"Where are you . . . ? Wait!" she called. "Chane, Shade, hurry."

With no choice, they trotted after.

By the time they caught up, Wynn found herself standing before a huge set of doors at the tunnel's end, but they were knocked outward into the tunnel. Each was one piece that must have been hewn from an immense tree trunk. Both had to be over three yards high. But both were broken like twigs by whatever had shattered the mountain peak above.

She stepped through to see Ore-Locks's expression no longer so impassive. His eyes shifted rapidly.

"What's wrong?" she asked, but he didn't answer.

They'd entered the center point of a great hall that ran lengthwise, left and right. It had taken some damage in the catastrophe, but was surprisingly whole. Chane and Shade came in behind Wynn, and the sight gave them all pause.

Six effigies stood in the hall, three lining each longest wall, but as with much of this seatt, Wynn was struck first by their sheer size. All of them were at least twice the height of Feather-Tongue's effigy at Dhredze Seatt. Even with her crystal, she could barely make out their heads high above in the dark.

She glanced at a large breach in the hall's right end, but then turned back to staring at the titanic stone statues. She and Ore-Locks both walked farther into the hall's center for a better look.

"The hall of Eternals," Wynn whispered.

"And these are all in one place," Ore-Locks added hoarsely.

In Dhredze Seatt, each Bäynæ had its own temple, except for the three warrior Eternals, who shared one temple.

"The main tunnel down connected directly to the passage leading here," Wynn noted. "This hall must have been open to the entire seatt." Then something else occurred to her. "Only six here?" she wondered aloud. "There are nine in Dhredze."

Ore-Locks appeared as perplexed as she was.

"I will start seeking an exit," he said.

Again, he turned away, as if the effigies suddenly no longer mattered. He walked over to stand between the nearest two.

Wynn felt Shade press against her thigh, but she watched Ore-Locks. For the first time, it dawned on her that he'd led them directly down here, and yet he'd never been here before. He was doing everything she asked, but always leading them. Was it her purpose that brought them here or his?

Ore-Locks rounded an effigy's base that was taller than his head and disappeared along the far wall. Wynn turned to quietly tell Chane her concerns, but he wasn't there.

Chane stood back by the broken doors, studying them, and Wynn hurried to join him.

Upon entering the hall of immense statues, Chane had looked for one without even thinking. Among the six present, none looked like the figure of Feather-Tongue that he knew. Perhaps that dwarven Eternal had been born after the war, lived in the aftermath, and was unknown among either Thänæ or Bäynæ in earlier times.

From what Chane fathomed, Feather-Tongue had been a scholar of the world rather than choosing to stay in any one place to teach. Perhaps he had gone among the scattered dwarves who had escaped Bäalâle, offering his tales and lessons. Somehow, he had proven himself worthy enough to be remembered and been elevated to Bäynæ.

Chane put that puzzle aside, for he had greater concerns. Control over Wynn's safety seemed to be slipping away with every step. While she studied the effigies, he went to the hall's far right end, looking into the wall's great gash.

A raw shaft went straight down, too dark and deep for his crystal's light to reveal the bottom. It may have always been there inside the stone and was only exposed when the wall had collapsed inward. But though rough surfaced, it seemed too round to be a natural rift. Why would dwarves excavate a vertical passage of such size, leave it unfinished and unusable, only to be exposed by the breach?

Chane turned next to studying the entrance doors. The hall was reasonably intact, so what had broken them? One leaned against the archway's edge, while the other had been knocked outward into the tunnel, its great hinges ripped from the frame stones. The remains of a rotating iron bar, nearly as thick as his thigh, was still bolted to the door. Clearly, this entrance had been sealed from the inside.

Half the bar was gone, shorn off near the center spin point. Glancing around, Chane spotted the missing half tucked in against the outer tunnel's wall base. His brows knitted.

The cataclysm might have caused some damage here, but judging by the doors' inner hinges and that bar, they would have more likely fallen inward. Yet there was the sheared bar lying in the outer tunnel, as if the hinges had been ripped from the stone as the door was forced outward.

"Chane."

He looked back to find Wynn hurrying over, with Shade trailing her.

"Where is Ore-Locks?" he asked.

She pointed. "He headed off behind that statue, looking for a way onward." Then she leaned closer, lowering her voice. "Does it feel like he led us here, like he knew where he was going?"

Wynn watched him expectantly.

"That is not possible," he answered, though doubt crept in. The dwarf *had* brought them directly to this hall.

"Is he leading us where he wants to go?" Wynn asked, not letting the notion drop. "Does he know more than he's told us . . . perhaps even about the orb?"

Chane had never truly cared what Ore-Locks wanted here. It had sometimes seemed the dwarf simply wished to know if the seatt was just a myth or if anything could be learned of his long-dead ancestor. It had not occurred to Chane that Ore-Locks might also be seeking the orb.

If so, Wynn was in more danger than Chane had thought. His first instinct was to take her from here, by force if necessary. But she would never forgive him.

"If he knows . . . anything," Wynn continued, "all the more reason to follow him, since I don't know where to look."

Shade growled in obvious disagreement, but Wynn turned and headed toward the effigies.

Chane checked both his swords for a smooth draw before hurrying after her. At the first sign of treachery, he would take Ore-Locks suddenly, killing the dwarf before he could react. That would end this foolish exploit.

"Ore-Locks," Wynn called.

"Here."

They rounded the last of the statues, the only female among them, and Ore-Locks stood before another archway. The dwarf's expression had altered, filled with relief or satisfaction. Then Chane took a better look at the archway.

Set deep between the thick frame stones was a panel of old, marred iron with a worn seam down its middle. The panel fully filled the arch, slipping into the wall on either side through a thick slot. It would be at least an inch thick, with two more like ones behind it. There was no lock, handle, or latch, nor brackets for a bar, and there would not be on the other side, either.

Chane knew those panels would open only for a certain set of individuals. His hand dropped to his sword hilt as he eyed Ore-Locks.

This portal matched the same impassable barriers they had once faced in Dhredze Seatt. One way or another, all black iron portals led to the underworld of the Stonewalkers.

Wynn became more suspicious of Ore-Locks by the moment. He was looking for something specific down here—and it wasn't effigies of the Bäynæ. His steady progress was beginning to border on manic, and he appeared to know where he was going, as if he had been here before.

"This must be opened from the other side," Ore-Locks said.

Wynn remembered how Ore-Locks's superior, Cinder-Shard, had passed right through such a portal. The master stonewalker had opened it by manipulating a series of rods in the wall on the other side that functioned as a complex lock. And Ore-Locks knew very well how these doors worked.

Panic hit Wynn as she realized he was about to pass through the wall. What if he didn't unlock the portal? The look of satisfaction on his broad face could only mean he was getting close to whatever he sought here. What if he just abandoned them and went on alone?

"Take Chane with you," she said. "You don't know what you'll find, or even if you can unlock it. You may need him to help force the portal open."

"I am not leaving you alone," Chane argued.

Ore-Locks turned his head, looking at Wynn. "No one could force a portal . . . it would take a dozen warrior thänæ, and even they might fail. If I cannot open it . . . I will return."

His tone dared Wynn to challenge his word. She didn't trust him, and he knew it. She tried to think of another way to stall him until she came up with something, anything else they could try.

Ore-Locks stepped straight into the iron and vanished.

"No!" she cried, slapping her hand against the portal, sending a thrum through the great hall. "Chane, why wouldn't you go? Now there's no one watching him, and we cannot follow."

"I am not about to be trapped on the other side, away from you."

How could he be so calm? Then another thought occurred to Wynn.

The locks for these portals had a combination for which rods were pushed or pulled into differing positions. Cinder-Shard, as master stonewalker of Dhredze Seatt, had likely set those combinations himself. How could Ore-Locks possibly know the combination here, set by a master stonewalker a thousand or more years ago?

She realized he'd never intended to bring her through, and panic threatened to overwhelm her. Had she come all this way to be left behind?

A rumbling grind of metal on stone made her lurch back.

The iron panel split, its halves slowly grating away into the frame stones on either side. The noise increased as the second, and then the third panel followed.

The portal was open, and Ore-Locks stood dead center, looking out at Wynn.

CHAPTER 23

Chuillyon led the way through the decaying, empty tram station and into a tunnel. He saw an archway ahead but was unprepared for the sight beyond it—a domed cavern as large as a small town.

"Oh, my," Hannâschi breathed.

Chuillyon stared up at the remnants of walkways that had once stretched between remaining columns as thick as some old trees of his people's forests. Column fragments and the ruins of huge stairways lay piled and scattered everywhere.

Even malnourished and exhausted, Hannâschi's awe and wonder were plain to see. Shâodh, however, appeared singularly unimpressed. He stepped through the rubble, glancing once at a skeleton still wearing a *thôrhk*.

"Fewer bodies here," he noted dispassionately.

Chuillyon almost winced, thinking of the grim fate of these lost dwarven ancestors.

"Did Wynn come through here?" he asked.

Shâodh paused, closing his eyes and taking a deep breath. His exhale thrummed briefly in his throat, and Hannâschi crouched beside a set of broken bones.

"So much death," she said quietly. "What happened here?"

"No one knows . . . as yet," Chuillyon answered.

She looked up, but her long hair and cowl covered half her face.

"This is the greatest archaeological find of our time," she went on. "Bäalâle is no myth. If there is evidence here—amid all of this—then we will have proof the war did take place . . . that it was not, is not, some overblown legend."

Shâodh's eyes opened, and he looked down at her with the barest frown.

In truth, Chuillyon had so single-mindedly followed Wynn that he had forgotten this possibility. But Hannâschi was only half-right.

"Such information must be kept from the public," Shâodh stated before Chuillyon could express the same notion.

Hannâschi rose and turned to Shâodh with her mouth set tightly. Clearly, she did not need his reminder, and seemed about to tell him so. This was not the time for a spat—although one might come later. Chuillyon decided not to mention it yet, but, in truth, even few of his peers at the guild could be told of this place until he understood more himself.

"Did she come through here?" he asked again.

Shâodh nodded once. "But we have another problem. I sense three distinct lives. The journeyor's protector cannot be one of them, and the majay-hì's presence is different. That leaves her and the dwarf."

"And so?" Chuillyon asked.

"Someone else is here, either with her or near her."

This was all Chuillyon needed: one more unknown variable. "Which way?" he asked.

Shâodh pointed south. "Do we follow?"

Chuillyon fought an urge to snap at him for that same tiresome question. Did Shâodh think they were going home to announce their great find and bathe in glory? They were here to learn what Wynn was after.

When Chuillyon did not answer, Shâodh held out his hand, helping Hannâschi over a pile of loose rubble. He kept hold of her hand as he led the way across the cavern. Chuillyon never missed these small familiarities between them. Neither had he ever commented on them. But that might have to change.

They passed more crumbling stairways and fragmented columns . . . and more remains of the long dead. After a good distance, Shâodh slowed, but he did not sink into meditation again. He gestured toward an archway at the cavern's south wall.

Just inside of it lay a small pile of blankets and canvas bags.

Chuillyon hurried over to see inside the tunnel.

*   *   *

Chane stepped through the portal last, finding himself in a narrow passage. Ore-Locks walked to an open recess near the door that held the grid of metal rods exposed by a sliding metal panel.

"No," Chane said quickly. "Do not close the portal."

Ore-Locks eyed him in surprise. "It will bar any pursuit if we are still followed."

"It will also lock us in. If we are forced to flee, we may not have time to stop and open it. Leave it open."

The dwarf did not appear convinced, but Chane had no intention of allowing him near those rods. Should Ore-Locks close the panel, he could leave them entombed and trapped.

Wynn held up her cold lamp crystal, illuminating the passage. "Chane's right. There's been no sign of followers since the vibrations on the tram tracks. Ore-Locks, what if you get hurt . . . or worse? The rest of us will be trapped with no means to get ourselves . . . or you out."

Her argument was rational and logical, and far less accusatory than what Chane was thinking. Ore-Locks finally nodded. It must go against his training and nature to pass through a portal without closing it. With the decision made, the strange, dark focus returned to his face, and he headed down the passage at a quick pace.

Shade rumbled low in discontent, watching him, and Chane shared her concern over the dwarf's shifting moods. He was obviously looking for something.

Wynn trotted after Ore-Locks. "Come on."

Within a few paces, Chane detected the floor's slight slant. They were going deeper again, and he tried to gauge their descent. When he reckoned they were about two levels lower, Ore-Locks stopped before a side passage. He turned his head, cocking it, as if listening.

Ore-Locks suddenly turned into the side passage, as did Wynn. She seemed to be just blindly following the dwarf.

"Wynn," Chane rasped, but she had already stopped.

Another iron portal blocked the passage's end. Ore-Locks did not even pause, but walked straight through the iron and vanished.

"No!" Wynn cried, rushing to the closed portal.

The smallest hope flickered inside Chane. Perhaps this time, Ore-Locks truly had left them. Without his obsession feeding Wynn's drive to go deeper, Chane might yet convince her to turn back. To his surprise, Wynn closed her fist around her crystal and pounded on the portal.

"Ore-Locks!" she shouted. "Open these doors now! Do you hear me?"

The words echoed loudly along the narrow passage, but Wynn only pounded harder.

Chane stood waiting, hoping, for her to finally halt in exhaustion.

Sau'ilahk drifted from the hall of the Eternals and through the open portal into a smaller passage. From a distance, he saw light down its gradual slope. The light suddenly dimmed by half and then spilled out of what might be a side passage. When the illumination faded from the passage's mouth, he followed carefully.

The sound of Wynn shouting and pounding rolled out of the side passage and toward him in echoes. He stopped and slipped close to the main passage's wall, prepared to sink into it. He had not caught her words—something to do with the dwarf—but she sounded more distressed than angry.

Something had gone wrong.

Sau'ilahk fled back to the open portal into the hall of the Eternals. He feared being sensed by the dog, and he could not move until certain of which way Wynn might go next.

A grinding sound rose in the narrow passage, rumbling all around Wynn, and she stopped pounding. When the last of the iron triple doors rolled away, Ore-Locks stood in the opening, but this time he looked angry.

"Do not disturb the peace of the honored dead," he ordered, and then looked to the crystal in her hand. "Close that in your fingers, and allow only enough light for sure steps."

With that, he turned away, heading inward beyond the portal.

Wynn glanced back at Chane and Shade, and then hurried after, entering a natural cave beyond a shorter passage. It all looked alarmingly familiar.

She walked a wide, cleared path between calcified, shadowy forms. A hulking stalagmite rose from the cavern floor, thick and fat all the way up to head height. Others were joined at the upper end by descending stalactites, forming natural, lumpy columns that glistened with mineral-laden moisture. But in the dim phosphorescence of the walls, some forms looked too big and bulky to have been made only by calcified buildup. To an unknowing observer, they might have been boulders at one time, now buried beneath decades of crust.

Wynn knew exactly what those protrusions were. She stood in the chambers of the honored dead, as she once had in Dhredze Seatt. This was where dead thänæ were entombed in stone, to be tended in eternal rest by the Stonewalkers of this lost seatt.

Ore-Locks glanced at only a few of the lone stone protrusions in this first cave. He moved to a nearby opening and stepped off the open path and into the next shadowed forest of such formations. Wynn followed, watching as he examined each one with a kind of mania before rushing for the next.

"What is he doing?" Chane asked. "Has he gone mad?"

"Shhhh," Wynn said. "Those aren't just mounds of calcified stone."

She didn't know why the Stonewalkers wouldn't allow bright light in these caves. They seemed to think it would disturb the dead they cared for. Wynn spread her fingers, letting just a little of her crystal's light seep out.

"Look," she told Chane, and he leaned in.

The top of one glistening stone protrusion narrowed over rounded "shoulders" to a bulk like a "head." This one had melded to the tip of a long, descending stalactite. The hints of features, like the face of a sculpture roughly formed and left unfinished, were barely visible in the light of Wynn's crystal.

The long-dead thänæ's eyes seemed closed, but there was no way to be certain.

Wynn couldn't tell if it was male or female. Its clothing was nothing more than the barest ripples in the glittering layers of minerals. The buildup had turned its hands into lumps. She glanced at other dark shapes about the cave's silent stillness.

"Honored thänæ, taken into stone," she whispered. "We are standing among the dead of a forgotten time."

No coffins or crypts. The Stonewalkers—the Hassäg'kreigi—entombed their most honored in stone itself. Left here for a thousand years or more, they became one with the earth their people cherished.

Chane backed up, looking all around without blinking.

Wynn knew he didn't fear the dead. He too had stood in those caves in Dhredze Seatt.

Chane's eyes suddenly widened. "One has been shattered!"

He rushed off the path.

When Wynn caught up, he was crouched over fragments at the base of one form. She froze at the sight of this desecration. From the size of the pieces lying all around, the dwarf had been large—tall—and the broken bits had been there long enough to bond to the cave floors.

She shook her head in sadness. Who would do such a thing, and why? There was no way to know, and she gripped her crystal tighter, peering about for Ore-Locks.

He still wove between the lumpy columns, studying every calcified thänæ he could find.

"What are you doing?" Wynn called to him.

Instead of answering, he broke into a jog and ran into the cave's wall.

Wynn stiffened, and then heard his heavy footfalls echoing through the caves. Shade took off toward another opening.

"Ore-Locks!" Wynn cried, following Shade's lead.

The next cave held only a few calcified forms. Ore-Locks was already running for another wall, his face twisted in urgency. Wynn started after him, but Shade barked.

Still moving, Wynn glanced back in frustration. "What?"

"Perhaps she has dipped into his memories," Chane said.

Wynn stopped cold, though Chane went on to peek into the next cave.

Shade padded closer, and Wynn dropped to one knee. She touched Shade's face, feeling bad for having snapped at the dog. In her own mania to catch Ore-Locks, she'd forgotten Shade's ways.

"Sorry," she said softly, closing her eyes.

An image of darkness filled her mind instantly. One of her own memories began to return. . . .

She held a cold lamp crystal out before a figure of stone, carved almost like an upright coffin, but with an engraving inside a raised, oblong panel about chest level. She traced the engraved markings with her finger.

. . . outcast of stone . . . deceiver of honored dead . . . ender of heritage . . . the seatt killer . . .

She reached the bottom—a final vubrí.

Thallûhearag—the Lord of Slaughter.

Shade had taken her back to the Chamber of the Fallen at Dhredze Se-att, those counterparts to the dwarven Eternals. Reviled for their rejection of dwarven virtues, their faceless effigies, chiseled in the form of iron-banded coffins, were locked away in the deepest place. One was worse than all others, and secreted in a small chamber of its own.

Inside the memory, Shade began to snarl.

In her crystal's light, a shadow of that lone effigy appeared to move upon the wall behind it. A baritone voice rose as if from the black basalt form.

"His true name was Byûnduní . . . Deep-Root."

Ore-Locks stepped from the shadows, his hand stroking down the effigy. He raised his eyes to where the head would be, as if seeing more than the mute form's representation. He placed both hands flat on the oval plate of its engraving, as if trying to blot out the epitaph.

"He does not belong here," Ore-Locks whispered.

The memory ended as abruptly as it began.

Wynn opened her eyes, still holding Shade's face, and realized what Shade was trying to tell her.

"Deep-Root?" she breathed.

Did Ore-Locks actually hope to find his traitorous ancestor among the honored dead of Bäalâle?

"What did she show you?" Chane asked.

"I know what Ore-Locks is looking for, and he will not find it here."

Rising, she ran into the next cave, and then the next. The farther in she went, the more the entombed forms became indistinguishable from the cave's glistening stone. She found Ore-Locks inside the fifth and last cave. He looked pale and stricken, down on his knees. When he saw her watching him, he stood up, his expression hardening.

She had no idea what to say. Her feelings were as mixed and blended as the remains of the dead and the cave's stone. She was angry with him for leading them astray. After the carnage they had seen above in the seatt, how could he ever have thought to find his genocidal ancestor here? Even if any stonewalkers had survived the seatt's fall, why would they ever place a monster among the honored dead? Or did Ore-Locks merely wish it so, as proof that the little-known tale of his treacherous ancestor was a lie?

But a small part of her pitied him. Was this truly why he had come all this way—to somehow change the truth of the past?

"We are finished here," he said coldly. "We move on."

"To where?"

"You wished to go lower." He strode past her, ignoring Chane and Shade.

Chane kept glancing about as they walked. When Ore-Locks neared where they'd entered, Chane slowed. Wynn stopped, wondering what was wrong.

"Feather-Tongue would find this tomb a tragedy," Chane said.

Wynn shook her head, uncertain what he meant.

"These thänæ are forgotten," he went on. "The tales that brought them here are forgotten. They will not continue in the memories of their people. These here are now truly dead, forever."

She hadn't considered that. First, Ore-Locks had tried to clear his genocidal ancestor's name in a place where the dead were forgotten, and now Chane waxed philosophical like a shirvêsh of Bedzâ'kenge. The world felt upside down.

"We have to go," she said.

He nodded and followed her as they hurried.

Ore-Locks was waiting by the portal. This time Wynn, Chane, and Shade all stepped out, and he closed the doors from the inside before passing through the iron to join them. They wouldn't need to enter that place again.

Ore-Locks still looked pale and sickened. He took the lead, and when they reached the narrow, sloping passage, he turned downward again.

A small part of Wynn wished to offer him some word of comfort; the wiser part knew that was foolish—and wrong.

Ghassan lingered near the entrance to the hall of the Eternals, noting the great gash in its far right end, but he did not step inside just yet. The wraith must be somewhere ahead of him. He did not wish to risk exposing his presence to it or to Wynn.

Footsteps and voices carried down the engraved entry passage *behind* him.

Ghassan looked back. Who else could possibly be down here? He could not make out the words, but he heard the lilt and guttural turn in those voices. Elves?

He hurried inside the hall. Quietly rushing down its length, he looked for a vantage point where he could still remain hidden. Then he froze midway.

The wraith lingered at an archway beyond the last great statue along the hall's far wall. Its back was turned to him.

Ghassan knew he had only moments before it might turn around or the elves would enter this place. He formed sigils and shapes in his mind, focusing on the wraith. He did not know if he could hide his presence from its unnatural awareness, but it was all he had left to try.

On pure hope, he ran between the statues on the hall's other side, ducking behind the shoulder-high base of the effigy of a dwarven warrior.

The wraith turned. It floated farther out into the hall, but did not look his way.

Ghassan stifled an exhale of relief. He remained rigid, listening to the footsteps approaching the hall.

Sau'ilahk thought he heard something and turned quickly. He saw nothing, but he was not given to hearing things that did not exist. He drifted to the hall's center and then heard something else.

Footfalls and voices carried from the hall's entrance.

It could only be Chuillyon and his companions. An overwhelming hunger flooded Sau'ilahk. Feeding upon Wynn was the only greater pleasure he could imagine than draining the old elf's life. But he could not lose Wynn now.

Sau'ilahk rushed back to the portal archway and saw her light far down the passage.

Ghassan peered out from hiding. Once again, he could almost not believe his eyes. Three elves in travel attire stepped through the hall's broken doors. The oldest of them led the way, followed by a tall, younger male and a beautiful female.

Ghassan fixed on the leader. He had seen that one many times whenever Duchess Reine of the royal house of Malourné had come visiting at the guild branch of Calm Seatt. He had heard the old one's name mentioned once or twice, and he tried to remember.

Chuillyon? What was an advisor to the royals doing in Bäalâle Seatt? It was certainly no coincidence.

"Look at their size," the woman breathed, gazing up at the massive statues. Beautiful as she was, she looked thin and exhausted, nothing like the hardened traveler Wynn had become.

Ghassan spoke Elvish well enough, and hoped he might learn more than expressed awe over the work of ancient dwarven artisans.

"This way," the younger male said, heading for the open portal.

Chuillyon slowed, glancing back at the hall's right end. He finally nodded and continued on with the others. The trio passed through the portal.

Ghassan exhaled in frustration. He now had more than one interloper between himself and Wynn.

Chane kept close as Wynn followed Ore-Locks. He gauged that they had gone down another two levels before the passage stopped at another sealed portal. There had been no further side passages along the way. Chane had a strange feeling that they had reached the end of their long descent, though he could not fathom why.

Perhaps it was the look of finality on Ore-Locks's face as the dwarf hesitated before that portal.

"What's wrong?" Wynn asked.

"Nothing," Ore-Locks answered.

The dwarf passed through the iron and, within seconds, the familiar grinding sound began.

Chane had not expressed his suspicions aloud, like Wynn, but he had become increasingly wary. Ore-Locks seemed to know exactly where to go and the correct sequences to open all portals. It was too easy, too convenient.

As the last of the triple iron panels slid into the arch's frame, Chane pushed past Wynn, stepping inside another great hall. But he instantly spotted its difference.

In place of the stone effigies there were huge basalt likenesses of coffins sealed with carved representations of iron bands. Chane knew where Ore-Locks had brought them, for he had been in a similar chamber below Dhredze Seatt.

This was another chamber of the Lhärgnæ . . . the Fallen Ones.

Chane hung back, blocking Wynn's entry, until Ore-Locks moved off. When he glanced back, Wynn was peeking around him. She paled at the sight of those basalt coffins.

He finally stepped forward, noticing that this chamber was in even worse shape than the hall of the Bäynæ. The left and right end walls each bore the same strange breach he had seen above—except the one on the left was wide, and the one on the right was taller and slightly narrower.

Though the stone coffin effigies were at least three times the size of those in Dhredze Seatt, two showed multiple fractures, and a third was half-shattered into chunks that lay across the floor. Again, there were fewer of them than in Dhredze Seatt.

Chane walked farther in, looking for any passage to another chamber or hall where one more effigy might have been set apart. There were no openings. They had truly reached a dead end. He turned to find Wynn examining the engraved, oblong panel on a basalt coffin. Her brow crinkled as if in deep concentration or thought.

Chane could guess at her concern.

She had followed Ore-Locks into the bowels of this dead seatt, and not a single clue or hint to the orb's whereabouts had been uncovered. Instead, they stood in this last hall, in the Chamber of the Fallen, with nowhere left to go.

"The symbols are worn, old, and hard to comprehend," she whispered. "But I've made out their titles, at least."

"Is Avarice here?" he asked.

Avarice was one of the Fallen Ones who she had learned of at Dhredze Seatt in tales of Feather-Tongue's exploits.

"No," she said, shaking her head. "He must have come later."

Ore-Locks had not bothered even glancing at the coffins. He stood before the wider breach in the hall's left end, looking into it. Then he walked the hall's length, as if to do the same at the other end. Wynn watched his every step.

Her eyes turned so bleak, Chane could barely stand to look at them.

"It's not here," Wynn said, her voice breaking with sudden catches. "The orb isn't here . . . and there's no place left to go. Perhaps it was hidden somewhere above, or worse, in the upper levels, buried where I cannot find it." She closed her eyes, leaking tears. "I've lost."

Chane pulled her toward him, not knowing what else to do. She dropped her forehead against his upper arm, gripping his cloak, his arm, and burying her face.

He hurt for her pain, but he was not sorry she had failed.

He was not sorry at all.

Suddenly embarrassed, Wynn released Chane's arm and pulled away, completely uncertain of what to do next. The thought of leaving empty-handed was too much after all this. She couldn't even look up at Chane, though she felt him watching her expectantly. She knew exactly what he wanted to do—just leave.

She turned her head and spotted Ore-Locks still standing by the taller, right-end breach. Why had he brought them down here after his futile attempt to find Deep-Root in the caves of the honored dead? He hadn't even looked at the basalt coffins of the Fallen Ones. Perhaps he knew what she would find: Deep-Root wasn't here either. Ore-Locks's ancestor had fallen for the atrocity committed here.

She stepped away from Chane, but he reached after her.

"Where are you going?" he asked. "This is over."

Evading his grasp, she went to the left-end wall and looked into its wide breach. Inside, another dark, raw shaft ran both up and down. She shuffled down the chamber, all the way to Ore-Locks.

The previous pale anguish on his face had been replaced by confusion. Obviously, he hadn't expected to find a dead end. Something final, perhaps, some last discovery, but not this.

"Not here," he whispered. "How could they not be here?"

Those words sharpened Wynn's awareness.

Ore-Locks was too focused in his task and far too knowledgeable for someone who'd never been inside this seatt. But someone else had been here—Ore-Locks's ancestor, that spirit who had supposedly called him to serve among the Stonewalkers.

Did that treacherous mass murderer guide Ore-Locks's steps?

Wynn's fear and revulsion of him magnified. In the face of her own failure, she lashed out at him.

"What are you looking for?" she demanded. "Deep-Root wasn't among the honored dead—he couldn't . . . never will be! So, what are you after now?"

Ore-Locks's red hair was dirty and wild, even bound back as it was. The beginning of a beard showed on his jaw. Confusion vanished from his face, and he turned on her in equal anger.

"His bones! Why else would I endure your ignorant judgments . . . endure traveling with *that*?" He pointed at Chane. "I found no truth here, but at the least I could have put him to rest. Now I cannot even do that."

Wynn stared at him, not knowing what to think. Everything Ore-Locks said sounded almost honorable, as if Chane had been right back in Dhredze Seatt. When Ore-Locks had come at her that night she'd found the coffin effigy of Thallûhearag, he had denied that his ancestor was that monster. If only he didn't wish to honor one who'd murdered thousands, tens of thousands. But if his ancestral spirit called to him now, deceived and used him even unwittingly, Ore-Locks still couldn't be trusted.

"It cannot end like this," he whispered.

No, she thought, *it cannot*.

Holding her crystal high, Wynn stepped to the tall breach, leaning in, and her heart jumped. This one wasn't a shaft.

"Did you look inside here?" she asked.

For an instant, Ore-Locks didn't appear to understand. All breaches so far had exposed raw, vertical shafts. Blinking, he gripped one side of the opening, pushing in beside Wynn. They both peered into a rough tunnel running off left and right from the opening.

Wynn's light only showed perhaps forty or fifty paces either way. The wall had certainly been broken by pressure when the mountain fell. She stepped into the raw tunnel, its floor as rough as the walls, and looked back as Ore-Locks followed.

Shade stood beyond the opening with her ears flattened and jowls twitching, and Chane glowered, his eyes narrow.

"Are you coming?" Wynn asked.

CHAPTER 24

To Chane's dismay, the tunnel behind the breach went on and on, deeper into the mountain. Each time he thought Wynn's perilous mission was finished, it began all over again. Worse, this tunnel was nothing like the ones above.

Roughly hewn, it had been gouged out in a rush, rather than skillfully excavated. Had someone been left alive after the seatt's fall? If so, why dig here, farther into the mountain's depths? Even more puzzling, the tunnel was surprisingly wide and without any supports, but the ceiling appeared sound. Chane could have driven a horse and wagon down this passage.

Ore-Locks still led them. Although his manic drive had resurfaced, he appeared less certain of his way, advancing more slowly. Wynn stayed right behind him, her breaths coming too quickly. When she looked back, her lips were parched.

"Drink," Chane said, pulling the water skin off his shoulder.

She took a long swallow and tapped Ore-Locks's shoulder. When he turned, she handed him the water skin. Once he'd finished, she dropped to her knees, set down her staff, and poured water into her hand.

"Here, Shade."

As the dog lapped, Chane noticed even deeper gouges in the wall. He took a few steps past Ore-Locks.

"Look here," he said.

Wynn joined him, holding out her crystal near the tunnel's wall. In some places, three gouges ran parallel, each one so deep they made no sense. Multiple strikes along the same lines would have been necessary to cut paths so deep, but to what purpose? He remembered the blackened wall in one tunnel far above, and the human corpses.

"I do not like this," he said.

"I know," Wynn whispered.

He knew nothing would stop her but another end to this new route. When she retrieved her staff, Ore-Locks moved on. Within twenty paces, the floor became cluttered with debris, and their progress slowed.

Chane looked ahead over Ore-Locks, trying to see how far the tunnel stretched, and then Wynn gave a small cry. She fell forward on the tunnel floor, and Chane moved quickly to help her, but Shade dodged around him, trying to get to her first.

"I'm all right," she said. "I just tripped."

She pushed up onto her knees and reached back, pulling something long and dark out from under her ankle. Dropping it instantly, she scrambled up.

Chane leaned over with his crystal for a closer look. It was a bone, big enough to wield as a club, and so aged that it had blended with the debris.

"Not from a dwarf," he said. "Thick enough, but far too long."

Ore-Locks waited ahead, but for the first time since Wynn had entered this rough-hewn passage, her eyes glowed with that old, familiar excitement.

"It's not human, either," she said quietly. "When I had access to the ancient texts, I found a mention in one of Volyno's writings that the enemy's forces may have tried to come in from beneath the seatt."

The knot in Chane's stomach returned. "What mention?"

"It was difficult to make out, and he also wrote 'of Earth . . . beneath the chair of a lord's song . . . meant to prevail but all ended . . . halfway eaten beneath.'"

"Eaten?"

"Ore-Locks, wait," Wynn called out. "Shade, come help me."

Chane was lost for a way to stop her as she dug through the rubble. Shade whined once and sniffed the debris, then huffed, scratching for Wynn to come look.

Puzzled, Ore-Locks came back. "What are you doing?"

"Looking for . . . here!" Wynn exclaimed.

She held up a large skull, having to use both hands. Chane took it from her.

Its back half was gone, and it was heavier than expected. When whole, it might have been the size of a mule or horse's head, but it was not shaped like any equine beast. Neither was it human or dwarven. Huge eye sockets were set wide to the skull's sides, and the long upper jaw was lined with a few remaining, needlelike teeth.

Chane had never seen anything like it.

"What was it?" Wynn asked.

"I do not know," Ore-Locks said.

"It *must* have been part of the enemy's forces." Wynn's excitement grew again. "That means it was down here for a reason."

"But did it come before or after the seatt fell?" she ventured, as if talking to herself.

Chane could see her mind working, and did not like it. "Either way, more important is how it died," he countered.

He looked to those three deep and long gouges in the wall. Shade huffed again, still digging in the debris, and this time Ore-Locks leaned over to grasp what the dog uncovered.

"I know this one," he said, holding up what was little more than the upper portion of a skull's face. "*Shlugga* . . . what you call a goblin."

Even Chane knew of goblins, having encountered a pack on his journey across the world to find Wynn. She had told him that some sages believed the Ancient Enemy had used these two-legged beasts during the war.

He kept his thoughts to himself. Unlike Wynn, he had never believed any war could have covered the world enough to blot out history. Before the Guild of Sagecraft, history would have always been a fragmented thing, subjected to "revisions" according to the desires of those who preserved it. But the scale of destruction and death here was beyond any territorial conflict exaggerated over ages to mythical proportions.

Multitudes had died here over a short period of time, at a guess. He could not help wondering what had happened. And what of these foreign bones in this deep, raw tunnel? What had made those distinct, deep gouges in the wall, and why?

Chane did not voice any of this to Wynn. Instead, he rose, peered down the dark tunnel ahead, and sighed in resignation. He knew they would simply move on.

Sau'ilahk drifted to the open portal of a hall filled with immense basalt statues like coffins. This chamber appeared to be a dead end, except for the gaping breaches in the end walls, but Wynn was nowhere in sight.

He went to look into the wide left-end breach and found a shaft going up and down. Carefully approaching the hall's other end, he found that this taller, narrower breach led into a tunnel. A good ways down it to the right, he spotted the faintest flicker of light.

About to slip in, he paused and looked back. Chuillyon and his companions would come soon enough. No doubt Shâodh was tracking Wynn's group. Sau'ilahk did not want to openly engage all three elves, but neither would he tolerate their interference. It was time to do something about Chuillyon.

But when Sau'ilahk looked down the tunnel, the faint light bobbed and winked. Wynn was moving again. There was no time to feed on Chuillyon here and now. What a disappointment, but perhaps something less personal but still deadly was required.

A simple servitor of Air would not be enough. Fire, in the form of Light, would also be required. It needed to be encased in Earth drawn from Stone, as well. A servitor of multiple Elements, in three conjuries, would cost him dearly. Then a fourth conjury had to intertwine with the others to give his creation the necessary spark of sentience.

He began to conjure Air. When its quivering ball manifested, he caged it with his incorporeal fingers and embedded it with Fire in the form of Light. A yellow-orange glow radiated from within his grip. Forcing his hand to become corporeal, he slammed the servitor down into the hall's floor stones.

Sau'ilahk's black form wavered as exhaustion threatened to overtake him. He was only half-finished, and the final two conjuries must be done simultaneously.

Around his flattened hand, a square of glowing umber lines for Earth rose on the hall's floor stones. Within that, a circle of blue-white appeared as he summoned in Spirit and inserted a fragment of his consciousness. In the spaces between the shapes, iridescent glyphs and sigils of white appeared like dew-dampened web strands at the break of dawn.

Sau'ilahk called on his reserves, imbuing his creation with greater essence.

His hand began to waver before him. He exerted his will to remain present and straightened, lifting his hand from the floor. All glowing marks on the stone vanished.

Awaken! he whispered in his thoughts.

Another glow rose beneath the floor's surface. It shifted erratically, as if swimming inside the stones. He raised his hand above it, fingers closing like a street puppeteer toying with strings, and the glow halted.

Stones bulged over it, and that light began to emerge. It rose out of the floor like a worm as thick as his wrist. Gray as the stone that birthed it, it wriggled away across the floor. Sau'ilahk had created such a servitor once before, with a gaping maw at one end, its body a vessel for poisonous gas.

Stop, he commanded. As it halted, he focused on its spark of sentience, and he drove it through the tall breach and into the tunnel beyond.

Hide in the wall facing the opening. When a life passes through, expel what you hold.

It would obey these simple instructions, drilled into its limited consciousness. Even if the two younger elves survived, without Chuillyon, they would turn back. Shâodh would insist.

Sau'ilahk drifted into the breach, weakened but satisfied, and he turned right down the tunnel to trail Wynn.

Wynn's thoughts turned over and over as she followed Ore-Locks. She wasn't as dismissive of Chane's concerns as she pretended, but her concerns differed from his. Clearly, he suspected that *something* had happened here after the seatt's fall, though just *what*, neither of them could say.

"What is that?" he asked from behind her.

She saw black on the walls and floor again, but it wasn't the same as before. Her crystal's light caused it to shimmer.

"*Chlaks-álêg*," Ore-Locks answered. "'Burning stone' . . . a vein of raw coal."

It crosscut their path where the tunnel floor dipped slightly in a circular hollow, as if a good deal of the coal had been dug out and removed from the floor and both side walls.

Chane slipped past Wynn into the left-side hollow. "And again here, look."

Both Ore-Locks and Wynn watched Chane trace his widely spread fingers along deep, long gouges in the black wall. This time there were four parallel grooves.

Wynn spotted places in the coal vein where it looked like chunks bigger than her head, or even Ore-Locks's head, had been gouged out.

"Ore-Locks, do your people use . . ." Chane began. "Do they use . . . beasts of any kind in mining?"

Wynn blinked at such a notion. What was he suggesting?

"No," Ore-Locks answered hesitantly. "Not that I have ever heard of."

Wynn didn't like where Chane was going with this. She glanced up the tunnel, thinking of those broken skulls. Did Chane believe something had survived the seatt's fall, something large enough to kill anything that remained or arrived later? Even so, any creature among the enemy's forces couldn't have survived all these centuries with so little to feed it. Unless . . .

Wynn began to worry. What if whatever it had been had taken away the orb for its master? Was the orb already long gone, as far back as the war? Her thoughts turned back to the few scant lines she'd read in the volume by Volyno.

. . . of Earth . . . beneath the chair of a lord's song . . . meant to prevail but all ended . . . halfway eaten beneath.

Something else came to her. Before leaving the guild at Calm Seatt, she'd stumbled on a forgotten dwarven ballad with one obscure word—gí'uyllæ, the "all-eaters" or "all-consumers." Even so, whatever had been here was either long dead or long gone.

"*A'ye!*" Ore-Locks said breathily.

Wynn swung around at his exclamation. His large hand was pressed into another depression in the coal. That hollow was so large that his hand looked small as he drew it along the depression's inner surface. Wynn slipped in, trying to see into the hollow as Ore-Locks withdrew his hand.

Under her crystal's close light, the hollow's back was smoothly cut in parallel grooves. These marks weren't like the ones Chane implied were made with claws. These were smoother, closer together, like . . . like teeth had bitten through the black coal.

She shook her head, reminding herself that whatever had been down here couldn't still be here. Then she heard a low, rumbling whine.

Shade stood off behind Wynn, not drawing near. The dog's jowls quivered as she flattened her ears, looking at that huge hollow under the crystal's light.

Wynn decided not to move on just yet. Whatever happened here warranted further investigation.

Chuillyon walked right through an open portal into a chamber similar to that of the Fallen Ones back in Dhredze Seatt. But this one was huge.

It still surprised him that Ore-Locks was leaving these portals wide-open. Such negligence would shock Cinder-Shard, though Chuillyon certainly could not complain. He could not have opened them himself, but how had Ore-Locks done so? How could even an errant stonewalker know the combinations for locks used a thousand years ago?

"What is this place?" Hannâschi asked, looking around with clear worry on her smudged face. "These effigies are . . . different from the last ones."

Shâodh examined pieces of a broken effigy lying on the floor. "What do the carved bands represent?"

This was the first openly curious question he had asked in a long while. Chuillyon had no time to explain dwarven vices or the place of the Fallen Ones in their beliefs.

He saw no other ways out of here except for two jagged breaches in the walls. The wider breach to the left of the entrance was just another vertical shaft, as in the hall of the Eternals. He doubted Wynn or the others had the equipment or skills to climb down.

He looked at Shâodh and asked, "Which way?"

The glance Shâodh cast back seemed almost hostile. The young man closed his eyes with a thrumming chant. When his eyes opened, he looked to the taller, narrower breach.

Chuillyon scowled in frustration. Perhaps he had again underestimated Wynn. As he approached, he held his crystal through the opening. It did not open into a shaft, and instead, he found a rough and raw tunnel running in both directions.

Hannâschi came up beside him and leaned in to see around the opening's sides.

"Well, onward again," Chuillyon told her tiredly.

A shudder shook the hall's floor, and he turned.

Shâodh still stood among the basalt debris, but his eyes widened as he looked toward the wide breach at the hall's other end.

Ghassan reached an open portal and carefully peeked around its edge. There was another massive hall waiting beyond, but this one was filled with near-black faceless and formless effigies. Representations of bands were carved in the stone all around each one, but they did not keep Ghassan's attention long.

Chuillyon's young male companion stood at the hall's center, while the old elf and the female looked into a tall breach in the right wall.

With no one looking Ghassan's way, he slipped in behind the nearest tall, black effigy. From his hiding place, he tried to hear what the others said, but they were all quiet. In frustration, he thought of dipping into Chuillyon's surface thoughts, hoping the old elf would not feel his presence.

But then Ghassan heard the sound of falling rock. Dust billowed from the wide breach in the hall's end just behind him. The floor shook and vibrated as he heard more debris tumbling down the shaft.

Ghassan froze, ready to bolt from the hall.

"What was that?" Shâodh said.

A cloud of dust billowed from the wide breach in the hall's end nearest its entrance.

"We should move on, as this place is not stable," Chuillyon said, and turned as Hannâschi stepped through the taller breach.

A ripple in the tunnel's inner wall caught Chuillyon's eyes. He instinctively lurched back, trying to grab for Hannâschi.

A loud hiss came as a cloud of umber vapors filled the tunnel inside the breach.

Chuillyon covered his face with a sleeve, as the cloud enveloped Hannâschi. She wheezed and choked as he snatched the back of her cloak and jerked. Then he caught sight of a wriggling form protruding from the tunnel's inner wall.

Only instinct kept him clutching Hannâschi's cloak as he threw himself back and fell. Muddy orange vapors spilled out of the opening, rising over the breach's top lip and drifting upward. Before Chuillyon could roll off his back, Shâodh knocked his grip free and pulled Hannâschi farther out on the hall's floor. He dropped to his knees, and she collapsed in his arms, her head lolling to one side.

"No . . . no!" Shâodh stammered, all composure gone from his horrified face.

Sau'ilahk saw Wynn's glowing light ahead and even heard her voice. From what he could tell, she stood at some dark crosscut in the tunnel.

"Keep searching," she said, her voice barely reaching him.

Sau'ilahk's excitement grew. He longed to drift closer, but he was too close even now. Yet he could not bring himself to withdraw. What had she found?

Wynn suddenly appeared to drop out of sight, as if she sank lower than the tunnel floor. By the glow of a crystal's light, Chane and Ore-Locks appeared to be on the crosscut's far side, and a fair distance away from Wynn.

"What are we looking for?" Ore-Locks called.

"Any more of the same," she called back. "Or anything unusual."

Sau'ilahk's urgency heightened. What did they search for?

A rumble carried down the tunnel from behind him, and he could not help turning to look.

Light spilled into the tunnel from the breach where he had planted his servitor. The elves must have come, but his stone worm could not have made that rumbling sound. He hung there, watching, until a crack like thunder echoed through the breach and down the tunnel.

Chuillyon regained his feet, prepared to repel whatever had assaulted Hannâschi. He drew his sleeve over his nose and mouth and looked through the breach, but he saw only the rough stone of the tunnel's inner wall through the thinning vapors.

A crack of breaking stone filled the hall.

Chuillyon whirled as the sound pierced his ears. More stones crashed down the chute inside the wide breach at the hall's other end. A billow of dark dust bulged out of the opening, and a charred stench filled the hall's air.

It was not dust, but smoke.

Flame bellowed out of that breach, reaching toward the hall's midpoint. Shâodh shouted something, but the fire's roar drowned him out.

Before the flames had begun to die, a monstrous form crawled out of the wide breach on all fours, its bulk spreading the cloud of smoke.

As the flames erupted, Ghassan tried running for the entrance, but he stumbled as he was assailed by searing heat. Something charged right through the fire, and he ran back behind the first effigy, rushing to its far side to see what was happening. All he saw amid the flames was something huge and four-legged, with a massive head on a long neck. It charged straight toward Chuillyon and his people.

Wynn tensed at the thunderous echo rolling down the raw tunnel. A soft, red light filled the passage's distant end back where the narrow breach led into the Chamber of the Fallen. But she froze before calling to the others.

A dark silhouette stood in the tunnel between her and that pulse of orange-yellow light.

Shade spun and lunged two paces past Wynn. The dog's growl began to twist into something akin to a cat's angry mewl, and her hackles rose in the light of Wynn's crystal.

Wynn's mind went numb. She knew Shade's sounds, but she couldn't accept what it meant, and kept whispering, "It cannot be. It cannot be."

Wynn couldn't take her eyes off the black figure framed by the orange glow farther up the tunnel. Then a crack of stone erupted behind her, followed by the sound of falling rocks.

Wynn twisted about as billowing dust and dirt rolled toward her.

"Chane!"

Chane was farther down the tunnel with Ore-Locks when three sounds stunned him in rapid succession. Shade let out a loud mewl of warning, and Chane shoved the cold lamp crystal into his pocket, reaching for his swords. Before he could draw them, he heard rocks falling overhead, and then Wynn cried out, "Chane!"

A cloud of dust and loosened earth filled the coal pocket between him and her, nearly blocking out her crystal's light.

Chane heard rocks crashing down within that cloud, and still he lunged forward. He felt Ore-Locks grab his cloak and jerk him to a halt.

"Let go," he snarled.

He turned in a frenzy, but faltered at the dwarf's gaping mouth and wide eyes staring upward.

Ore-Locks shouted, "It is coming from—"

The rest was drowned in a thunder of crashing rock. Dust filled the air around both of them. Chane grew wild to reach Wynn as he looked back for her, but that choking cloud obscured everything.

Something lashed at him out of the dust.

He caught only a glimpse of a great, snaking tail with a barbed end, and he tried to duck. Its bulk caught him across the chest like a swinging tree trunk and slammed him against the tunnel wall. As the world darkened for an instant, he heard a metallic clang, and then Ore-Locks cried out.

Chane crumpled to the floor as the snaking tail whipped away. He clawed at the tunnel wall, trying to get off his knees, but a sudden pain made him fear he had been broken inside. Dust began settling over fallen stones in the crosscut, and he struggled up, looking for whatever had attacked them. At first he could not see Wynn at all, for something blocked his line of sight.

He barely made out the huge tail as its barbed end scraped the stone floor. Though the creature faced away from him, he could see it was taller and broader than a draft horse. Its back nearly reached the ceiling. Wynn's light from beyond it exposed something else shifting on its back.

Folded leathery wings covered its upper body.

Chane saw the glint of scales all over it, down across its flexing haunches to its taloned rear feet. But the light around it was the wrong color, orange instead of the white from a sage's crystal.

The creature shifted suddenly, stepping away up the tunnel with a scrape of claws.

Chane's panic sharpened as he finally spotted Wynn and Shade beyond the creature. But he also saw that the flickering orange glow came from far beyond them.

"Run!" he tried to shout, but his maimed voice was drowned out by an echo of falling stones. As he drew both swords, for an instant he thought he imagined . . .

Someone stood in the tunnel's darkness between Wynn and the distant orange light.

That light suddenly died, leaving only Wynn's glowing crystal, and all that mattered to him was reaching her.

Wynn saw a monstrous head snake out of the dust cloud, and the whole creature followed with a grinding scrape of claws upon stone.

Shade lunged back around her, barking and snapping.

The reptile opened its long mouth, and an acrid stench stung Wynn's nostrils. It hissed as clear fluid spilled out of its maw. A shower of spittle sprayed out as its large, sooty rows of teeth clacked together . . . and sparked.

"Shade!" Wynn screamed, grabbing the dog and throwing them both toward the tunnel's far wall.

Spittle ignited, and flame burned along the wall where they'd been standing.

Wynn hit the far wall, toppling over Shade. She tried to keep Shade down as her staff clattered away across the floor. A curtain of fire spread along the far wall and the ceiling above from whatever the creature had spit at them. Wynn felt her forearm begin to sear.

Her sleeve was on fire!

She thrashed and whipped her arm against the tunnel floor, smothering her sleeve. While flailing, she caught a glimpse up the tunnel.

Before the flames died, Wynn clearly saw a black robe and wafting cloak illuminated by the fire.

She almost lost her fear of the beast coming at her as she saw *him*.

Sau'ilahk was there, watching her.

As flames suddenly erupted near Wynn, Sau'ilahk rushed halfway to her. She had not yet led him to the orb, and he could not let her die. Somehow she grabbed the dog and rolled clear, evading the worst of the fire.

Sau'ilahk still heard a roaring far behind him, but it did not pull his attention. He could only stare at the winged, reptilian creature filling the tunnel beyond Wynn.

That noise behind him, and the blast of orange light at the breach, could mean only one thing. There were at least two of these creatures down here.

Sau'ilahk did not think Wynn could escape them. Perhaps he could save her, but she had already led him into the seatt's deepest place. The search could not reach much farther.

He had no fear of these creatures, no matter how long he remained. Their teeth and claws, even their fire, could not touch him. He could search at his leisure, ignoring them.

Wynn froze, staring at him, as if not believing her eyes. The sight of her stricken face sparked a sudden joy within him, and then he saw the creature behind her open its maw again.

A howl echoed sharply up the tunnel.

Shade charged toward Sau'ilahk. Chane rushed the creature from behind. Wynn scrambled for her staff.

Sau'ilahk had always hoped to kill her slowly. But the orb was all that mattered now.

Wynn would die, anyway, her last sight being that of him.

Sau'ilahk focused down the tunnel past Chane, past Ore-Locks, as far as he could see. And he blinked through dormancy.

Wynn almost screamed in anguish as Sau'ilahk vanished, and Shade snapped at empty air like a wolf gone mad. Amid terror, Wynn spun to face the creature behind her. She couldn't help thinking that Chane had been right all along.

The wraith had survived and would now beat her to the orb.

The last thing that should happen was for the orb to fall into Sau'ilahk's hands—to be reclaimed by the Enemy for whatever purpose it served. She couldn't allow that at any price.

Whirling back, she saw Chane charging the creature from behind. She raised her staff, hoping to blind the creature before it spit fire again. Its maw was open and fluid dripped out, but it didn't clack its teeth again.

The creature raised its large head, and its black orb eyes stared up the tunnel at Shade. Wynn was caught in hesitation when it suddenly snaked its head back around. Chane dodged aside, but the creature looked beyond him, fixating on Ore-Locks still lying against the tunnel's side.

Wynn jumped a step as its head snapped back, but again it looked toward Shade. She heard scrabbling claws as Shade rushed by her, but her only thoughts were for the orb.

"Chane, no!" Wynn shouted. "Sau'ilahk is here, and he's gone to find the orb. Don't let him take it. Nothing else matters!"

Shade lunged in, snapping at the creature's face. But the massive reptile only lifted its head out of reach. Chane didn't stop at Wynn's plea, and he came at the beast from behind.

The creature merely lashed its tail.

Chane ducked under, rolling to the tunnel's other side. The tail's barb shattered the wall where he'd stood, scattering chunks of rock everywhere.

"Chane, listen to me!" Wynn cried.

The creature fixed its eyes on her.

Chane regained his feet, still within reach of its tail. He held both his dwarven blade and the old, shortened one. His pale face was twisted like an animal's about to snarl. She'd seen this before. He was lost in fury and a hungered drive to get to her.

How could she make him listen?

"Nothing matters but the orb!" Wynn shouted at him, and then ripped the cover off the sun crystal.

Chuillyon saw the reptilian monstrosity coming at full charge, and he bolted to the left. If he could gain its attention, he might draw it away from Shâodh and Hannâschi.

It came at him rapidly in a mass of scales, jaws, and thrashing wings. He ran between two of the huge coffins, but when he glanced back, it was not coming after him.

The monster swung its long head around, fixing on Shâodh, who stood between it and Hannâschi's prone form.

"Keep moving!" Chuillyon shouted. "Give it two targets."

With a quick blink, Shâodh appeared to understand, and he ran for the hall's other side.

The creature swung its head toward him, fluid dripping from its mouth. A singular thought pounded in Chuillyon's mind.

Someone had to survive.

He had not told anyone else of this journey. Even if they did not catch Wynn, one of them had to tell the guild of this place, about the proof found here, and that she'd come seeking something more.

Chuillyon glanced at Hannâschi on the floor, barely breathing, her long hair in a tangle across her face. Even at the cost of leaving her, one of them had to escape.

The creature followed his gaze. Its huge, dark eyes focused on Hannâschi's prone form. It opened its jaws wider, as if about to spit.

Before Chuillyon could act, he heard Shâodh cry out, "No!"

Shâodh ran toward the creature, waving his arms. "Here! Over here!"

The creature pivoted at his noise, spitting, and its jaws clacked.

Chuillyon's cry drowned under the flame's roar.

Shâodh's face filled with horror and his mouth gaped for an inhale. His scream never came out, and Chuillyon cringed back between two basalt coffins as the air ignited.

Flames erupted from the creature's maw, lighting the whole hall in an orange-yellow glare. Amid fire, the barest shadow of Shâodh crumpled like cinders burning too quickly in a forge.

Everything happened too fast for Ghassan to react. He saw the young elf waving his arms and shouting to draw the creature away from the girl.

Ghassan dashed out to do something—anything—to help. Then fire burst from the creature's maw, engulfing and incinerating the young elf.

The floor was covered in flickering, small flames, as if some ignitable fluid had been sprayed across the stone.

Ghassan's mind raced. What could he do—what could anyone do—against such a monster? In desperation, he began drawing shapes and sigils in his mind's eye, chanting quickly but softly as he focused on the creature. Perhaps he could befuddle its mind.

His thoughts hit a wall, and then a backlash struck him.

Ghassan reeled against the base of one basalt statue as the whole chamber dimmed before his eyes. He forced his eyes to stay open, and the blackness faded. He never had a chance to ponder what had gone wrong.

The creature swung its head again, this time looking at him.

Chuillyon watched as the creature looked toward the hall's entrance. He silently crept forward between the immense basalt statues, following its gaze.

There was Ghassan il'Sänke. Still in shock, Chuillyon could not comprehend how the Suman sage could be here.

Il'Sänke pushed off the base of the basalt coffin, wavering as if injured or ill.

Chuillyon looked numbly at the flames still writhing from blackened stone around the lump of Shâodh's charred remains. He could see no way to reach the hall's portal, and the nearest breach held some trap that had struck down Hannâschi. Shâodh was gone, and Hannâschi appeared barely alive. And what could one Suman metaologer do against this thing that had come out of the other breach?

Again, someone had to survive to tell of this place. No matter Wynn's reason for coming here, or what she sought, the guild had to know of the seatt's existence and of a monster in its depths.

Something had to come from all that this had cost.

The creature's head whipped back toward Chuillyon, and he peered around the coffin's base. Its maw opened once again, spittle dripping from its jaws to the floor.

Ghassan gained his feet and took a stumbling step as he began to chant.

"No!" Chuillyon shouted.

Ghassan froze in silence.

"Go!" Chuillyon shouted. "Tell our own of this place. Go . . . now!"

Ghassan's brow furrowed as either anger or frustration passed across his caramel features. But Ghassan was so close to the open portal. He could escape this hall.

"Get ready to run!" Chuillyon called. "I'll distract it."

He steeled himself, hoping that when he died, it would be quick, if not painless. But he saw no choice. Ghassan was the only sage here with a chance.

Before Chuillyon could move, Ghassan bolted.

Chuillyon saw the Suman run straight for the wide breach from which the creature had emerged—and not for the exit out of this place. Chuillyon was stricken cold as he watched Ghassan launch himself into that opening and fall from sight down the shaft.

Chuillyon could not breathe. His mind went numb as any frail hope withered, thinking that all this would die with him. Why would Ghassan kill himself in such a futile manner? Did he fear the creature would pursue him, and he preferred another death?

Chuillyon was alone as he heard claws upon the hall's floor.

The creature rushed him, and all he could do was retreat to the wall between the coffins. The reptile came too rapidly for him to dart along the wall, and its head thrust in at him only an arm's length away.

A sadness like no other crushed everything inside of Chuillyon.

Ghassan's self-destructive act, Hannâschi's helplessness, and Shâodh's burned bones overwhelmed all other thoughts as he looked in the creature's black glistening eyes.

He could not bear any more sadness and loss. All he had left was a moment to pray.

Chârmun . . . fill me with your absolute nature . . . in my sorrow of failure.

"Nothing matters but the orb!"

Chane heard Wynn's shout on the edge of his awareness, but it brought only a ripping sense of denial. Hunger, fury, and his love for this woman tangled, becoming one and the same. Then he heard her chanting softly and saw her thrust out the staff's uncovered crystal.

Chane lashed out at the winged creature's tail with both blades, trying to make it turn on him.

"Chane, don't!" Wynn cried. "Go!"

No searing light filled the tunnel.

He halted, looking to her. Why had the sun crystal not ignited? Wynn raised her shocked eyes to the end of the staff. Something had gone wrong. Chane would have screamed if he had a true voice.

But the creature did not spit fire again.

Shade snarled and weaved, trying to stay between it and Wynn. The scaled beast raised its head out of reach, but its attention was fixed on Shade.

Wynn bolted forward. She tried to slip by, but the creature's neck snaked down and cut her off. It would not allow her to pass. She locked eyes with Chane, and tears rolled down her cheeks.

The desperation on her face knifed Chane in the chest. She grew still, looking at him, and her voice was frighteningly calm.

"If you care anything for me," she called, "you will listen. What matters to me here is who I *am* . . . and it matters more than even what I mean to you. Go after Sau'ilahk. Get to the orb first."

Chane took another step.

Wynn shook her head, and this time her voice was barely audible.

"If you love me, then go . . . for me."

Chane shuddered.

Those words stung him more than if she had simply told him to leave her and never return. To deny what she asked and save her, or to do as she asked and lose her, was crueler than any choice she had ever forced on him.

He let out a hiss of anger and panic. The feral thing at the core of his nature struggled beneath the violet concoction that had kept him awake since they had first headed under the mountains. He could not take his eyes off Wynn, even as she turned to face the creature hovering just beyond Shade's bared teeth.

The creature was poised in stillness, but for how long?

If you love me, then go . . . for me.

Chane cringed in anguish as Wynn's plea kept rolling through this mind. How could he deny what she claimed by not doing what she asked?

All he could do was turn and run down the tunnel.

Ore-Locks had barely regained his feet. As Chane rushed by the dwarf, he snarled.

"With me—now!"

Ghassan kept falling down the shaft, out of control, still dazed by the backlash of his failed sorcery on the creature. Chuillyon's demand that he flee still left him shocked, but there was much more at stake here than just revealing the discovery of Bäalâle Seatt. Chuillyon had not seen the frightening hints in the translated poem.

Ghassan feared whatever Wynn might find and remove from this place. He had to learn her true purpose at any price. As he fell, he had no time to regret leaving the old elf to such a death.

Wynn did not yet know that the wraith had followed her. It had not killed her, so it could only be using her for the same purpose as Ghassan sought. If her search had anything to do with something left behind by enemy forces, the wraith could not be allowed to reach it first.

Ghassan had to survive, just as Chuillyon had said.

His shoulder clipped the shaft's wall.

He tumbled as his body careened off the jagged walls. A rock protrusion ripped his sleeve. Even dazed, he knew he could hit bottom at any moment, and he forced his mind to focus amid vertigo.

Ghassan closed his eyes, seeing only the shaped sigils igniting in his thoughts. With air rushing past and ripping at his clothing, he pushed against the shaft's walls with his will, trying to slow his rapid descent. But all he felt and heard were bits of stone breaking when he collided with the walls, and he barely heard clothing and skin tear as he plummeted through the darkness.

CHAPTER 25

Wynn looked into the creature's face. Her attempt to ignite the sun crystal had failed, though she'd done everything right.

Shade's snarling suddenly ceased.

An ache grew in Wynn's head as she saw the creature fixate on the dog.

A cacophony, like a thousand leaves, began blowing about inside Wynn's skull. It grew to a deafening pitch until she whimpered and dropped to her knees. She clutched Shade tightly. She couldn't even save the dog, only hold her and wait to die.

Shade's memory-words rose in Wynn's thoughts above the scratch of leaf-wings.

—*Fay-born*—

The creature's head swung toward Wynn. What was Shade trying to tell her?

The roar in Wynn's mind drowned out everything else. All she saw were great black eyes within a reptilian face boring into her until everything went dark.

There was only blackness.

Wynn's chest hurt and then began to burn, as if she'd held her breath too long but couldn't let it out. She sensed motion but her limbs wouldn't move.

It was so familiar, but amid growing panic to breathe, she couldn't remember why.

Blackness faded, but only a little.

She exhaled hard and couldn't stop shaking as she gasped, unaware of where she was. Every muscle in her body clenched and wouldn't release. Something pulled at her thoughts, but it wasn't the crackle of leaf-wings.

It was monotonous and endless, like a wind shrieking inside her head. Words rose out of it in fragmented whispers.

. . . they come . . . liars, deceivers . . . assassins, murders everywhere . . .

The wind inside her skull seemed made of even more than those words, so many whispers that she only caught these broken pieces. Her own thoughts were drowned by the gale, as the first thing she saw was a dim hearth.

Orange-red coals within it barely lit the space where she stood. She stood surrounded by plain stone walls, in a room without a single piece of furniture. Its empty state heightened her awareness until her focus snapped sharply to the left.

She hadn't even thought of turning, but she did.

. . . trust no one . . . not ever . . .

At those whispers out of the gale, Wynn looked to an archway in the room's left wall. It was nothing but another portal into blackness, for the hearth's dim light didn't penetrate the space beyond. She wanted to back away, to find any path out of here, but . . .

"Vra' feilulákè . . . bhâyil tu-thé?"

Not a word of that cry made sense, though it rushed from her own mouth with a frantic urgency pushing toward rage. But it wasn't her voice that she'd heard.

Wynn's fear mounted.

She was lost inside a memory. But whose? Was Shade doing this? She focused hard, trying to see the world she last remembered—the rough tunnel, the winged reptile, or Shade.

None of this came to her.

Where was she? Who was she? Without answers, she wrestled with what she'd heard to hold off the fear-fed whispers trying to drown her reason.

The first word had been vocative, masculine—she knew the language!

She'd been speaking Dwarvish, but either she hadn't heard it right or she didn't know the dialect. She couldn't recognize the word's root. Only the suffix "-ulákè" barely made sense.

It meant "like" or "alike."

"Vra' feilulákè! Bhâyil tu-thé?"

Wynn's throat turned raw as she repeated the deep shout. A rustle of leaf-wings rose in her mind. Not many, just one this time, like when she'd listened in on Chap as he'd communed with his kin. The first words she'd uttered repeated in her head, this time in every language she knew: *Brother-of-like-flesh . . . are you here?*

Whomever this memory belonged to, Shade was not the one passing it. Shade had called the winged creatures in the tunnel Fay-born. Did those leaf-wing sounds come from them? Was this how the Fay would finally get to her, kill her, while she was trapped and lost in some memory?

Something moved beyond the archway.

It wavered from side to side, staggering forward through the dark. Large, dwarven hands covered his broad features, smothering his haggard, rapid breaths. One eye peered at her through his thick fingers. Then his left hand slid off his face and clutched the archway's side. Though his other hand remained, its fingers curled upward into his red-brown hair.

This "like" brother—"twin" brother, at a guess—had a broad jaw, once clean-shaven and now shadowed with days of stubble. His eyes were sunken in dark circles, as if he hadn't slept in many nights. He was young, or might have seemed so, if his face weren't twisted in horror.

For an instant, Wynn thought she knew him, but that wasn't possible. She didn't even know where she was—or who she was. Nothing about this place was familiar.

. . . loved ones now hunt you . . . they are coming . . . be ever watchful . . .

The brother's gaze darted quickly about, searching the hearth room.

He heard those gale whispers, just as she did!

. . . never close your eyes again . . . not ever . . . not until they all die . . .

His jaw muscles bulged as his hand jerked from his head, haplessly tearing out tangles of hair. That hand balled into a massive fist.

Wynn saw the same rage in his face that she'd heard in the voice of this memory's owner, the other brother. She rushed forward, grabbing the brother's vestment's front with one large hand. She felt her other hand groping for something at her waist.

"Why are you still here?" she shouted in the deep voice that was not her own. "I told you to leave, while you still could. *Get out of here!*"

The brother froze, his fist still raised. Then the gale grew once more in Wynn's mind.

. . . if they see you, kill them quickly. . . . They will kill you, if they can. . . . They will; you know this. . . .

Wynn's lower hand clenched. She jerked hard, though she barely glimpsed what she gripped. Her gaze remained locked on the brother as he pulled a dagger from a sheath on his belt. He raised it, point downward.

The leaf-wing came again in Wynn's head.

I am with you—hear only me. Hear the quiet I bring to your thoughts.

Wynn froze as the brothers faced each other, each ready to strike the other down.

A scream carried from somewhere distant.

Wynn released her grip and backstepped, not knowing what she—he—was doing. She spun toward the distant sound.

Then she saw what had become of the furniture.

Chairs, stools, an oak table, and even a large chest were piled against the door of this place. Everything from this room must have been thrown against it in blind desperation. When her focus turned back, the haggard brother stared toward the door, as well. His eyes were wide in fear as he shuddered and looked at her.

"Come . . . come, please," he begged, stuttering. "Come with me."

"No," Wynn answered. "Go alone, as I told you."

"Do not do this!" the brother shouted, advancing one step, anger returning to his face. "Your brethren have fallen, like the rest . . . though first, did they not? They locked the people from the temple . . . and you helped them? In this plague of madness, where are the people to go even if any could think to leave . . . if any could escape?"

He stepped farther out into the hearth room.

The brother's vestment might have been russet, but it was too filthy, and there was too little light to be certain. His gaze dropped downward, and whoever Wynn was here and now followed that gaze. Wynn saw what she held.

The long, triangular dagger, its base as wide as his fist, had straight edges that tapered directly to its point. Its polished guard and pommel were almost silvery, and bits of the hilt that showed around his broad fist looked lacquered in pure black.

It was the blade of a stonewalker.

Wynn cringed within that imprisoning memory, not wanting to accept what that might mean. The gale whispers rose, as if called by her fear. The single leaf-wing didn't return until the stonewalker—she—raised the blade.

This is not the one you must kill.

Wynn felt the stonewalker falter as he—she—looked at his brother.

Cling to me alone.

She sensed no true comfort in those words, and they gave her none. That leaf-wing voice didn't speak to her. It spoke to him, the owner of this memory. She heard it, felt it, only because he did.

Wynn began to doubt even more.

Those words couldn't have come from the monster in the tunnel. They were just part of this memory. What was it that had come to this place? What spoke to this stonewalker?

"By our blood, remember me," she—he—whispered. "But once you leave here, never speak my name again. By our blood, I bind you to this . . . let me be forgotten by all."

Shock rose on the brother's face as he shook his head in disbelief. The instant he opened his mouth to speak, the stonewalker turned.

Wynn saw the wall coming at her as he raced toward it, into it. She remembered why that first, suffocating blackness felt like it had entombed her. Stonewalkers could move through anything of earth and stone. But even that didn't silence the gale whispers inside of him, inside of her.

She didn't want to see anymore. But as he raced through open tunnels, passages, and chambers, she couldn't look away or close her—his—eyes.

He never paused, always running for the next wall, but Wynn saw things . . . heard things. Between the silence and blackness of each dive into stone, wails of manic fear and rage echoed in every space.

Two dwarven women tore at each other until one ripped the other's throat open with her bare hands. She'd barely let the body fall when she whirled toward a male with his back turned. She threw herself at him, her stained hands reaching around to tear at his face.

A young female shoved an old man aside as they both tried to get through a door. She slammed it shut in his face, though he pounded on it as the sound of heavy boots closed upon him.

A red-spattered warrior beat upon the fallen with his mace, shrieking at them to get away or he would kill them all. They were already dead, mangled beyond recognition, yet he wouldn't stop.

A silent dwarven child felt her way along a wall. She couldn't see because of the blood running out of her hair and into her eyes.

At the center of a large chamber filled with tables and stools, an elder male crouched upon a greeting-house dais. He rocked slowly, whispering to himself as if in prayer . . . and then he laughed in hysteria as his gaze flitted about at nothing.

The blackness of stone came again and again. Each time, Wynn wished it would be the last.

Let her stay in that cold, encasing darkness, where she—he—would see nothing ever again. She didn't want to know more of the madness, the whispers, waiting with each return of dim light. When it came again, she would've whimpered if she'd had her own voice.

And the stonewalker halted.

It was darker here than any other place, even more than the home of his brother. It was almost quiet, except for a pounding in his ears. Wynn didn't want him to turn around, but he did.

A great archway filled her sight. Its double doors were shut, sealed with an iron bar that rotated on a rivet larger than her arm. It wasn't broken like the last time she'd seen it. The muted rumbling of thunder reverberated through those doors.

There were people out there, on the other side, pounding to get in.

"What are you doing?"

At that menacing whisper, the stonewalker grabbed for both blades on his belt. As he twisted around, Wynn saw immense, dark forms in the hall. Great silhouettes of statues reached toward a ceiling lost in the pitch-black heights. Three each lined the hall's longer walls, and Wynn knew where she was. She was still in Bäalâle, in its hall of the Eternals, but not as she'd found it. It was whole, as if from another time, long ago. A flickering light caught her eye, and she—he—watched an approaching flame.

That torch's light illuminated the bearer's reddened face of broad features and gray beard. His eyes were so wide, the whites showed all around his black-pellet irises. Firelight glinted on the steel tips of his black-scaled armor.

The old one was another stonewalker.

"You would let them in!" he accused.

"No . . . not anymore," Wynn answered in the deep, masculine voice.

"Liar!" the other hissed, and his free hand dropped to a dagger's hilt. "Where have you been? To your prattling brother?"

Wynn didn't answer, but felt her—his—grip tighten on the hilt of his battle dagger.

"Is that how it started?" the old stonewalker whispered, creeping forward. "All of them turning against us, once the siege began. What deceits did you spit into the people's ears . . . through your brother?"

And the whisper gale rose again.

. . . *no one left to trust . . . never turn your back . . . they are coming for you . . .*

His hand slipped from the dagger's hilt. Wynn felt pain as the young stonewalker slapped the side of his own head. The leaf-wing rose instantly, its voice too loud over the gale of whispers.

Listen only to me—cling only to me.

Its crackling skitter smothered all thoughts from Wynn's awareness.

"No . . ." the young stonewalker moaned. His other hand slapped his skull as he shouted, "Leave me be!"

"Leave you be?" hissed the elder, almost in puzzlement.

Wynn realized the old one hadn't heard the leaf-wing.

"Why would I?" the elder went on. "You—you did this to us, traitor. You and your brother . . . made them come for us!"

"No," he groaned. "My brother has no part in this."

"More lies!" shouted the elder, jerking his blade from its sheath.

Do what is necessary and come to me.

At the sound of that leaf-wing, the young stonewalker closed his hands tighter on his head. And the elder dropped his torch and charged.

"Keep your treachery," the old one shouted, raising the dagger. "Byûndunî!"

Do not listen. Come to me.

The young stonewalker squeezed his skull ever tighter, trying to crush that voice from his head. But Wynn didn't feel the pain. She only shriveled within upon hearing his name.

She tried frantically to escape once more to the real world, to escape this memory of Byûndunî—of Deep-Root—of Thallûhearag, the Lord of Slaughter.

Sau'ilahk raced down the tunnel, following a conjured servitor of light to break the darkness. The tunnel began to intersect with smaller, branching passages, but he kept to the main one, always heading downward into the mountain's depths.

His servitor shot into a small cave, and Sau'ilahk halted at the dead end.

Upon seeing no breaches, passages, or another way in or out, his frustration threatened to boil over into rage. Where could he look now? How many narrow tunnels had he passed along the way? The orb had to be here somewhere!

Then he saw the bones.

There were so many, and they were so old that they blended with the loose stones and rubble on the cave floor. Some were still embedded at the base of the far wall, and he wondered how this could be. Had the rest that were lying about been dug up? Curiosity quelled frustration as his thoughts turned to what little he knew of this place.

Beloved's forces had breached the seatt, and then a catastrophe struck. The mountain peak had collapsed, killing both sides during the siege. He had wondered over the centuries what could have created such devastation.

Sau'ilahk had seen no more bones along the tunnel, but he was deep down now, and the bones here were numerous. Something had happened here, something had been . . . dug up? Turning one hand corporeal, he began digging, scattering loosened debris and bones. Then his fingers scraped something hard and dense.

Calling up his reserve of consumed life, he turned his other hand corporeal and began tearing away more loose rubble and dirt. He kept clawing and scraping on something hard as stone. The more he dug around it, the more he felt it was too round and almost smooth.

He frantically brushed the dust from its gritty surface.

It was a globe slightly larger than a great helm, made of dark, near-black, stone. Though faintly rough, its rounded surface was too perfect to be natural. The large, tapered head of a spike protruded atop it. When he rolled it slightly in the rubble, he saw the spike's tip sticking out through the globe's bottom. Spike and globe were one, chiseled from a single piece.

Waves of joy inside him mixed with an unexpected outrage.

Made by his god, by Beloved's own will, the orb . . . the Anchor of Spirit had been left like forgotten rubbish among dirt and bones. Perhaps the catastrophe had caught the Children who had brought it. That they had been buried among Beloved's minions, his tools, brought some satisfaction to Sau'ilahk. And the anchor had remained where it had fallen in a long-forgotten time, waiting for him to claim.

He would be beautiful again and forever young. The promise made to him so long ago would be fulfilled. This time, he had not been betrayed.

Beloved, he whispered with his thoughts.

Through that whelp of a sage, his god had led him to his own salvation. Drawing deep on his reserves, he turned his whole body corporeal and picked up the heavy orb, finally, after a thousand years. As his cloth-wrapped arms closed around it, he just stood there, and relief made him almost wearier than anything else.

He looked down at what he held and went numb inside.

In those ancient days, he never actually touched the anchors. Only the Children were so privileged. He had seen one on rare occasions when one of *them* carried it out for a purpose his god had commanded. But he knew of them, all five, each one an anchor binding one Element of Existence. Each one enslaved a different primal component for his god's bidding.

Although the orb lay dormant in his arms, he should still be able to feel its essence. Through his Beloved, through his own nature as an eternal spirit, he should feel the core of its elemental nature and the spark of Spirit trapped within it.

The spark was not there.

Sau'ilahk stared at the orb in his arms. He sensed something from it, but its presence felt deeply . . . grounded? There was nothing within it close to his nature as a pure, undying . . . spirit.

He looked about the cave. Anguish returned, swelling into horror.

Those reptilian creatures must have dug into this place in the seatt's bowels. The state of the bones suggested something else had happened here. Beloved's forces must have tried to dig in under the seatt, to come in from beneath before anyone here realized. But in the end, they must have been discovered.

Something had gone horribly wrong. Beloved's forces had died here, buried under the mountain along with their enemies. And here was the orb.

But what would the orb of Spirit be worth in this place? Nothing, now or then. This was *not* the orb of Spirit. It was one of the others, perhaps the orb of Earth? He had been following Wynn all this time . . . only to find the wrong orb.

At that truth, Sau'ilahk began to moan.

Dust and dirt stirred as conjury-twisted air gave a voice to his pain. He began weeping, and his growing rage turned into a wail. His shrieks filled the deadend cave with so much wind that pebbles scored the walls and bones rattled across the floor.

Sau'ilahk screamed, *Betrayer!*

He had been cheated again by the half-truths of his god, as he had a thousand years ago with the promise of eternal life.

A hissing whisper rose in his thoughts. *Do not despair.*

Sau'ilahk was beyond caring if he offended his god, and he screamed back, *Wellspring of lies . . . of deceits!*

He dropped the orb. Rubble and bones crackled under its weight, along with a metallic clang. Hope of beauty and eternal youth withered, and the pain of renewed loss was too great to bear. He screamed at his god once more.

The sage is dead, burned to nothing! What would you have me follow now!

The hiss assailed him again.

She lives . . . but if you choose to no longer obey, servant, then seek on your own.

Sau'ilahk's shrieking wind died. If Wynn lived, why would his treacherous god allow him freedom to do as he pleased? What could he do that he had not tried already in a millennium of searching? He was done with this place, and his misery made him wish to be gone.

That whisper like reptilian scales sliding over sand tore at him again.

Every anchor has its chain, its handle, by which to haul it, just as every portal has its key by which to open it. Did you not hear the key speak?

He was too anguished to care about more taunting hints, but Beloved went on.

Since you no longer hear me, servant . . . perhaps you will remember having heard it.

Sau'ilahk stood still, suspicion growing within him. What was this non-sense about chains, handles, or keys . . . for the anchors of Existence?

He looked down at the one he had dropped.

The orb just lay at his feet, but there had been a sound when it fell that was wrong. Not the dull crack of stone upon stone, or even bones, but a metallic clank. He crouched, forcing one hand corporeal again, and shoved the orb aside.

In the depression its bulk had made was a spot of ruddy golden hue.

Sau'ilahk quickly slapped away dirt and dust until it was fully revealed. Before him lay a thick and heavy circlet of a rusty-golden metal, neither brass nor gold. Its open ends had protruding knobs pointing directly at each other. Its circumference was covered in engravings, though he could not read those marks.

Sau'ilahk remembered seeing such an item before. Once when he had wit-nessed one of the Children departing with an anchor, an orb, it had worn just such an open-ended circlet about its pale neck.

He glanced toward the orb and saw something more in the tapered head of its spike.

There were grooves about the right size for the circlet's knobs. Was this key, this handle, how an orb was truly used? Even so, what good was it to him? This orb was not the one he desired.

I need no key to a place I do not wish to go, he projected. *Nor a handle for something I do not want.*

This time, no answer came—and Sau'ilahk heard the footfalls echoing down the tunnel.

There was more than one pair, and both were too heavy to be Wynn. If one of them was Chane, Sau'ilahk was too weak to deal with that irksome undead.

Frustration made him hesitate, and then he snatched up the circlet. He had no way to carry it without remaining corporeal, so he turned to the cave's rear wall.

The last of his energies fueled one final conjuration as a maw opened in the stone.

Sau'ilahk shoved the circlet in, to be retrieved later.

As the maw closed, leaving only raw stone, dormancy took him completely, and he vanished. For now, he was done with this place . . . this tragically disappointing place.

Wynn was lost in loathing inside the memories of Deep-Root. She was shaken back to awareness when the elder stonewalker's furious cries were suddenly cut off. The blackness of stone enveloped her again, and all she heard were the gale of whispers inside Deep-Root.

. . . they are coming . . . not one but many . . . soon they will find you . . .

A dim glow rose all around as the leaf-wing pushed the whispers down once more.

Ignore them, and hear only me.

Wynn—Deep-Root—stood in the dim phosphorescence of the caves holding the honored dead, but he didn't move an inch. He kept twisting his head rapidly, looking about, and the glimmering walls and shadows whipped too quickly in Wynn's sight.

She didn't understand what had happened in the hall of the Eternals. How had this mass murderer escaped the insane older stonewalker?

Deep-Root took a slow step, placing one foot carefully, and then another. He was trying to be silent. Then he crouched amid the calcified dead, placed his hand on the cave floor, and grew still.

Wynn felt—heard—distant sounds, as if his hand could pass them directly to her ears or her thoughts. She—he—was listening through stone, as Ore-Locks had in the tram tunnel.

Running boots pounded, and Deep-Root twisted to his right.

Wynn saw only a crushed wall beyond columns made of joining stalactites and stalagmites. More footfalls sounded, more running feet, and Deep-Root twisted farther around.

The sound suddenly cut off as he looked to the wall he'd come through.

"Honored Ones," he whispered. "Give me sanctuary!"

Wynn wanted to scream at him for such a plea, but she had no voice. The leaf-wing came instead.

They cannot. Cling to me against the madness. . . . Come to me.

"Silence!" he snarled. "You are nothing but more of this plague upon my people."

I am only with you since my coming. I hold this piece of calm, of silence, anchored within you.

"Get out!" he shouted, forgetting all caution.

I am what gives you this respite, free of what eats at all others. You already cling to me for this.

"You are the worst of what has come! Leave me alone!"

The leaf-wing seemed to fade, but not completely. It was still there, somewhere, holding off the gale. But the moment of near silence left Wynn lost as to what any of this meant.

Then kill me . . . if you can.

That one crackling utterance smothered Wynn's despair and stoked fear in its place. What was that voice trying to do in goading Deep-Root? Then she heard a loud, wet smack.

Deep-Root whirled about as a thrum rose through him from the cave floor. Wynn felt it as she spotted the shadowed form of another stonewalker in the next cave opening. He had just slapped his hand against the stone.

She'd seen that before in the underworld of Dhredze Seatt, but she'd never known how the Stonewalkers' signal for alarm truly worked. It was like a rapid quake running through her, and she could actually follow its sound through stone to its origin.

Heavy boots struck the cave floor, and Deep-Root turned again.

Yet another Stonewalker rushed at him from out of a cave wall.

I wait beyond the farthest place to fall. Can you live long enough to reach it?

Deep-Root bolted, and Wynn heard the shouts of his pursuers echoing through the caves of the Honored Dead. He ran straight through calcified columns and walls of wet stone, swerving each time he reappeared to leap into another wall. And then one time, the blackness of stone didn't pass in a wink—it went on and on.

Wynn felt her lungs might rupture before she—he—took another breath.

What was the "farthest place to fall"? Or was it truly a place one could go?

Besides Deep-Root, there was one thing lower than this worst of traitors; that was the enemy—Beloved, il'Samar, the Night Voice. Was it speaking to him, toying with him through a false protection from the madness that ate through this seatt amid a siege? Where were those other whispers coming from?

Blackness broke, and Deep-Root exhaled, though not with the exhaustion Wynn suffered in the stone. It didn't affect him at all. Perhaps it didn't affect any Stonewalker. He turned in the near dark, feeling along the wall.

His hand settled on something made of crisp angles and smooth surfaces, and he stroked it once. Amber light rose all around.

Wynn looked upon the Chamber of the Fallen.

Deep-Root's eyes locked on something that was wrong in this place—or was wrong to him. A great gash showed in the hall's far end—exactly like the one Wynn had found. But he hesitated, stiffening, as if he had never seen it before.

"I am coming for you!" he threatened, walking slowly, watchfully, toward the gash. "I will tear you out of my head."

And I have been waiting . . . since I came for you.

Wynn didn't want him to go anywhere near that gash. Something inside there was trying to use this murderous traitor for its own purpose. One malevolent force was manipulating another in this place, and she could do nothing to change it.

Deep-Root leaned through the gash, looking up and down the tunnel beyond it.

A heavy footfall echoed through the chamber, and he began to turn.

"Hiding among the Fallen?" someone shouted. "Running to your own . . . you traitor!"

The pound of their boots echoed like war drums. Three stonewalkers charged down the hall between the great basalt coffins.

Deep-Root fled into the gash, at first turning left. But something there glowed in the dark, like coals heating up under a harsh breath. He whirled and ran the other way down the raw tunnel—the direction that Wynn had gone herself.

She heard the footfalls and shouts of the others now in the tunnel. Deep-Root halted, listening to them coming nearer. He took a step toward the rough sidewall.

A soft, red glow rose in the tunnel's distance behind him.

Wynn heard a crack like breaking stone echo down the tunnel. Again and again it came, faster and faster, as it drowned out the pounding echoes of heavy boots. Three silhouettes of stonewalkers up the tunnel halted and looked back.

A hissing roar hammered Wynn's—Deep-Root's—ears and made the stone vibrate. Deep-Root sucked a breath as flame erupted up the tunnel.

It engulfed those three silhouettes before he could shield his eyes against the glare. Screams rose and were quickly smothered by crackling fire, and then the roar faded. Wynn saw one broad form aflame throw itself at the wall. It didn't pass through but toppled back, crumpling like the other two. She watched them come apart like cinders under a hot blaze.

The blast died away, and the only light left came from burning bodies and the scant flickering flames clinging to the floor, walls, and ceiling, as if they'd been splashed with oil. Beyond the dwindling flames, something came striding forward. The tunnel shuddered under its heavy, rhythmic steps.

Its head appeared, its jaws widening slightly.

Deep-Root looked up into the black orb eyes of a gí'uyllæ, an all-eater.

This was the all-but-forgotten word of his people for these winged reptiles. Wynn had other names for it, equally little known among other races, like . . .

Wêurm . . . thuvan . . . ta'nên . . . dragon.

This one was so much larger than the one Wynn had faced. Its back scraped the ceiling, grinding off bits of rock. Deep-Root reached for the tunnel wall as he lunged.

No, not this time.

His hand rammed painfully into stone and did not pass through. He didn't look back, but ran down the tunnel, away from the burning remains and deeper into the dark.

Wynn hadn't expected this place to be so similar to what she'd found, no matter that this beast was even more futile to fight. A part of her wanted it to catch her—to catch *him*—even if this was only a memory. Whatever happened, it would change nothing.

But if it did catch him, it wouldn't know of her. If he died would she die with him while locked in this memory?

Deep-Root slammed hard against stone in the dark. Wynn lost all feeling from his body for an instant. When awareness returned, he groaned upon the tunnel floor, reaching for his face. Touching his head only brought more pain.

Frail red light slowly lit the tunnel's dead end.

Deep-Root rolled over, scrambling up as he drew both daggers. Wynn didn't need to feel anything from him to know how much fear filled him now.

There was the dragon, filling the whole tunnel as its spittle dripped flames upon the stone floor. It just stood there, watching her—watching Deep-Root—as the chaos of the gale whispers grew to a storm.

Listen!

That leaf-wing crackle barely lessened the gale. At first, Wynn heard nothing, and Deep-Root wouldn't turn his back on the creature. Even if he were foolish enough to attack, his blades could do nothing to it.

They come. Listen . . . hear them and know . . . all here are lost.

The voice took away the gale's edge, making its cacophony of whispers grow distant, as if pushed back beyond the rough walls. Wynn felt a vibration beneath her feet.

Deep-Root hesitantly crouched, keeping his eyes on the dragon. He laid down one blade and flattened his hand on the stone. That vibration grew stronger, echoing through him. To Wynn, it was like listening to stone crack under some tool; it kept cracking and breaking and tearing without pause.

Something was coming up through the earth below the seatt.

She had seen the madness spreading here, but if enemy forces outside had blocked all entrances, why dig underneath, and why so fast? Surely they could hold this place until everyone within perished.

Yes, all will be lost. This is written in stone. But in death, what might come if you can kill me?

Deep-Root stared into the dragon's eyes, glistening with fire flickers like polished obsidian orbs. His blades were but slivers against an enemy of such size. The beast let out a rumble that made Wynn want to cover her ears. Deep-Root rose and backed against the dead end.

The dragon began retreating up the tunnel, its bulk too wide to turn about.

Stay here in the dark, listening and unseen at your end . . . or follow me. Either way, you will die, as written in the stone of your bones. But what purpose will death be remembered for, one day to come? Choose.

Its spittle no longer flickered with small flames, and the tunnel grew dark. Only the sound of the creature's steady retreat marked that it was still there, until it backed over the charred remains of stonewalkers. Blackened bones crackled under its clawed feet.

Wynn didn't know what she would've done in Deep-Root's place.

He took one hesitant step and then another as he followed. Once the dragon backed up to the breach into the Chamber of the Fallen, it turned about, heading up the dark tunnel's other way.

There were too many turns in the dark where unseen side ways could be felt in the walls. Wynn had long past lost track of where she was. But each time the way branched, Deep-Root followed the scrape of the beast's movement against the tunnel's stone, until he stopped at the sight of flame flickering in its maw.

It turned into a wide passage that sloped steeply downward. Again he followed. A long way down, it emptied into a vast cave, and the air of the place choked him. Wynn felt suffocated, as well, for the stench rose from a large, long pool of viscous fluids that filled most of the cave's bottom.

Soft light flickered red-orange. To one side of the cave, on a slope of rock, the dragon dripped ignited spittle that burned there well away from the large pool.

Sheath your weapons. Do not create even one spark in this place, or we perish to no purpose.

"What is this place?" Deep-Root choked out. "What is in that pool?"

I have eaten and disgorged all of this, weakening myself without true sustenance since my arrival. I am now prepared to die, if you can kill me. First, listen . . . and hear them.

The dragon lifted its head, looking to the cave's distant rear wall.

Deep-Root hesitated, but the beast merely stood waiting. He sheathed his blades and crept around the pool, never taking his eyes off the dragon. It watched him in turn. When he reached the cave's wall, he placed a hand on its stone.

At first he barely heard anything.

Higher.

At that command, he tried to find purchase in the wall for his foot. He reached upward, and the farther he went, the more he felt—heard—the same sound of endlessly breaking stone as in the dead end.

Deep-Root stretched as high as he could, until his thick fingertips touched where the wall curved into the cave's ceiling. The whisper gale rose to a roar in his head, as if he'd stepped into the storm's heart.

Wynn lost all awareness in that torrent.

When it finally faded, she was looking toward the pool, but it was sideways and low, as if Deep-Root lay on the cave's floor. She was sick with dizziness. Deep-Root moaned and pushed himself up as the leaf-wing voice came again.

They call themselves the in'Sâ'yminfiäl, the masters of frenzy. To the few who have ever escaped them and yet never have seen them, they are known as the Eaters of Silence. They have driven the peace from your people's thoughts—and driven them mad. Nothing can stop this now.

Wynn knew of whom the dragon spoke. She'd learn of these sorcerers, once in service to the Ancient Enemy in the forgotten war. If she'd had her own voice, she could've asked so many questions. But she was only an observer, reliving all this through Deep-Root's eyes and ears.

Your blades are worthless. Something greater is needed to breach my bowels, once I ignite what is left within me. And then . . .

The dragon looked to the pool, and Wynn went numb.

She didn't understand why it needed to be impaled, but it intended to somehow ignite all of the fluid it had disgorged. This place would collapse in an explosion, pulling down those who were right above, digging their way into the seatt. And she knew it would shatter this whole realm.

There is little time, for I cannot prepare all this again. Even now I fade in starvation. That is why I have made certain that what is done here is enough to reach them, no matter the cost.

Every question Wynn wanted to ask vanished as Deep-Root's breath caught.

The way out through the range will become their way, if they take this place—and they will. It is what they seek to gain as quickly as possible, at any price.

Wynn envisioned the map she'd sketched in her journal, looking for what lay just to the north of here.

But the price to stop them is even higher. To halt those who would breach this place, all here must die by our choice . . . though they would be lost just the same.

Wynn began to see the choice the dragon offered; it was no choice at all. Sacrifice an entire people to slow or cripple the enemy's advance, but with no certainty that it would bring ultimate victory. Or wait and hope that more of the dwarves here might yet escape this place of madness, but at the cost of the enemy achieving an unstoppable advantage.

She knew the path the siege forces would secure, for she had traveled it, and then nothing could stop more of them from following. The Slip-Tooth Pass would take them into the north, unseen until too late. The very tram tunnel that she had used would lead them right to it.

Unlike the horde of undead buried by time in the plain beyond the Lhoin'na forests, nothing would stop an invasion of the living from swarming over it, even into First Glade. Perhaps that was what they were after most of all, that one place the undead couldn't go. And then what would become of the Numan nations? Without First Glade, there would not even be a fragile sanctuary for the few who could reach it.

There is no more time. Either believe or not. If so, go and find what is needed. But if you die before it is your time, all is lost.

Wynn shrank in self-recrimination for all that she'd thought of Deep-Root in the passing season.

He turned and fled into stone.

Wynn choked for air, still immersed inside the memory.

Over and over Chuillyon prayed until the rise of Chârmun's presence within him grew into a pure silence, as if he were alone and all that was left alive in this world—as least for one more moment.

And that moment lingered on and on . . . too long.

Chuillyon clung to Chârmun's presence as he barely cracked open his eyes.

He stood there . . . alone . . . staring toward the dark breach where il'Sänke had madly thrown himself to his death. Even the flickers of fire on the stone had died, leaving only trails of smoke filling the air.

Where had the creature gone? Why would it leave him alive? For an instant, he wondered if his prayer to Chârmun had affected it, but that was a foolish thought.

From the moment Hannâschi had fallen, he had barely had the wits to think or feel anything. His gaze drifted to her, lying on the floor, and then continued onward, stopping at the charred pile that had been Shâodh.

Chuillyon quickly looked away from that unbearable sight, and it shook him from complacency. Only moments before, he had been ready to face death. He walked to the hall's end and dropped down beside Hannâschi. With a touch of his fingers, he found she still breathed weakly.

"Hannâschi?" he said softly, but her eyelids did not flutter.

Chuillyon picked up her fallen crystal, still bright with her warmth, and he looked into the breach beyond her.

He had no idea how or if Wynn had managed to pass the trap in the tunnel wall, nor how to do so himself. For that matter, Wynn would fare no better than Shâodh if the beast had gone her way.

His curiosity, his pride and arrogance, had cost Shâodh's life. Hannâschi was poisoned and might yet follow her loved one. And someone still had to survive to tell of this place, of what happened here . . . of what waited here.

Chuillyon lifted Hannâschi's frail form, which weighed so little in his arms. He realized he would not be able to pump the cart by himself all the way back beneath the range. They were nearly out of supplies, and they would not survive. He needed to get Hannâschi directly out of the seatt, into the open air, beneath the sky, where he could find food and build her strength before starting the journey home.

"Chârmun, be with me," he whispered. "Guide me out."

Ghassan lay stunned at the shaft's bottom. He had not been able to slow his descent enough and had hit hard. Afraid of moving too quickly and injuring himself further, he carefully drew his legs up toward his stomach, feeling for any sharp pains. His need to move on overrode fear of injury, and he pushed himself up.

Flashes of pain in his back and right leg nearly made him fall again. He fought them, and his arms did not give way. None of his bones seemed broken, but he was bleeding from multiple cuts and scrapes. His clothing was torn and shredded in many places.

Once he gained his feet, he found himself at the head of a downward-facing tunnel, though he had no idea where he was or how deep he might be. He took his first steps forward, and then a shrieking blast of wind rushed up the tunnel. It made the tatters of his cloak rise and thrash.

He knew that sound. He had heard it when facing the wraith in the streets of Calm Seatt.

Ghassan stumbled along the wall, following that wail.

Chane and Ore-Locks kept running, down and down. Chane had sheathed his short blade and pulled out the crystal Wynn had given him to light the way. All he could do was trust that Ore-Locks might guess the correct passage to keep descending.

The dwarf stayed in the main tunnel, never turning aside into smaller ones. Wynn believed the orb would have been guarded someplace deep in the seatt. This was all Chane had to go on in trying to fulfill her desperate plea.

He tried not to let himself think and kept running.

If you love me . . . then go, for me.

Was this the only way to prove his love? If so, then love was unfair.

Without warning, a shrieking wind tore up the tunnel.

Ore-Locks stalled, wide-eyed, and Chane darted around him without a pause.

"What is that?" Ore-Locks huffed from behind.

Chane did not answer, though he knew that sound. Wynn had forced him to sacrifice her for the orb, and he would not let Sau'ilahk have it.

As suddenly as the wind and noise had started, it died.

This time, it was Chane who faltered. He stood, listening for anything, but all was quiet. He bolted onward, and there were no more side passages along the way. A dead end appeared ahead, and he skidded to a stop in a small cave.

Ore-Locks stumbled in after him, panting too heavily. The cave was otherwise empty, and the wraith was nowhere to be seen.

Chane began to panic as he looked back up the tunnel. Had Sau'ilahk already found the orb and faded away? No, even in Calm Seatt the wraith had only been able to carry off transcription folios by hand. It had not even been able to make one follow it as it slipped through a scribe shop's wall.

"Look!" Ore-Locks said, panting. "What is it?"

Chane spun around and then froze at what lay in the back of the cave.

He and Welstiel had trailed Wynn and her companions seeking an orb secreted in an ice-bound castle in the frigid Pock Peaks. Magiere had found it on a pedestal, guarded and revered, in the center of a four-way stone bridge over a deep, volcanic fissure. Its resting place had been impressive . . . intimidating. This one lay abandoned, covered in dirt and dust and old bones.

Chane stepped closer, looking down at the globe of a dark material with a tapered spike piercing down through its center. Suddenly, this all seemed too easy.

"Is *that* what she has been seeking?" Ore-Locks asked.

Chane did not care to explain. A hunk of carved rock was not worth her life. But he had found it, seemingly undisturbed, and so quickly.

"Take it," he told Ore-Locks. "We go back now!"

The dwarf hefted the orb, appearing surprised at its weight, but he wrapped it under one arm while still carrying his iron staff.

"No!" someone snarled.

Chane whirled with his dwarven sword aimed point out. A tall figure limped into his crystal's light. At first he was uncertain who it was, and then he shook his head, not believing his eyes.

"Il'Sänke?"

The domin was a torn and bleeding mess, bracing one hand against the wall at the cave's mouth. He did not enter but stood there, blocking Chane's way.

"Give it to me," il'Sänke ordered, his voice low and hard. "Whatever it is, it must be protected. You and she are nowhere near capable of that."

"Who is this?" Ore-Locks demanded, taken aback that Chane and the intruder knew each other. "What is this . . . *thing* you all want?"

Chane kept his gaze locked on il'Sänke. His first instinct was to kill the man where he stood. But il'Sänke was more than a sage, perhaps more than a highly skilled metaologer.

For an instant, Chane almost considered giving up the orb. Even if he reached Wynn and found her still alive, after all she had suffered and all she had risked, how could he face her if he did so?

"Do not defy me," il'Sänke said, his voice deadly cold. "There is more at stake than you understand."

Chane tensed, ready to charge and strike.

Il'Sänke's gaze turned on Ore-Locks. As his bloody right hand shot out toward the dwarf, he began to whisper unintelligibly.

Chane knew what was happening, had seen it before. He quickly side-stepped between the two, breaking il'Sänke's line of sight to Ore-Locks.

Il'Sänke's eyes widened. He shook slightly as anger washed over his dark-tan face.

Chane suddenly remembered something that il'Sänke might not know. They all had abilities, powers, not just the domin. They could do things most people could not.

"Ore-Locks, go!" Chane said. "Take it into stone!"

It was a desperate move, but he saw no other choice.

"Neither one of you leaves with that!" Ghassan shouted, losing his composure.

He pushed off the wall, limping forward and shifting left around the cave wall.

Chane shifted too, keeping himself between the domin and the dwarf. He was losing precious moments, and desperation broke his control. The beast inside him surged, struggling against the violet concoction he had taken upon heading under the mountains.

Chane whirled with a wild slash at il'Sänke and shoved Ore-Locks toward the cave's rear wall.

"Go!" he rasped.

Ore-Locks started in surprise at the sight of him. Chane knew his eyes had lost all color, his features likely twisted into something feral. He did not care as long as Ore-Locks listened.

With one last glance, Ore-Locks backed into—through—the wall, and Chane turned on il'Sänke.

*　　*　　*

Ghassan's breath choked off as the dwarf simply sank into the cave's back wall and vanished.

Then Chane turned on him.

He couldn't help stumbling back at the sight of Chane's altered face . . . colorless eyes, elongated teeth, and twisted features. Chane rasped like a snake or a voiceless, rabid dog as he thrust his sword.

Ghassan flashed a hand in front of himself, focusing on the steel.

The blade swerved slightly at his gesture, striking into the wall at his side. He tried spinning away before the blade slashed across at him, but sharp pain in his right knee made his leg buckle. Ghassan tumbled down along the cave wall.

Bloodied and weak, he could feel his strength ebbing. He raised a shielding arm and tried to scramble back before Chane struck him down.

The blade never fell, and he heard only the sound of running feet.

Ghassan peered over his arm at an empty cave. When he flopped over to look up the tunnel, all he saw was a form fleeing by the fading light of a cold lamp crystal.

Ghassan rolled back, his heart pounding, as he looked at the cave's rear wall. None of this made sense. There was not even a hint of the dwarf's passing . . . and the orb was gone.

He had read Wynn's journal accounts of what she and three others named Magiere, Leesil, and Chap had found in a castle among the highest icy peaks of the eastern continent. The description of their find matched what had been under the dwarf's arm.

And where was Wynn, if Chane still . . . lived?

Pieces of the poem tumbled through Ghassan's head.

> *The Children in twenty and six steps seek to hide in five corners*
> *The anchors amid Existence, which had once lived amid the Void.*
> *One to wither the Tree from its roots to its leaves*
> *Laid down where a cursed sun cracks the soil.*
> *That which snuffs a Flame into cold and dark*
> *Sits alone upon the water that never flows.*
> *The middling one, taking the Wind like a last breath,*
> *Sank to sulk in the shallows that still can drown.*

And swallowing Wave in perpetual thirst, the fourth
Took seclusion in exalted and weeping stone.
But the last, that consumes its own, wandered astray
In the depths of the Mountain beneath the seat of a lord's song.

The anchors of the creation *were* the orbs. The poem was a puzzle, giving clues to their locations. Wynn had figured this out before he had.

There were others orbs hidden by the Children of the Ancient Enemy.

Ghassan struggled up, biting the inside of his mouth against the pain in his knee. What could he do now? Go after Chane, try to dip into his thoughts, and find where the dwarf might have gone?

That would not serve him. He had tried to hear Chane's thoughts once before and found nothing, as if the man—the undead—was not even there. Even if he could find the dwarf . . .

What if Wynn had sent those two on purpose, so the dwarf could take the orb? No one would know where he had gone, so that not even she or Chane would have knowledge of its new location.

Anxiety set in, and then a strange paranoia grew within Ghassan.

Had he underestimated her? Could Wynn be that devious? Did she know what he was . . . what he could do? Did she understand he was more than some guild practitioner of thaumaturgy or even conjury?

Did Wynn even suspect sorcery still remained hidden in the world?

He put a hand to his mouth, smearing blood across his face in the process. Perhaps he had been reckless to jump down that shaft. His body now betrayed him.

The medallion against his chest suddenly warmed. Amidst his turmoil, he ignored it at first. He had no wish to speak with Mujahid, and he waited for the medallion to grow cold again. It would if he did not answer.

The warmth did not fade, and he finally grabbed it.

What? he demanded.

Return now. Make all haste.

It was not Mujahid's voice in Ghassan's head, though he recognized it. His thoughts cleared at her urgent words.

"Tuthâna?" he whispered. "What . . . what is wrong?"

I cannot say, even in thought, for . . . It has awoken and might hear.

Ghassan's breath caught in his chest. *How did this happen?*
Hurry.

The medallion cooled in his grip. He plied his will upon it, crushing it in his hand as he tried to reach out for her.

"Tuthâna!"

No answer came, and he lingered, not daring to think of what his comrade's warning might mean. Some part of him felt like he had been defeated by the seatt itself, but he could do nothing more here. He had been away from his kind for far too long, and it appeared the worst had happened in his absence.

He had to reach home . . . quickly.

Ghassan limped up the tunnel, taking the side passage that led back to the shaft. He would have to crawl out the same way he had come in, the only sure path he knew.

If *it* had escaped, he could waste no time searching for another exit.

When Ghassan reached the shaft's bottom, he closed his eyes and focused all of his will, and he began to rise through the dark.

CHAPTER 26

Still lost in the memory, Wynn—Deep-Root—emerged in the glistening caves of the honored dead. He stepped out of stone, placing each foot slowly, fearful of making any sound. Then he crouched to feel the cave floor with one hand.

The leaf-wing still skittered in Wynn's mind, holding the whispers at bay, but beyond its influence, Deep-Root felt the gale whispers. They were distant, moving erratically, but they were out there, searching for him. He had no more time for caution.

He began searching quickly among the calcified figures and paused before one.

It was tall for a dwarf. Though mineral crust obscured details of its form, it held something long and narrow against its chest in a double grip. The object appeared to reach all the way to the cave floor, unless decades and centuries of buildup had dripped down to make it look so.

"Forgive me," Deep-Root whispered as he drew one heavy dagger. "I beg of you, grant me absolution for this sacrilege."

With a single, quickened breath, he struck the first blow.

He stabbed and hacked until Wynn saw a glint of tarnished and mottled steel. Then the sound of running boots echoed among the caves. Deep-Root dropped the dagger and grabbed the top of the object with both hands. Calcified stone fractured and broke as he wrenched it from the figure's grip.

Wynn thought she saw the petrified remains of dwarven arm bones as the figure's hands broke off, still bonded to the object. She wanted to cringe at the sight of them.

The footfalls grew loud and near.

Deep-Root whirled, and all he could do was raise the object he held. A blade cracked against it.

Pieces of calcified stone exploded around the impact as he saw another stonewalker with a maddened expression before him. Chips shot into his face, and even Wynn flinched at their patter. Deep-Root groped at his belt for his other dagger. The other stonewalker's hand closed into a massive fist, and he struck low.

Wynn felt the pain as if her own abdomen had been hit. Breath rushed from Deep-Root as he toppled back against the calcified figure.

"Your bones will not rest here!" the other stonewalker snarled. "We will leave you to rot with those outside who try to come for us."

His features glistened with a feverish sweat and were so twisted that Wynn couldn't tell if he was the same elder from before. Then she saw his blade coming again.

Deep-Root tried to block. The stonewalker's blade slipped off the object Deep-Root held up and tore down the left side of his scaled armor. Wynn heard steel-tipped scales screech under its passing.

Deep-Root cried out as he jerked his last dagger free. He slammed the long, crusted object into his attacker's face as he raised his blade. The stonewalker's head jerked in another spatter of calcified stone. Deep-Root swung downward, and his blade sank point first into the neck of the stonewalker's armor.

There was a wet, grating sound, like steel across stone—or bone—but the stonewalker didn't fall. He reeled back, his mouth gaping as he choked. Blood began seeping between his teeth and over his lower lip.

Wynn heard Deep-Root's dagger clatter on stone as he looked in horror at what he'd done. More footfalls and shouts echoed through the caves, growing louder and closer. Deep-Root raced across the cave and into a wall.

There had been no choice in what he'd done, and Wynn knew this. But in the darkness of stone, her own shame began to grow. She realized what he was about to do.

Deep-Root leaped out of stone into the dragon's deep cave. Mute whimpers escaped his mouth with each sobbing breath.

Wynn heard the echoes of pursuit rolling in from the tunnels above this place. When Deep-Root raised his sagging head, for a moment all she saw was a watery blur through his eyes, until he dragged the back of his hand across his face.

The dragon stood waiting in the middle of the viscous pool. It hung its head, its breath weak, but it gave Deep-Root not a moment's rest.

Strike below my last rib, upward into my chest, as if toward a heart. But only when I have begun my last flame and swallowed it down. Only then . . . only upon my command.

Deep-Root raised the stone-covered object in his hand.

So much of its mineral crust had broken away that Wynn saw parts of a long, thick blade. He grabbed the lumpy hilt, breaking away the remains of calcified fingers. With one hesitant glance up the sloping passage, he gripped the cleared hilt and slammed the crusted blade against the cave's wall. He beat it again and again until the sword's blade was nearly clear.

Every ringing blow sharpened Wynn's panic. It would be heard everywhere in these tunnels.

A shout erupted just before a splash.

Deep-Root turned wildly. Another of his brethren splashed toward him through the pool, and then came a slap upon stone that hummed through his bones. Up the sloping tunnel, another stonewalker had her hand firmly against the tunnel's rough wall. The sound of a blunt impact and rapid splashing pulled Deep-Root's attention the other way.

The dragon's head slammed against the wall as it staggered sideways in the pool. A stonewalker whipped an iron staff back for another strike.

Deep-Root splashed toward the dragon, but the beast suddenly righted itself.

Its head whipped around, its maw widening, and then it dipped its head and its mouth snapped shut with a crack. Half of its assailant vanished amid torn bowels. Spatters of blood rained down on Deep-Root.

Wynn suddenly shrieked, though it was Deep-Root's voice that cut loose. He arched away from a deep pain in his back so sharp that everything dimmed before Wynn.

When her sight cleared, she saw that he'd turned, knocking aside someone's arm. Yet the pain only increased as he chopped down with the sword.

The blade cleaved through a young stonewalker's skull, and Wynn saw the dwarf's face split open.

Deep-Root groped at his lower back, and Wynn felt the protruding hilt that he grabbed.

Now . . . before our deaths are wasted.

Deep-Root instantly released his hold on the blade in his back and turned.

The dragon lifted its head toward the cave ceiling. Amid a nerve-tearing clack of its jaws, flickers of fire rose between its teeth. Wynn thought she heard Deep-Root whispering something, over and over, but she was lost within herself.

If she'd been there, she would've done anything to help him. If nothing else, she would've thrown herself in front of any adversary to give him even one more moment to succeed. Inside of him, inside of this memory, she couldn't help but wonder . . .

Would she be trapped here to end along with him?

Deep-Root rushed in, placing the sword's point against the dragon's side, still whispering frantically.

Remember him . . . his words . . . our end, my children.

Before Wynn fathomed those last leaf-wing whispers she heard, Deep-Root threw his bulk against the sword.

A world of fire erupted, and then there was only whiteness. There was no one left to hear the silence in place of those gale whispers.

Wynn cried out as the memory ended. Remnants of the forgotten events washed though her with heat that couldn't be real.

Deep-Root and the dragon had sacrificed themselves, along with a seatt gone mad, to stop enemy forces from gaining access to the northern lands.

A multitongued voice rose in Wynn's mind.

Remember!

That word hung alone in the whiteness, which grayed and grew darker.

A flicker like a flame rose—but not in the dark. It reflected on twin obsidian orbs so large they blocked out everything else. Those twin eyes watched Wynn, as the dancing shimmers of orange-red within them spread everywhere in the dark . . . spread like memories in Wynn's mind.

As the last of Deep-Root's images faded, a fresh ache assaulted her. It was like something fiercely pulling at her thoughts, and she felt her own memories rising.

The world went black again for an instant. Then she saw herself moving backward in time, each memory coming more rapidly than the last. First was a clear image and the sensation of the pump cart as it moved, but it was moving backward. Every memory flowed in reverse to another as she relived . . .

. . . driving the wagon down the Slip-Tooth Pass . . .

. . . the attack of the Fay in the Lhoin'na great forest . . .

. . . traveling with Chane, Shade, and Ore-Locks on the ship as they journeyed toward Drist . . .

. . . fighting the wraith in the underworld of Dhredze Seatt . . .

. . . being shunned by her peers in the guild at Calm Seatt . . .

. . . Chane crouching on the ground near a stable, when he first handed her the scroll, lonely hope in his eyes . . .

. . . Shade diving from a dark street to protect her from the wraith . . .

. . . the journey from the Farlands to her homeland with Magiere, Leesil, and Chap . . .

And the images came even more rapidly.

. . . Sgäile lying dead under a willow tree . . .

. . . Chap helping her remove ancient texts from the ice-bound castle's library . . .

. . . battling Welstiel's feral vampires in that castle . . .

. . . jumping from a burning elven ship into a lifeboat with Osha . . .

. . . facing Most Aged Father before the council of the an'Cróan . . .

. . . sobbing with her head on Chane's bloody chest after Magiere cut off his head. . .

. . . standing beside Leesil as he uncovered the remains of the five races sacrificed for Magiere's birth . . .

. . . drinking mint tea with Chane, before she knew he was an undead, as they pored over historical parchments in peace and quiet at the guild annex in Bela . . .

Memories rushed back and back, until she stood in the central council hall of Bela. Leesil, Magiere, and Chap came walking down the broad passage. She looked down at Chap and then smiled up at Leesil, seeing his amber eyes for the very first time.

"Stop!" Wynn cried out.

Her shoulder suddenly ached, but her life continued to race by, as if it were only these tiny blinks of time.

Memories suddenly halted, leaving her in darkness, but the pain in her shoulder sharpened. Behind a leaf-wing's cacophony, broken words echoed over and over.

—*Wynn . . . come back. . . . Wynn . . . wake up*—

Wynn opened her eyes to Shade standing above her. Shade's jaws were clamped on her shoulder, biting through the cloak, as the dog pulled and shook her.

"Don't," Wynn moaned, reaching up.

But lying there on the tunnel floor, the unfamiliar *presence* remained inside her head. The sensation was nothing like the feel of sharing memories with Shade, or Chap's multilingual voice in her head. It was harsh and unbreakable, and Wynn clamped her eyes shut again.

It was so deep inside her that she could feel emotions that weren't her own. Hope and suspicion, spite and hesitation, all crawled about inside her, as if that presence was searching for something.

Wynn cracked open her eyes.

She looked up into twin obsidian orbs in a reptilian head that filled her view. The dragon stared down at her, unblinking, its presence so deep inside her that she began to sense something of it in turn.

It was a descendant of the one who'd come for Deep-Root. It had been waiting here for so long . . . for something. That other, greater dragon and that forgotten and fallen stonewalker raised one question in Wynn's mind.

Where was Ore-Locks?

A pounding sound overlayed with the grating of massive claws finally broke through her haze. She lifted her head at the vibrations in the tunnel floor beneath her back.

Another dragon, not quite as large as the first, crawled down the tunnel from the direction of the breach into the Chamber of the Fallen. Shade released her grip on Wynn's shoulder and turned to snarl at it.

The second dragon halted, fixing on Shade.

Wynn was frozen in confusion. A soft sound of lighter footsteps echoed from down the tunnel into the dark. When she looked, a light came bobbing up out of the dark behind the first dragon.

Chane ran into view, and Wynn pushed herself up to sit. He had his sword in one hand, and his eyes sparked without color in the light of his crystal. His features were twisted with panic and blind rage, like that night back in First Glade.

The first dragon snaked its head back toward him, and Chane raised his blade.

"No!" Wynn shouted.

Chane saw Wynn on the tunnel floor with the reptile's massive head hovering over her. The sight magnified his fear until even the beast within him struggled to rouse from under the violet concoction that kept him awake. He raised the sword, ready to strike once and slip past to Wynn.

Shade snarled and whirled the other way.

But then Chane saw the second winged monster up the tunnel, and his self-control drained away completely. He lunged as the first one turned its head his way. Wynn cried out, but he only heard her panic and not her words. As he swung, the nearer creature drew its head aside, opening its maw with a hiss. Not even the threat of all-consuming fire cut through Chane's madness to get to Wynn.

"Chane, stop it!"

He heard Wynn's call at the edge of his awareness, distant and echoing, like something tapping him awake from dormancy.

"He's not what you think," she shouted, her voice echoing in the tunnel.

Chane faltered before he swung. Those words had not been for him—but for whom?

The question awakened reason, and Chane stopped no more than a sword's reach from the creature's jaws. He smelled its breath, hot and stinking like something akin to smoke and oil. The stench cleared his thoughts a little more.

Rushing in blindly would not save Wynn. Somehow, he knew this.

Chane fought for reason, struggling to swallow down the hunger and rage and the half-awakened beast inside him. The reptile's maw slowly closed, but it did not turn from him. He kept his sword cocked upward as he looked at Wynn.

"Did you find it?" she called to him, her voice desperate.

It? What did she mean?

Wynn glanced once down the tunnel, beyond him. She appeared less afraid of those creatures penning her in than of something else.

Chane remembered the orb.

"Where is Ore-Locks?" she asked in alarm. "Where's the wraith?"

Chane's clarity sharpened, and he cowed the stirring beast inside him.

"Ore-Locks . . ." he began. "I sent him. . . . He took the orb into stone before il'Sänke could take it."

Wynn's eyes widened. "Il'Sänke? What are you—?"

"He is here. He tried to take it."

"You gave the orb to Ore-Locks?"

Chane faltered in shame, not knowing what to say. He had let Ore-Locks take the one thing she sought at all cost, because reaching her mattered more to him than anything.

"I had to," he finally answered.

To his surprise, Wynn nodded. "It's all right. He'll come back."

Chane stared at her, dumbfounded by her sudden calm. She knew no such thing.

"You did everything right," she said. "Everything."

At a complete loss, he stood there looking at this small woman who had brought him halfway across the world. He understood only that she was alive, whole, and unharmed. This was all that mattered.

Wynn watched in relief as the soft but pale brown color flooded Chane's irises. He lowered his sword. Before she could take a step toward him, multitongued words exploded in her head.

There is more to learn . . . and to discern.

As before, she felt emotions—hesitation and suspicion and doubt. She spun sharply to see the second dragon coil and turn, heading back up the tun-

414 · BARB & J. C. HENDEE

nel. Shade rumbled, backing up, but then she turned, rounding Wynn with a nudge. Yet when Wynn looked back at the first dragon, she found it still blocking Chane's way. Before she could say anything, more words filled her head in every language she knew.

Not this unliving thing. It will no longer defile this place of sacrifice.

The dragon had seen all her memories. It should know better.

"You know how I see him," she answered. "Without him, I wouldn't be standing here. And the orb wouldn't have been saved without him."

You saved nothing!

At those sharp words, Wynn heard Shade yelp, and everything darkened for an instant before her eyes. The dragon swung its head away from Chane and turned on her. Its jaws parted in a hiss as spittle struck the tunnel floor.

We have no faith in your kind, no trust in you to keep a prisoner of Existence out of the claws of the first slave. The shackled one is not for you! We give the anchor of Earth only to the blood of the sacrifice. It is now his to protect. Move on . . . or die with your walking dead!

Wynn forced herself not to flinch at a flickering flame sparking between the creature's grinding teeth. Her mind raced over its words.

The "blood of sacrifice" was clearly the descendant of Deep-Root. But Ore-Locks was gone, and she didn't know where he was or when he would return. The "anchor" had to mean the orb itself. But the strange reference to a "shackled one," a "prisoner," and keeping it from a "first slave," left her bewildered.

What did any of this have to do with the orb?

More than you deserve to know.

Wynn stilled her thoughts, for every one of them was exposed to this ancient being. She looked at Chane, and as much as she feared shattering this very fragile respite, she couldn't accept leaving him after what he had done.

Then it is upon your life that he comes.

Again, the reply came before Wynn could speak. She carefully waved Chane to her. Without hesitation, he sidled around the creature, coming to her as quickly as he could without breaking into a run. The open relief on his face pulled at Wynn.

"Put the sword away," she whispered. "Don't draw it again, no matter what happens."

Chane shook his head, his expression hardening, and the color began to fade from his eyes.

"Trust me," she said.

He tensed at her urging. She wasn't certain anything she said or did would get through to him. Finally, he slid his sword back into its sheath.

The dragon watched his every move.

The second one had stopped up the tunnel, as if waiting. Wynn headed after it, with Chane behind her and Shade in the lead. The first creature followed, and soon all Wynn could hear was the sound of claws scraping stone.

"Where are we—?" Chane began.

She quickly glanced back and shook her head at him. There was so much she had felt in the ancient memories of these beings. She knew they were descended from the one who'd sacrificed itself with Deep-Root. They had been here, one generation after another, guarding the orb, but for reasons she couldn't fathom.

That they continued to fulfill their ancestor's stand against the enemy was clear. But whether they were truly allies was not so certain. They wanted something from her, and she didn't believe she would walk out of this seatt unless she fulfilled whatever they required.

Soon they passed the breach into the Chamber of the Fallen, but the lead dragon continued up the tunnel's other way. Along the winding passage, Wynn saw it pause briefly ahead at turns, breaks, and splits in the tunnel. They kept on at a pace that forced her into a half trot, and soon she emerged in a pocket of deeply sloping stone.

The smaller, lead dragon settled on a rise of stone near one of the side walls. The surface beside it was strangely smooth, though it slanted toward the pocket's roof. Wynn squinted, letting out a bit more light from the crystal in her hand.

There were ragged marks in the walls, as if clawed into the stone, but the longer Wynn looked, a pattern began to emerge.

You will wait here . . . for him.

She looked back to find the first dragon inside the pocket's opening, blocking the way.

"I don't know where Ore-Locks is," she answered. "How could he find us here?"

The blood will come to its own.

As if on cue, heavy footfalls echoed from the tunnel beyond the pocket.

Ore-Locks appeared at the opening, carrying the orb under one arm and the iron staff in his other hand. At first, Wynn could only focus on the orb. She remembered how heavy the orb of Water had been. She was astonished he could carry the orb of Earth with one arm.

At the sight awaiting him, Ore-Locks's eyes widened. He backstepped, leveling his staff one-handed at the first dragon. It didn't even look at him, but shifted to make room for him to enter.

"Ore-Locks," Wynn said, waving him in.

He blinked at her, hesitated longer, and then cautiously crept down the passage.

"What is happening?" he asked.

The answer lashed every other thought from Wynn's mind.

Look upon the last words, and speak them to him.

The second dragon swung its head toward the marred wall.

Wynn stepped closer, examining the claw marks. "I cannot read these," she said, but words began filling her head.

Chane watched Wynn's face as she flinched. Words poured from her mouth in Numanese as if she performed a recitation.

> *May I be forgotten for what I do.*
> *May I die in Eternity for the choice I make.*
> *May the necessity never be used to forgive me.*
>
> *Let my people live again, but without the horror that I am.*
> *Let my name be forgotten by all but one.*
> *May only my brother . . .*

Wynn faltered, and her breath caught sharply. She covered her mouth, and a tear slipped from her left eye.

Chane put a hand on her shoulder, but before he could speak, she went on.

May only my brother . . .

And again the words seemed to catch in her throat.

. . . remember me,

As I was before this fall.
In that, by our blood, I bind him,
To silence my name forever.
I, Deep-Root, of the family of Rain, Tangle-Root clan of the
Laughing Crag tribe in the nation of the Seatt under a Lord's Song,
wish to be no more.

Chane felt Wynn shudder at every word, though she had faltered twice on one phrase. The brother mentioned in the verse had been admonished never to tell of Deep-Root, should that brother have actually survived what had happened here a thousand years ago.

Wynn heard every word in every language she knew. She could never have read the gouges on the wall, for those marks of these creatures were utterly unknown to her. And even so, what they'd recorded was from a lost dialect of Dwarvish.

The dragon guardians had recorded and passed down the last words—the last whispers—of Deep-Root damning himself to eternal death.

Without remembrance, he chose to pass into nothingness rather than the afterlife of this world in his people's beliefs. He cut himself off from them. The few who remembered only the title of Thallûhearag were no better than Wynn in their ignorance.

But Wynn had recited less than what the dragons had read into her thoughts. Strangely, neither of them had reproached her for this.

A command erupted in her head.

You will tell him everything we showed you of the past.

Wynn turned around. "Ore-Locks . . . Ore-Locks, I'm . . ."

He looked so stricken that she faltered at where to begin. She looked to those marks on the wall, and then to the floor—to anywhere besides his face. She began recounting what she'd lived within Deep-Root's memories. She never heard a sound from him. When she came to the moment of Deep-Root's choice, tears were running down her face. Her knees went weak and she sank.

Strong hands caught her from behind. Chane held her up, and she let him, but not once could she bear to look into Ore-Locks's face. Not even as she finished.

"I'm sorry," she kept whispering, but it sounded weaker, more inadequate each time.

Ore-Locks still said nothing. And then Shade broke the silence with a snarl.

Wynn raised her eyes just enough to see Shade stalk toward the dragon by the wall. Shade looked so tiny before that great being, but it shifted immediately out of Shade's way, never causing the dog to pause. She paced at the pocket's back and then craned her neck, looking at Ore-Locks.

A pile of blackened shapes lay beside Shade's forepaws. She lowered her muzzle to them as the multitongued voice spoke to Wynn again.

Tell him to take up his blood . . . take what is his.

Wynn blinked hard, wiping her face with a sleeve to clear her eyes. She squinted at *bones* by Shade's feet. There weren't enough for an entire body, but she realized whose they were.

Those were the last remains of Deep-Root. The dragons must have unearthed what they could find over the centuries.

Ore-Locks set down the orb and his staff, and he slowly walked over. He fell to his knees before the bones, and just knelt there in stillness. When he started to reach for them, Wynn pulled out of Chane's hold, frantically trying to strip off her cloak. Chane helped her, and she clutched it as she approached.

Almost afraid to come too close, she held back until Ore-Locks looked up.

Anger crossed his broad face. She couldn't bear it, and dropped her gaze as she held out the cloak. When he didn't take it, she crouched to place it on his folded knees.

"They say the orb is only for you," she whispered. "You are its guardian now."

He still said nothing, and Wynn watched only his hands as he began lifting the bones one at a time. He was so slow and gentle, as if any one of them might crumble to ash.

Wynn watched Ore-Locks place each bone in the small cloak, but she never looked up into his eyes.

CHAPTER 27

All the way back through the seatt to the tram station, Chane kept a careful watch, peering into a thousand darkly shadowed corners. Once, he made Wynn sit and rest while he claimed to scout ahead, but that was not all he did. Out of everyone's sight, he took another half dose of the violet concoction. They were far from out of danger yet, and he could not afford to be taken by dormancy.

When they finally crawled through the makeshift hole at the cave-in, he was not surprised to find two rather than one pump cart on the other side. Il'Sänke must have come on the second one, but the domin seemed to have vanished.

Chane wanted Wynn as far from this place as possible, and he quickly put her and Shade aboard. Then, he and Ore-Locks began pumping for the long journey back. Still, Chane watched the shadows, though il'Sänke was not foremost in his thoughts.

He found no vindication in being proven right about the wraith. Much the opposite. He had terrorized Wynn before this journey began, in the hope of planting doubt in her certainty that the wraith was finished.

He wished he had been wrong. He wished he could beg her forgiveness for what he had done.

Days and nights followed, but by the time they made it through the long tunnel and emerged again into open air—taking refuge where the Slip-Tooth Pass met the Sky-Cutter Range—only one thing preoccupied Chane.

Wynn appeared broken; he could not save her from everything, most especially herself.

Too often, when she had sought what was most crucial or necessary, others paid the price. While he did not care about that, it was unbearable to watch her sit hunched before the campfire. He stood outside camp, where the firelight barely reached him. Even with Shade's head in her lap, Wynn looked at nothing but the crackling flames.

"Why did you tell me to go . . . when that Suman found us?"

The sudden question broke Chane's train of thought. He swiveled his head to find Ore-Locks standing a few paces to his right. But the dwarf was not looking at him, only at Wynn.

Chane took too long to answer, and Ore-Locks finally turned to him. Only a hint of suspicion and revulsion lingered there, but in that moment the dwarf asked about, perhaps he had seen who Chane truly was.

"Why did you risk her," Ore-Locks went on, "and trust me . . . when she would not? How did you know you could trust me?"

"I did not *know*," Chane answered tiredly. "There was no *knowing* anything at all."

It was not that simple. It was also not a real answer, but Chane did not have one yet.

How could he say that a part of him had not cared what happened to the orb, as long as he could reach Wynn? In doing what she asked, he had still made that choice to trust Ore-Locks. It had come and gone in an instant, when reason and knowing had been lost.

Only the beast had remained, half-aware behind Chane's desire for Wynn, or so it seemed now. This frightened him, even as he obsessed over it.

"You should get some rest," he said.

But Ore-Locks still stood there, watching Wynn.

In one piece of luck, they had found both horses nearby, drinking from a mountain brook. The animals were in surprisingly good shape and fit to pull the wagon. However, as if to quell this bit of fortune, Chane found three other horses, as well, along with three elven saddles tossed into the brush. He did not know what this meant, but it supported Ore-Locks's earlier claim; they had been followed, and not just by il'Sänke. Perhaps the Suman sage had not been on the second cart.

Who had ridden those other horses?

"Shade and I will go hunting," Chane said. "After that, we will stop only for food or to rest the horses. I will keep us moving at night, and you will in the day, with Shade to keep watch with you. We will find a way to cut through to the coast rather than go anywhere near the Lhoin'na . . . especially with what you now carry."

Ore-Locks sighed, nodding as he folded his arms.

Chane stepped slowly into camp but stopped short, not wanting to startle Wynn. Even as Shade lifted her head, Wynn did not move. She showed no sign of even hearing his approach. Chane was uncomfortably aware of Ore-Locks out in the dark, more so than the dwarf even knew. For Wynn's guilt toward the wayward stonewalker was anchored by something more.

In the seatt, when they had reached the pump carts, and before even starting the journey back, Wynn requested—insisted—that Ore-Locks never openly speak of Deep-Root.

That name had been erased, replaced with a title that even those few who remembered it wanted forgotten, forever dead. Deep-Root had wanted his name buried. He had not wanted anyone to know the truth, that his brethren had gone mad and turned against their own people.

After Wynn made this request, Ore-Locks had turned on her with the first words he had spoken since finding his ancestor's bones. The entire incident was burned into Chane's memory forever.

Wynn had stood in silence, offering no defense, as Ore-Locks verbally tore her apart. On some level, Ore-Locks must have known she was right. Still, he assaulted her with the anger and pain he had locked away—as there was no one else to take the blame.

Chane had stood there in silence.

Though he had tensely watched Ore-Locks for any sign of violence other than words, he never interceded. Wynn would not have wanted him to. Perhaps she knew Ore-Locks deserved a chance to vent his anguish.

In the end, Ore-Locks had fallen silent, exhausted.

Even if he had wanted to clear his ancestor's name, what proof did they have of the truth?

There was no proof.

The world knew nothing of Deep-Root. Those who knew the title of Thallûhearag—the Lord of Slaughter—knew only what it meant and not why. They wanted to forget even that. As to Deep-Root's true fate, Ore-Locks had only the words of a scaled creature guarding a tool of a forgotten enemy.

The tale of how Ore-Locks had acquired such knowledge would be far less believable than the reviled legend of Thallûhearag, even if proclaimed in the most aggrandized telling that any greeting house of Dhredze Seatt had ever heard.

All Wynn could offer Ore-Locks was agreement to let him tell Cinder-Shard everything. The master of the Stonewalkers, who had taken in the youngest son of the Iron-Braids, might believe such a tale. Ore-Locks could lay his ancestor to rest among the honored dead of Dhredze Seatt, no longer forgotten, no longer eternally dead, at least not to him.

Chane watched Wynn before the fire, but he could not send her off to sleep. Beside her bedroll in the wagon's back was another reminder of how little had been gained for her, as well. Yes, the orb lay there, hidden beneath a tarp, but what did that matter? Chane could not understand how or why he had obtained it so easily when the wraith had gone on ahead of them. And where was Sau'ilahk now?

Nothing was this easy. They could not be so fortunate. In that, he had no faith.

Worse still, Chane wondered why Wynn kept so silent as she stared vacantly into the flames.

All along the coastal journey north, from one ship to the next, Chane and Ore-Locks kept watch to see if they were followed. Between Sau'ilahk, il'Sänke, and perhaps some mysterious elves, there were too many who had followed them into that dead seatt.

Chane took pains to make Shade understand that she was to stay awake in Wynn's room during the nights. He removed his ring more often to clear his own awareness on deck, though he never sensed anything, and Shade never raised warning.

Winter had passed and spring encroached by the time they reached port at Calm Seatt. They walked the city streets, making their way toward the guild. But when it loomed ahead along Old Procession Road, Chane suddenly stopped.

Wynn took three more steps before realizing. Chane faltered at first, for there was something more he had put off telling her.

"I am leaving," he said abruptly.

Wynn's startled face made him regret his choice of words, and he rushed on.

"No. . . . Do not be . . . I am going with Ore-Locks to Dhredze Seatt, to keep the orb secure until he takes it into hiding with the Stonewalkers. It should be . . . safer there than anywhere else. Even if Sau'ilahk still follows, he would hesitate at ever entering that place again."

Her face was pale with exhaustion, and her eyes just as bleak as that night by the campfire.

"I should come with you."

"No, go inside, and *stay* there," he ordered, then caught himself. "For me, please. Sleep in your room, eat something decent, and rest. Ore-Locks and I can travel faster if we travel by . . . his method."

Wynn looked at him for a long moment, realizing what he meant, and finally nodded. "All right."

"Do not leave the guild," he said firmly, and looked at Shade to make certain she understood. "Ore-Locks will arrange a schooner to return me across the bay. I should only be away two nights."

He was surprised by the distress on her face. Did she fear he might not come back? He began digging into his pack until he felt a cylinder of old, worn tin.

"Here," he said.

Chane held out the case containing the ancient scroll that had once led him to her. The same one that bore a poem as yet fully translated, its parts having led them this far together. Giving her this was the only thing he could think of to assure her.

"For safekeeping," he told her, and he turned to head back to port.

Something grasped his hand.

He did not turn or even dare look down. He was too afraid, for there were still too many unanswered questions between them.

But he squeezed Wynn's hand once before letting go.

The following night, Chane stood alone in the temple proper of Feather-Tongue.

He stared up at the massive statue of that Bäynæ—dwarven Eternal—who had been missing from the great hall of Bäalâle Seatt. The oil lanterns in their brackets cast upward shadows on its features, and Chane could not help feeling as if it watched him.

Ludicrous notion.

In one blind moment, he had stepped into a sacred space, not knowing what would happen. He had not even thought about it. Not as he had when Wynn first brought him to the temple's outer doors. Not as he had when they had walked the outer hallway beyond this round chamber, and he had flinched, drawing himself back, at each opening into this chamber.

Now he stood, whole and unbroken, in a sacred space.

All around him, the walls were marked in engraved emblems he could not read, though he wished he could. Then he heard the heavy, booted footfalls approach the temple proper's opening behind him.

"Is it safe?" he asked without turning.

When no answer came, Chane lowered his gaze and looked back.

Ore-Locks stood inside the archway, dressed in the black, scaled armor of his brethren. He looked up at the statue of Feather-Tongue, frowning in puzzlement. When he lowered his gaze to Chane, that same perplexed expression remained.

How strange it must appear to Ore-Locks that a monster with a mindless beast within should be found standing before a patron of knowledge in a place of faith.

"I brought what you asked for," Ore-Locks said, stepping closer, "though I wonder why. Do not eat them raw, since they must . . . be . . ."

Ore-Locks faltered, for what would a Noble Dead, an undead, want with food of any kind?

"They are not for eating," Chane replied. "Something else . . . something for Wynn."

Taking the cloth from the dwarf's hand, he opened it and found a pile of strange little fungi, or mushrooms, grown only by the dwarves. Their caps were unusual, spreading in multiple branches that flattened at their ends, almost like tiny leaves. Muhkgean, they were called. Along with the white flowers of the Lhoin'na, they were one more component from the list in the *Seven Leaves of Life* to create a healing concoction.

He was careful not to touch the mushrooms with his bare hands. After what had happened with the *anasgiah*, he would take no chances.

"Thank you again," he repeated. "How can I reach you, if necessary?"

Ore-Locks paused. "A head shirvêsh at any temple can contact Master Cinder-Shard. Send word here, and I will receive it by dawn or dusk."

A moment's silence passed between them. Ore-Locks looked up at Feather-Tongue once more and then glanced sidelong at Chane. A bit of old suspicion and hardness resurfaced in his broad features, though it faded after a perplexed shake of his head.

"The world I wanted is still buried," he said. "Changed to something I do not want."

"It has not changed," Chane said quickly. "It has always been what it is. All that changes is what we know—or believe—though it might be other than what we wish."

Ore-Locks nodded and hung his head, staring at the floor stones.

"A schooner waits below, as promised. Make sure you board and get below tonight. It leaves at dawn," he muttered, then raised his eyes to Chane. "Safe journey . . . and a little peace, while it can last."

By the time Ore-Locks's footsteps faded down the long hall to the temple door, Chane finally turned to leave.

Walking through this place of . . . belief, he pondered everything he had been through in the past few moons, thinking on what he himself truly believed in.

He believed in Wynn.

The Wynn that he now knew was a far cry from the vision born on the first night they had met. In the guise of a minor young noble with scholarly interests, he had visited a small barracks refurbished for sages in the faraway capital of his homeland. That escape into the realm of the living had quickly died at Magiere's appearance, that half-living, other "monster" who had taken so much from him.

Chane's illusions of Wynn had taken longer to pass. From their first night over a rickety table strewn with ink bottles, quills, and parchments, the air laced with the scent of mint tea, she might have been all he would have wanted as a companion . . . in life.

How much had changed since then—and how much had not. He had watched her fall bit by bit from his greater vision of all that her guild and she represented. Then she had struck him down with four words.

If you love me . . .

That utterance did not confirm that she felt the same for him. This was not something he could yet risk believing—putting his faith in—in place of knowing. But that challenge had trapped him, forced him beyond all reason and knowing. Perhaps only instinct had led him through that crisis.

How could he love her and yet deny what she believed in?

The answer had been with him, in him, since the moment she had spoken those four words.

Whether he accepted the way Wynn saw the world or he believed any part of what she saw to come did not matter. If he ever wanted her, he had to want what mattered to her. It was necessary to believe in her.

If he were ever to mean anything more to her, she had to be the heart of his faith.

Dusk had passed by the time the schooner landed the next night. Chane disembarked and made his way back to the Guild of Sagecraft.

He walked right through the inner bailey gate, for not one city guard had been posted outside. Even the outer portcullis was left raised. No attendant came out to greet him.

It seemed a season without death had fostered some irrational notion among the sages that this place was once more safe. Or perhaps the sight of the city's oldest castle, a bastion of knowledge, being locked up and guarded was no longer acceptable before the people's eyes by the royals of Malourné.

Either way, it was a fool's arrogance to Chane.

He grew angry as he strode out of the gatehouse tunnel into the inner courtyard beneath the light of the great torches above him. Where was Wynn, left so exposed here—in her room, in the common hall, or perhaps the library or archives? Uncertain, he turned toward the southern barracks, where all upper apprentices and journeyors were housed.

Without breaking stride, he slipped a hand into his pocket and drew out the cold lamp crystal Wynn had left with him. He rubbed it, quickly and briskly, across his thigh.

Entering the barracks, he made his way up to the door of Wynn's room and opened it. Just as he was about to step inside, movement down the passage's dead end caught his eye.

"Sir . . . ?" a frightened, wavering voice asked.

A small form in a tan robe came out of the shadows. It was a little girl with freckles and pigtails. Chane remembered her as the one who had been arguing with her friends about Shade that night when Wynn first told him the council had approved their journey.

Eyes wide, head craned back to look up at him, she held out a piece of parchment, and her voice wavered.

"Journeyor Hygeorht said to give this to you if you returned this evening."

Chane took the parchment, unfolded it, and read it.

> *Chane,*
> *All is well. I'm down in the archives and will return soon. Wait for me in my room.*
>
> *Wynn*

The words brought a mix of annoyance and relief. He had wanted her to stay out of sight, but at least the need to search onward may have pulled her from too much despair. He paused, looking again at the note's script. He had not even thought about it in his distraction with the messenger.

It was written in the Begaine syllabary, though the symbols were purposefully simplified.

Why had Wynn done this? Why had she sent this child in pigtails to give it to him? Then he remembered the initiate telling her friends she was fluent in Begaine.

So many secrets, so much of importance was often written in the syllabary. Remaining with Wynn, believing in her—in her cause—would be more complicated than he had ever imagined. Until last night, he had never given it this much thought amid his fantasies. If he wanted her, and her world, more changes had to be made.

"Kyne . . . is it not?" Chane asked, looking down at the girl.

Puzzlement began to outweigh the nervousness marring her small features. She nodded but did not speak.

"I have heard that . . . Wynn says . . ." he began, and faltered in the attempt. "She told me you grasp the Begaine syllabary better than most . . . for your age."

She cringed at the sound of his maimed voice. Her lips parted as if to speak, but she could not find her voice.

"You will teach . . ." Chane started to demand, and then halted. It took effort to force a softer tone. "I would like . . . be grateful, if you could assist— tutor—me . . . when you are able."

She blinked once and then twice more, but did not move.

"Please," he added too sharply.

Chane's patience thinned quickly in the waiting silence. Suddenly, she took a step closer. In her slow approach, her gaze kept flicking to the glowing crystal in his hand.

That lure had the effect he expected, as predictable as a dropped pouch of coins at an alley's mouth when he hunted in the night streets of a city. Or at least it caused enough confusion to make her wonder against her fear of him.

She moved even closer and glanced into Wynn's empty room.

No doubt she had seen him before with a journeyor who had wandered the world like no other and returned with wild tales, and with a dark majay-hì out of folklore. What the girl did not know—what no one here knew for certain— was of the monster who had followed Wynn across half a world.

Kyne looked up, her voice still lost, and only nodded again.

Chane held out his free hand, and she took it.

Her tiny palm felt overly warm and a bit sweaty. She jumped at his grip, likely too cold in her own. He led her down the stairs to where the parallel passage through the keep wall at the back of these barracks emptied into the initiates' outer ones.

"Your message is delivered," he said. "Go to bed."

Chane watched as she scurried off, though she glanced back at him several times. When she finally vanished from sight, he made his way back to Wynn's room. Closing his hand over the crystal as he entered, he peered out the window to the inner courtyard below.

No one was out there, and he stood waiting in the dark, watching for Wynn.

The beast inside him strained at its bonds, but he pushed it down, focusing on one truth. He would now viciously guard this place—as well as all who resided here, worthy or not.

And he would do so for as long as Wynn would allow him.

EPILOGUE

Wynn sat in an intersection alcove, deep in the guild's catacombs, while Shade lay on the floor, watching her. Upon the night of her return, she'd sought out Domin High-Tower to give proper notice that she was back. She preferred to deal with him rather than Premin Sykion, but her effort hadn't mattered.

The impassive way that High-Tower looked at her suggested he already knew. Some word must have reached him, and he'd merely dismissed her to her quarters. He hadn't even told her to remain on grounds; he didn't have to.

So much had happened over the course of a single winter.

Wynn had watched helplessly as her guild began to curl up on itself, one faction or branch turning against the others in distrust, suspicion, and secrecy. The Fay had come for her again, manifested in anguish and anger like some avatar of a divine force called by a wild priestess. In dead Bäalâle Seatt, the forgotten gí'uyllæ—the all-eaters, the dragons—whose generations went back to the first animate life that had walked in Existence, were found guarding a weapon and waiting for the blood of Deep-Root to come.

And in one desperate moment, Wynn had bent Chane to her will by his love for her.

In that, she'd revealed that she knew how he felt, though she couldn't even consider how she felt about him. That was too much, yet too little a thing, in the face of everything else.

The light of a cold lamp exposed one open book upon the table before

Wynn, and the sun crystal staff leaned beside her. Chane's scroll lay nearby, as did her new journal of short, cryptic entries in convoluted Begaine symbols. This single, brief journal was all that she needed now that she had Shade.

The old journals that she'd burned weren't truly gone. What they'd contained was now even farther beyond anyone's reach than ashes. On the nights she'd sat alone with only Shade, preparing scant, cryptic notes in the new journal, she'd silently read every line in the old journals, over and over, until . . .

Shade had echoed back every word.

Shade might never speak with Wynn as Chap had done, but Shade could do one thing perhaps even better than her father. Along with any memory Wynn recalled, once Shade understood something, she remembered it—perfectly.

What better place to hide secrets than with the one who would never forget the smallest detail? Who better to secure knowledge than such a companion, a majay-hì from whom no one could forcefully take it?

Shade understood why this was necessary. Perhaps she would finally come to understand the risks Wynn had taken—would continue to take.

A whining rumble made Wynn stiffen on her stool, and she looked up.

Shade stood before the alcove opening leading back toward the stairs up to the guild. She'd been fidgeting more and more as the night grew later.

"Stop!" Wynn said. "There's no one else down here . . . and I already took you outside after dinner."

Just like with Shade's father, Wynn sometimes slipped up when frustrated or exhausted. She forgot the powerful spirit and unique intelligence hidden in the guise of a young animal.

Others saw them as majay-hì, mere mythical beasts of awe. Even most Lhoin'na, who regarded them as sentient and free-willed, treasured them with too much reverence to understand them as individuals.

Wynn knew better, which added a spike of guilt to her burdens.

"I'm sorry," she whispered, expecting a petulant retort in broken memory-words.

But Shade merely returned to Wynn, not even grumbling. With a sigh, Wynn propped her elbows on the table and dropped her forehead into her palms.

Three of the five orbs were still missing, and what had finding the second one truly accomplished? Chane had kept it from Sau'ilahk, but still, Wynn knew next to nothing of the orbs' creation or purpose other than that the one now with Ore-Locks had been used somehow in an attempt to breach Bäalâle Seatt. But how else were they used?

Wynn had little to go on except for Magiere's mistake with the first one, the orb of Water, when she'd blindly opened it in the cavern below the ice-bound castle. Did Magiere have the only way to open an orb, with that tool she'd been given?

The tool might look something like a dwarven *thôrkh*, but it wasn't one. So what good was it, if all it did was unleash an orb's effect without control? What purpose, if any, might there be in finding all of the orbs, beyond keeping them from falling into the hands of the Ancient Enemy?

More lies and deceits weighed Wynn down, more suffering for others because of it, and one more secret.

That last one, which held no discernable bearing upon any greater questions, was something she dared not tell to anyone, most especially Ore-Locks. It made her sick inside after what she'd already done to him—forbidding him from clearing Deep-Root's name. Only Shade knew this additional secret by now, but Wynn couldn't stop thinking about it.

One phrase she'd seen clawed into that cave wall had made her falter twice.

May only my brother . . .

She looked down at the open book: an original lexicon of dwarven root words, compiled over centuries from archaeological recoveries. An abridged copy was available in the upper library. But what she sought here in the original wasn't a confirmation of what she knew. Rather, she'd hoped it would prove her wrong and free her from another burden. Even when she'd asked Master Tärpodious where to find it, she had known it wouldn't let her escape the truth or her deceit.

Beneath Bäalâle, she'd heard an ancient name. It had come as the dragon recited Deep-Root's last words, damning himself to eternal death. That name had filled her head in every language she knew, by whatever translation she would've given it at first. She hadn't grasped the ancient Dwarvish until she'd focused on the Numanese that came with it. It had choked off her voice.

May only my brother, Softly-Spoken, remember me. . . .

Why the orb's guardians hadn't forced her to repeat it only confirmed why she hadn't. Perhaps they'd known what she feared, should Ore-Locks hear it.

Wynn glanced at the last set of cryptic Begaine symbols in her new journal. The strokes were so tangled, so truncated that only she would be reminded of what they meant.

Bhedhägkangâva . . . Softly-Spoken.

If Ore-Locks had heard it in the Numanese she'd spoken, perhaps he wouldn't have caught the hidden connection. As a cathologer steeped in language, Wynn had missed it only for an instant. Pronunciation changes in the Dwarvish root words hadn't hidden it from her. And suffixes, prefixes, and alterations for creating verbs, nouns, adjectives, and adverbs had remained mostly stable over a thousand years.

Bhethäg was an adverb in the vocative for a proper name. Its root had to be something like *vetheg.* It was listed so in the lexicon.

Vetheg, vedhegh; see vedzagh in contemporary usage.

Its most accurate translation in Numanese was "softly," but the more literal, if less meaningful, might've been "featherly." *Vedzagh—vetheg—*was the root for "feather."

Kangâva had been less clear, but she'd worked it out. The vocative of a past-tense verb, its root was something like *changa* or *changasa.*

Changasa, changaksa, chenghak; see chenghaksé in contemporary usage.

"Spoken" was the precise meaning in Numanese, but the more literal would be "tongued." The root *chenghaksé—changasa—*meant "tongue."

The name of Bhedhägkangâva—Softly-Spoken—would need to change only so slightly over so many centuries to . . .

Bedzâ'kenge.

Feather-Tongue had been Deep-Root's twin brother. The repercussions Wynn now hid with that name were overwhelming.

Ore-Locks had barely succumbed to her reasoning as to why he couldn't speak of Deep-Root to anyone except Master Cinder-Shard. From the beginning, he'd been silently obsessed with one thing: to clear his ancestor's forgotten name and restore his family's heritage.

Wynn had denied him that right, to do what was right.

If he'd heard that brother's name, desperation and a great heritage would've made him unstoppable. She'd seen fear, hatred, and revulsion evoked from Shirvêsh Mallet at her naive mention of Thallûhearag. Sliver and High-Tower were vehemently sickened by their elder brother's passion for a long-dead ancestor that had called him into service among the Stonewalkers.

If Ore-Locks had proclaimed who Deep-Root was, what his ancestor had done and why, he would've been denounced by any who still remembered Thallûhearag. Without verifiable proof, at even a testament from Wynn, a mere "scribbler of words," Ore-Locks would've turned to the name of Deep-Root's brother as his last salvation.

What would happen if Ore-Locks publicly claimed that the forgotten worst of the Lhärgnæ, the Fallen Ones, was blood kin to a Bäynæ, an Eternal?

Feather-Tongue was revered as a paragon of knowledge and wisdom, but also for a cherished heritage. That meant everything to any dwarf with faith, as it did to Ore-Locks. Wynn had seen her own people let belief override reason to the point of denouncing fact . . . or worse.

Ore-Locks would've been branded a heretic, at best. His family would've suffered more than they already had. And at the worst . . .

Any head shirvêsh, even Mallet himself, could've incited righteous outrage. Neither Ore-Locks nor his family would've been safe—not even High-Tower. Any dwarven family, clan, or tribe coming after the domin would rouse the guild to his defense. And the royals would have used any means to defend the guild. They already had against Wynn's efforts.

The people of Malourné and the dwarves of Dhredze Seatt had been neighbors, allies, even comrades for over four centuries. Those connections could not be destroyed simply because one stonewalker yearned to clear his family's heritage by any means.

Wynn couldn't face the chance that any of this might happen. She'd stolen Ore-Locks's final hope of absolution and locked it away. She'd sacrificed his chance to be free of a hidden heritage to the Lord of the Slaughter.

Wynn had been raised, nurtured, trained to seek the truth for all to hear. Another choice like this crushed her down even more. Every muscle in her small body ached as if that growing weight were real. If anything more dropped upon her, she felt she might break. And there was more to come; she knew this.

Except for Shade, Wynn felt alone in this moment. There was no one far enough outside the guild for her to trust. There was no one here who knew enough and believed in what would come . . . not even Chane.

Shade's low rumble cut through Wynn's growing anguish.

"All right, we'll go," she whispered.

Shade's rumble grew to a snarl.

Wynn almost sighed. Was Chane coming? Maybe he hadn't received her message—or he'd ignored it.

—not . . . Chane—

Shade's hackles stood on end. Her ears flattened as she bared her teeth and glared through the opening at the alcove's rear.

Wynn snatched up the staff as she dug into her robe's pocket for her glasses. Did she sense some other undead?

Shade suddenly twisted her head, looking to the opposite opening among the four ways into the alcove. Her head whipped twice both ways before she turned again toward the front opening.

—behind—

Wynn shoved on the glasses and ripped the sheath off the staff's crystal. Shade's snarl sharpened again as Wynn barely turned toward the rear arch, and she almost glanced back.

A dark form crept around the rear entrance's left side.

Wynn thrust the staff out as shapes and phrases for its ignition raced through her mind.

The sun crystal ignited.

"My eyes!"

That strange cry came the instant that Wynn's glasses blackened. She couldn't see anything except the sun crystal's dimmed point of light.

"Put that thing out!"

Wynn spun at the snarling command behind her, but still held the sun crystal toward the first intruder. The glasses began to adjust.

Beyond Shade's tense form, Wynn barely made out a tall figure outside the other alcove arch. It was dressed in a heavy cloak, with one gloved hand held up to shield its face within the cloak's hood. Beside it stood the shape of a huge canine.

Shade wasn't snarling anymore.

That is enough, little one. It is all right now.

Those strange multilingual words barely filled Wynn's head when a cry rose behind her.

"My eyes! Ah, seven hells, Wynn, you've blinded me!"

She spun back, staring at the first intruder, now standing in the alcove's corner between two of its openings. This one had both gloved hands clamped over its face. Only then did it dawn on Wynn . . .

Both intruders were speaking Belaskian.

Wynn instantly snuffed the sun crystal's light, and only the cold lamp's softer glow lit the dark alcove.

The figure before her was slight, tightly built, and obviously male. Beneath the cloak and the wool pullover, the collar of a leather hauberk protruded. There were unusual weapons lashed to his thighs. Around the gloved hands clamped over his eyes she thought she saw tendrils of white-blond hair.

Fright and guilt flooded Wynn at what she might've done. She dropped the staff across the table and rushed at him.

"Leesil?" she whispered, and grabbed at his hands, pulling them down.

There was his caramel-tinted face. Faint scars showed on his jawline, and those feathery eyebrows weren't quite as slanted as a full-blooded elf. He opened his eyes, blinking several times.

Wynn was still panting in fright, and then . . .

He winked at her with a sly grin. "You're just too easy to play. You know that, don't you?"

He was still blinking through a squint when Wynn sucked in a shocked breath. All the joy and relief at seeing him once more faded under fury at another of his stupid tricks.

"You . . . you . . ." she stuttered. "You . . . *bastard!*"

She punched him straight in the chest.

Steel rings lashed on his armor beneath the pullover bit into Wynn's knuckles. She snatched her hand back in a cringe of pain.

"Hey, what was that for?" he asked.

Looking into Leesil's frowning face, Wynn lost any irritation he always sparked with a jest. She threw herself at him, knocking him into the alcove's corner.

"Take it easy," he warned. "You going to crack my head open on the wall now?"

She just held on to him.

"Wynn?" Leesil asked, but she couldn't answer.

His hand slid across her back as he wrapped his arms around her in return. She was shaking when he clamped his hold tighter. She lifted her head and saw the concern in his slightly large amber eyes.

Wynn barely regained composure as she rose on her toes to kiss his cheek.

"What do you think you're doing with my husband?"

That caustic jibe came from behind, and Wynn quickly turned her head.

There *she* was, nearly as pale as a corpse.

Magiere pushed back her hood, letting loose her black hair. The cold lamp's dim light barely raised a shimmer of bloodred in those locks. Magiere closed on Wynn with a typical scowl, though she smiled, as well.

Wynn twisted away from Leesil and quickly reached out, grabbing the edge of Magiere's cloak. With a sigh of burdens dropped for the moment, Wynn buried her face against her tall friend.

"What magic are you toying with this time?" Magiere asked, and the rumble in her chest hummed against Wynn's cheek. "I'd have thought you'd have learned your lesson by now."

With her friends' arms around her, Wynn looked up to find Magiere glaring toward the staff lying across the table. Wynn wasn't certain, but she thought she saw Magiere's irises go pitch-black. Now they faded quickly to their normal rich brown.

"Where's Chap?" Wynn asked as she peeked around Magiere.

Here.

She saw him as his answer filled her head. His silvery blue-gray fur shimmered in the low light. He stood outside the alcove archway, but he was looking down the outer passage. Why didn't he come to her?

Wynn rushed over, dropping to her knees, and slipped her arms around Chap's neck. Just before she buried her face in his fur, he whipped his whole tongue across her face.

"I missed you so much," she whispered, and then suddenly remembered Shade.

Is that her . . . my daughter? Is that what you call her?

Wynn lifted her head. Of course he hadn't known. He'd been long gone from the Elven Territories before Lily had given birth to their children.

"Yes!" she answered, looking about and finally following Chap's sightline. "I named her . . . or she named herself . . . after . . ."

Wynn looked down the passage.

So little light leaked from the alcove that she barely made out Shade's form, but that light sparkled in Shade's eyes. Wynn heard Shade begin to growl.

Why would she do that? It was obvious these were friends, and especially with her father finally here.

"What . . . who is that?"

Magiere stood behind Wynn in the alcove's archway and was looking down the passage.

"One of Chap's children—his daughter," Wynn answered.

"What?" Leesil tucked into the archway next to Magiere.

Wynn looked at Chap. "You didn't tell them? Why?"

In their separate ways, they are both fixed on those they consider family. It would have been another contention, another distraction from what had to be put before ourselves.

"How?" Leesil interrupted, unaware of anything passing between Chap and Wynn. "Who's the mother?"

"The white majay-hì, I'd guess," Magiere barely whispered.

It sounded almost sad to Wynn.

Leesil huffed, perhaps a half laugh. "Why, Chap, you ol' dog, you."

Instead of chiding him for crudeness, Magiere looked away.

"Shade?" Wynn called out.

Shade was barely more than a black shadow hunkering and growling in the dark. Those pinpricks of eyes vanished, and Wynn heard the click of claws on stone recede in the distance. She was about to call out when Chap interrupted.

Let her go. There is nothing here for her . . . except you.

"Yes, there is," Wynn returned. "You're her father."

No . . . only the one who forced a purpose on her through her mother. That is all I am to her.

Wynn was confounded, much as she partly understood the problem. She didn't ask him why he had done that, didn't tell him he shouldn't have. She couldn't imagine being without Shade. But there was so much in her head that she had to let some of it out.

"What of the first orb?" she asked Chap, but it was Magiere who answered.

"First? How do you know of the other one?"

Wynn looked up into Magiere's eyes. "There are five, but how would you know—"

"Five?" Leesil asked sharply.

Magiere stared down at Wynn and then turned away into the alcove.

Leesil ripped off his cloak and tossed it too hard toward the table. It slid off to the floor, but he left it there. He pushed his hands through his hair, almost covering his ears for an instant.

One sleeve of his wool pullover was raggedly torn off. Long, parallel scars ran along his forearm, like the marks of claws. Leesil had a tendency to gather scars, but Wynn had never seen these before. He shut his eyes hard.

Magiere glanced at him as she dropped onto the one stool at the table.

The orbs are safe. I have seen to that.

"Orbs?" Wynn echoed back at Chap. "You had one . . . I found another."

Chap turned his head to look at her, his ears falling for an instant.

"That leaves three," she added.

No, if your count is correct, there are two left.

Chap gazed down the passage, though no one remained there to see.

Wynn was lost, uncertain what it all meant, but for one thing. Wherever her friends had gone to hide the first orb, they had uncovered another one.

Suddenly, she wanted to go over what little she had copied from Chane's scroll and try to see which one they had found. And that thought made her turn.

Magiere glanced sidelong toward Leesil, as if she wouldn't look directly at him. He had his back to her and remained so. Neither said a word, not even to each other. And there was something more.

Wynn began to panic as she watched Magiere sitting in cold silence.

Chane would soon return, and Magiere was here.

Wynn looked to Chap, wishing she could just be with him, be with all of them, and try to bring Shade back. But an awful question lingered around her, as if it hung out there in dark of the catacombs beyond the reach of the cold lamp's light.

"What happened to you," Wynn asked, "all of you . . . in the Wastes?"

Though she waited, Chap didn't answer—not yet.